THE BONE BRICK CITY

To Mike

FOUR WINDS - ONE STORM

THE BONE BRICK CITY
BOOK I

BY
AARON HOLLINGSWORTH

❈
Eightfold Wrath Books
Kansas City

Cover Art by Stephanie Hollingsworth

This book is also available in audio book form and narrated by Steve Vito.

Acknowledgments

If not for the influence of the following people this book would have never been what is has become: The Hollingsworth Family and all our cousins, particularly my sister Katherine who helped me add new dimensions to my characters in the very beginning. The Richardson Family for being a second kin to me. The Jacobs Family for all I have now. Sifu Larry Thornhill for teaching me the White Dragon Way. Sheryl Shreve for your selfless efforts in correcting my many mistakes. David "Dax" Bauer for encouraging me to raise the stakes and write a better ending. Laurie Douglas for pointing out a need. Cody Kiser for your friendship and encouragement. Mark "Corwyn" Jameson for teaching me the word "theurge". Mallory Rose for telling me what had to be removed. Josh Hoefle for your feedback. Eric Durbin for your wisdom and support in all things. Jennifer Bauman for the exchange of feedback. John Jervis for being the closest thing to a real theurge in this reality. Lisi Chance for your sharp eyes and help. And my loving and supportive wife Stephanie, the mother of my children and source of my magic. Thank you all.

This book is dedicated to the memory of Dorothy Hollingsworth, a loving and encouraging mother.

Introduction

Sherlock Holmes said "Once you eliminate the impossible, whatever remains, no matter how improbable, must be the truth." How then does one solve a mystery in a world where nothing is impossible? Moreover, how does one write such a mystery and create such a world?

In an effort to develop something original it is easy to just rebel. Rebellion itself tends to become its own cause when this happens. But as the years of cultivating these ideas went by I've slowly learned that new ideas are meaningless unless they are properly applied; and then propriety and rebellion become strange associates.

I could have just set this story on a far off planet, alternate dimension, or some planar environment full of celestial or infernal influence. Instead, I strove to create a new kind of cosmology, a new kind of setting where the mundane and exotic can coexist.

I could have employed fantastic races of Tolkienian extraction to people this setting. Instead, I strove to create new races with their own cultures. In the beginning, I even tried to not include humans in this work (but the loathsome creatures still managed to infest it like everything else).

I could have created a pantheon of gods and planar hereafters. Instead, there are no gods and no afterlife. But there are still souls...

Developing a new magic system proved the hardest part, how to make the impossible possible. It had to be more than just ancient words that alter reality. It had to be more than just an energy only some select few were born with. My answer was found in philosophy, speculative thought for speculative fiction. Philosophy is like magic in that it seems to change the world around you once you've been exposed to it.

The story is told in a third person omniscient style, whereas most modern literary works are told from a single viewpoint per chapter or per book (whether it be first or third person). This was not an intentional act of rebellion for originality. I just grew up reading comic books and watching shows that where told from the 4th wall or camera's point of view. In such stories, the audience is shown what's going on inside and outside every character on a moment by moment basis. This may be an odd change for readers who like to "wear" characters.

It is immense fun developing these ideas. But originality is nothing without skill, and developing skill is where the fun ends. As this is my first effort, I hope the only difference between it and my final effort will be some degree of skill. And that's all I have to say about that.

As for what is not original, I've cherry picked my favorite elements of comics, manga/anime, westerns, tabletop RPGs, Saturday morning cartoons, martial arts flicks, horror films, adventure movies, and of course, fantasy/sci fi novels. My influences are too many to name, but a savvy reader may be able to tell where certain elements came from. In fact, I challenge them to do so.

May this new mythos bring you what you seek and more.

-Aaron Hollingsworth March 2014

Dry Wind of the Northwest-
the Ground bleeds Fire from your Tall Mountains,
Cold Wind of the Northeast-
from Icy Peaks the Rivers cleave the Land,
Wet Wind of the Southeast-
Clouds over Hill and under Dome of Huncell,
Hot Wind of the Southwest-
Burn away that which blocks the path of Life,
Four Winds- One Storm,
Destruction and Birth in a Mandala of Weather,
Clearing Debris from the Sacred Path,
Discipline of Nature,
Liberation from Delusion,
Greed, Envy, Anger, Torpor, and Pride,
The Living Lies of Suffering and Waste, Muses of Evil,
The Tail of the Drake had a Will of its own,
The Dragon spun around fast to catch it in its Jaws,
In such an action,
The Tornado of Existence began its Cleansing Rotation,
Still echoing throughout the Ages.

-ancient Buresche Drakeri text
translated by Mazil Whortshellean

<u>Prologue</u>

Dahms Capgully loved riding his bicycle to and from the marketplace. He would pedal there each day through the bumpy streets, selecting the various components for his dinner. On this particular day, he had chosen to take home and enjoy a whole roasted duck, fried potato slices, coleslaw with chunks of broccoli, and a bottle of mulberry wine. He purchased the items and placed them in a wicker basket mounted to his handlebars. Before leaving the marketplace, he also bought a bouquet of daisies for the vase in his den.

Although he was middle aged and twice divorced, he was still a romantic. The bright, fresh flowers reminded him of when there was a woman living with him. He still got along with his ex-wives and had no serious regrets about them. Both marriages lasted well over a century. That wasn't so bad for Drakeri. Both resulted in happy children and strong friendships between them all. And there was always the prospect of another love, or so he hoped.

That was the real reason he rode a bike instead of being taxied by some hulking foreigner with stones for brains. He was trying to lose weight and get fit to attract a new mate. With each rotation of the bike pedals, he felt himself grow closer to shedding his unwanted torso fat.

He took the long way home, weaving his way between steed-drawn coaches and taxi-pullers. Up ahead, he saw a jumble of wagons in a traffic jam.

"A wheel must have broken off," he thought.

Seeing that the sidewalk was empty, he opted to take it. He feared his duck would get cold if he waited too long.

"Ah, duck!" he mused, taking in the wafting aroma of the cooked bird in his basket. He felt the gentle bumps from the cobbled sidewalk beneath him. Recalling a song from the bright days of his childhood, he began to sing as he pedaled.

> *"Oh a duck has wings and a quacking bill,*
> *And lots of feathers to fight the chill,*
> *They have webbed feet with scaly skin,*
> *A duck can walk or fly or swim,*
> *Oh a duck lays eggs in a grassy nest,*

And tasty fish they like the best,
But duck is also a tasty meat,
And you can cook one for a---"

Before Dahms could finish the verse, an unseen mop handle poked out from the corner of an alley way, jabbing through the spokes of his front wheel, bringing his pleasant ride to a jolting halt. He flipped over his handlebars, tearing his basket loose. As the top of his head dashed against the rock hard ground, his food and flowers spilled around him. Dazed and stunned, he faced the alley to see what had tripped him. A thick boot crashed into his nose, and a bubbling burst of pain flared inside his skull.

A swarm of coarse hands dragged him into the alley. The salty blood from his nose flooded into his bristly beard. He tried to look up to catch a glimpse of his attackers through watery eyes, but all he saw was a flash of dark light. He felt his eyes blink and he winced from the sting. But he could see nothing at all.

It was more than just blindness. His confusion was amplified by fear and helplessness. Distantly, his soul sensed his body being pounded and stomped. His spirit shuddered, also feeling the pain that his body endured. He heard his attackers speak words that he had heard all his life, but could no longer understand.

The hands assaulting him began to paw and search. They removed his wallet and coin pouch, slipped off his wrist watch, and yanked off the chain necklace that held two very old wedding rings.

The last pain he consciously felt was a sharp stab in his thigh and warm fluid running down his leg. At first he thought it was piss. But he heard his heart pounding in his ears, and the fluid gushed in time with it. He heard his attacker's footfalls fading away from him. As cold emptiness crept inside his body, he knew that he was dying.

He wanted to call for help or comfort, but could not. He once heard that a person's whole life flashes before their eyes before they pass away. He wanted that now. He wanted it badly. He wanted to see the days his children were born. He wanted to recall the moment his first grandchild smiled at him. He wanted to see the faces of the women he had loved and lost. But even in his mind's eye, all he saw was that terrible black void.

His soul departed the way all souls do in this world when the body stops working. It exploded into thousands of fragments, each one soaring in a different direction. And wherever life begins, however it begins, the souls fragments of the recently dead bond with others, forming new souls in new bodies.

Dahms Capgully was now a part of everything that was beginning.

Chapter 1
The Bushwhacker, the Chimancer,
and the Runaway

◇

In a cluster of georganic cells called Draybair we begin our story. These cells are not ordinary cells. They are Huncells. And each one is big enough to hold its own realm of people and places. They are connected by a series of tunnels many miles long, allowing inhabitants to travel from one Huncell to another. Of course, not everyone is welcome everywhere.

"Hey, Rev?" asked the shorter man.

"Yes, Will?" returned the taller man.

"How many o' these...whudya call 'em...*tellfone poles* are in a mile?"

"Forty two, if I am not mistaken. Roughly."

"Roughly, huh?" the shorter man scoffed. "Mighty odd number fer mile markers. Odd meanin' strange, mind you."

The taller man regarded the circular, brick-covered columns on either side of the road on which they were walking. "I have read that marking miles was not their original purpose."

"Oh?"

The taller man, Hindin, raised a great silvery hand to point at the poles. "Their primary purpose was to suspend miles and miles of lightningwire to relay energy and messages. But since the Omni-war, the local Drakeri have preserved their wooden cores with brickwork. Rather simple masonry, I must say. But effective, nonetheless."

Will, the shorter of the two, glanced up and scoffed. "Fevärian expansionists an' their lightningwire. I wonder why they never put 'em up back home."

His friend nodded at the statement. "Perhaps because *your* people never let them occupy your huncell as long as the Drakeri."

Will grinned and squared his shoulders. "Dang round-ears overstayed their welcome, that's why." He peered into the

15

distance at the city they were approaching, and his grin melted. "Hope that we don't do the same here."

The distant garden of towers had beckoned them for two days. Night fell as the two men set foot on streets of cobbled stone. It was now too dark for them to behold the famous architecture that had earned the city its nickname: Embrenil, the Bone Brick City. After weeks of walking and hitching rides, they had finally reached their destination.

The ornate streetlights cast their pale glow on the two travelers. Will unknowingly hunched his broad shoulders, so unnerving was the worm's eye view of the colossal buildings. It was his first time in a city so huge.

He was young in the face, with the slight hint of crow's feet at the corners of his blue-gray eyes. Although he stood just under the height of most males, his hands were drastically large with all the fingers the same length. They were tanned, rough hands that any old farmer would recognize as 'honest'. His booted feet were also big, with heels as wide as a steed's hooves. Soft, sandy blonde quills adorned his head, eyebrows, and the tips of his ears. He was a Tendikeye, a wingless Bukk. And although he did not have quill-covered wings like others of his kind, he still had that same wild glint in his eyes.

The dust coat he wore was dark green with the right side of the collar flared up while the left side lay flat. Strapped to his back was a rectangular carrying case made of rawhide. As he walked, his open coat swayed back and forth, revealing what looked like a pistol. More than a few Drakeri natives glanced at him with wary curiosity or contempt. He pretended to ignore them.

His companion was easily a foot taller, resembling a bald, steel-skinned statue. He was neither thin nor bulky, but lithe and very well toned. He wore a pair of loose-fitting brown canvas pants, iron sandals, and a long sleeved hooded leather jacket with a black satin sash tied about the waist. His eyes were two finely cut green emeralds fixed behind eyelids of steel that gave him a calm, studious look. He carried a bulging duffel bag big enough to hold a corpse. The natives barely noticed him. To them he was just another Malruka, a *Child of the Ground*.

Ignoring the odd stares the pair received, they made their way to an open diner. The indigo-skinned customers and staff only filled half the dining room. The natives' eyes, black with

16

three irises each, ranging from bright gold to dark orange, turned to the strangers. For a split second, all those eyes seemed disturbed. Before the door could fully close behind the two men, the natives went back to their eating and conversing.

The strangers waited to be seated, but the three waitresses looked tired and busy. The tendikeye tilted his head toward an empty booth. The tall malruka nodded, and they made their way to it. The table had not yet been cleared of the mess left by the previous patrons. Without saying a word, the two men stacked the messy plates and gathered the dirty utensils. With cloth napkins they wiped the rings of water beneath the glasses. After piling the mess neatly at the edge of the table, they sat down and conversed.

"I am glad you decided to do this. I think it will be good for you," Hindin said, sounding somewhat parental. The half-melted candle between them brought out his warm smile.

"Whatever it takes, Rev," Will answered in his native drawl. "Brem's bound to hear 'bout me 'ventually. Pullin' this job off oughta send up the right signal," the tendikeye bukk spoke with a slight grin and eyes holding a relaxed assurance. He slung an arm along the edge of his upholstered seat and let out a tired sigh.

"The day will come, my friend," Hindin agreed. "But the reason that the *meantime* is called such is because it means the most. We are here to bring peace."

"And I'll find a whole world o' peace when them maxim-chuckers hit dirt!" Will exclaimed with a cold eagerness. Then a loud creak in his stomach woke him from his zeal. "What's keepin' that waitress?" he asked, looking around.

The three waitresses had gathered for a chat. The tendikeye opened his ears and sorted through the sounds of customers yacking and utensils clinking. His eyes stared at nothing as his sharp ears redirected their edge.

"I'm not going to," whispered one waitress.

"But it's *your* area!" argued another under her breath.

"Give them time, Will," his friend assured. He drew out a folded newspaper from his bag, and flapped it open in a fast, smooth motion.

Will snapped out of his listening and rolled his eyes. Prejudice he could deal with, but not hunger. He looked over at his steel-skinned companion. There were plenty of his kind in

Doflend, mainly in its cities. What prejudice did *he* have to fear? But a tendikeye bukk amongst all these Drakeri? He pushed the idea from his mind. He was more interested in what Hindin was reading.

"So, we get here too late?" Will asked, lighting a cigarette with a red tipped match.

Hindin read over the article, his gem eyes shifting to find the answer. "I'm afraid so." He read in a deep, round-toned voice. "Another victim of the 'Mystic Mafia' was hospitalized three nights ago due to severe blunt trauma and mystical blindness of an unspecified theurgy. The city guard has yet to reveal the victims' identities. This is number six in a strain of similar assaults in the past month. Only one victim has died from these attacks. Dahms Capgully, a retired brick layer."

"Sounds like more mystic gut snake," Will responded with a smirk. "Mystic Mafia, my foot! Any theurge worth his salt in organizin' is better off runnin' fer office."

"Mmm." Hindin shifted in his seat and pointed down at the paper. "Blinding maxims are highly illegal to the public and reserved for military and high ranking city guards. This law was passed in 1656 A.T. Or was it 1657 A.T.? Here, let me check my books."

Hindin was just about to reach into his duffel bag full of his little library when Will stopped him.

"It don't matter none, Rev."

Hindin straightened back with impeccable posture. "Anyway, the law passed two hundred years ago. So, some younger Drakeri might not know it."

Will looked out over the small crowd of his fellow customers. The different shades of purple skin he was used to. Their triple-irised eyes that never shifted from side-to-side annoyed him. Their hands having three fingers and one thumb bothered him, too. And all those narrow ears that rose into two points. The culture itself. It wasn't that he hated them; learning their ways was a hassle..

He and Hindin stood out like sore thumbs on a plate of noodles.

"How long these city draks live again, Rev? Twelve hun'erd years or so?"

"By average," Hindin answered promptly. "But they tend to always act the age they look for some reason."

18

"Prob'ly 'cause they've been domesticated by the cultures they borrowed from," Will speculated. He glanced around without turning his head. He took a thoughtful puff and exhaled. "Anyway, back to the mission."

"I thought we were calling it a *case*. It cannot be a mission for no one has sent or dispatched us."

Will's broad shoulders dropped in frustration. "Well, why not call it a goal or aim then?"

"Why *not* a case? Or maybe, objective? I like objective. It means all of these things." Hindin's face lit up, exposing perfectly chiseled marble teeth.

"Well, we can't call it a *case* 'cause we ain't detectives, no matter how many of them dang books you read."

Hindin nodded with sympathetic understanding. "So, objective it is."

"FINE! What kind of victims we talkin' 'bout?"

Hindin took a quick glance at the paper. "Various ages, occupations, and social standings. There have been six thus far. None of whom were ever even acquainted. All were robbed of money and jewelry. The nature of their injuries was all similar: beatings, minor stab wounds, and permanent mystical blindness. " As the malruka explained, a question formed in his mind. "Academic scholars of the theurgic arts are usually quite well off. Why choose such an under-productive way to increase their wealth?"

Will put out his cigarette. "Maybe they're bored. Maybe they ain't scholars and not so good at maxim castin'. Maybe just plain no good." He stood up from the table. "That waitress ain't comin'. I'm gonna go walk around a bit. See if anyone else is this friendly."

Hindin frowned as he watched his friend get up to leave. "Do not pick any more fights out there," Hindin advised.

"Aw, Rev, you know the fights always pick me," Will shot back with a cocky grin.

Will had room to be cocky. The two deadly pieces of steel on his belt only made up part of it. He was a country boy in a foreign city. But he did not see that as such a bad thing. His ears caught the unmistakable howl of a locomotive's steel throat in the distance. The evening gloam had shifted to night. The ancient cobblestones of the street ground mutely beneath his wide boots. He blew out smoke and drew in the air of the city.

"Better to stick out than be stuck in," he whispered to himself.

✦

"You can do dis, Polly," she told herself as she shivered in the warm air. She stood for several minutes, staring across the street at the barbershop with thoughts and emotions colliding into one another. The hooded drakeri girl, barely eighteen years old, bit her lip and made up her mind. Forcing herself across the street, she muttered under her breath, "Just keep moving. Got nothing to lose." The brass bell on the front door made a *tink-tink* as she went in.

"Hullo, Miss," greeted the barber as he snipped an older man's hair. "How can I help you?"

"I..." she paused as her mind froze. She could not believe how nervous she was. "I'll wait and look around," she said. Quickly, she turned and tried to look interested in some photos on the wall.

"Sure thing. I'll be done here in just a minute."

As the barber went back to his work, Polly looked over to study him. He was in his late thirties, despite that he looked her age. That was one perk of being Drakeri. After the age of twenty, every hundred and fifty years equaled ten years compared to average races.

She studied the elderly Drakeri in the chair. The weight of a thousand years had sagged his wrinkled skin. He seemed comfortable sitting in that chair. Familiar and broken-in.

He smiled at her and spoke. "I wouldn't trust this rascal, honey. He only knows how to give one kind of haircut. If I were you, I'd run to the nearest beauty salon as fast as I could!" The customer chuckled at his own jest.

"Ah, now you keep quiet, Lurcree. He's only kidding," the barber assured her.

Polly nodded quietly as her heart pounded in her ears. She closed her eyes and tried to regulate her pulse.

Soon the barber finished up, and the older Drakeri dropped a handful of grotz coins on the counter. They were square pieces of metal with holes punched through the centers. The two men shook hands and exchanged friendly words of parting.

The older man tipped his head to the pretty young girl as he left the pair alone. "Be seeing you," he told them as he exited through the jingling door.

"So," the barber said, startling the mysterious girl, "What'll it be? A trim? Shorten?" He began to sweep around the chair.

"Oh, um...j-just shorten it, I guess," Polly stammered, removing her gray secondhand cloak. She was shorter than most girls, but her limbs were well toned. She was at that age where girlish cuteness was betrayed by womanly endowments. She untucked her wavy hair and let it fall free to her waist.

The barber stared with mouth slightly open. "Miss, you sure you want to cut *that* off? I know women who would hex their mothers for that shade."

Polly flinched and studied the strands of silk sprouting from her head. It was dark purple with natural light violet highlights, giving it a dreamy depth. Her eyes then locked with his.

"Cut it all off," she replied harshly.

The man stepped back, a bit surprised by her sudden change of tone. "All right, Miss. Please, have a seat."

She sat down as the kind faced man wrapped a cloth around her neck and shoulders. She could not help but stare at his hands. She wanted so badly to cry into them.

"Seems a shame though," he shrugged. "Let me guess; some boy broke your heart?"

She swallowed hard. "No, Mr. Yonoman. Nothing like dat," she said with lowered eyes.

The barber hesitated, scissors in the air. "How'd you know my name?"

"Dis is Yonoman's Barber Shop," Polly smiled slightly. "At least dat's what de sign says." Her voice spoke with a girlish tone and a slight raspiness, as if she had recently gotten over a harsh cold. Her accent, though somewhat refined, caused the man to delay his response while trying to understand her words. Chumish accents could be rather confusing.

Yonoman laughed politely. "Yep," he agreed, starting to snip. "Got this place from my dad after his arthritis worked up. Hope to pass it on to my son in a few centuries."

Polly tensed.

"Unfortunately, he's into that awful music they play nowadays. Thinks he can play the sitern. But hey, it's not his only ambition. He has a special gift, you see. He's receptive in Subjective Kinetics. To think; my son; an actual theurge!"

A silver framed picture sat on the shelf by the mirror. Polly reached to pick it up. "Dis him?" she rasped.

"Yep," he answered with pride. "And my wife, Dinnala. Got an anniversary next month."

Polly closed her eyes, feeling like she'd been hit with a mallet in her chest. Her hand shook as she set the picture down.

"Any other kids?"

Yonoman put down the scissors and picked up a comb. "Nah. One's enough."

Those words were like a shard of ice into her heart. Her mind raced for something to say. She'd come all this way and put all her hope ...

"Done!" the man announced triumphantly, snapping her out of her thoughts. Polly's eyes opened and she looked up. Her eyes darted briefly to the man in the mirror before settling on her hair. Now cropped short, it curved under her chin. Her hair parted on the right side now, she smiled, despite herself, on how different she looked.

"Tank you," she whispered.

"No problem, miss," he replied, dusting her off. "That'll be fourteen grotz."

"Oh!" Polly gasped, thinking of her nearly empty purse. She hadn't intended to get a haircut. "Um," she patted around her pants and pulled out a pathetic looking brown bag. She looked in it hopefully and her face fell. "Great, Polly," she told herself, "now you have to run."

"Say," the barber blurted, trying to sound off handed, "How about we get a picture?"

"A picture?" Polly squeaked.

"Yep, see, every time a cut turns out so exceptional, I get a picture done and hang it on the wall as examples of my work. You get your haircut for free this way." He winked at her.

Relieved and full of gratitude, she nodded. She knew that no such deals were made in this simple old shop. It was an exceptional feeling. The thought of *him* being so unfairly kind to her clouded her mind with inexpressible joy.

He ran a quick comb through her hair, tilted her chin up, and had her sit still. Taking a portrait of an old customer off the wall, he flicked the glass pane with his fingernail. In seconds, the image dissolved, leaving only a clear glass plate in an old dusty frame. He held the small window-like frame a few paces from Polly's face.

"Okay, say 'Pepper-Jack'!" he encouraged.

"Pepper-Jack", she repeated shyly, rolling the *r*.

It was the first time in a long time she could not resist smiling. She looked in amazement as her image mystically appeared in the glass. "You also are a theurge?" she asked with visible curiosity.

"Me? Oh, no!" the barber chuckled. "This was just a gift from an old customer. The man who just left, actually." He turned the glass pane around for a look. "Say, you take an excellent picture! Thanks for letting me cut your hair for it." He gave her a playful wink, and once more, she could not help but smile.

But, alas, less than a minute later, Polly heaved a heavy sigh as she stepped back into the breezy city streets. She took a single look back at the man behind the glass. He had hung her picture up; and now swept her severed hair into a pile on the floor.

"Goodbye, Papa," she whispered.

Walking the cobbled sidewalks of Embrenil, she felt knots form in her throat and stomach. She was losing a battle with grief. She came all this way, only to let her fears and uncertainty win. It was not as if she expected him to be able or willing to help her. He would only get hurt or worse. There had always been a stinging hope for acceptance. But that hope did not betray her, so much as she betrayed it.

She stopped in mid thought and pinched the seven-pointed septagram tattoo on her forearm. It was a habit she picked up whenever her mind grew too muddled. The mark was a design composed of four black lines and three red lines.

"Flow past it all," she told herself. "Blood must flow."

She glanced around at the market venders putting up their wares for the day. She had no money left for food, but luckily there was a fountain nearby.

"Water is better dan nothing," she thought. *"Might as well fill up on it."*

23

The urban maze of streets emptied of all life except for her as the huncell walls grew dim. Night fell in the huncell known as Burtlbip like a bowl of darkness placed over the concave realm.

As she lifted another handful of water to her mouth, the smell of cheap cologne stung her nose. It was so strong she almost choked on her drink.

"Hey, precious. What a night it is!" said a shrill voice in her left ear.

Polly's eyes shifted to look at the man next to her. The male Drakeri stood imposingly close to her. He was dressed in a faded denim suit, and grinned sharply as he tugged the brim of his matching hat. Such an outfit was the usual attire of a fleshbroker.

She glared at him. Her eyes inadvertently focused on the two gold teeth in front of his fiendish smile.

"Name's Cecil. What do they call you?" he inquired, as his cold eyes wondered here and there.

She gave no answer. Her boots did all the talking as she tried to walk away.

"Hey now!" he called, padding after her. "Don't you coldshoulder me, luscious. I see you might have money troubles. Just so happens I'm looking to hire a girl like you." He made a grab for her arm. "You got the build and everything!"

She looked over her shoulder, locking one turned eye to his. "Go," she demanded. "You have nothing to provoke my interest." Each word came out colder than the last. With a shake of her arm, she broke his hold and continued walking. Sadly, it was into the wrong alley. Dead end.

Polly's eyes widened. She felt both of Cecil's wiry hands caress her shoulders. His touch made her feel itchy all over.

"Tsk-tsk," came a sound from his teeth. "Is that a Chume accent you have?" he teased. "Not many of us spend so much time there. Supposed to be full of all kinds of crazy. Wild Energies. How about you show old Cecil some of that wild energy, luscious?"

A hush fell over Polly's mind. "No need," she answered.

Suddenly, she dropped to her haunches. Her cloak puffed out from the fall, blocking the sight of her changing position. Now on all fours, she brought her right knee to her chest before launching her heel into Cecil's knee joint. The fleshbroker bent down as his leg snapped backwards, inhaling for the scream of his life. But Polly already had tucked and rolled, letting her other heel clobber his jaw in the process. He stumbled shoulder first into the alley wall, letting out a faint squeak.

Polly's rosebud lips curved into a vicious smirk. Wrapping her fist in a bit of her cloak, she rattled Cecil's world with three dainty knuckles of wrath. Cecil was done for the night. Polly was not.

"You won't be needing *dose* anymore," she purred, producing a small knife.

Lynda was just about to close up her fruit stand for the night. The dark hours were known to be full of undesirable characters. It had been that way for centuries. Her wariness was fully primed as a wingless, armed-to-the-teeth tendikeye approached her stand wanting service. Worse yet, he was the haggling type.

"Five grotz."

"Two?"

"The price is five grotz a piece."

"How 'bout three?"

"Listen, pointy! These are high quality jububes imported from Gurtangorr. Five and no less!" the hefty woman demanded.

"Gut snake!" Will exclaimed. "Most're still green an' the ones that're ripe are covered in purple dots! You can't fool me, lady. I know that's a sign o' them goin' bad."

"These are all I have at the end of the day. If you had been here earlier, you could have gotten fresher. Besides, the green ones are good for digestion."

Will gnawed at the end of his unlit cigarette. He was in no mood to be tongue lashed by some old drakeri hag. His information hunt had turned up nothing. No one wanted to talk to him. And those who did were little different from this woman.

"Look, ma'am," he started, trying to sound polite, "I know 'bout three minutes ago, you sold a dozen to a drakeri fella fer twenty. He was yer last customer 'fore me. Now, I'd hate to think that a sweet gal like you'd be discriminate. That's...what...'bout two grotz a piece almost?"

The vender pursed her lips in thought, looking him up and down. "That was when I thought no one wanted anymore. Supply and demand, sir. Be on your way!"

Will's eye twitched in frustration.

Without warning, a high pitched yell woke him from his bad mood. He turned toward the sound, dropping a hand on his holstered side arm. His long pinky and index finger coiled around two separate triggers. He drew the weapon a half inch. The old vender caught a glimpse of him grasping what looked like two revolvers connected at the butt handles.

Will's sharp eyes narrowed as his gaze ranged over a string of alleys in the lamplight haze. He wondered which the noise had come from. "*Could it be the Mystic Mafia?*" he thought with slight hope. He was hungry and cranky. The sudden prospect of a skirmish excited him.

Far down the street, Polly sprinted out of a dark alleyway. Her hooded cloak flapped behind her as she ran. Will saw her face only briefly. He hesitated, not sure if she was the one who made the scream. He then saw a figure crawl out yelling after her.

"Bith took my teef!" Cecil cried. "My gold teef!"

Will squint his eyes and looked over at him. By his standards, the man wasn't hurt *that* bad. And he certainly was not blinded in any way.

He searched again for a second glimpse of the running girl, but she was gone in the night.

"Great, just a common thief," he told himself. "Not my problem."

It was morning at The Goose Egg Inn. *Transients Welcome* read the sign out front of the ramshackle establishment, and Will and Hindin were no exceptions. They sat at a splintery, stained table in a large room that served as both the lobby and dining hall. Will was finishing off his second helping of bean curd as Hindin walked in with the morning gazette.

Hindin shook his head as he unfolded the morning paper. "Perhaps we should both go out to ask the locals. Malruka are more common here. They might tolerate me enough to answer

26

our questions. Not that I wish to upstage you." He sat and began to skim the articles.

"Gut snake," Will let out the words with a smoky sigh.

Hindin's eyes glinted in amusement. "Are you still not accustomed to city life, Mr. Foundling?"

Will raised a quilled eyebrow. "Ain't no room to run here, Rev. I mean REALLY run. So many folks shoved together, a man can hardly breathe."

"Mmm-hmm" Hindin replied, standing back up. "I could use some open air myself, not that breathing is a personal concern. The buildings are a bit cramped on the inside, but the architecture is stunning. Since we arrived late yesternight, I suggest a stroll to fully enjoy it."

"I don't *stroll*, Rev."

"Very well. I will stroll. You can tag along. That's what sidekicks do, yes?"

Will laughed. "In yer dreams, boy. What about the objective?"

"A wise man once said that answers are best found in inspiration when examination proves useless."

"Huh." Will paused in contemplation. "So, he only said that once?"

The steel man chuckled and shrugged. "Well, I am sure he said it many times to make the saying catch on."

The two men didn't have far to go. After a few blocks of hustle and bustle, Hindin, towering over most, spotted another of his race. This malruka stood an easy ten feet tall, with massive arms and short sturdy legs. His upper back hunched over and was armored with a bronze plate crowned with large dull spines. His forearms had matching plates with intricate ridges. He pulled around a huge cart full of crudely upholstered seats.

"Excuse us, sir!" Hindin called, waving his hand in the air.

The taxi puller raised his head and smiled. "Where to, fellas?"

"Oh, we do not need a ride, sir. My partner and I wanted to ask you some questions about the city."

"We're new," Will added.

"Questions? Um, sure. I need a break anyway," the bronze behemoth took a seat on the sidewalk. "My name's Richard Armbakk. And you to are...?"

Hindin's eyes widened. "You are a member of the Armbakk family? The proud descendants of Zyearvu Armourback? The famed malruka who said 'We lived to fight. Now we fight to live!'?"

The taxi puller smiled. "You know your history, friend. Yeah, that's us. We can all trace our ore back to him."

"How did you end up here in Doflend?" Hindin straightened his already perfect posture and crossed his arms. He was prepared to listen for hours.

The friendly behemoth nodded his shiny head as he talked. "Well, I was a middle child out of ten brothers. I wanted to see other huncells. Not just lug rocks around all day. I asked my father for leave. He granted me twenty years to travel abroad. Doflend has been my home for eight of them thus far."

"Oh yeah? How do you like it?" Will asked, with doubt in his voice.

"I love it! There's so much to see here. The people that come through are quite interesting. At first, I thought it would be boring pulling a cart around. But with all the conversations that I've had and heard and all the sites of this city; it's been great." Richard gave them a quick look-over. "I take it you two are tourists?"

"Excursionists, actually," Hindin corrected. "We are on a pilgrimage of justice and skill-honing. Myself, for seven years now, my friend here for only the last few months."

The taxi-puller gave a nod. "Yeah, I thought about giving that a try, given the family's history. But our design is now more just a sign of our heritage. We're built for wars, but that doesn't mean we have to chase them. Heck, guys like me end bar fights just by standing up. I did a caravan job once, though, pulling and guarding. It was this crazy old theurge and his laboratory equipment."

"Speaking of theurges," Hindin interrupted with a bright smile. "What have you heard about the Mystic Mafia?"

Richard scoffed. "Only that the press is milking it. People get mugged here in Emby all the time. The only thing special about these cases is that a theurge is behind it. I swear, it's all some customers talk about. That this blinding effect also puts the victim in a dream-like state or something. They still get beat up and robbed just the same."

"So, you think there's more to it than that?" Will asked.

"Maybe. Could be possible. The police say that jewelry is stolen, too. It might be jewel thieves. Maybe we malruka should be worried, too," he half-joked about the fact that all malrukan eyes are made of precious stones. His own were sapphires.

"Let us hope it does not come that far," Hindin jested in response. "Thank you very much for your time, Mr. Armbakk. It was an honor meeting you."

"Sure thing. I hope you find the pissants. But, uh, before you leave, may I ask *your* name, sir?"

Hindin covered his mouth for a split second. "Oh, how rude of me! Please, grant your pardon. I am Hindin Revetz, son of Diyomead."

"Revetz, eh?" Richard stood up, and peered down at Hindin. He could not help but notice how short and plain he was compared to him. No intricate designs, nor armor-like skin or bulky muscles. "Sorry, but I've never heard of *your* clan," he declared with a confused frown.

Hindin smiled. There was a restrained positivity in his expression. "You may before too long, sir."

"Oh, agave, you look famished!" Polly heard as she passed a plump woman running a fruit stand. Before she could tell the woman otherwise, her stomach let out a deep growl. Reluctantly, she moved toward the stand and picked up a piece of the sweet treasured fruit.

"Um." She timidly reached in her pocket. "How much are dey?" She pulled out 17 of the square grotz coins. It was all she had left from Cecil the Flesh-broker's wallet though she kept the two gold teeth. She had already purchased a warmer change of clothes and a meager breakfast.

"Normally I charge twelve for twenty grotz," the vendor said."But you look so hungry; I'll let it slide for today. Here, take a few," the lady insisted, packing the ripe fruit into a paper bag. "Just tell everyone you know that you got them from me. Okay, agave?"

"T-Tank you!" Polly stammered, taken aback by the sudden kindness. She accepted the bag and nodded slowly into an awkward bow. "I don't tink I've tried dese before."

"You've never had jububes?" the lady exclaimed, raising her eyebrows. "That accent... Where were you raised?"

"I..." Polly struggled for an answer. "Tank you again!" she cried out before running off. The last thing she meant to do was have people ask questions, let alone stand around and answer them.

A few blocks and back streets away she came to an empty alley. Nestled against a building were some large empty shipping crates abandoned by one of the many venders at the marketplace. She crawled into one with a hole kicked in the side. This had been her home for the last two nights. Tucking her knees under her chin, she eyed the large fruits and tried to relax. If she ate one a day, she'd have four days of food. If she filled up on water, maybe she could stretch it out to six or seven. But she would start to get weak and become an easier target. The city had run out of options for her. There were plenty of places to hide, but more people to see her. She did not want to press her luck. She had to pick a safe direction. Sadly, she knew little of this country's geography, and picking the wrong escape route could prove devastating.

A sudden crash snapped her out of her thoughts. She peeked out of a broken hole in the crate. A tall young male wearing an Embrenil Academy sweater had tripped over some nearby debris. She could see why he had not noticed it- a black halo of energy encircled the young man's eyes. *"He's been ensorcelled!"* she thought. *"It's a sensory curse."*

Four other young men surrounded him. They wore loose tunics, wool jackets, and leather hats with eye-shading brims.

"Typical ruffians," Polly thought. She hugged her knees tighter and pinched her tattoo. *"Dey'll probably just rob him, rough him up, and run off."* She tried to convince herself.

The taller ruffian wore a faded yellow bandanna around his neck and a smile on his lips. He stood over his prey, gloating. He put something shiny into his jacket pocket. Polly felt an unsettling chill emanated from him. *"Dis one's blood burns to spill de blood of others!"* she thought. She fought to keep still and ignore her trembling veins. *"Save your energy,"* she thought. The ruffians stomped and kicked at the boy mercilessly as they laughed and growled like a pack of dogs. The blinded boy seemed only partially aware of the thudding shoes. He swayed and flailed wildly until a kick connected with his temple. He went limp and still. Polly felt a vicious tug like fish hooks in her heart.

"Leave the class ring and the wallet. That's all traceable," the tall one ordered as he unsheathed a knife from his belt. "Only get the money and what we need this time. I don't want anymore problems."

"You have dem anyway," came Polly's voice from behind them.

The four turned, surprised by the sudden presence of the petite young woman. But that was not all that startled them. The gold in her pupils shifted to a glowing red and the veins under her skin popped and swished around like epileptic worms. The four ruffians froze in momentary shock as the veins multiplied and grew longer. She raised an arm and yelled *"Blood for blood!"* focusing her energy at the blood lusting leader. He shook and spasmed as blood poured out his nostrils. His blade hit the ground as he twitched like a puppet out of control. The thief closest to him squatted to pick it up, but his face met the toe of Polly's boot. His nose collapsed and he saw the blinding color of pain.

"Shunting slag!" another yelled at her. "You think you're the only mystic in Emby?!" He dramatically backed up and tossed off his cap. Long dreadlocks fell to his shoulders. He raised his hands as if holding a ball.

"A burnt child fears the fire!" he exclaimed, harnessing the power of the maxim. Bright cinders manifested, concentrating into a small round flame. He seemed impressed with himself as the flame swooshed and crackled.

But that moment of vanity used up any time he had to react. Polly had already raised her hand and responded with *"Blood is thicker dan water."* A dark thick spurt of blood shot out of her wrist and onto the burning orb. The flame hissed and burst into a red cloud of steam, stinging the eyes of fire starter. As he covered his face with his arms he felt the solid thump of her boot bash into his groin. His balance and sense of pride were lost as he fell.

The fourth ruffian, who was broad and stocky, charged to tackle her. But just as he closed in, she saw him. From one forearm and quickly the other, her squirming veins popped out and surrounded his arms like a thorny cage. They snagged his flesh like barbed wire through his sleeves. Polly turned and spun

31

on her heels, redirecting his momentum into a wall. His face bounced off the bricks before he even had a chance to scream.

"Not another move! Not another trick!" came a voice behind her.

Polly looked over to see the leader standing once more. He was also clutching his knife again. He held up the beaten college student and rested the blade on the boy's throat. The blood from the ruffian's nose had smeared across his face.

"No!" she thought with sudden guilt. *"The effect was too weak! I used it too fast!"* Her veins made a splishing sound as they slithered back into arms. The three injured ruffians stumbled up and limped over to hide behind their leader. All glared at her in varying mixtures of anger and fear.

Polly focused on the victim. He flailed gently like a child trying to awake from a nightmare.

She took in a slow breath and said "You let him go. I let you go. Dat means you win." She focused her eyes on the leader."If you kill him, you will only be a dead winner," she warned.

The leader's eyes flickered in desperation. "Fine," he answered, trying to stay calm. He moved forward, still using the boy as a shield. He began to push him forward. Polly reached out to take the boy's hand when suddenly; the leader yanked the boy back.

"On second thought!" His eyes grew cold in a sneer. The dagger flashed as he drew it across the boy's neck. Before she could react, the ruffian pushed the boy onto her. Blood gushed into her face and chest. His weight slammed her into the ground as the ruffians sprinted off. She tried to get him off her, but he clung tight as air whistled out of his split neck. Her stomach lurched at the smell, and she used that disgust to find the strength to roll him off. She wiped at her eyes with the hem of her shirt. His blood was in her eyes, nostrils, and mouth. She rubbed her face and blinked hard several times. When her sight returned, she saw that the boy was dead.

Beginning to tremble, she clenched her teeth. It was too late to heal him. If only he hadn't been pushed on her, she might have been able to return the blood and seal the wound. It all happened in less than a minute. She failed and had to run away again. Soaked in blood, she got up and ran the opposite way the gang had left. At the end of the alley, she ran into more young people wearing Embrenil Academy shirts.

"Are you alright?" one girl asked.

But Polly was already sprinting away. She ran, knowing they would find their classmate murdered, and knowing that she would be blamed for it. The moment anyone saw her seven-point tattoo, the symbol of the Crimson Theurge, she would not escape the penance of the law.

❖

Will and Hindin stood in awe of the fossil filled wall of a shipping dock building. Actually, Will struggled to light his cigarette as Hindin prattled on.

"One must admit; the fossil-filled architecture in this city comes close to grandeur of the stained glass edifices of Vempour. What truly sets this city apart, my friend, is its unique brickwork. Seven thousand years ago, its founding peoples mined the nearby mountains for building stones. But what they discovered was that the rock itself was full of petrified bones, shells, and carapaces of beasts from millions of years ago! To think, my friend, the bones on this building and others throughout the city once belonged to creatures that not even the oldest beings among us can recall."

"Gah!" Will shouted in disgust, tossing a pack of matches to the ground. "You got to be a fire mystic to get a spark on these cheap things." He turned to the large steel man next to him. "And how is lookin' at these old bones s'posed to help? We ain't tourists, remember?"

"What should we do?" Hindin asked, shrugging. "Keep approaching strangers and beat up random punks in hopes of getting a drop of information?"

"Works in other towns," Will mumbled. For a moment he forgot his inkling for a tobacco fix, and looked at the buildings his friend seemed so intrigued by. This was his first time in a large city in daylight. And as his thoughts came to him, he shared them with Hindin.

"Rev, this place has a presence about it. These streets are a lot wider than the dusty roads of some old boom town. But they don't look it 'cause the buildings are so dang tall. You remember that narrow mountain pass in Gurtangorr?"

33

"Yes," Hindin answered.

"Well, these streets feel just like it, all cramped an' channeled out. Some of these buildings are twenty stories tall, fer goodness' sake! How can people live so close to each other an' still stay civil?"

Before Hindin could reply, a terrified scream erupted from across the street.

"Davil!" Across the street a group of students gathered around an alley, a shaken girl stumbled out. "She killed him!" she screamed in a panic, pointing desperately down the sidewalk.

Will's eyes focused as he saw a darting girl in a gray cloak weaving between the passersby. Two things clicked in his mind: one, she was the thief girl from yesternight, and two, she was soaked in fresh blood that caught the sheen of daylight.

"Aw, gut snake!" he shouted, tossing his cigarette on the ground.

"Will?" Hindin asked.

"It's that gal from yesternight!" Will exclaimed as he started after her. Polly could run fast but could not outrun a tendikeye. He only needed a few well aimed leaps before he tackled her from behind. His strong arms easily captured the petite's body and stunned her as they rolled onto the ground.

In a second's time he had one arm pinned to her side as he held on to her squirming waist. Her wet clothes and hair reeked of blood and bile.

"Rev! It's her! The thief!" Will shouted back to his partner.

Hindin did his best to clear a path through the crowd. He even resorted to picking a few of the smaller pedestrians up like confused toddlers and setting them off to the side.

Polly writhed against whoever had grabbed her. With her free arm she clawed at the large hand pinning her. She didn't care who it was, she would hurt him bad enough to get him off her! One of the hands about her waist let go, probably to try to grab her clawing hands. She latched onto his wrist, and that is when she felt it.

Thick, deep, and loud. His pulse was strong and booming. So loud she couldn't hear anything over it. She never felt a pulse like this before. It beat again, loud enough to startle her. Purely by reflex, she focused her will to push back against the thunderous heartbeat.

34

Will's mind blanked white with pain as he yelled and let go. His arm cramped up as all the blood rushed up out of it.

Polly rolled away and stood. She looked down at a spiky headed beast with green scaly skin. No, wait. That was his coat. His skin was a weird tan color.

Everyone around stood back as Hindin broke through the crowd. His expertly cut emerald eyes met Polly's red ones and a challenge was made. He took a smooth, relaxed fighting stance and bellowed for people to back up. They immediately stepped back. His stance was deep and his bearing was studious.

"Whadya do to me?!" Will yelled, still on the ground, gripping his arm.

"You'll live," she told him, before focusing her attention squarely on Hindin. Polly summoned her veins from her forearms and used the iron in her blood to harden them. She had never fought a Malruka before. And by the looks of this one, she did not want to.

"And what of the poor man you just killed?" Hindin asked calmly.

"I-I didn't," Polly protested, panicked. "But I saw who did! Let me go!"

Hindin was not taking chances. "Surrender without hostility, and I shall do you no harm. But I will not let you go."

Before she could answer they heard the clicks of carbine rifles around them.

"Embrenil Civic Police! Halt!" a gruff voice screamed at them.

Two local police guards emerged from the crowd. They wore burnt orange leather armor with a brass badge in the center of the chest. They aimed squarely at Polly and Hindin. Will still clutched his arm on the pavement, wincing at the pins and needles as it woke back up.

"Make no sudden movements or you will be petrified!" warned the officer targeting Polly, his nervous eyes roaming over her spiked veins.

Hindin eyed the carbine rifles. They were no doubt loaded with *petrarounds*, or theurgic ammunition. They did no damage to bodies, but turned anything they were fired at to inanimate stone. Even malruka were not immune to their effect. And by the time it wore off, they would wake up in jail with mean headaches and stiff joints.

35

Hindin and Polly raised both their arms. Will, to his dismay and embarrassment, could only raise one.

One of the officers put a whistle to his lips and blew a harsh, loud note that quieted the streets of the market place. In less than a minute, more guards came. They put handcuffs on Will and Polly and took their weapons. Polly's throat grew tight. She could feel the dead boy's blood going dry on her face.

An officer cautiously approached Hindin. In his hand he held what looked like a scroll only a few inches wide. "Your hands," the officer demanded.

Polly watched as the officer wrapped the roll of parchment around the malruka's wrists in a figure 8 pattern. She looked for scribed mystical runes on the paper, but saw none. "How can dat hold him?" she wondered.

"We got a cold one here!" another cop yelled, looking into the nearby alleyway.

The oldest of the officers looked at the three outsiders, glaring. "By the authority of the Chief Justice of Embrenil, I arrest you three. Keep your tongues still unless you want them turned to stone. You are to come along peacefully and remain in our custody until justice finds its mark. Nod if you comply."

They did.

Chapter 2

The Man in the Silver Helmet

◈

The Embrenil Civic Police Department building took the shape of an arch that had fallen backward on the corner of Primary St. and Cradle Blvd, curving like a thick stone rainbow that lay on its back. Rows of clear windows arced inward on its front and outward in the rear. On its sides were the petrified exoskeletons of two giant arachnids, forever frozen in yellow-orange stone. The structure was three stories high, one story deep, with many stories resolved, and few left open. Above the front entrance was a grand and tall veil of bright orange. Upon it read the words *All Who Enter Shall be Judged*. It was a double meaning, of course. The accused would be judged as guilty or innocent. And the police who worked there would be judged for their efficiency. On the first floor in a grand office sat an old Drakeri of eight hundred and forty two years. He was still spry and regal, for the invigorating surges of purpose and duty still pulsed within him.

Chief Judge Waltre Taly rarely let himself have a bad day. After having thousands of suspects sweat before his gavel, witnessing all flavors of fear, he had learned the secret of not worrying. This, he believed, allowed him to make more sound decisions.

Will, Polly, and Hindin were processed individually into the police station. After giving separate statements, the three were brought before the bench of the Chief Judge for their hearing and sentencing. The Chief stood behind the bench reading each statement as he stroked his graying purple mustache. His expression was stern but eerily relaxed. He glanced up at Will and Hindin first.

"Mr. Revetz and Mr. Foundling. First off, why are two outsiders snooping around my city? Why do *you both* feel the need to investigate a case you have no stake in, personal or professional?"

"We came to help, sir. To offer support," the tendikeye answered.

"Why?" the Chief asked harshly. "What's in it for you? No reward has been offered."

Will took a deep calming breath. "Well, if yer obligated to pry, yer honor: then I'll let you in on my agenda. I'm lookin' fer a man called Brem Hoffin. He's a wingless bukk like me. Years ago, before he skipped town, he said that if I ever wanted to find him, I'd hafta make a name fer myself in Doflend. I figured solvin' a big city conundrum might get the old coot's attention."

The Chief eyed the tendikeye for a chain of moments, watching, waiting. Then he asked "And why is it so important that you find this man?"

Will flexed the muscles in his jaw and shook his head. "It dudn't concern you, yer honor. All you need know an' all I need say is I got a reputation to build an' a certain man to find by doin' it."

The Chief Judge raised his eyebrows. "Well, my boy. You are off to a good start by getting arrested." He shifted his cold gaze to Hindin. "And why are you with him?"

Hindin raised his chin politely. "A few months ago, this man saved my life. I am honor bound by my philocreed to see him reunited with his mentor."

The Chief scoffed. "Does that make you his servant?"

"His friend," Hindin corrected. He leaned forward, raising his hand to his mouth as if to tell a secret. He spoke in a loud whisper. "Though I must admit, your honor: I often *serve* as his conscience, too."

The Chief blinked his eyes, wondering whether the steel man was joking or serious. Then the old man realized that he did not care. These two made their choice. And now he made his.

"You are both charged with the following offenses: disturbing the peace, public brawling, unregistered firearms, and investigating without a permit," he stated in one calm breath.

"Since when do you need a permit?" Will raised his voice as if his favorite toy was taken away.

"New law, son. It was passed by the city council only 43 years ago," the Chief replied, already tired of Will's tone. "This city once crawled with foreign mercenaries and excursionists like

38

you. Each one of them seemed to have their own interpretation of what justice was. They became every bit a menace as the criminals they hunted. These days, if you wish to give the department hands-on assistance, I alone can grant approval. And guess what, son: Your chances aren't looking so great. I know a glory seeking hothead when I meet one. This department doesn't need your kind of help."

Hindin nodded calmly, "It makes sense if you think about it. The new law, I mean."

"Ah, shut up, Rev!" Will pout-shouted.

Taly's head turned to Polly. "As for you Miss Gone. One count of murder and theft and several other counts of assault pending investigation. You also share a public brawling charge with these gentlemen. Whether you are or are not the killer, you still abandoned a crime scene. Furthermore, *hemopathy* is illegal in this country. Highly illegal, given its philocreed." He leaned back, taking in her concerned expression with his cold eyes. "Now, I've read your statements and this is how it will be; for you gentlemen, I'll reduce your sentence provided you plead ignorance here and now."

Hindin did not hesitate. "We do, your honor."

Will rolled his eyes and resisted fidgeting, "Yes, sir."

Chief Taly's mouth smirked with approval. "Good, good. Now, you have three choices, either thirty days in jail, a two thousand grotz fine, or a round in the Red Dirt arena as gladiatorial defendants. If you win, you are free and cleared of all charges."

Now it was Will and Hindin's turn to smirk. Hindin answered with a big grin, "We choose to risk our lives for the amusement of the masses, your honor!"

Taly stamped their papers. "Good. Foreigners never disappoint the crowd." He turned to Polly. "As for you, Miss, we have to wait a few more hours for the coroner's report. He's using some post mortem theurgic techniques to ask the victim what happened."

Polly was shocked at the man's words, "You have a necrotheurge for a coroner? I have heard it takes a dark pnuema for such practices."

"The same can be said of your path of casting, little lady," he replied, eying her seven point tattoo. "It's standard procedure if the body is fresh enough. The soul is mostly long gone, but traces of it remain."

She looked down at the floor. Hindin glanced over at her. She looked more like a lost child than a murderer. He could not help but feel pity for her.

"But even if you are innocent, the other charges still stand." The Chief banged his gavel. "We will inform you when the coroner is done. You boys will have your bout in three or four days. Enjoy your stay with us."

Each was taken to a separate ten foot by ten foot cell. Hindin politely hunched as he was escorted through the six foot tall doorway. Will could feel the cold presence of the bars surrounding him. Polly choked on despair, but hid it with a neutral face.

The tendikeye sighed as he sat on his cot, slapping his huge hands on his knees. He turned his head to his friend in the adjacent cell. "Hey, Rev. What's a pnuema?"

"Soul," the malruka answered. "But it is an out-dated connotation."

"Hey, guys! How's your hammer hanging? You here to let me out yet?" The voice came from the cell across from Will's. It was from a creature none of them were surprised to see in a drakeri jail- a human male, and a big one. He stood optimistically at the bars, staring at the guards. He was over six and a half feet tall and built like a brick dung house with a slight gut. He wore a shabby black leather vest over a stained white sleeveless shirt. His dark arms were thick with muscle and covered in crude tattoos. His blue jeans had natural holes where the knees had worn through. But the most distinctive thing about him was his helmet. It was a single solid piece of a simple design. It covered nearly all of his face, only allowing the gleam of his big brown eyes. Tarnished abstract etchings made the head piece fearsome and elegant all at once.

One guard turned to him and wagged a finger. "You know why you're here, Fevärian! Cut the dung!"

"Aw, come on!" the human pleaded casually. "*I'm* the victim here, man! That girl lied and said she was 20!"

"She was only 16!"

"Well, she *felt* 20!" he quipped back with a shrug and a hardy chuckle.

Another guard, a curvy drakeri woman with the hips of an exotic concubine, responded to the exchange. "Play nice, boys," she smirked.

Polly Gone sat against the back wall of her cell, next door to Will. She saw that the right side of his coat collar was flared. It bugged her. Was it some kind of style or did he just not care? His gray eyes were studying her up and down. She wondered what went through his mind. What kind of thoughts was he entertaining? Was he the poaching type of hunter? Was he planning to gut and skin her for messing up his arm?

"It isn't my fault dat de energy hurt your arm so bad," she said defensively. "How was I to know a tendikeye had tackled me?"

"The arm's fine now, thanks," he answered flatly. He locked eyes with her and cocked his head. "Do you swear you didn't kill that man?" he asked as if she might not have understood the question.

She nodded, trying to find her voice. "On my philocreed, I swear. I tink and hope dat de victim saw deir faces before dey blinded him." She hung her head and closed her eyes. "I...I doubt his pnuema shattered peacefully."

Hindin was listening as he approached the cot in his cell. "Metaphysical fission," he said solemnly. "Slate teaches us that without facing the impeding doom of one's own spiritual deconstruction, one can never find wisdom in the present moment."

"Slate?" Polly asked, looking up. "He is your King, no? King of de Malruka?"

"His word is law for his word is truth," he answered, about to sit down on his cot. "But his title is not *King*. He is The Life Father." As his weight settled into the cot, it snapped and collapsed into a pile of wood and cloth.

The brutish human burst out laughing. "Sorry, Two-Ton, but these aren't stone slabs like in malrukan prisons."

"Why am I not surprised you've seen the inside of other cells?" Will called out with a sneer.

"Are you okay?" Polly asked the malruka semi-discreetly.

Hindin looked up and nodded. "It is not the first time furniture has collapsed under me," he tittered, smiling and dusting himself off. "On another note, I hope that you *are*

41

innocent, Ms. Gone. And I hope you hold no ill will toward my partner and me."

She shook her head and cracked a smile. "My leg got scraped up a bit when your tendikeye tackled me."

"*His* tendikeye?" Will fumed at the girl. "I ain't his pet!" He kicked his cot hard enough to make it flip over. "And it ain't like yer bleedin' still."

"I only bleed when I want to," she snapped back coldly.

"When is that?" the human broke in. "Once a month? Oh, wait. It's every ten years for you girls, isn't it?" He laughed madly then stopped with a straight face. Then laughed again.

"Have you always worn a helmet?" Polly sneered at him. "Even as a child?"

The tall brute laughed at the comeback. It sounded like his whole world was being refreshed. "You three are my kind of crowd! Allow yourselves to make my acquaintance. My name is Sir Röger Yamus, independent Black Vest and part time mercenary," he declared with a formal bow.

"Hindin Revetz," the stone man returned calmly. He raised a steel eyebrow. "'*Independent* Black Vest, you say? I take it you are a former Fevärian retainer of some sort. Would that not make you instead a *former* or *ex*-Black Vest?"

The human smiled with his eyes. "Lord or no lord; my duty hasn't changed. Only now, I choose what causes I take up." He shifted his cheerful gaze to Will. "And you are?"

The tendikeye looked unimpressed as he flipped his cot back over. "Will Foundling, Harker at'cher service."

"A Harker?" Röger grinned as his eyes widened. "I've known a few Harker's in my time. Not the best duelists, but pretty handy on a nature hike. Why aren't you bushwhacking back in Cloiherune? Were you discharged or did you run out of rebels to dismember?"

"Neither," Will responded flatly, turning away and crossing his arms.

Polly was still giving him a dirty look. "You don't act like a Black Vest. I heard dey were polite."

"The *Code of Word and Deed* should be only used in moderation," he said as if listing a rule. "Much like hot tempered Drakeri girls."

Polly rose up so fast even Will was startled. "I'm not hot tempered, you dirty round ear. And if dese bars weren't in my way I would make you choke on blood for insulting me." Her eyes brimmed with animosity and frustration.

But Röger's eyes shone with satisfaction. He looked over at Will like a frisky school boy. "Anger makes this one more beautiful." He winked smugly. "Want to see how beautiful I can make her?"

A hiss echoed from Polly's cell.

"Go easy on him, Miss Gone," the female officer urged, reentering the cell block. "Mr. Yamus has a big fight tomorrow." She carried a clip board as Chief Taly followed behind her.

"The coroner's report came early," announced Taly, taking the clip board. Polly held her breath. The chief flipped through the pages. "You are hereby dismissed of all murder and assault charges. However, the other charges stand. Two years in county lock up, ten thousand grotz fine, or a bout of penal combat at the public arena? Either way, I don't want vagrant blood witches in my fair city."

"I will fight for my freedom, if I must," she answered with lowered eyes. "I have no money. So the sooner I can fight, the sooner I'll depart your city."

Taly smiled in satisfaction. "Not that we aren't enjoying your pleasant company, but I'd agree that it's for the best. You'll need to wait a couple of days." He signed a page and handed the board to the lady officer. "Hmm, maybe we'll be able to arrange for you to fight one of these lads," he mused, tapping Will's bars with an ink pen.

"Dat won't be necessary," she answered, glancing at the others.

"Very well," Taly shrugged. He turned to the caged brute and made a face like he had just bit into a lemon. "As for you, Yamus..."

"Yes, sir, am I free to go?"

"Hardly," Taly sighed, nodding to the curvy deputy to explain the terms.

"You're booked at the Red Dirt at 3:50. You'll be given your weapons an hour beforehand to warm up," she said professionally. "Any questions?"

"Yeah, what exactly am I fighting? Monster? Theurgical construct?" He looked over at Polly. "Feisty mystic?"

The woman smiled and cocked her head to the side. "The paper says, Röger Yamus vs. Question Mark. My guess is it's a secret they're keeping from the public to sell more tickets. Must've worked. I hear the place is sold out."

Röger's calm joking dissolved into jittery concern. The last thing he wanted to do was fight in front of a big crowd and be forced to reveal more about himself than he wanted. Mainly, revealing his brains against some wall. He eyed his fellow cell mates, and an idea sprouted in his mind.

"Say, Chief, is there a way to put three more question marks on my side and have these three join me?"

The Chief raised an eyebrow. "Are you suggesting a team battle?"

"Yeah!" he exclaimed, stepping back from the bars. He put his hands on his hips and shot glances at his cellmates. "Come on, guys! Care to break out a few days early?"

"It sounds ... plausible," Hindin responded.

"Sure, why not?" Will nodded. He regarded the human brute with a bemused wariness.

Röger took a knee and turned to the Chief. He looked up like a man about to confess his love.

Taly looked over at Polly. "Miss Gone?

She didn't need to think about it. It was a faster way out. "Yes," she answered gravely.

Taly rolled his eyes and nodded. "Very well. I'll see what I can do. Lights out!" He clapped and the room's temperature dropped as the lantern's dimmed. "Get some sleep," he ordered before taking his leave.

Polly crawled onto her cot and covered up with a thick wool blanket. All the while, she watchfully eyed Will. He simply stood there in his dark cell and eventually struck a match against a steel bar to light a cigarette. As the light shone on his face, she caught another glimpse of his collar. It was still flared on the right side.

"Why don't you fix your collar?" she asked him, bearing her teeth. "Do you tink it makes you look stylish or someting?"

She felt his eyes shift toward her in the chilly darkness. It was then that she realized it was her own fear that annoyed her. She knew that he could not see her. But his cool predatory glare caused her paranoia to stir.

"It's a custom, is all," he answered calmly. "We tendikeye answer certain questions 'fore they get asked by what we wear an' how we wear it."

44

She furrowed her brow in confusion.

Will flicked his flared right collar, the finger making a loud pop on the leather. "This means I am unmarried without little ones. If the left side was popped; that'd mean I was hitched up an' probably with little ones. If both sides are up; it means I'm a widower or maybe divorced."

"What if both sides are down?" she asked.

"Means yer on yer way to the brush pile."

"Brush pile?"

Will laughed dryly. "Means yer either dead or about to be." He took a long puff before telling her "G'night, Miss Polly. Rest up to keep yer best up."

Later, in his pristine office, Cheif Taly considered the day's decisions. The girl was a living witness for a major case, but mystics of her ilk could not be trusted. He doubted that Will Foundling was the tendikeye's real name. No family in all of Cloiherune would turn down the blessing of a bukk child. Plus, he seemed too well adjusted to be an orphan. Unrefined, yet polite. The malruka was clearly insane. His good manners just covered it up. And as for Mr. Yamus, the Chief had him pegged from the get-go; a brash marauder looking to have a bit of sport with the locals before fleeing the law. It was the Chief's personal and private belief that humans and tendikeye, due to their shorter life spans, were more prone to disorder, base behavior, rash violence, and bad hygiene. Besides, the local arena had a new attraction to showcase. What better candidates than rootless outsiders? All things considered, Waltre Taly had a good day.

The Red Dirt Battle Arena was a large wooden stadium on the edge of the city's oldest district, Soularde. It was created as an elaborate way to execute convicts, pitting them against each other or some captured monster. Over time, the government invested in hopes of scaring offenders straight, making it bigger and with more menacing attractions. Survival would always mean freedom to those who did not want centuries in prison or a formal execution. It was a full blown event center complete with concessions. One of the most popular treats sold was meat left over from the slain arena monsters. It came in all forms from bun cradled franks, meat kabob, and of course, hamburgers. "Waste not, want not!" venders shouted in the rows. Everywhere, there were banners sporting the NcRay Beer logo. And of course, there was always a booth open to take bets.

Due to a high sex drive and a low judgment, the human Sir Röger, was to face an A class threat known only as "?". Normally, sneaking out of windows was a C class charge, but rumor had it his verbal suggestions to Chief Judge Taly on what to do with his gavel raised the level of punishment.

The tall brute stood in the locker room, swinging a large two-handed axe to warm his muscles for the bout. He looked over at his teammates.

The malruka stood gazing out the bars at the first A class battle. A sex offender with a club took on a twenty foot tall birdbeast called a *Magmacock*. The pretty Polly sat with her knees tucked under her chin, expressionless. Röger sighed through his nose, *"Great. A polished rock and an angst filled teenager."* he thought. His eyes rolled to the one person he thought might be helpful.

The bukk swung a polished steel blade, cutting wide circular arcs in the air around him. The sword was mirror polished with a small black marking on one side that the human did not recognize. The arm length blade curved in a smooth crescent. He seemed to be going over a mental library of stepping patterns. Röger took note that there were no blocks or parries in Will's bladeplay. But his footwork was quick and deceptively defensive. Each cut he made was a fast, clean slash meant for a one hit kill. The weight of his heavy hand added deadly momentum to each swing. There was no mistaking it: the kid really was a Harker.

"It's too bad they won't let him use his gun for this fight," Röger thought. *"I'm only going to see half of what this boy can do."*

"Hey, Yamus!" an officer called from the other side of the bars, "You're next."

Röger set his axe down on a wooden chair and lifted up his billblade sword. It was a long, double edged sword with a wicked hook at the end. It was originally designed to hook the legs of a war steed or rip a rider off one. He strapped it to his back and took up his axe.

46

The arena attendant's voice boomed through the stands. "Are you ready for our mystery event?!" Over seven thousand excited voices erupted in reply. The eastern entrance gate swung wide and the four fighters walked into the arena. The red clay dirt that gave the arena its name layered the floor, better to hide the blood with.

At one end of the battleground was a smoking crater where the last defendant had last stood. Pedophiles never got much of a chance.

"Ladies, gentlemen, locals, and visitors, we have a rare team battle today with a select group of warriors from all over the Cluster!" the announcer called over a bellowing crowd. "First is the tenacious tendikeye from Cloiherune, Will Foundling!"

Will raised his sword politely, but offered no smile. Tendikeye loved fighting. But their ideals toward it differed from Drakeri. Sparring for sport and entertainment was fine. But death duels were usually private matters settled between hated enemies. He did not cotton to the idea of having to kill a yet-to-be-known opponent.

"Next: the marvelous, the mysterious, mesmerizing mystic, Polly Gone!"

Polly hissed and shrank into herself. She hated crowds. She hated being stared at. Too many people, too many eyes on her. Too big of a risk.

"Next up, the team powerhouse!" the man called, "Hindin Revetz, Malrukan ... Chimancer?!"

A slight hush fell over the crowd. Here and there, mutterings of puzzlement could be heard.

Polly's ears perked. "*Chimancer?*" she thought with confusion and curiosity. She had learned about a rare theurgy that mingled martial arts and nerve energy. But such practitioners were always beings of flesh and blood. How was it possible with a *Son of Stone*?

"And our last defendant, Röger Yamus, the Fevärian," the announcer finished flatly.

"That's SIR Röger Yamus the Black Vest, mud-humper!" Röger rumbled, giving the finger to the announcer's booth.

The announcer made a gesture of his own towards the large chained door at the end of the field. The crowd quieted down to listen.

Röger looked over at Will. "Should we have planned a strategy, bukk?"

Will gave him a slight grin. "Why bother? There's no tellin' what's behind that door. No plan is the best plan."

Röger nodded in agreement, but his helmet hid the unease in his eyes.

"Originating from the deepest forest of Ses Lemuert," the announcer began.

"Aw, hell," Will spat.

"I give you the greatest, most dangerous beast ever released in our arena, truly a mountain of madness!"

"Oh my," Hindin fretted.

"Behold! The one, the only, Sizzagafiend!!!"

"SHUNT!" Röger cursed, scraping the dirt like a bull.

The gates clanged open with ear-piercing reverberation. The beast climbed out of the entrance as a large spider does from a small hole. Its spindly limbs carried a massive body that seemed both reptilian and insectiod. Two canoe-shaped pincers curved down like foreboding mantis claws. Its long neck swayed from side to side like a viper about to strike. It had the terrible head of a gaunt hooded cobra with spider-like mandibles protruding from a fang filled mouth. The mouth opened wide and shrieked, dripping slime from its jaws. It was one of those sounds that scrapes down one's back and lands at their feet, pinning them to the spot.

Röger's eyes widened inside his helmet. "They wanted me to fight that by myself?!" he shouted angrily.

Will's heart sank. He felt crippled without his pistol. He had been growing edgy since the first cheer from the stands. At that moment, as his body shook, he let those nervous shakes settle into a hard trained focus.

His large feet blurred as he charged the beast, kicking up red dust behind him. Making a darting twenty foot jump, he swung his blade at the long neck of the Sizzagafiend, wasting no time, and landed the hit around mid center.

The beast reacted with a twitch as if trying to dismiss an itch. Will sprung back, quickly examining the cut he made; only a foot long and an inch deep cut showed, not even an eighth of the width of its neck. The beast hissed, coming down at him with one of its massive pincers. He leaped back, the strike missing by mere inches as a cloud of red dust shot up from where the pincher had landed.

"These claws are gonna be a problem, Rev!" he called out to Hindin.

Hindin replied as he charged the massive claw. "Sir Yamus!" he called. "Would you mind attacking its left side, please?"

Röger lifted his axe high and ran toward the left claw. "Sharing is caring, so they say!" He leaped in the air, a forward flip increasing his momentum for a downward chop. He slammed down the curved axehead onto the creature's canoe sized claw. The beast lurched and shrieked as the exoskeleton of the claw cracked. Green ichor oozed from the jagged crack. Distracted by the pain, it noticed too late as Hindin shoulder charged its other claw. The force of the stone man's tackle caused the pincher to shut. In a lethal bear hug, the malruka wrapped his arms around it, holding the claw closed.

Another shriek went through the spectators. The beast slapped Röger away with its injured limb. He felt the air forced from his lungs as the massive limb slammed into him. He landed on the back of his head, slamming his chin into his chest. He rolled limply, kicking up a cloud of red dust.

Will watched as the Sizzagafiend tried to lift Hindin and throw him as well, but the stone fighter only gripped tighter as he was lifted barely a few feet off the ground.

Out of the corner of her eye, Polly saw Röger land. "He's not moving! His neck broke!" she thought as terror seized her.

The tendikeye to her right darted forward and jumped high, aiming once again for the long neck. Hissing, the beast weaved out of the way and tried batting the man with its wounded claw. Will kicked the bloody pincher as it came at him, sinking his heel into the pulsing wet stump. Once again, the creature screamed either out of pain or frustration. It chased forward after Will, dragging Hindin on its right limb. But after a few steps, it realized that Hindin was the easiest target. It snapped at his legs with its powerful maw, trying to pull him off. But the malruka's grip was strong and his legs were too hard to be hurt by its teeth.

"His head is lowered!" Hindin yelled to Will.

"Got it!" Will called back, leaping again at the cut he made earlier. He followed the line of the cut, tracing it with the

49

edge of his yashinin blade in a flash of steel. The beast made a loud gagging sound and let go of Hindin's legs.

It responded with a surge of rage, biting at the tendikeye. Will dodged, but his dust coat got hooked on one of its teeth. It hoisted and threw him a good thirty feet into the air, ready to catch him in a big bloody bite. But before the Sizzagafiend could consume its falling prey, the five foot long sting of Röger's bill blade sword caught its side. The beast's jaws snapped shut before Will fell. With reflexes like a caffeinated cat, he landed on its snout, jumping and twisting to land near Polly.

Röger, now covered in red dirt, tried to remove his sword, but opted to leave it in instead. Limping and rubbing his sore neck, he dashed for his axe several yards away.

"Hey! Mystic girl!" he yelled at Polly. "Can't you throw a fireball or somethin' useful?!"

"My theurgy doesn't work like dat!! I only have influence over blood!" she yelled back. She was too scared to be amazed that he was alive. She had not planned on being so useless. She was used to taking on things close to her size and safely sneaking in close. But in the barrage of large blades, larger pincers, and huge monster fangs, she could see no safe way to join in. "I can't get in close enough to do anyting!" she cried.

The tendikeye fumed through his nostrils. "All you had to do was ask!" Will yelled, his face grim.

Before she knew it, the tendikeye scooped her up onto his shoulder and started running with her to the Sizzagafiend, her head facing away from the beast.

"What?!" she squealed. "Get your meat fists off of me!"

"Rev, play paperweight a little bit longer!" Will called to Hindin, ignoring Polly's demand.

Hindin nodded, though his arms were getting tired from holding the massive pincher shut.

"Sweetheart, time to make yerself useful!" the charging tendikeye told her.

"How?!"

"Do to that thing...what you did to my arm!" He jumped passed the beast's snapping jaws, crashing with her onto its back. She looked down at the gaping gash Will made earlier. It was twice her arm's length away. She tried crawling to it, but the monster started bucking.

"I have to get to dat wound!" she cried.

"I'll start a new one!" Will answered. Gripping the sword's handle with both hands, he jammed it straight onto the beast. But the blade made a thud sound, and only the tip of the point sank in. "It's all bone back here!"

Polly did her best to stay steady. But the jarring motions only flung her further from her mark.

"Timber!" Röger bellowed from the floor beneath them. He had retrieved his axe and hacked away at the beast's spider-like legs.

It gave Polly the chance she needed. Pouncing on the front of the creature's neck, she drew her dagger and stabbed it into the exposed wound. She found its pulse like she had on Will the day before. But this time, instead of pushing against it, she pulled!

At that instant, every injury that had been made on the fearsome Sizzagafiend gushed a green sticky liquid. The pressure was so great, that Röger's stuck sword shot out like an arrow into the dirt. Will and Polly rolled off its back and onto the ground as the beast writhed and twitched through its agonized shrieking. Hindin let go of the partially-crushed pincher, hoping to dodge the spray of monster blood. But he had no such luck. All of them, including the first three rows of the crowd, got drenched in the thick green ichor. The Sizzagafiend rolled onto its back and shrieked no more. It curled into a gnarled ball and died, its wounds making gurgling, dripping sounds.

Cheers and applause roared through the arena as the four defendants emerged from the goo. The glory of their victory marred by red dirt caked together with green sludge.

Hindin's hands made scraping sounds as he wiped the sludge off his steel-covered body. "Well done, Miss Gone," he told Polly cheerfully.

She smiled weakly. "Tank you. Call me Polly."

Röger and Will kept their eyes on the twitching carcass. When it finally stopped, they exchanged nods for a job well done.

Then, in a theatrical sparkling puff of smoke, the announcer appeared beside them. "And your winners" he announced as announcers do. "Without a single casualty...!" He paused and gestured to Hindin. "Psst!" he whispered "What's the team name, stonebro?"

Hindin glanced over at the others, and then leaned over to whisper in the announcer's double pointed ear.

51

The portly showman stepped forward, raising his hand. "Ladies and Gentlemen! Four Winds-One Storm!!!!"

The bathing facilities at the Red Dirt Battle Arena were usually adequate and practical. Each washroom provided a modicum of privacy, a wide floor drain, and a hand operated pump connected to a furnace heated water tank. Every defendant would usually receive a towel and a bar of soap after surviving their fight for freedom. But for the four combatants that now occupied the room, a few exceptions were made. Polly received a cheap wooden comb. Hindin got a cup of crude oil to keep from rusting. Will received a cigarette. And Röger got a second bar of soap. It was the least the staff could do for them, considering the massive profit the arena had made from their battle.

"Just what the hell does Four Winds-One Storm mean?" Röger called out to Hindin from his stall.

"It is from an old poem in one of my books," he called back as he tied his black sash around his waist. "Would you like me to recite it?"

"Uh, maybe later. A men's washroom isn't exactly a place for poetry."

Will came out of his stall into the main change room with Hindin. He wore only a clean pair of jeans and his boots. On his bare chest hung a military dog tag with two feathers fixed to the chain on either side of the small name plate. He did his best to rinse off his dust coat in the shower spout and then began the meticulous endeavor to clean the finer points with a damp rag.

Röger could not help but notice Will's attention to detail to every inch. He took a step closer and his eyes widened in his helmet. The dark green dust coat was made from the scaly skin of some reptile. The scales themselves were as wide as sword tips. *"Whatever beast that skin came off of,"* he thought *"it was a lot bigger than the one who wears it now!"*

In the washroom adjacent to theirs, Polly finished rinsing her hair out. She was now even more grateful to have it short, since it was easier to clean.

"Miss Gone?" called an attendant's voice from outside. "Chief Judge Taly is here to see you all. He requests that you all meet with him in the men's locker room in five minutes."

"A-Alright," she answered timidly. *"When? When will dey just let me leave?"* she thought.

She waited a good four and a half minutes before knocking on the men's room door.

"No, no! Let *me* get it!" she heard someone say on the other side. Röger opened the door wearing nothing but a towel and his helmet. "Enter at your own risk, milady!" he chuckled with a bow.

She gave a sour look and walked past him. Hindin gave her a smiling nod, which she quickly returned. Will paid no attention, still concentrating on his dust coat and still neglecting to put a shirt on. His tanned skin looked so odd to her, in contrast to the various shades of purple on her people. It was stretched over a mass of well crafted muscle. Drakeri tended towards lean, lengthy bodies, even the strongest of them. But this tendikeye was wide *and* tall. She found it strange that he seemed to take up more room with his shirt off. Her eyes fixed on what looked like a faint trail of quills growing down the center of his toned abdomen. Suddenly, he looked up at her with suspicion in his eyes.

She twitched, startled by his stern face.

"How'd you do that?" he asked.

"Do what?"

"Them're the same clothes you came here in an' they're clean and dry. How'd you git all that blood out?"

Polly raised an eyebrow and smiled. She looked around and found a blood soaked rag on the floor. "Dis your shirt?" she asked him, picking it up.

"Well. It was," he replied with a half grin.

Then, before his eyes, the shirt started to drip. From top to bottom, it began to drain of all moisture onto the floor. In seconds, it was a clean dry shirt again.

"Dat is why dey call me a crimson theurge. All secrets hidden in blood are mine to control and influence. I walk upon de Red River, de path of Life and Death," she explained, smiling proudly.

Will stared at the shirt blankly, then back at her. "If it's all the same to you, Miss Polly. Toss it. Thanks, but no thanks."

53

"But...what is wrong?" she asked, suddenly confused. "It is not torn or anyting."

"He does not trust or rely on theurgy," Hindin answered for him. "Please, do not be offended. It is simply his way."

Before she could ask anything else, Chief Judge Taly entered the room.

"Well done, kids!" Chief Taly praised, clapping his hands. Accompanying him was a deputy carrying an arm load of cloth wrapped items. Will glared up at the men, wiping off his dust coat. Thankfully, snake skin didn't stain.

"Are we free to go now, sir?" Hindin asked.

"Yes, yes," Taly replied, gesturing to the deputy. The deputy passed out the items that had been collected from them when arrested: Will's guns, Hindin's books, Polly's jubube fruits and two gold teeth, Röger's smoking pipe and everyone's money pouches.

"Sign the arena forms on the way out. Be sure to fill them out properly. I'm too old to chase down morons who forget to punctuate." He and the deputy then turned and exited out the door through which they had entered.

Hindin tied his meager pouch of grotz coins to his sash.

"Son of a nagging slag!" Röger exclaimed, looking into his pouch. "Not one cop pocketed any coins!"

"Maybe they were too impressed by what we did out there" Will smirked.

Röger laughed and looked at his three fellow outsiders. "By the way, thanks for helping me out, everybody. Taking that thing on alone would have been a pain in the ass."

"No problem," Will replied. "Better that than wait weeks for our own battle. Consider us even, Rög." He offered his hand.

Röger's eyes gleamed under his helm as he shook the large hand of the tendikeye. For the *quilled race,* handshaking was usually reserved for family or, in rare cases, fellow soldiers. This break in tradition for the sake of respect was a rare treat for most humans. He turned his attention to Polly. "Hey, Polly! You can do my clothes too if you want!"

"Fine. Dat will make *us* even," she replied in an annoyed tone.

She darted over to his vest, jeans, and t-shirt and began draining them. She had to avert her eyes from him as he put each piece on as she finished with it. He chuckled as he dressed.

54

"Dere, I am done," she stepped back and regarded the three men she had fought along side. "It was...nice meeting you three. I hope events go well wit' you all. But I must leave dis city as soon as possible. Goodbye." With that she turned and walked toward the exit.

"Polly, wait!" Röger padded after her. Will and Hindin followed as well. The four of them left the dressing room area and entered a hallway going toward the spectator stands.

"But Polly!" Röger pleaded. "You don't have to leave this town! There's still so much to see and do." He put an arm around her waist. "Let me give you a tour of the city. Buy you meals and stuff. I can tell by that wacky accent you're not from around here!"

"Dere something wrong wit' de way I speak?" she hissed, making a sharp turn down a corridor leading to the open arena.

"Aw, Polly, come on!" He begged as they came out amongst the almost empty area seats.

"Now I'm jealous, Sir Röger," a female voice called from the nearby stands.

Both looked up to see the curvaceous female guard from the holding cells. She was off the clock, her uniform replaced by tight blue slacks and a green sleeveless blouse.

"Feyna, my love!" Röger exclaimed, turning himself and all his attention toward her. Polly didn't know whether to be insulted or relieved. "You came to see lil' ol' me? Why, I'm honored!"

Will and Hindin caught up just in time to watch the scene between the two.

"I'm a free and honest man now, Feyna." Röger boasted.

"*Free* I'll agree with."

"I owe you for sneaking me that extra blanket," he winked.

"I thought you already repaid me with what we did *under* that blanket."

"I know a great inn at the west side of the city."

"I know one closer."

A loud gunshot coupled with a woman's scream interrupted the flirtation. A herd of people rushed toward the opening gate.

"Retaeh's Breath!" Feyna cursed, drawing her badge from her bag and dashing toward the crowd, elbowing her way through.

Will was the first to arrive through the clearing and scowled at what he saw. An elderly man lay twitching in the arms of a woman who was desperately trying to keep him alive.

"Help! Th-they shot my Dympner!" she shook his limp body. "They did something to his eyes!"

"Clear the way!" Feyna shouted, waving her civic badge.

Will felt something rush past his arm and saw Polly kneel by the old couple. She lifted the man's shirt and circled her index and center finger around the bullet wound. The crowd whispered in amazement, for not only the bleeding stopped, but the blood seemed to return back into the hole.

"He's not waking up!" the woman clutching her husband cried.

"The bullet needs to be removed," Polly told her.

"Then re-remove it!" she shouted.

"I'm no doctor!" Polly shouted back.

"These men are." Chief Taly said, appearing with three men dressed in white. "They work for the arena, taking care of survivors. They can help him," he assured the elderly wife, as they put him on a stretcher. Taly smiled approval at Polly. "Good job. You've proved your usefulness, young lady."

She smiled, surprised by the gruff man's compliment.

Turning to Will, the Chief's eyes hardened. The old drakeri paused and furrowed his brow before saying "You still want that permit?"

"Does a krilp make gut snakes in the jungle?" Will replied with a nod.

Taly looked to Hindin who nodded as well. "Fine, this is obviously growing more serious with a daylight attack in a crowded area. Is it just you two or ...?" he faded off, looking at Polly and Röger.

"She is the only one we know who has seen the attackers," Hindin whispered to his partner.

"She's just a pick pocketing thief, Rev," Will stated, not bothering to whisper.

"That's it!" Polly yelled, jumping to her feet. "I am not a thief, you tan-skinned beast!"

56

"Then what are ya?!" Will shouted leaning his tall frame over the much shorter woman.

"I...I..." Polly faltered. Her eyes shifted to his shoes. "I am no one. I am from de shelter of Nyupe Shan Zahn here in Embrenil. I am an orphan."

Chief Taly lifted an eyebrow at her words, but said nothing.

Will's hard gaze softened. Some of the color seemed to leave his eyes. But before he could respond, Röger slapped his thick arm across the tendikeye's shoulders.

"Count me in, too, Taly!" he grinned.

"You?" Will exclaimed.

"Hey, I said I owed you one for helping me out," Röger returned. "And I may not look it, but I used to be a pledged Black Vest in Karsely. I won't slow you kids down."

Hindin's smile was broad with approval. "Will, the Black Vests are a very elite order, disciplined in investigating and nullifying mystic threats. Sir Röger has proven his worth as a warrior, in spite of his shortcomings as a hedonistic pervert."

"And what about her?" the tendikeye tilted his quilled head toward Polly.

"I like her very much and you should, too."

Will looked back into the drakeri's golden three-irised eyes. He recognized a familiar determination and stubbornness.

"I can point dem out to you," she offered with cold truth in her voice.

"Chief Taly," Hindin grinned as he raised his chin, "make the permit out to Four Winds-One Storm!"

Will groaned and sighed as he glared back at his partner. "Rev, remind me later to put a dent in yer ass fer comin' up with that name."

The Chief Justice looked at them with wary eyes. Watching them interact, he wondered if he was making a rash decision. "Alright then. But just so you all know: The permit only grants authority to assist the department. No pay or monetary rewards. There's an old proverb around here; *You can't buy justice.* You would be considered volunteer investigators. Still interested?"

Before anyone else could answer, Röger Yamus stepped forward. "Fame and fortune be cursed! Out classing the E.C.P.D. will be reward enough!"

The Chief Justice made a sour face and turned to Hindin. "This is my city. Things are to be run *my* way, understood? Don't let this go to your heads."

Hindin gave a formal warrior's bow. "We are grateful for this task, your honor. May this exchange of trust guide us to our goal."

Thirty-seven minutes and half a pitcher of beer later, Röger had a theory about the Mystic Mafia muggings. "They were assignments. *Projects* is a better word. They're dumb punks working for someone who's training them for something bigger."

The group had retired to the Goose Egg Inn and sat in the tavern below. The lovely Officer Feyna *volunteered* to tag along with them to provide police information. It was late evening on a week day, so the dinner crowd had left, leaving them relatively alone. The group traded ideas and speculations over plates of the house special; barbecued bat with meat loaf.

"De attack on de man in de crowd," Polly started. "It was a message to me. Dey had no guns last time in dat alley. A bullet can out-dash any maxim. But on de other hand; dey might have changed deir minds after seeing de fight with you three dere, as well. Dat should have scared dem off and deterred dem from shooting de man. But dey did it anyway...because it was an order. It must be as you say," she gave a slight nod to the human.

"Polly," Hindin asked, "do you think the one who attempted the fire maxim was the blinding caster, as well?" He had his journal out, ready to take notes.

"Maybe, but I doubt," she answered. "All theurges have a philocreed path, or group of maxims dey live by dat also allow dem to redefine reality. De practitioner must be inherently tuned to de energies dey are learning. Pyrotheurges, cryotheurges, hydrotheurges, even chimancers, like you, Hindin, should and usually do master each art before tuning demselves to another path.," she paused, readying her drink. "If I only knew the theurgy of de blinding effect, or the maxim that causes it."

"So, the two maxims ain't related. That means there's two teachers helping 'em out?" Will asked.

Polly looked at the jubube juice in her glass. "Yes or no. It takes decades to master a theurgic path. You must have complete faith in your *philocreed* to do dis. De thief mystic I fought in de alley, his faith was rather weak. I could tell from de small amount of flame he produced. None of de victim's were blinded by heat or light, fire's two main aspects." She paused, taking a sip of her drink. "Den again, pyrotheurgy *is* de most common theurgy for Drakeri. Maybe...maybe...oh, I don't know..." she cradled her cheek in her palm and slumped, defeated, in her chair.

Will put down his beer glass. "But they're obviously workin' for someone in addition to trainin'. Has to be someone with money to buy 'em off an' time to teach 'em. Or have access to someone to teach 'em."

"But robbery? There are better ways to train than that," Hindin argued.

"What was swiped?" Röger asked, reaching for Hindin's journal. The malruka swiftly picked up the cracked cover book. "Geez, grabby much?" the human whined.

"It's written in malrukan. I doubt you could read it, especially with my bad hand writing," Hindin added defensively.

"What? How hard can it be? Marukan writing is just a rip-off of old Fevärian. You 'rukes based the scientific elements on a code during your rebellion. That rebel code is still used today, even by you. But just so you know, your people's spelling has been all wrong from the start."

Had Hindin blood, it would have filled his face. "I will admit our early lack of formal education resulted in a few inaccuracies. But that was far from our fault, human." His steel brow furrowed. "Besides, the standards in language we have developed is not without its own dignity. And I doubt you could appreciate our writing unless it was tattooed to a female's lower region."

Silence hit the small room like a hammer. Polly stiffened, holding back a giggle. Even Officer Feyna cracked a smile. Polly glanced pleadingly to the tendikeye across from her, hoping he would be able to break up a possible fight. Disappointingly, he sat back and put both hands behind his head. His expression told her nothing of what he might do.

"Shoot, man," Röger spoke first, "you've got some brass!" He smiled at the steel and stone giant.

Hindin raised a finger. "Actually, I am a steel coated, red granite -- "

"He means ya got guts, Rev," Will interjected.

"Oh," Hindin uttered, suddenly calm again. "No, I don't have those either. Some malrukan fathers give their sons hearts of gold as symbolic gestures..."

Röger laughed loud in that barking way of his. "Didn't mean to offend, but most men I meet - malrukan or otherwise - tend to treat me like a fool who'd sooner sleep with a reporter than read the newspaper, not that I wouldn't. But I notice more than you think." He touched the temple of his helmet and scratched it softly, cocking his head to one side. "Like how an iron coated red granite malruka, a creature that lacks a basic nervous system, can channel chi?" Hindin's eyes darkened slightly or maybe it was a trick of the light.

Röger continued. "Because all malruka, when built, are given an allotted lifespan of two hundred years. This amount cannot be added to but can be taken away, such as criminals having fifty to one hundred years subtracted for severe crimes. If able to draw chi into oneself, similar as Polly described with mysticism, or theurgy, one could increase one's energy thereby lengthening one's life past the two hundred years." Röger slowly placed both hands on the table, palms down. "A most illegal act in your country, am I right?"

"By my Blood!" Polly thought. What had she gotten herself into! She thought these were supposed to be good guys! And Hindin - he was a goody-goody compared to the other two. If he was as bad as Röger was implying, then how evil could the others be?

Hindin Revetz smiled and nodded as he set down his journal. "An interesting theory, Sir Röger. But your study of in ways of chimancy is clearly from hear-say." He raised his massive palm, revealing a gold circle in its center. "When I was constructed, I was built with a functional circulatory system made of refined gold strands running throughout my body. The golden outlets draw energy through the openings in my feet and palms. I have a chakra reserve housed in seven places in my body that allows this energy to be stored without interfering with natural life energy. Not only is it a path of energy, theurgy if you will. But it is a path I was built to be attuned to. My mother deserves most of the credit."

"MOTHER?!" Röger shouted. "How the hell can you have a...?"

"My mother," Hindin continued, "meant no harm in building me, but as I was something new, something different, I was deemed an illegal construct and was asked to leave ..."

Röger let out a long whistle. "Pot calling the kettle black," he muttered bitterly.

"What?"

"Nothing. Look, big guy," Röger sighed, adjusting his helmet, "I meant no harm, but I just got out of jail and am in no mood to get tossed back in. A man's business is his own so long as it doesn't get me killed, jailed, or forced into a vow of celibacy." He extended his hand. "Are we in good standing?"

Hindin's broad smile lightened the whole table. "Good? Yes. There is no offense in the pursuit of knowledge." Hindin shook the offered hand and immediately disguised his shock at Röger's steel-like grip of bone and flesh.

Will leaned forward, resting his elbows on the table. "Well, now that we got that settled; back to the case."

"I thought it was an objective?" Hindin muttered.

"Shut the shunt up, Rev!" Will snapped, annoyed. "Now, Miss Feyna..."

"OFFICER Feyna," she corrected.

"Officer," the annoyed bukk repeated with a forced smile. "What's the department know that it ain't sharin'? Röger asked what was taken from each victim. I'd kinda like to know that, too."

"Money and jewelry. We tell the pawn shops to keep a look out for the stolen items. But I doubt all of them are honest, if any."

"What kind of jewelry was it?" Hindin asked her.

"Wedding rings, old watches, class rings, necklaces, etc."

"Were any of dem theurgically charmed?" Polly asked.

"No. None of the victims reported anything like that."

Will rubbed his forehead. "Another dead end," he shrugged and hung his head. "I got a feelin' we'll keep hittin' 'em if we don't get a proper rest-up. No offense, Officer Feyna, but the room and board at the station house ain't exactly the epitome o' comfort."

"None taken, Mr. Foundling," she winked. "First thing tomorrow, Taly will have a carrier deliver a copy of the case details and permit regulations."

Hindin nodded in agreement. "It would be best if we all called it a day. I suggest we all meet at this table tomorrow morning."

"I can't," Feyna shrugged. "I have to work tomorrow."

"Aw..." Röger made a sad puppy-dog noise.

"But..." She whispered in the ear-hole in his helmet.

The burly man stood up in a jolt. "Guys, that sounds like a great idea! See you all tomorrow morning!" He then took the officer by the hand and led her upstairs, both leaving a trail of laughter.

"Slut," Polly muttered under her breath.

"Which one?" Hindin whispered to her.

"G'night, all," Will sighed as he rose from his chair. The remaining three then disbanded to their separate rooms.

As Polly locked the unfamiliar door behind her, she hung her head in doubt. These men were brave, and certainly capable of defeating the gang she encountered. But they were not detectives anymore than she was. Finding these four murderers in a city of seven hundred and eighty thousand could take weeks or months; if ever. Would it be enough time before her cover was blown?

She slept in her clothes, just in case.

Malruka do not really need sleep. Their construct bodies only tire and fatigue if pushed beyond normal rigors. However, Hindin always found that letting the mind shut down for the night was a good way to process information. And after soaking in a few chapters of the recent year's Monster Almanac, he smiled with an amusing thought and then slept.

As for Röger; never mind how he got *tucked in.*

Will was the last to drift asleep. He expected the innkeeper to charge a higher rate for letting him sleep on the roof. The discount was a relief on his wallet and his mind. He had not slept under the *hunveins* since entering the city.

Thousands of miles over the land in every direction, snaking trails of light coursed through a dome ceiling of living stone. The dome spanned over every land and sea in this Huncell like an overturned bowl. And flowing throughout this enclosure were the sources of light in this world: *Hunveins.* They shone blinding-bright during the day. But on a dark, cloudless night like this one, they were clear and brilliant. Like frozen rivers of smooth lightning, they stretched for hundreds of leagues over the landscape.

The Goose Egg Inn was in a dark part of the city, which suited Will fine. The only lights he was aware of were the ones high above the city and the cherry cinder on the end of his cigarette. With each soul caressing puff and wide eyed stare upward, he cleared his mind of all recent events, getting his head straight, pushing all past impressions out of the way. He didn't wish to forget anything, just to keep from remembering. Before taking in a last long gaze up at one of nature's marvels, he closed his eyes and smothered the cinder into a roof tile. The *Hunveins* of Burtlbip over Doflend were indeed beautiful. But they were still no match for the *Hunveins* of Cloiherune, the home he ached for every hour of every day. In a sigh of smoke and restlessness, his last breath before sleeping seemed to say, "Where are you, Brem?"

Like a butterfly exits its cocoon, Röger waking is a unique process though a less than stellar a sight. Just as the light of day crept between his eyelids, he shifted his shoulders and rolled onto the cold wood floor. Landing with a loud thud, the floorboards bowed slightly beneath his weight. He sat up to stretch and yawn, wearing nothing but his trusty helmet. After using a bedpost to help himself up, he gave his butt a scratch and looked around his room.

Officer Feyna had already taken her leave. There was a half full glass of water near a half empty pitcher on the dresser. He made a sleepy, bleary-eyed grin as he guzzled what was left.

He made his use of the room's thunderjug as he stared absently at a print of geese on the wall. There was one more clean shirt left in his back pack. He decided to save it for later. After putting on what he had worn the day before, he went to the mirror on the wall.

He looked to see a man wearing a mask. It was more than just the helmet covering his face. He wore the facade of an oaf, a shameless hedonist who hid behind a wall of bad jokes and sportful sex. He was not a natural comedian, and he knew it. He was the only one to laugh at his crass remarks. That was the whole point, wasn't it? He *had* to stay in a good mood. He *had* to blow off steam in a positive way. And Feyna, --health and happiness find her-- she knew how the game was played. She calmed him down with her touch and embrace after his brush with death. Röger never let on to her how strained he was from being jailed and forced to fight. Or how grateful he was for her company. Without her, or these new found allies, his façade would have melted into something terrible.

He turned and went downstairs.

Will and Hindin had already claimed a table. The two men were occupied by the words of the day. Will read over the Embrenil Gazette while drinking coffee from a tin cup. Hindin was gleaning details from some official document. Near him was a shredded envelope.

"Good morning, guys," Röger greeted cheerfully. "Is that the adventuring permit?"

"Mmm," Will answered, still reading to himself while munching on a raw potato.

"Oh," Hindin started, not noticing Röger until he spoke. "Good morning, Sir Röger. Yes, it is." The tall steel man rose up and gestured to an empty chair. "It arrived not five minutes ago. Please, sit."

Röger obliged. "What are they serving?" he asked. "I smell eggs and pig strips."

"You mean *bacon*?" Will asked in a cranky tone. "A bit out-dated on yer meat grammar, ain'tcha?"

Röger smiled. "Need any help readin' them thar letter-drawin's, bumpkin?" he fired back with his best tendikeye imitation.

Will let out a slight chuckle. "Naw, I did well enough at the schoolhouse to get by." He folded the newspaper and handed it to the human. "Can you believe this?" he muttered.

Röger opened it up to see an article on yesterday's Red Dirt battle. He looked it over and then read aloud. "In a valiant fight to earn their pardons, the four jailed foreigners displayed unorthodox skills to defeat the dreaded Sizzagafiend. The group calling itself *Four Winds-One Storm* became instant fan favorites. Due to the massive bloodbath that took place, many locals are starting to refer to the Red Dirt now as the GREEN Dirt Battle Arena. The promoters are considering changing the name if the Sizzagafiend's blood never fades...blah blah blah..." He lowered the paper and looked at Will. "It goes on saying

64

nothing but good things about us. It doesn't even disclose what our charges were. I don't get it, Foundling. Why are you so annoyed?"

"It ain't on the front page! Our names'll be fergotten in two days!" the bukk huffed.

"Will," Hindin started, sounding parental. "When we find the Mystic Mafia, I am confident that the press will give us enough recognition."

Röger sat back and studied the mismatched pair. "So, you guys are in it for the fame."

"Naw, just me," Will answered smugly. "Now, do you wanna order them pig strips while they're fresh? I'm content with this here potato."

The human grinned, determined not to let the subject get changed. "Why do you want all that attention, country boy? I can tell that you're not comfortable around paved roads and towers. You're the type of kid that cuts his teeth hunting monsters for small, remote villages. Maybe you pulled a few escort jobs for wagon trains, country stuff like that. Why urban detective work when it's not your element?"

Will smiled like he had nothing to hide. "I hafta make a name fer myself in Doflend. This city's my chance. Let's just say I wanna expand my options."

Röger nodded, thinking "To each their own". He raised his hand to flag down the waitress. "Hey! Triple serving of pig strips right here!"

Polly slowly made her way down the steps. The three men looked up to see her with her arms folded. Her hair was a mess. She looked at nothing but the empty chair meant for her. Will nudged it out with his boot from under the table. "Take a load off," he said flatly.

Polly sat down. Her movements were stiff and sluggish.

"Good morning," Hindin greeted politely.

She glanced around at the three men she barely knew but with whom she was about to share a meal. The air was thick with stale tobacco and sizzling swine fat. She struggled with a runny right nostril and clogged left one. The morning was too bright.

"It's cold down here," she grumbled. "Is anyone else cold?"

It was an awkward meal, to say the least.

Hindin cleared his throat. The others turned their attention to him as he began to read. "The crimes consist of thus: 5 counts of grievous assault, 1 count of assault with a firearm, 6 counts of armed robbery, 2 counts of murder..."

"Wait," Polly interrupted. "Only two of de eight victims were killed?"

"Ain't you read the paper?" Will asked. "You even witnessed one gettin' his neck split."

Worry crept from Polly's stomach and into her eyes. "How did the other victim die?" she asked tensely.

Hindin flipped through the small stack of pages until he found the coroner's report. "It says that the victim, Dahms Capgully, died of blood loss from a stab wound. A narrow blade was introduced into the top of the left thigh, delivered via a stabbing thrust, angling into the femoral artery."

Will shook his head and scoffed. "Lucky shot is all it was."

Polly pinched at her tattoo. "Dat was not luck. It was ignorance." She stared out at the space between her face and the table. Her mind assembled the pieces. "De femoral artery is nearly impossible to hit wit' a stab like dat. An upward or...or even a sideways slash is de best method."

"Most of the victims had at least one knife wound in either their arm or leg," Hindin added.

Polly's teeth clenched. A lump formed in her throat. "Den dat means it was an accident. None of de victims were meant to die! So, if I had not interfered when dose four thieves robbed Davil Pert, den dey wouldn't have killed him!" She began to pinch her tattoo. "I thought I was saving him ...But I only ended up enraging de leader. Dat is why he cut his throat and it's all my fault for getting involved!"

Hindin raised his hand abruptly. "Enough!" he commanded firmly. "You did not know. You could not have known."

Her regret gave way to anger. "Dat bastard wit' de yellow bandanna. I could sense in him de desire to kill. If dese men are following orders to not kill anyone, den he must be sating his desire by only stabbing deir arms or legs."

Röger had an idea. "Well, maybe he was ordered to do that, too. Maybe it's for a blood maxim. You know, like making a voodoo doll or something."

"Doubtful," Polly dismissed, at first. "But den again...blood as a component is...plausible."

There was a short pause before Hindin broke the silence. He shook the police report to catch everyone's attention.

"As I was saying. Eight counts of illegal maxim casting, 1 count of attempted murder, and a number of counts of unlawful conspiracy." After listing out the names and addresses of the surviving victims, Hindin added "And here is the strangest thing about the victims: not one of them remembers hearing the words of the maxim as they were blinded. This means that the effect was not brought about by conventional theurgy."

The table was silent for a moment before Hindin spoke again. "We must not hesitate to ask them anything that comes to mind. And remember this: This is a mystery involving the supernatural, so the facts cannot always be trusted. A fact can be warped and twisted by a maxim. Without the proper understanding, we will be lost and confused. So, feel free to theorize and speculate. And whatever you do, keep your eyes and minds open." He glanced over at Will before addressing Röger and Polly. "Would the both of you please excuse Will and me for a moment?"

Röger shrugged, feigning apathy.

"Why?" Polly asked.

"It will only take a moment," Hindin answered.

Will and Hindin walked behind an archway, just out of view in the lobby.

"I suggest we pair off when visiting the victims. We can gather information faster that way."

"Makes sense," Will answered, with a quick nod.

"Added to that, recommend that Sir Röger go with you. If he goes with Polly, he may become....distracted."

"Will do, Rev." Will cast a suspicious look toward the lobby. "And it'd be best if the witch keeps with you. You not havin' blood an' all."

Hindin frowned. "I'm sure she would not appreciate that."

"What? Goin' with you?"

"No, being called a witch. She is a theurge, like I am. Our only differences are the paths we follow."

Will sighed and rolled his eyes. "Cut it out, Rev. It's how I was raised. You know that."

Hindin looked at him. His eyes said everything that the back of his hand wanted to.

Will took the hint. "Fine." He had the utmost respect for his partner's feelings. Fear was never a factor.

Hindin nodded four quick nods. "Today, my friend, it will be you who must watch over an unruly companion, not me. Sir Röger has the maturity level of a middle grader. Remember to exercise sensitivity and understanding with these poor souls."

The tendikeye smirked. "Good thing these folks are blind. They might have less impulse to turn us outsiders away. 'Least you got a Drakeri to tag along with."

Hindin continued in his parental tone. "But bear this in mind, Will. They have possibly been blinded for life, unless the caster is slain or voluntarily disengages the effect. The authorities have yet to find the assailants. We have been given a chance to out-do said authorities. However, there is more to being a hero than slaying the enemy and out-doing the competition."

"Aw, here we go again!"

"Quiet. You have to be a comforting hope for these victims. Let them know that we do this by choice, not for money or prestige. As we live, we have but one goal: Bringing these ruffians to justice."

The tendikeye raised a curious eyebrow. "Is fame the same as prestige?"

Chapter 3
The Victims List

❖

Davil Pert, the boy who was murdered in the alleyway, was a mere 21 years old. In his third and final year at Embrenil Academy, he was well on his way to become a master irrigator. But when his throat was slashed open, that goal was forever denied. His family lived fifty miles away. Tomorrow, a city employed rider would deliver the news, along with his cremated remains and a few belongings gathered by his dorm mates.

Dahms Capgully was 574 years old. With his two ex-wives, he had three daughters, four sons and twenty one grandchildren. His body was also cremated, and the ashes were mixed with clay to make a ceramic figurine of himself called a *Towma*. It was placed reverently in the Capgully family shrine with the *Towma* of his ancestors.

The team agreed that visiting these two victims' families would be a waste of time. They wanted firsthand accounts, and none of them could converse with corpses.

❖

"We meet again, brother," Richard Armbakk cheerfully declared when he saw Hindin.

"Is this your usual routing area?" Hindin asked, as he helped Polly into the wagon sized cart.

"No, sir. Only the Union Guild works like that. I work the whole city as an independent."

"Does the Guild ever...give you trouble?" Hindin asked, slightly arching an eyebrow.

The bulky taxi-puller laughed. "Once. But after a short discussion of fists, we came to an arrangement: I mark up my fare by one and a half times their going rate."

"How fortunate for us," Polly miffed.

69

"Aw, don't sweat it, though. My legs may seem short, but I'm one of the fastest in the city. I charge by distance, not the time it takes to get there."

"In that case," Hindin started as he took his seat. "How much would one day's services cost? We are on official business now for the ECPD, and efficient transportation is exactly what we require. Are you up for the task, Master Armbakk?"

The taxi-puller pondered the offer a moment. "How many stops?"

"Three before returning here," Hindin answered.

"Only three? That shouldn't take the whole day! Let's make it 40 grotz. Plus tip, of course."

"There may be long periods of waiting between stops," Hindin warned.

"Aw, don't worry about it! I won't need a bathroom break! Where to first?"

Darb Wesley had a low voice with a handsome nasal croak. The middle aged Drakeri sat dejectedly by his apartment window. His cast-covered leg was propped up on a pile of books atop a small foot rest. He sat in a green upholstered chair that was covered in nappy fuzz. It looked itchy, but still comfortable. The lack of sleeves on his shirt revealed a red heart tattoo with the letters M, O, and M. The tattoo had a newly made scar on top of it. The living room was littered with coffee spoons, yet the only cup in sight was in his right hand. In his left hand was a small mirror held and cocked forward at his left temple.

"This is the only way I can see you," he addressed the mysterious young beauty on his couch and the malruka standing behind her.

By looking closely, they could see that the man's eyes were all black, yet in the reflection they were a normal deep orange.

He went on, "Ever since that night three weeks ago, I've had to look at things through this."

"What about the mirror in your bathroom?" Hindin asked.

"Well, I can't exactly carry that one around, but, yes." Darb gave out a light chuckle. "Any normal mirror works. But it's awkward, especially when hobbling on a crutch."

"Do any other reflective surfaces work?" Polly asked.

"Windows, but only a little. I tried coffee spoons and my knife's blade, but I got nothing. All I can see is what is in the mirror. All around it is a dark weird haze."

"Did your leg get broken in the attack?" Hindin asked.

"No, this was from my first attempt at walking down stairs with the mirror. I had to walk sideways."

"What was it like when de maxim was cast on you?" Polly asked.

"All I remember is walking past that alley. Then the darkness just hit me. It was like being in the dark on mushrooms and salvia. I didn't know who I was or where I was. But I could feel those bastards kicking me and stab me in the arm. Without my senses or sense of self, it was like drowning in helplessness."

"And what did dey take?" Polly asked.

"My wallet, which had my picture card, about 60 grotz, pictures of a few old girlfriends, and a buy-one-get-one-free hamburger ticket for Mrak's Burger Stand. They also took my ring and my watch."

"Tell us about the jewelry," Hindin asked with concerned eyes.

"It was just a plain old spoon ring. Silver and old. I got it at the local flea market. The watch was no sign of wealth, either. I got it back in 2715, I think. I replaced the band a few times. Also got it at the flea market. I get most of my stuff there, this chair, these books...that couch you're sitting on. The watch was silver, too, like the ring. When I got it appraised the man said it was worth about 200 grotz." He sighed and hung his head. "The beating they gave me...I've had worse. But the darkness increased my fear as it was happening. Weird, huh?"

Polly and Hindin pondered silently for a moment. Hindin cradled his chin between his thumb and forefinger.

"Is there anything else you remember?" asked Hindin. "Anything that comes to mind?"

Mr. Wesley shrugged again. "I'm still getting that druggy feeling. It's worse in the morning waking up. I can't even see things when I dream. When I'm awake, I can't even imagine images, like my mom's face or this coffee cup. All I see is myself

71

and whatever else this mirror catches. As I look in the mirror I think *Here and there I stand to face me.* Crazy, huh?"

"No, Mr. Wesley," Hindin replied with a sympathetic frown. "You are merely having a natural response to an unnatural effect. Thank you for your time."

The drakeri man nodded and managed to crack a smile. "Sure thing. If you find those punks before the cops do, feel free to pay them back for ruining my tattoo."

Polly and Hindin took their leave. They walked carefully down the stairwell exchanging ideas.

"I have never seen a blinding effect like dis," Polly confessed.

"There is more than one kind?" asked Hindin.

"Several. My own version works by forcing out blood through de skull sockets. De vision becomes flooded. All dey see is red."

Hindin blinked and stalled. "That is...rather gruesome."

Polly shrugged and kept walking. "At least it's not permanent."

Chan Burster steadfastly refused to let Will and Röger into his flat. They caught just a glimpse of him before he had slammed the door, the quick impression that he was fat, curly haired, with glasses and a hook in place of his left hand.

"Mr. Burster, please. It's fer yer benefit, I assure ya." Will had been pleading for three minutes as Röger stood by, silent.

"I don't want your help!" came a high, cheek-echoing voice.

"Let me," Röger insisted, stepping to the door. "Hey, Chan! You okay in there, buddy?"

"Go away!" Chan yelled back.

Röger glanced at Will with a playful glint in his eye. "If you let us in and answer a few questions, I'll show you some naked pictures of my mom! Very tasteful!"

"I'm blind, you moron!" answered the voice.

Will's head snapped back to Röger. "Do you really got pictures of ...?" he began to ask, but he cut himself off when it clicked that the human was full of merde.

Röger pounded the door. "Hey, Chan, what's the word? C'mon, buddy. Whatchu need? Is there anything we can get for you? Groceries? Beer? How about I get my buddy here to make run for us? We'll all just sit down, pound a few cold ones, and figure out how to catch those little dung-clumps who jumped you. I got a 15 lb. axe that'll split their skulls and everything underneath!"

There was a long pause from behind the door, until finally--

"NcRay Light." Chan replied.

"You got it, buddy," Röger answered. He plunged his hand into his coin pouch and pulled out a hand full of grotz. Handing it to Will, he urged, "You heard the man, harker. Go."

"What? Why me?" Will asked, glancing down at the money in his hand.

"You're faster. Now, go! Beer! Now!"

Will rolled his eyes and turned on his heel. *"He didn't even count it,"* he thought as he bolted down the apartment hallway. He came to a squared spiral staircase. "I'm keepin' the change!" he yelled as he leapt over the banister. His green dust coat flapped wildly as he swung, flipped, and slid his way down three flights to the bottom.

He thanked his luck that there was a liquor store nearby that opened this early. Minutes later, Will was back at the door with a six pack of bottled NcRay Light. The hall was empty but behind the door, Will could hear two voices chatting and laughing.

"Hey!" Will yelled, as he pounded on the door.

"Come in!" Chan answered. "It's open."

Will burst in to the apartment. From wall to wall (which wasn't very far) it was packed full with trash and clutter. There were old newspapers, take-out boxes, beer bottles, and large articles of clothing strewn everywhere. The smell of the room was thick like old socks and cheese. Röger and Chan were seated at a rickety old card table, passing back and forth an onyx labeled bottle of what stank like cheap whiskey.

"You rump-stuffers!" Will exclaimed, as he walked across the room and opened a window without asking. "You made me get beer when you had whiskey here the whole time?"

The two men chuckled and one of them farted. Chan lifted a piece of broken glass near his face to see out of the reflection.

Röger pointed at the six pack of beer in Will's hand. "Darn it, Will! Don't you know that you shouldn't mix drinks? Now you have to drink all of those!"

Will scoffed and smirked at the challenge. "I outgrew beer when I turned 16! We start our kids off on this swill!"

Twenty affable minutes later, the three men got along famously. The inevitable mixture of beverages broke the social ice. In that time, Chan explained how he could only see out of a glass mirror's reflection. The piece in his hand came from his bathroom mirror. The hook on his left stump was an old reminder never to steal again. He also made an attempt to convince the two visitors that it was the fault of his condition that his apartment was a mess. The atmosphere was cool and comfortably stagnant as Chan told the tale of the Mystic Mafia's assault.

"I'd just gotten out of Banlee's. It's a bar in the Westpear District. Lots of music bars that sell fried catfish and overpriced imported beer. They had a bunch of kids hacking at their costly instruments. They claimed to be an azule band, but it sounded like pigeon merde to me.

"But anyway, these four jerks came in. I doubt any of them were above a hundred. They were hardly paying attention to the band. I figured they were waiting to make a gray dust deal. The gray dust business has always rode the coat tails of the music business. The point came to where I checked my watch and paid my tab. As I went out the front door, I saw them get up out of the corner of my eye. I wasn't ten steps outside when I heard the doorbell jingle again behind me.

"I started to walk faster and get nervous. The district is sometimes sparse on Trokday nights, so I couldn't get lost in a crowd. It only took a glance back to see them before I started running. They ran to one side of me, forcing me to take an alley. Once I got in, everything went black.

"I swung my hook around hoping to hit one. I felt it catch and heard a scream. So I reared back with my fist to cold cock him, but someone grabbed my arm. They pulled me off my feet and beat me. A huge thud came down on my head, smacking my face into the ground. Ruffians broke my glasses, the jerks! This is my old pair I have on. I know I'm blind now, but wear them out of habit. Anyway, I woke up the next day in the police infirmary. They patched my face up and put seventy stitches total in my calf and shoulder. The bastards slashed me up while I was out cold."

"What did they make away with?" Röger asked.

"My wallet. The watch my uncle gave me. My arrowhead necklace. Luckily, they left my hat." Chan gave a flick to the brim of the black fedora.

"What was so special about the arrowhead?" Will asked.

The blind man smiled. "Bought it off an old tendikeye when I traveled the Ashes Road. He said it was used in the Skirmish of Thistletongue Hill. Didn't know if it was true, but I liked the story."

Will Foundling cracked a sad smile. The Ashes Road was the main highway of his home huncell, Cloiherune. He had only walked it once. But still, that was enough to miss it.

Röger rolled his eyes. "That's probably all it is: a story!" he laughed. "I've been on that road half a dozen times. No matter where you go, there's a monument to this battle and that. And plenty bead and feather necklace-peddling locals to take advantage of tourists."

"Let's get back on the case," Will reminded them sternly, dismissing his homesickness. "What about yer uncle's watch, Mr. Burster?"

"My uncle got it from his uncle, too'" Chan explained. "Apparently, it was over two thousand years old. Naturally, it had to be fixed a few times. He ended up putting in more money than what it was worth. He left it to me before he died back in 2265. He was my favorite uncle, Uncle Shnerd."

Röger nodded, smiled, and gave Chan a friendly pat on the shoulder. "Well, hey. Thanks for all your help, man. But we got two more people we need to see. Do you need anything else before we go?"

"Um, yeah. I'm kind of nervous being blind with all these beer bottles lying around. I'd hate to step or fall on one. I've been cut up enough," he added with a nervous laugh.

"Sure thing," Röger answered cheerfully. "Where's your trash can?"

Chan raised his hook. "That's the thing: All empty NcRay bottles need to be brought to the nearest curb for daily pick up.

It's part of some new city ordinance for recycling. The brewery reuses the old bottles."

"Does it make the beer any cheaper?" Will asked with a sly grin.

"I wish," replied the blind fat Drakeri.

"So, it's kinda like the milk man!" Röger laughed. "Only, they don't leave any fresh ones behind!"

The three men had one more good laugh before Will and Röger headed out. Röger opted to carry the wooden crate holding several dozen bottles down. As they walked down the hall and stairs, Röger couldn't help but study the bottles. They were all slender in the middle, like Officer Feyna's torso. Not unlike an hourglass. The label read *Now designed for a better grip!*

"Yeah, right!" he thought as he scoffed. *"It's just a way to put less beer in there!"*

❖

When two common men such as Darb Wesley and Chan Burster get beat up and blinded in a city such as Embrenil, it is hardly a cause for public worry; illegal activity is common in such crowded areas, mystical or not. But when a daughter of one of the city's Council members was beaten and blinded, it became the talk of the city. With every attack that came after, the topic grew hotter as paranoia reigned. Newspapers flew off the stands.

Yrot Aundi's deluxe apartment was now a glass prison. Her well-to-do father thought it would brighten her spirit to fix enormous glass mirrors to her walls. The elegant butterfly wallpaper had been covered up. Her fancy photograph collection had to be taken down and stored in a closet.

She sat on her bench in front of a black piano detailed in green leaves and red roses. Yrot was glad to have strangers in her home. She usually sought them out in order to harvest inspiration. Hindin and Polly gave her reflection the utmost attention as she told them her story.

"I was at an art gallery when nature called. In the bathroom I noticed that two of the three stalls had two sets of legs."

"Did you not think that odd?" Hindin asked.

"Art galleries attract many types of people," she answered with a shrug. "I figured it was something I didn't want to know about."

"Just as I got finished, I opened the stall door and there was this flash of black. It moved like light, but looked like darkness. I couldn't see anything. It made me feel very dizzy. Something was tugging at my purse, so I held it tighter. Then I felt this awful slap to my cheek. It turned me sideways and knocked me back. My hip hit the toilet as I fell. Someone punched down onto my head repeatedly. It was horrible!"

The woman's voice cracked at the last word. Tears welled up in her pitch black eyes.

"I felt them pull my rings off, my bracelets, and earrings, too. They took my purse. It contained my cosmetics kit, 1,500 grotz for buying a painting, and my timepiece. I let them have anything without a fight. But they wouldn't stop hitting me. I tried to scream, but it was like I'd forgotten how. I couldn't even cover my face!" The tears fell.

Still, she went on. "Just when I thought it was over, I felt a sharp pain in my arm. One of them stabbed me with a knife. After that, they left. Someone found me five minutes later."

Polly had listened straight-faced the whole time. As she watched the woman dry her eyes, she asked. "Is dat piano a Shambrute?"

"What? Um, yes. Yes, it is. You know of the brand?"

Polly stepped over to get a closer look. "De company is no more. Only seventy-three are known to exist. Dere are many imitations, though." Those last words reeked of doubt.

Yrot stood up carefully and stepped away from the bench. "It is genuine. See for yourself." There was a definite challenge in her tone.

Hindin was a bit put off by Polly's apparent disinterest in the woman's story. Still, it got her to stop crying, at least for now. He shifted his attention to his mysterious companion. "*Who is she?*" he thought. "*Is she really an orphan like Will?*"

Polly sat and examined the keys for a moment. Her violet fingers pressed on them lightly, but not enough to make a sound. She felt the weight of the cool ivory rise up as she lifted off. Then, with a focused intensity, she pounded her fingertips into the keys. The sound was startling at first. Her four-fingered hands marched from left to right and leapt over each other in a cascade

77

of horrendous scales. Notes of august grandeur shot into air like a storm of arrows. Like a small tremor, the music seemed to shake the room. Hindin felt his emotions ready to collapse, so expressive was the intricate tapping of keys. Yrot's mouth gaped in astonishment.

Polly looked at her and talked as she played. "I have seen de men who attacked you. Dey escaped me. I am almost convinced dat de one who stabbed you did so because he enjoyed it. But dat does not make it so!" With every few words, she incorporated a musical phrase. "He may be collecting blood samples to further a goal. Are you of royal blood?"

"No," Yrot answered timidly.

"Are you a virgin?"

"No."

"Is your family line cursed?"

"I don't think so."

"Are you a first born?"

"No!" Yrot cried, now getting confused and frustrated. "What does that have to do with anything?"

Polly stopped playing. "Because all I would have to do is taste a teaspoon of your blood to know everyting about you wit' in de last month. I could thumb through every memory until I found someting to use against you. Do you have any enemies?"

"I'm sure my father might. He has quite a following."

Polly shrugged and sighed in frustration. Her hands clawed out an angry melody in a tic-toc rhythm. "If dese thieves were after your father, dey would attack only members of his constituency and family. De other victims are not members or employees of him. So, no. Dat will not do!" She turned her head, studying the blind woman like a missing piece of a treasure map. Yrot trembled at the reflection of Polly's calculating eyes. Polly stopped playing. She stood up from the piano and placed the mahogany cover over the keys. A cruel smile curved on her lips and her eyes glinted with solemn joy. "You are right," she told Yrot. "It *is* a real Shambrute."

There was a long awkward pause before the astonished Hindin asked "Where did you learn to play like that?"

Polly was immediately troubled by the question. Stammering, she answered. "At de orphanage. A sister dere gave me lessons."

78

"She taught you to play with a *Flanzien* arch?" Yrot asked with growing suspicion.

Polly shook her head, not understanding the question.

Yrot explained. "The way you raised your elbows and bent your wrists, that is called a Flanzien arch. Back in feudal times, the royalty had proper ways of doing everything, from how to hold forks to greeting certain people with certain gestures. It was all very formal and strict. And any commoner caught using these sacred customs would be punished horribly. Those rules were done away with after the Socionomic Revolution."

Hindin looked at Polly, waiting for some kind of response.

Polly at first looked perplexed, but swiftly, her attitude changed. "I am sure dat it is only coincidence. Dose times are long gone. And it was probably just a habit de sister picked up. De sister who instructed me."

"Is there anything else you can think of, Ms. Aundi?" Hindin asked, trying to change the subject back to the case.

"No," she answered sternly. "You may both go now."

The two left silently. Hindin bowed as he went through the door. Nothing was discussed as they made their way back to the busy street. Hindin gave Richard Armbakk the 'let's go' look. As they both took their seats, Hindin glanced over at his companion.

"Royalty?" he thought.

❖

"I told you: You cannot attend the auction without an invitation!" the stout yet foppish gatekeeper yelled.

"And I told you: We ain't here fer no blasted auction!" Will answered, getting red in the face.

"Just let us in!" Röger pleaded. "I need to pass water!" The beer and whiskey from earlier had run its course through his system.

The gatekeeper shook his head. "It is simply not possible. Mr. Rohlend is selling off the rest of his paintings today. His condition is forcing him into retirement."

The two armed men saw beyond the gate a quaint house of stone. Doors were propped open by various lawn ornaments as drakeri sophisticates shuffled in and out. Easels were being set

79

up for paintings. Plain wooden folding chairs were set in rows for the many attendees to sit on and remark on the weather. A trio of fiddlers were tuning up their finely polished instruments. Röger's eye was caught by a table of food tended by two fetching female caterers. One was petite with wild spiky hair with blue highlights. The other wore too much make up. But to Röger it was a plus. They were serving bison franks, pepper sprout corn loaf, coffee brownies stacked into a brick pyramid, various wines, and fruits of every color.

"What do we need invitations for?" Röger asked indignantly. "Maybe we have the money to buy a painting or two!"

The gatekeeper looked snobbishly at their clothes. "I highly doubt it, sir."

"Now you've insulted me!" the human snapped. "Do you see the quality of this axe? This sword? These are highly functional antiques. This helmet was a gift from an autocrat!"

The little man laughed in Röger's shielded face. "Even if it were true and you did have the money to bid, you could not come in! This auction is only for those who truly appreciate art!"

"Art?" Will asked accusingly. "Let me tell you somethin' about art. You ain't gonna find it in no painted piece of canvas. Art is turning a piece of canvas into a useful tent fer the night. Paint ain't fer conjurin' up the face of some poncy aristocrat. Paint is fer bringin' out the hatred on yer face fer yer enemies to see! Art is that moment when yer sword splits the torso of your enemy. There's two ways to enjoy killin': The wrong and easy way is to put aside yer regard for life. To become a monster. The *artful* way is to see that the technique you been workin' on fer years does work and works well. Now, if you don't mind, go in and tell Mr. Rohlend that two dedicated investigators need his help findin' the Mystic Mafia gang. You do that and I'll give you an attaboy."

"But..." the gatekeeper began.

Will cut him off. "If you think a man's sight is more important than a few thousand grotz, then do it."

The keeper nodded and turned away toward the house. As he walked he thought *"Now, why can't I find a cute man that's that assertive in this city?"* The stout drakeri went to a few other helpers, buying time for the interview. He then went into the house for several minutes. He then came out nodding and smiling at the two visitors.

"He'll see you, but only for five minutes. The auction is behind schedule as it is."

Will bowed slightly. "You have our thanks, sir. May yer luck be the right kind."

The keeper fought a blush as he opened the gate door. "Follow me, please."

"Bathroom first!" Röger winced as his eyes began to water.

Standing over a throne of porcelain, Sir Röger achieved a momentary state of zen. When he at last finished answering his call to nature, he splashed his hands in a basin of cool water and dried them on his jeans. Opening the commode door, he proclaimed "Okay, ready to go!"

He and Will were led down a busy hall, passing more helpers hauling out paintings. At last they came to a spacious den where the last of the art was being fetched.

In the far corner of the room sat a man in a comfortable red leather chair. He wore a dark blue suit of satin and suede. On his well pronounced nose and sharply pointed ears rested a dark pair of shades with rectangular frames. His bark brown hair was long and tinted with streaks of blonde. His pliant looking hands were placed on an ornate ash cane topped off with a brass knob.

"Here they are, Horce," the gatekeeper told him.

"Thank you, Tweng," the blind man replied, smiling with a handsome overbite.

"I'm going back to the entrance now. There may be more guests coming." The stout man turned and left, too busy for parting words.

There were no other chairs nearby and neither of the two visitors asked to sit down.

Will initiated the interview with haste. "Mr. Rohlend, my name is Will Foundling. This is my associate, Röger Yamus. We're on the trail of the four or more outlaws that've assaulted you and several others. If you wouldn't mind givin' us a personal account of yer run-in with 'em, we'll be well on our way to catchin' their sorry asses."

The blind man laughed softly. "Where are you from, Mr. Foundling? And how does one acquire such a surname?"

Will paused for a moment. "In the Swordocracy of Cloiherune unwanted children are given the name to forever indicate their status, even if another family takes 'em in. The name can't be passed on unless their child too is unwanted. Say, did you know that you might still be able to see if it's out a mirror's reflection?" Will changed subjects without missing a beat.

The artist's smile widened. "Oh, yes. But the people who came to purchase my works don't know that. A blinded artist's work is nearly the worth of a dead one's. Should I ever lay eyes on those street crawlers again - if it's ever possible to see anything again - I should like to thank them. This auction will make me a wealthy man."

"So, the attack made you famous," Röger remarked.

"It did. All my life, I've lived off commissions. And they were few and far between. Every piece out there today is a project I did on my own time. Each one is something I created because I wanted to. And now they are going to be sold and divided amongst rich strangers. With that, my immortality is assured."

"Well, that's a burden off my mind," Will sighed with dismissal. "So, how'd it happen? Where'd they stab ya? What'd they take? Y'know, yer not the only one who's havin' a busy day."

Before Horce could respond, Röger cut in. "We only want to help you, man."

Horce Rohlend leaned forward and grimly gripped his cane. "The police have already heard the answers to those questions, tendikeye."

Will leaned in as well. "Yeah? Well, I can listen a lot better'n they can."

The artist leaned back in his chair and sighed. "Fine. It happened upstairs in my bedroom. It was the middle of the night and I was fast asleep. I woke up to the sound of loud footsteps. I could hear them all around me. Voices echoed all around as things were getting smashed. I couldn't see anything. Not because it was dark, but because they blinded me in my sleep. I felt this sharp pain in my arm. Someone sliced open my bicep. Then something heavy hit me in the head. I awoke the next morning calling for help out of my window."

"What'd they take?" Will asked.

"My silver statuette of Nulal."

"Who's that?" Röger asked.

"One of Doflend's great Renewal painters. I suggest you study him. Anyway, they also took my gold pen and ink set, my crystal hummingbird collection, a few silk shirts, my savings box containing 145 grotz, my watch, and ...um...Are you guys *cool?*"

"What do you mean?" asked Will.

"Yes!" Röger answered. "We are cool. There's nothing to worry about."

Horce smiled. "Good. In that case, I lost three ounces of dreamweed, too. There's no doubt now that it's all been smoked away!"

Röger hung his head. "That's a tough break, man. It also reminds me: I should pick some up somewhere."

Will rolled his eyes. "I doubt a little 'smoke n' stoke' was their motive. Did you know you were in any trouble, Mr. Rohlend? Did you owe someone money?"

"No," Horce answered. "Nothing like that. Now, if you'll please excuse me. I have an auction to attend to."

"Thank you fer yer time," Will growled coldly. "We'll show ourselves out."

The artist rose from his chair. "Would you both mind escorting me outside, please? This cane is a bit tricky."

"Only if you let us hit the catering table on the way out," Röger replied.

"Fine, fine," agreed the artist.

"Score!" the human thought.

When Hindin Revetz had awoken that morning, he had believed himself a decent judge of character. But as the day wore on, he became wary of his young companion. He had chosen her to come with him for a few reasons, among them that there were two women on the victims list. A malruka and a woman seemed a good choice to talk to them. He had always gotten along well with flesh and bone females. They tended to regard him as a gentle giant or well behaved doll. He had believed Polly to be a reserved, soft spoken introvert. But there was something in that piano that brought out a cold, domineering aspect.

Polly Gone was silent and slumping in her seat. She stared blankly, letting the swaying of the wagon rock her back and forth. She had lost her self control, and was now paying for it. She ran away to escape that way of being: cold and cruel. But a part of it had rubbed off on her. She tried to put out every emotion like lights in a house before getting too sick. The passing sight and smell of butchered animal carcasses hanging at a butcher stand didn't help much. She thought of how that poor woman had been so upset, and that she didn't even care. She had no tolerance for someone who couldn't get over a simple beating. That woman had no idea what *helpless* was. But it was all wrong, this way of thinking. She knew it in her heart of hearts. The guilt of not caring mingled with the pride and comfort of detachment like a bad mixed drink. *"Dere's no escape from it,"* she thought. *"It's in my blood."*

"Polly," Hindin started softly, yet still startled her. She looked up into the stone man's perfect emerald eyes. "Polly, we are about to visit another woman who was blinded and beaten. We must employ every virtue of compassion and understanding."

The crimson theurge nodded mutely as her guilt doubled inside her stomach.

The taxi cart eventually stopped at a circular tower called Crodolet Flats. Inside, a grand spiral ramp fixed to the inner wall spun its way up level by level. After making their third lap up, they came to Flat 12. Hindin gave the door a rap with a single finger. It made for a loud knock that didn't sting the ears. Polly could feel her pulse pounding throughout her body. Her eyes flashed red as she regulated it with her will.

The door opened fast and wide. Before them stood a regal woman in her autumn years. She wore an orange and red silk robe and a pearl necklace that gave off a pale pink glow. "May I help you?" she asked, her eyes blinking rapidly for a second.

"Good afternoon, Madam," Hindin greeted with a low bow. "We are independent, city sanctioned investigators working on the case concerning Miss Sinala. My name is Hindin Revetz. This is my friend, Ms. Polly Gone. We realize that this is a difficult time for Sinala. And that, given the nature of her attack, no time would be a *good* time to ask for an interview. Nonetheless, we humbly seek an audience with her, so that justice may be served."

The woman placed her hands upon her hips and tilted her head in doubt. "And how would justice be served, I wonder? Do you plan on making it so that the last thing they see before getting their eyes stabbed out would be their balls sliced off?"

"It can be arranged," Polly thought to herself.

Hindin gave a look of utter sympathy. "Madam, the ruffians' apprehension is our only goal. And I believe with her and your cooperation, that goal can be achieved. Please, Madam."

The lady sighed and frowned. "My poor great, great grand baby never did anything wrong. She would have never been fooled into some dangerous situation." She looked at the two visitors as if waiting for some response.

"I know," Hindin replied warmly.

The lady's gold irises darkened with the beginnings of tears. But she blinked hard to prevent them from escaping. "Come in," she said. "I'll get her. She's in her room."

Hindin and Polly found themselves in a living room full of silk tapestries, wax candles that smelled of honey, and empty bird nests set on shelves. The older woman was just about to proceed down a hallway when Polly stopped her.

"You are fabrication mystic, aren't you? An Artificer?"

The lady turned around with poise and fluid grace. "Yes," she answered plainly. "But my philocreed stems from wonders naturally created by animals and the elements. I do not bother with machines."

Polly stepped forward with a formal curtsey. "Yours is a philocreed path to be admired. Like de noble silkworm, spider, clam, and sparrow; theurges of your craft create many wonderful tings."

The lady smiled. "And your path is?" she asked, inclining her head.

Polly hesitated. "De Red River," she answered. "I walk it."

The woman's smile melted. She glanced over Polly's apparel. Worn out white sneakers, faded blue jeans, a brown leather belt, a gray t-shirt, and a gray cloak. She looked Polly dead in the eye. "It is my understanding that a crimson theurge must wear red to work her wonders."

Polly pulled her shirt collar aside, revealing a cherry red bra strap.

The lady cleared her throat and looked impressed. "Very subtle, my dear. Now, if you'll excuse me." The lady turned once more and left.

"Fabrication mystic?" Hindin asked in a whisper.

"I'll explain it later," Polly whispered back. "If you anger her, don't let her touch you."

A few minutes later, the lady returned. Her hands rested on a younger woman's shoulders, guiding her as they walked. The girl looked as though she hadn't rested in days. She wore a yellow housecoat with matching slippers. If her hair hadn't been a tangled mess and if there was no scar on her face going from her chin to her earlobe, she would have been gorgeous. The older drakeress sat her down in a silk covered love seat with spider web-like doilies on the arms and back.

"What do you want to know?" she asked, hunching as she sat. Her face was as pale and calm as a corpse.

"Everything," Hindin answered. "Please, leave nothing out."

"Fine," she replied, producing a thin cigar and a small box of matches. "I hate these darn things. But I can't roll my own without seeing it." She lit the blunt cigar and took a puff before starting her story.

"I was walking home from Elsie's BBQ. My arms were full with an order of ribs and bread. It's only a few blocks away, so I didn't bother with a taxi cart. I was about half way back, when I heard a voice behind me say *'Hey, can we help you carry that?'*. I turned my head to look, but this flash of darkness hit me. It was like being drunk or stoned or both. Someone slapped the food out of my hands. Then I felt them grab my arms and legs and carry me off into an alley. They pulled off my jewelry. If I resisted, they hit me. So, I ended up getting hit a lot. One of them stomped on my chest. Couldn't do much after that." Sinala took another agitated puff on her cigar. She let the smoke out slowly before continuing.

"One of them had a knife. He stuck it right into the tip of my chin and yanked it hard to my ear. Then they ran away. I had to crawl out of the alley. The people who found me say I was screaming, but I don't remember it."

Polly was surprised at how calm and cool the woman was. "What possessions did you lose?" she asked.

"Like I give a care about a few pieces of cheap jewelry," the woman snapped. "I was more upset about the ribs."

"It might give us a lead to their motives," Hindin offered.

Sinala shook her head in dismissal. "A pair of slate earrings, five fake gold rings with faux stones, my brass dragon pendant, and my old silver watch. There. Are you happy?"

"Yes." Hindin answered calmly. "For now I see a pattern. Thus far today, we have interviewed three victims including you. It occurs to me that wealth is not the motive of these four miscreants, not directly from the victims anyway. This blinding effect would be put to better use against richer targets. No, you and the others were chosen for one and/or two reasons: silver watches and non-lethal wounding."

Sinala shrugged and shook her head. "Everyone on this town carries a watch. Ever since lightning destroyed the clock tower at city hall."

"But *silver* watches..," Hindin argued. "All of you were robbed of one."

"Yeah, so? They're pretty common, man. You and those idiots at the police station can't accept that these attacks are random. Well, maybe they at least do. And that's why they sent you on this wild goose chase."

Polly spoke up. "What about mirrors? If you can see out of dem like de others, den dat is another pattern."

The blind woman gave a slight nod. "Yeah, I can. But I choose not to. In this darkness, I'm unable to imagine what happened to me. There's not one single image in my head, and I kind of like it that way. And even if these cloacas get caught and this effect gets lifted, I don't want to have to look at them. Especially the one who cut me."

'Maybe you won't have to," Polly replied. No one but the older woman saw that she gave her sheathed dagger a slight caress as she spoke. "I witnessed dem murder dat college student two days ago."

"So, that was you that the police arrested?" the older woman asked as if offended. "They thought for even a moment that a teenaged girl was committing these crimes? Did they forget about what happened to her?" She pointed at Silana with her thumb. "Oh, that Chief Judge of theirs is going to get a piece of my mind!"

"Grandmother, please calm down," Sinala pleaded as if embarrassed. She faced out to where Polly's voice was coming from. "Tell me about it. How was it that you found them?"

Polly started her story slow, choosing her words carefully.

"I was homeless, just out of de orphanage. I had no place to stay except a large old crate in an alley. As I was sitting dere inside it, I saw dem out of a knot hole. Dere were four of dem and de victim. Dey ambushed him, and stomped at him as he lay dere blind and confused. So, *I* ambushed dem. I would have ended it quickly. Dey were clumsy and slow. But one of dem, de leader no doubt, grabbed de boy and put a knife to his throat. I had no choice but to let dem regroup. He said he'd let de boy go, but he didn't. He cut his throat and pushed him on me. I tried to save his life, but too much blood escaped too quickly."

Sinala nodded when Polly finished. "See? That proves it. You only found them by chance. Unless someone gets caught in the act in this city, no one ever gets arrested! You people are wasting your time!" She stood up and stomped toward her room. The older woman made an attempt to guide her, but Sinala brushed her hands away. "I can do it!" she shouted. She felt her way down the hall and disappeared.

The grandmother cried softly into her silk sleeve. "She wasn't like this before. This isn't how I raised her. It was those vile monsters!" She gazed at Polly. "I only wish her soul to be healed."

Polly raised her head. "Before any wound can be healed, it must be cleansed. You may rest your hopes on our backs, mistress."

The lady sniffed loudly and stopped crying. Her aura of dignity returned in her face. She held out her hand saying "Lend me your dagger a moment, girl."

Polly drew her blade by the handle. With a flick of her wrist and a roll of her fingers, she now held it by the blade. Reverently, she placed the knife into the woman's palm. The lady took it and immediately ripped the leather off the handle as if it were paper. She touched the wooden grip with her fingertip. As she pulled it off, a single white strand could be seen, connecting the fingertip and handle. She then let go of the knife with her other hand, but it did not fall. Instead, it spun in midair. Like a spool collecting thread, it pulled out yard after yard of the shimmering line. Back and forth she moved her finger, coating it with the web-like thread. When it was finished, the handle was smooth and ivory white. The lady plucked it out of the air and presented it to the young mystic. "I have charmed your weapon. My spirit goes with it, for our philocreed paths cross over the same purpose. From now on, it will never leave your grasp unless you will it to."

Polly took the dagger, noticing the balance had also improved. "And who do I have to tank for dis gesture?" she asked.

"You may call me Keevantha."

Polly smiled as she flipped the dagger back into its sheath. "I somehow doubt dat to be your given name."

"And what kind of name is *Polly Gone*?" the lady replied, with a haughty grin.

The crimson theurge maintained her smile and almost laughed. "Tank you for your time and your gift, Keevantha Bladespinner. By my philocreed, it will bring your bloodline justice."

The 5th Ward, also known as 5-Town, was not like other districts in the city. The buildings were newer, yet looked older due to shabby construction and decades of neglect. Will had seen poverty before, but never on the mass scale of this city slum. The street lights were covered in rust and very few even worked. The kiln-crafted bricks that made up the building's skins were blemished with uncountable cracks and chips. The few faces he saw were of grim-eyed humans peeking from behind rotten door frames and shattered windows. Trash and junk were piled high on the street corners and alleyways. The tendikeye loathed the place more and more with each step.

"This place ain't right," Will murmured with wary eyes.

"Sure it is," Röger replied calmly. "We should be there soon."

"That ain't what I mean," the tendikeye shot back. "This whole set up. The air's too stiff. The buildings're too close. Not enough daylight gets through. I can't spot a single potted plant. Nuthin' grows here. This place looks like a big...a big mistake somebody made."

"Does it make you miss the forest?" Röger asked.

Will swallowed with a dry throat. "I'd take a desert over this place."

"Relax, man. It won't be long."

Will could not hide his disgust. "How does a place like this come to be, Rög?"

Röger kicked a rusty food can as he considered the younger man's question. "This place is one of many. Every major city in Doflend has one. It's called a ghetto, which in old tongue means *get out*. It's a place for unwanted people. These humans are descendants of refugees from a war that happened a century ago. The war had many names depending on what side you were on; The Meodeck Secession, The Free Blood Rebellion, The War for Purity...all dignified names for a series bloody exchanges. It got so bad that there were people on both sides that just wanted to escape it all. So, they flooded into other huncells, like this one, all in search of a better life." The Black Vest looked down and scoffed bitterly. "Funny thing was; they were all still full of patriotic blood. And it was not uncommon for them to form gangs that clashed, sometimes violently, with each other over issues that didn't matter anymore. They had left the war, but the war had not left them. So, the cities built up the ghettos as quickly and cheaply as they could, and forced the humans to live in them.

"And all these years later, even though the patriots are long dead, our bad habits remain, I'm sad to say. We can't even trust each other. War does that, you know. Ruins everything." He glanced up and took a deep breath before saying "Heads up. Company."

Just as soon as Röger finished speaking, a rough, skinny human approached them. His hair was cut very short and he wore a brown wool jacket. He walked with a careless, clumsy swagger. It made Will think *"If he walked like that in the wild, he'd twist both his ankles."*

"Hey, fellas! How are you on this fine evening?" the man asked with a broken smile.

The two warriors stopped, silent and observant of the stranger.

"Relax, fellas," he said, still smiling. "I'm just collecting donations. Whatever you can spare. Whatever's weighing you down."

Will raised his chin and glared at the stranger. He rested his hands on the handles of his gun and sword. "An' how do you expect to collect these donations, son?"

The stranger stopped about seven feet from them. He laughed out loud as he scratched his stubbly cheek. "I don't expect to do anything but collect your money and maybe a few of those fancy weapons. But my trigger man, though..." He pointed at a window two floors up behind them. Another human male held a rifle with a mounted scope. His head and arms were out the window, pointing the barrel at Will and Röger's backs.

Will looked back and forth at the two robbers. "Nice ambush, mister," he said to the one on the ground. The man grinned with victory in his eyes. Will returned the smile, but before anyone knew it, he stepped between the rifleman and Röger. "Take yer shot, you son of a slag!" he hollered with fury burning in his eyes.

Before Will finished the sentence, the shot was indeed taken. The bullet cracked through the air, hitting him square in the chest and knocking off his balance. The tendikeye growled as he reset his stance. Faster than thought, his pistol was out. It was a Mark Twain Special, arguably the best sidearm ever created. It resembled two finely crafted revolvers connected at the butts. His index finger and pinky hugged the top and bottom triggers. The two 10mm barrels were connected by a steel plate with a heart-shaped notch cut in its center. It made a stuttering *KA-KRAK*, expelling two angry pieces of lead. They hit their marks in unison, one blowing off the man's right cheek and ear, the other destroying his left elbow. The man wailed in agony, letting his gun fall to the sidewalk. It broke into three useless pieces upon impact. The sniper fell back into the safety of the building, screaming.

Will spun around, clutching his chest with his free hand. He barely had time to see the impact of Röger's fist bash into the other man's teeth. It seemed like the man fell sideways as he flew a good ten feet away. He was out cold before he landed, grazing a lamp post on the way.

"That's a heckuva punch!" Will thought as he winced from the pain in his chest.

"Are you okay!" Röger shouted as he turned back around.

Will smiled and rubbed his chest, but the pain was so great he collapsed to one knee.

"You shunting idiot!" Röger exclaimed. "Why didn't you try to dodge it?"

"'Cause it woulda hit you," Will answered, gritting his teeth.

"Shunt!" the human yelled. "We should get you patched up!"

"No need, Rög." Will stood up, dropping his hand to his side. The shirt he wore had a hole in it. Inside, a huge welt was forming on his chest. Upon that welt was a blood blister the size of a fingertip. Just below that Röger could see the feather adorned dog tag necklace Will wore on the inside of his shirt. "It's gonna hurt to breathe fer awhile," he coughed, putting back his pistol.

Röger was no fool. He heard the sound of that rifle. He knew all too well what they could do to a flesh and bone body. Will should have had a hole through him as wide a temple door. "Will", he started, looking very serious and a little scared. "What's wrong with this picture, man? Why aren't you dead?"

Will looked off to the side and took a deep hurtful breath. He looked at the two concerned eyes inside the silver helmet. "Theurgy," he answered gravely.

"Theurgy?"

"Yep," Will answered, not sounding too proud. He spat on the ground, getting the taste of the word out of his mouth.

"Let me get this straight: Aren't you the man who says he doesn't need to rely on mysticism?"

Will made a sad grin. "It ain't like I got a choice. Hindin and I've been all over this huncell. So far, no theurge's been able to diagnose the energy. Fer some odd reason, bullets bruise and swords scratch. I've been this way my whole life."

Röger nodded in amazement. "Is this why you left Cloiherune? Because it's a crime to use it there?"

"You could say that. I don't deny its usefulness. But to me, its nuthin' but a curse. Someday, I hope to get it lifted an' be able to go back home. By the way, you smell somethin'?"

Röger took a whiff from the air. "Is that...? What is that? It smells like something off a spice rack."

"It's chives," Will explained. "It's a cousin to the onion. I give it off whenever I get hurt enough to kill a normal man. That make sense to you?"

"Weird." Röger agreed, leaning in and sniffing some more.

"I know. It's why I smoke. Throws off the stink."

Röger regarded Will and nodded. "Well, Mr. Foundling. It seems that you yourself are also a mystical mystery. But don't worry. I understand the value of secrets. Yours is safe with me. Come on. Let's get a move on before we attract more attention."

Will smiled and the two started up walking again. But after coming to the unconscious ruffian on the ground, Röger said "Wait a sec." He bent over and rolled the man onto his stomach. "There," he said tenderly. "All better. We don't want this dung-clump to drown in his own blood."

"Such a gentleman," Will said with a chuckle.

"I know. What about your man in the window?"

"What *about* him?"

The two men continued walking.

A slight whimper could still be heard from the window up above.

The old man known as Dympner Bhakta didn't need to stay at the hospital. He could afford his own house nurse. Although they lived in the worst part of town, Dympner and his wife, Yennej, made a handsome living as landlords. Over the last century, they'd witnessed four generations of humans grow and fade in their shabby apartment building. The last hundred years since the Fevärian Civil War started had indeed been profitable. They cared for their tenants the way a rancher cares for their herd. They knew every tenant by name, as well as the tenants' family trees four generations back. Dympner was a retired military man who had served his country as a field cook. In his one hundred years of service, eight centuries back, he had seen little combat. So nothing could have prepared him for the hot piece of lead that was fired into his abdomen at the battle arena yesterday. Upon their door hung a sign reading Do not disturb. All matters will be dealt wit*h at a later time. -Yennej.*

A large, tanned hand pulled the cord that rang the doorbell.

"*Lousy tenants!*" the old wife thought. "*Can't they read the sign?*"

She undid the three locks that secured her door. "What is it that is so important that...?" Her words ended at the sight of Will and Röger out in the hallway.

"Evenin', ma'am," the tendikeye greeted.

"Hey there," Röger added, squaring his huge shoulders and giving her a wink.

The lady squinted her eyes, searching her memory. "I know you two!" she proclaimed. "You were the two fighters at the Red Dirt. You were there when my husband was shot."

"Yeah, that was us." Röger answered proudly. "And now we're on the case to find the ones who did it! We suspect it may be the Mystic Mafia."

"No merde," the woman returned flatly. "He sure as death wasn't blind *before* we watched you kill that beast. What is it you two want?"

"We'd like to talk to him, Mrs. Bhakta," Will answered.

"Well, so would I!" the woman fired back. "But the nurse has him so drugged up that he doesn't know his ass from a canyon."

"You were right there with him," Will said. "Maybe you could answer our questions."

"I'd be happy to," she replied, sounding more annoyed than happy.

"May we come in first?" Röger asked.

"No. And keep it short." The decades of being a slumlord hardened the old biddy's heart.

Will saw that the time for pleasantries was over. "What'd they look like?"

"All four of them were young, not even two centuries old."

Röger asked next. "What kind of clothes did they wear?"

"Plain clothes, all of them. One of them wore his hair in long, messy braids. One was tall, with a yellow rag around his neck. He's the one that blinded him. The gunman had a broken nose. I didn't get a good look at the fourth."

"So, you saw the maxim get cast," said Röger as he crossed his arms. "What did it look like? How did he do it? What were the words he used?"

The lady felt hassled as she recalled the incident. "He pulled out this little round mirror from his pocket. He held it up to my husband's face, and this dark glow flashed out and clouded Dympner's eyes. Just after that, they shot him and ran."

"So," Röger pondered. "He didn't even say the words of the maxim?"

"Nope. It just came out of the mirror."

94

"So, they didn't take anything either?" asked Will. "His coin pouch? Jewelry?"

"Nothing," the lady answered.

The three people stood there for a moment, each thinking a different thing.

"Well, is that all?" the woman asked with thinning patience.

"Yeah," Will replied. "Fer now, anyway. We'll be back if we can think of anything else. Hopefully, yer man'll be better by then. Good night, Mrs. Bhakta."

"And good night to you, sir. Both of you." the old woman slammed the door shut. The sound was followed by the fast clicks of its three locks.

Chapter 4
Blood and Broken Glass

◈

The clocks in Embrenil, and indeed every well kept clock in the vast Cluster read 5:83, eighty three minutes passed the fifth hour. In this sunless world time is measured in a different way. By tens and hundreds are the passing moments counted. One hundred seconds to the minute, one hundred minutes to the hour, ten hours to the day, ten days to the week, ten weeks to the month, one and half months to each season, and six months to the year. 1 o' clock is called Morning, 3:50 is called Noon, 5 o'clock is called Evening, and 7:50 is called Midnight, and is still the witching hour. It was the ten-fingered and ten-toed humans of Fevär that made the first clocks, with the number 10 governing most of their calculations. But worry not about having to learn a new system of time. For you may take this knowledge or leave it. Morning will still be morning, and Evening, evening.

Polly and Hindin waited fifteen minutes for Will and Röger to meet them back at the Goose Egg Inn. Supper was being served by a lukewarm staff. The small dining hall was full of hungry transients, slurping their broth and shoveling their potatoes. Will noticed that the beer being served tasted much like what he had earlier that day. When he asked the waitress, she confirmed his suspicion, saying "Of course it's NcRay beer! What else should an honest inn serve in this town?"

The four teammates sat around a wobbly table (which they were lucky to get to themselves with such a crowd). There, they shared what they learned with many an idea and theory.

"It might have something to do with paintings," Röger suggested. "Horce Rohlend is a painter. Yrot Aundi was at an art gallery when they attacked her. Maybe those two are connected."

Polly shook her head. "I doubt any of his paintings were featured at de show she attended. His attack came after hers, and he was not dat successful until after he went blind."

Will blew out a lung full of smoke. "Miss Polly, yer the mystic here. You ever heard of anybody castin' maxims out of a mirror?"

"No," she replied. "Dat seems very strange. Maxims are usually cast through de hands, and need to be spoken aloud unless it directly effects de theurge. A focus instrument can be used, such as a wand, a staff, or weapon dat de mystic is attuned to. It channels de energy better."

"Like your dagger!" Hindin happily declared, proud of his deduction.

"Exactly," Polly smiled. "Perhaps de mirror itself contained de energy, and de possessor only had to activate it. And a mirror's reflection is de only ting de victims can see. Either way, *mirrors* must be part of de energy's philocreed path."

"What kind of theurge uses mirrors?" Will asked.

"Perceptionists," Hindin and Polly answered accidentally at the same time. They exchanged amused smiles. She made a courteous gesture with her hand, allowing him to further explain.

"The best perceptionists claim they can undo and reshape reality, but most are manipulators of the first five senses. Many, however, only focus at mastering one sense at a time. Sight and hearing, naturally, are the most popular. In this case, it would be sight manipulation. But rather than tricking the eye into seeing something that is not there, it simply sees darkness. So, perhaps they are not technically *blind*. They simply see nothing but a dark void. And if, perchance, a mirror is the cause of the effect, then a different mirror could partially disrupt it. Which is why they can see out of reflections!"

"But only reflections from mirrors and window panes," Polly added, her enthusiasm growing with Hindin's. "But wit' window glass, only a vague reflection can be seen. Both are made of glass. Dat could mean someting, too."

Röger leaned forward with his elbow on the table, trying to look cool. "You know, Polly, they say that the eyes are the windows to the soul."

Her smile grew into a sneer. "Be serious, you pelvis-head! Dis is no time to flirt!"

"When would be a good time?" he asked with sparking eyes.

Polly grinned a big toothy grin. Seductively, she stood up and stepped to him. She placed her three smooth fingers on the side of his thick neck. As she lightly brushed them down to his shoulder, Röger didn't even have time to feel tired. His helmed face splattered in his bowl of diced potatoes.

Will jumped out of his seat. "What'd you do to him?!" he gasped.

"Nothing dat wouldn't happen eventually," she answered as she sat back down. "He's dreaming now. Of me, most likely, de dirty skirt chaser."

Will started to get angry. "This ain't a time fer fun and games, missy. We got a case to figure out, and we need him awake. Now, he didn't mean you no harm. So, how do you wake him up?"

Polly gritted her teeth and glared at the tendikeye. "Like dis!" She reached over and slapped the back of the human's helm. It startled him awake and made him sit up. A wet chunk of potato was stuck in his helmet, blocking his left eye. He looked confused up at Polly as warm potato broth dripped off his face and onto his shirt. A mad laughter erupted from her. Hindin couldn't resist joining in. They both laughed uncontrollably. Röger picked the potato out of his helmet and ate it, still not sure what had happened. Will chuckled in spite of himself. Then, he too, lost his control. And as he did so, Polly noticed that he did indeed have a nice smile, different from his usual cocky grin.

Röger took a gulp of beer, and stared at them all like they were crazy.

Night fell, and three of the four teammates retired to where they had slept the night before, all save the tendikeye. It was raining outside, so Will couldn't sleep on the roof. All the other rooms were taken, so he opted to share Hindin's room. Hindin had little use for a bed anyway, so he sat cross-legged against a wall. But both men were too busy speculating to sleep.

"A princess? How ya figure?" Will asked, rolling his last cigarette for the night.

"It makes perfect sense," Hindin replied. "Yrot Aundi pointed out how she played the piano, that it was an old style reserved for royalty only. Furthermore, she has a thick Chumish accent."

"Yeah, it's annoyin', like she dudn't know how to talk right. I have a helluva time try'na understand what she's sayin'. What's yer point?"

"Well, Ms. Aundi also explained that the old Doflend royals were overthrown. I have read that some of them went into exile to Chume. Maybe Polly is someone of that lineage. Oh, and by the way: She speaks quite eloquently, especially when you get her talking about theurgy. I bet she was formally trained in her blood powers just like her music. You should really hear her play sometime. But she may go a little crazy when she does."

Will started to get cranky. He had laughed so hard earlier that it made his sore chest hurt even more. "Rev, if you like this girl so much why don't you marry her?"

Hindin gasped from surprise. His eyes widened as an idea popped into his brain. "That's it!" he shouted.

"Rev, I was only kiddin'!" Will told him with a worried voice.

"No. I know now why she ran away! To escape an arranged marriage! Think about it!"

Will didn't want to think about it. He wanted his excited friend to pipe down. He pulled his pillow over his face. "Go to sleep!" he yelled through the feathers and cloth. He threw the pillow at the malruka's face.

Hindin caught it with ease. "Will, what if she is? What if someone is after her?" There was honest concern in his steel face. "Maybe we should go find that orphanage and make sure."

Will sighed and shook his head. "She *does* have someone after her, Rev. It's them four punks that're terrorizin' the city. I do believe now that when they shot that one man, Bhakta, they were sendin' a message to her. They blinded him to make sure everyone knew it was them. But they didn't stab him or take nuthin'. We ain't got time to investigate her when she needs our protection."

"Oh, I see." Hindin replied, as if understanding a secret code.

"You see what?" Will asked.

"Oh, nothing. Goodnight, Will." He gave his partner a studious eye before closing them both.

❖

The sore muscles in Polly's legs kept her awake. Even the pressure of fabric was too much and she was left with no choice but to sleep without her shoes and blue jeans. Though it was unusual for her, she had grown accustomed to the room. She hung her red bra and dagger on the bedpost. Pulling off her socks, she carefully wiggled and stretched each of the two large toes on each foot. She curled into bed wearing only a pair of white cotton panties and white tank top.

She thought about the nearly four week walk it took to get to the city. She had assumed her legs could stand up to anything after that. But after a day of climbing stairs to talk to strangers, they were tender in all the worst places. She could have used her power to give them a good massage, but it was getting late, and it would be too messy a job.

While out with Hindin, she had hoped to walk by the Nyupe Shan Zahn Shelter, her old orphanage. It had been, in truth, twelve years since she had been there. *"Is Sister Tercha still dere?"* she wondered.

Big raindrops padded gently against her window. It made a soothing sound, like blood splattering onto a marble floor. She hated that she liked killing, but it was part of her philocreed. It had to happen soon. The power bonded to her very heart and mind depended on it. She hoped that the leader of that gang would be her next sacrifice. Looking up at her newly upgraded dagger, she felt shame collide with pride. Killing was a part of her philocreed, and philocreed was a part of her soul. *"Oh well. It could be worse,"* she thought. *"At least I'm not a slut like some girls."*

Abandoning the attempt to sleep, she decided to get up and watch the rainstorm. "Four Winds-One Storm," she whispered to herself. She rather liked the name. For a few seconds, lightning lit up the street below. She could barely make out the few figures beneath her window that walked up and down the sidewalks. It made her happy to be off those streets, where the people and weather were too unpredictable. She noticed the faint cast of her own reflection in the window glass. At first it saddened her, for it reminded her of the mystical picture taken by the man that fathered her, her reason for coming to Embrenil in the first place. But then another thought came to her like a bolt of lightning.

"Dat's it!" she yelled. "Dat's de secret of de blinding effect!"

Suddenly, the window shattered with a loud bang. Polly was knocked to the floor onto her back, her breath knocked out of her lungs. As she tried to breathe, blood rose up from her mouth like an overflowing cup. She wanted to scream, but couldn't. There was too little air, and too much red liquid. She rolled onto her side and felt the full intensity of the pain in her chest. There was no doubt it was a sizzling hot bullet, for the upper part of her left breast was pumping out spurts of blood by the shot glass. Immediately, she caught the blood with her hands, and rubbed it into her white shirt. There was no time and no strength to get up and put on her red bra. She had to wear red to activate her powers. She prayed that her shirt soaked up enough color in time.

"Polly! Are you okay?!" Will pounded on her door. "Answer me!"

But Polly could not. All she could do was slap the wet floor and wheeze out a gurgling noise.

Hindin rumbled something she couldn't hear. "Naw, I got it!" Will yelled. The solid wood door flew in two feet and landed flat on the floor. Will was inside in a flash, followed by Hindin.

"Gut snake!" Will exclaimed when he saw Polly lying there. Her shirt was completely soaked in blood. He immediately ran over to her, starting to scoop her up off the floor. "Polly! Polly, you stay awake now, y'hear!"

But Will knew it was too late. He had been through enough skirmishes to know better. The light in Polly Gone's eyes was almost out. He looked in them as felt his own eyes sting with growing tears. "Polly, I swear to you we will find them! They ain't gonna git away with this!" He looked down to see her lips moving. He had trained to read lips, and there was no mistaking it. She was saying *I'm sorry*.

"Yer sorry?" Will asked as he blinked. "Fer what?"

Without warning, Polly wrapped her arms around his body. The thorny veins burst from her arms and wrapped around the two of them like a cocoon. She bit fast and hard into the young man's neck. *"Dere it is!"* Polly thought. It was that same strong pulse she had felt once before.

Will screamed like a little girl and panicked. "Git her off me, Rev! Git her off!!!"

102

The malruka lightly tugged at the veins, not sure if he should rip them off or if that would damage both of them even more. He suddenly became terrified for them both. There was no choice. Now was the time for his chimancy.

With his heavy steel hands he lightly thumped the girl on two special places on her bottom rib and upper jaw. Her veins retracted as she went limp, and slithered back into her arms. Will was motionless as well, lying next to her. Both were very pale and still, but breathing.

Röger suddenly appeared in the doorway. "What did I miss?!"

The malruka opened his mouth, but no words came out. He closed it, shaking his head. It was indeed a rare occurrence when Hindin Revetz did not know what to say.

The 3rd Ward Temple of Health was once the mansion of a powerful count. After the democratic revolution of 811 A.F., it became just another museum. For over a thousand years, it was one of many historical landmarks with a guided tour. As the city grew and changed, so did its historical policies. A wellness temple was needed in the area. So, the city council voted that the building held the least amount of historical significance. The antiquities within were removed and stored in a vault. Today, a large plaque on the eastern corridor gives tribute to the nearly forgotten count. There it read:

It was within these fossil laced walls there once dwelled Count Dredma of Embrenil. He was as wealthy as he was mysterious, for it is still unknown where he came from. He was known, however, to throw lavish parties for the local lords, ladies, and public officials. He is also credited for financing many trade ship companies on the eastern coast. In his later years, it is believed that he relocated to the foreign land from which he hailed, leaving behind a mansion full of exotic and priceless art. To view some of these artifacts, visit the local city museum.

It was state law for each city to have at least one temple of well being. Because of this, healers of all kinds had little want for employment. Because these temples were primarily funded by the state, they had to report all criminal related injuries to the civic police. By morning, the police were on their way.

Will woke to the sound of sandpaper on steel. He sat up in a comfortable, yet unfamiliar bed in a plain white room. Hindin sat on a stone bench by his bed side, sanding off small traces of rust from his head and torso. His jacket lay across his lap. "Good morning," the malruka huffed, not looking up from his work. His face had a look of annoyance.

"Rev, you rusted! What happened?"

"I had to carry you through the pouring rain. The hood of my jacket flew back as I ran. It was dark and we got lost a couple of times trying to find this place. Not a single taxi cart could be found in such weather, much less one that could pull us all."

"Does it hurt? It looks pretty bad."

"I would compare it to the time you wrestled that monstrous poison oak plant. Rust is the malruka's rash, I suppose."

Will suddenly remembered yesternight. "Wait. What about Polly? Is she okay? What did she do to me?" He touched his fingers to his neck, feeling for the bite wound.

"You are completely healed," Hindin assured. "Even the bruise on your chest is gone. They used theurgy to heal you. I was told that it did not take much, given your highly conductive race. You should be grateful, even though it goes against your way."

"But what about Polly?" Will grew impatient. "Don't evade the question, Rev! I have to know if she's okay!"

Hindin just kept sanding as he searched for what to say. "I'm not quite sure. They managed to remove the bullet and heal her wound. But..."

"But what?" Will asked.

Hindin stopped sanding. "I'll have to finish this later. Get dressed and we will go see her."

Will threw on a white robe provided by the temple. Beside it was a pair of slippers that his huge feet had no chance of fitting into. "Okay, let's head,' he ordered with an air of command.

As they walked down the great hallway, they passed a few of the female helpers. "I see that the *big boy* is awake," one of them said as they passed Will. The two ladies giggled as they went on by.

Will turned to his friend. "Hey, where's Röger at?"

Hindin just shrugged. "We are in a hospital full of nurses in form-fitting outfits. Your guess is as good as mine."

Polly's room was just down the corridor. Hindin placed a hand on Will's shoulder. "You will find this unnerving," he warned before knocking on the door.

"Just a moment," an older woman's voice called out. After what Will perceived as at least a moment and a half, the door was answered by a thick-waisted, kind faced woman in a white smock. "Ah, Mr. Foundling, you're up!" She smiled like an eccentric aunt as she pinched his cheek. "And how are you feeling, sir?"

"Are you the mystic who did it?" he asked timidly.

She shook her head. "No, that was Sister Julya, the third shift healer. I'm Sister Caberetta. I handle all the first shift services."

"Well, thanks all the same. Can we see Polly, please?"

As he walked in, Will saw nothing but a small tendikeye woman standing by the window. She was strikingly beautiful, with shapely quill-covered wings, dark tanned skin and blue eyes that shone like diamonds. Rarely had Will ever seen so fetching a creature.

"I'm sorry," Will apologized with a nervous laugh. "We must have the wrong room."

"I don't tink so, Will," the young beauty said in a Chumish accent.

Will eyes widened. His ears did not mistake him. That was Polly's voice coming out of her. He looked closer at the girl, trying to make sense of the situation. "*It does look kinda like her*," he thought. "Polly?' he asked at last.

She nodded and took a short breath, saying "I'm afraid so."

"WHAT THE HECK IS GOIN' ON HERE!!!" he hollered, startling everyone in the room.

"Calm down, Will," Hindin urged, placing a hand on his shoulder.

"Mr. Foundling, this is a place of rest and healing. Please quiet down!" Sister Caberetta admonished with an accusatory finger.

Polly stepped forward, and Will stepped back to keep his distance. "I am sorry, Will, for taking your blood. I truly am. But I had to do it or else die on dat floor."

Will put his hands up in front of him, warning her off. "I don't care 'bout that right now! Why are you...? How did you get...?"

Polly explained. "Whenever I drink dat much blood from a creature, I have two choices. One, I could know every thought dey had in de last year or so. Or two, I could take on de characteristics of deir form. In dis case, I chose to mind my own business." She raised her large five-fingered hand and admired it. "To tell de truth, I like dis shape much better dan a bear or a dog."

Will made a look of disgust. "You drank the blood of bears and dogs!?!"

She flared her upper lip into a sneer. "It was only one bear! And how dare you judge me?"

Just then, Röger appeared in the doorway. Lipstick kiss marks were all over his helmet. "What did I miss?" he asked in the same tone as the night before.

◈

"Twenty-three hun'erd grotz?! We ain't got that kinda money!" A pervasive helplessness invaded Will's being. All his training and years of buskwhacking could not have prepared him for the subtle wrath of the temple's healing bill.

The tendikeye and his teammates had gathered at the temple's billing station. A pudgy, stern-faced drakeress in her middle years sat at a neatly kept clerking desk flanked by a wall of shelf compartments filled with papers. In her right hand she wielded a fountain pen. Underneath the pen's unfriendly brass point, a piece of paper was being tortured by the woman's mechanical scribbling. With cold ruthlessness, she filled out the form that filled Will with numerical dread.

"Please, Miss," Will implored. "I 'preciate what y'all done. But I didn't ask fer it. Neither did Miss Polly here."

The clerk shook her head once as she scribbled. "But it was necessary, Mr. Foundling. Both you and Miss Gone sustained serious blood loss. If the sisters here had not given their aid, you both would be dead, if not sickly weak."

Polly seemed partially distracted by a picture of rabbits on the wall. "And yet we do not have de money to pay you, madam. How can we settle dis debt?"

The clerk gave her a queer look and then regarded Will. "Since none of you are permanent residents of Embrenil, and thus uninsurable. The only option is too give you a fifty percent discount. However, if you cannot make that payment; it can result in banishment from the city or even jail time, depending on the mood of the Chief Justice."

Will sneered and balled his fists. "The last thing I want is to deal with *him* again!"

Hindin tapped Will's shoulder with the backs of his fingers. "Will, how much do you have?" he asked.

Will hunched. "270, I think."

"I have been saving," Hindin said. "I can add 712."

"I can give 6," Polly added with a shrug.

"You still need 152," the clerk groused.

The three teammates looked back at Röger.

"What?" he defended. "Polly was shot in the line of duty! The ECPD should pay for it!"

"You wanted to join our team, didn't you?" Polly argued. "Den pay up so we can leave. I can't wait to try dese wings out."

"Röger rolled his eyes. "Okay, fine. But 160 is all I got. After I *lend* you the 152, don't expect any more."

As the four of them emptied their pouches and pockets onto the clerk's desk, Will smiled humbly at the Black Vest. "Thanks, Rög. I mean it. I just don't get why the healer's hafta charge so much."

Röger shook his head bitterly and made a slight growl. "Don't blame the healers. Blame the government. Blame nearly any government, especially Karsely. Almost every big government throughout the Draybair Cluster keeps a tight lid on their healing theurges. And the only thing that can pry that lid is ridiculous amounts of money. And you know why?" He cast the clerk a dirty look. "Because when wars are fought, like the Fevärian civil war between Karsely and Meodeck: it's the healers that keep the troops going. And darn near every healer I've known had a heart of gold and an unselfish willingness to help.

But the governments know how valuable they are. So, what do they do? They give them jobs in a nifty place to cast their maxims, like this dump! Or worse; they put them in their military until their faith shatters along with their theurgy. They make it illegal for healers to practice their art in private, because they're afraid that the healers might be seduced into joining

107

freedom fighter/terrorist movements. That and they know that when people are sick or hurt, they'll pay any price to get better! Nearly every major government runs things in different ways. But they all agree on one thing: *He who controls the Healers, controls the people!*"

"That is quite enough, sir!" the clerk's hand slapped down on her desk as she rose out of her chair. "I'll have you know that the true reason healers become civil servants is to discourage roving Excursionists like you from getting themselves and others into danger. Theurgical healing should not be abused by reckless adventurers in search of cheap thrills."

Röger took a brief moment to look the woman up and down. "Lady, you wouldn't know a cheap thrill if it slithered up your leg." He turned and grimly marched toward the exit doors.

The others followed.

"Sir Röger," Hindin gasped, walking along side. "I had no idea you had such a grasp on political history."

"History? Oh. Yeah. Just the things I care about, really." He pushed the doors open and started to descend the temple's grand front steps.

Will hung his head with his thumbs hooked into his pockets. "Where're we gonna stay when we're broke?"

Polly seemed oblivious to everyone else's concerns. She was too busy enjoying her new form. She giggled as she leapt five or six stairs at a time. Her dark black wings allowed her to land softly on her tip-toes. She had just escaped and cheated death. There was no sign of trauma, or seeking of comfort or reassurance. She was alive and well. That's all that mattered to her for the moment.

"When are you gonna come out outta that?" Will asked, not knowing what to think of her new appearance.

Polly laughed. "De effect only lasts for a day. But since I'm a tendikeye, it may only last a few hours."

"Can't you cancel it or somethin'?"

"In any other form, I could. But tendikeye can't work theurgy, remember?" She took an even greater leap, whirling like a dervish to the bottom of the stairs. She landed facing up at them, grinning. "I have no doubt dat it will wear off soon. But I am in de mood to make de most of it. Either way, dose four ruffians might tink I'm dead. And if dey don't, I am now in disguise, no?" She gave a tilt to her hips and raised her chin as if celebrating some small victory. "Besides, before I was shot yesternight, *I* figured out de secret of the de blinding effect."

"Well then, let us hear it!" called a thick male voice from behind her.

Polly whipped around to see two strangers, a man and a woman. The man wore a burnt-orange leather jacket that reached down to his mid thigh. He wore two over-sized bronze gauntlets that resembled the hands of a full-sized malruka. His purple goatee was neatly trimmed and pointed. His amber eyes were all business. The woman was slightly taller than him, also wearing burnt orange, only her outfit was tight fitting like a second skin. Around her right wrist was one end of a pair of manacles. Its long, long chain spiraled up her arm, around her statuesque torso, and down around her left leg with the other end latched around her ankle. She wore her long violet hair in tight, neat braids that descended to her well-toned butt. Both she and her male companion sported badges of the Civic Police Department.

"Good morning," the man greeted with a slight bow. "You must be Four Winds-One Storm. I'm Detective Rafe Azell. This is my partner, Jana Swarbule. We are the detectives assigned to the Mystic Mafia case."

"Wait," responded Hindin. "It was my understanding that we were put in charge of the task."

The detective smiled and shook his head. "That's not quite how it works, Mr. Revetz. You were given permission to assist the department. We have an obligation to earn the public's tax grotz."

Jana Swarbule smiled like she was teaching numbers to toddlers. "We understand that you've been visiting the victims. We also received word that one of you was shot yesternight." She fixed her eyes on Polly. "Are you Polly Gone?" she asked.

"Yes," Polly answered suspiciously.

The officer raised her eyebrow. "I'm confused, Ms. Gone. It was our understanding that you were a drakeress and theurge of some sort."

Polly made a sour face at the woman. "I was almost murdered yesternight. Dis is a disguise, if you must know."

"Oh, we must," answered Rafe as he raised an oversized gauntlet. "We must know everything that you know, and everything that you do. All of you. That's how it works."

109

"So you can eventually take the credit?" Will asked as he stepped up to Rafe.

The detective stopped smiling. "Our only goal, Mr. Foundling, is taking down those four thieves. Glory is for heroes, kid. Cops have no use for it."

Will groaned and rolled his eyes. "Rev, please, you handle this," he told Hindin as he turned away shaking his head.

Hindin cleared his throat, looking humble, yet dignified. "Please, pardon us, Detectives. We are unfamiliar in your ways. We must return to the Goose Egg Inn to gather our belongings, for we have run out of funds for room and board. If you would walk with us, we would be obliged to share what deductions we've made."

The two detectives accepted the malruka's offer, and complimented his good manners. As the six of them walked, Hindin and Polly gave a detailed summary of what the group discovered. Will and Röger hung back a few steps in observant silence. As they walked the final block to the Goose Egg Inn, Polly shared the discovery she had made at her window the night before.

"Glass," she said plainly. "Mirrors and windows are made of glass, which is nothing more dan forged sand dat had been melted wit' fire. One of de ruffians tried a fire maxim at me. He might have learned it from whoever created de mystic blinding mirror. It must be some kind of geotheurgy and pyrotheurgy, using minerals and heat." Suddenly, another idea came to her. "Wait! Yesternight, Röger told me dat de eyes are de windows to de soul. Windows, Hindin!"

The maruka's eyes widened. "Of course! A window is a portal that gives access to sight!" Hindin exclaimed. "Perhaps that is why the victims were left alive! It could be that the blinding is a kind of mystical link to their spirits. We chimancers call the head's part of the soul the *crown chakra*. It controls both sight and thought, which explains the blindings AND the victims' lack of certain mental functions, such as mental visualization. They could have partially drained the energy from the crown chakra!"

"It's very possible!" the blood mystic agreed.

"Wait, wait, wait." Detective Rafe interrupted, squinting his eyes. "You're both saying that we could be dealing with a soul thief?"

"Yes!" Hindin replied with glee. "And *that* would explain why the victims all suffer from a strange, druggy feeling. Their souls could slowly be draining out of them!"

The two cops gave each other the same look of concern. Detective Jana pulled out a wire loop with several grotz coins strung upon it. "Here," she offered, pulling off several of them and handing them to Hindin. "Courtesy of the Department. At 5864 35th Street there is another inn called the Rotten Cherry. As you've said; the Goose Egg is no longer safe. Go there and lay low while my partner and I look into these ideas of yours. We'll be sure to contact you in a couple of days."

"Thank you, Detective," Hindin said with a formal bow. He held up the money and gave an additional nod of gratitude.

"You're welcome." Detective Rafe replied. The two cops turned and walked away.

The Rotten Cherry Inn was an architectural oddity. *Mess* would be a better word. In its eight hundred and sixty years, it has had almost two dozen different owners, each one believing they possessed a knack for the hammer and saw. Various additions were built. A doorway had been bricked up to reinforce a wall to support a new level. Crudely made secret passageways were obvious to the untrained eye. Heavy tiles meant for floors were poorly glued to a few walls, so once in a while; one or two would fall and break. Hard wood floors had been put down over old carpet. Various scavenger bugs scuttled about in vast colonies hidden inside the rotting walls. The faded paint schemes of each room seemed to clash violently with the next. Even the roof had three different types of shingles; wood, clay, and rusted tin. The stains in the mattresses were mysteries better left unsolved.

The current owner, Selbrum Jyxx, was a long-winded, middle-aged hot shot. He rented out room and board to anyone who could pay, although his preferred customers were lost souls. The divorced and the abused, runaways, drug addicts, the mentally and socially handicapped, and the lonely elderly who had made too many mistakes in their lives: These were his kind of guests! For amongst them, he could seem suave and cultured. He would advise and preach to them his more experienced point of view, and put them down in subtle ways. He would often take advantage of his female tenants, and offer a rent discount for sex, then later run them out like they were cheap whores.

His younger brother, Wickurdo, tended the tavern hall. He was always too busy for such fun, although he did enjoy his work. He supervised one cook and two waitresses as he tended the bar and lit cigars. In the corner of the smoky hall, he had a low-rent pianist, who sometimes also huffed and puffed sloppily on a mouth harp. The weary musician survived primarily on tips and complements.

It was mid afternoon, and the tavern was nearly empty. A barely legible sign advertized a lunch of roasted pigeon with corn chips and salsa. The four teammates sat at a thick topped square table. Will and Röger spoke little as Hindin and Polly continued their buzzing discussion on theurgy.

"It *has* to be soul related," Hindin declared enthusiastically. "For in my homecell, Slate the Great Father, gives us life through our eyes. When we are punished, varying portions of our life force are drained out *through* them. All of our eyes are crystalline substances, such as emeralds, diamonds, or even colored glass. Geotheurgy!"

"But I am again having doubts dat de victims' stab wounds are part of it." Polly replied. "Only a crimson theurge like me can use blood in pnuema related maxims. And only a dedicated master, at dat."

"Do you know someone who would?" Röger asked.

Polly hesitated, recalling an unwanted memory. "No," she replied. It was a lie. "Not since de time of de Gloam Crusades has dere been such a master. And dey were all hunted down by Slate's forces." She gave Hindin a sort of sideways nod as she mentioned his homeland's ruler.

"I hope you inherited no ill feelings from such events, Polly," Hindin said gravely.

"None at all, Hindin. De forebears of my path were evil. Besides, I like you."

"What about me?" Röger asked, in a randy tone.

"I am starting to learn tolerance," she sighed, rolling her new blue eyes.

Röger snickered and nudged Will with his elbow. "Hey, you should give it to her: She makes for one foxy tendikeye! Or was it just that she used *your* blood, pretty boy? Do you have a sister that cute?"

112

Will looked far from amused. He peered over at the girl who had subdued him with her theurgy twice in the last four days. "Miss Polly," he started. "I consider myself a seeker o' truth. I want to figure out this mystery as much as anyone. An' I truthfully believe that yer expertise has helped us out greatly. Fer that I thank you. But in the meantime, I seek another truth: Who exactly are you?"

"I-I've told you," she stammered.

"I know what you told me. But I've heard tales of monsters that drain blood out of necks to survive."

She saw the trigger fingers on his hand twitch slightly on the table top. "I am no hemogoblin!" she yelled, standing up from her seat. "It was de only way I could've survived!"

Will's face didn't change. "If you say so. And what about yer theurgy and yer knowledge of it? Do they teach that to little kids in orphanages? How to play with people's blood? Rev here thinks yer some kinda princess escapin' an arranged marriage. Who are you really, Polly Gone?" He stood up from the table.

"Why do you need to know?" she cried, fear edging into her voice.

Will frowned slightly. "Because yesternight, as I held you while you was dyin', I was wishin' it was me that got shot. I *want* to trust you. I want the four of us to work together to figure this thing out. Please, Pol, you can tell us."

Polly took a deep breath and tried to keep from shaking. "I am escaping my teacher. Is dat good enough for now?" Her eyes were pleading.

Will and Hindin looked at each other, both thinking roughly the same thought. Will turned his face back at her, wearing a curious grin. "Ain't that somethin'. And the main reason I'm in this crazy huncell is that I'm *lookin'* fer mine!" He laughed and slapped his knee as his eyes sparkled with astonishment.

Polly blinked her eyes, thrown aback by Will's sudden easy-going attitude.

The tendikeye smiled and flipped out the dog tag necklace he wore under his shirt. She saw the two falcon feathers that adorned it were fixed on with strands of rawhide.

"My teacher, a man called Brem Hoffin, gave me this right before he left my village. Left me this pistol an' blade, too. Taught me all I know about harkin' an' the wild. Then one day,

113

he's gone! An' the old coot leaves me a note sayin' *If you want to know who you really are, make a name for yourself in Doflend. I will find you.*"

"So, you really aren't military, are you?" Röger asked, seeming a little disappointed.

"Brem was. He was hardcore Dasaru, a master of the sword and pistol. He did special operations fer the empire, and other sneaky ooh-gosh-neat-stuff."

"Why did he train you?" Röger asked, leaning on his elbow. "Of all people, why'd he teach some backwoods farm boy? Special ops masters in my huncell tend to only give private lessons to rich kids."

Will shrugged. "He said he was retired, that he wanted to rest somewhere quiet fer awhile. He taught me in the meantime as a way of keepin' up his own practice." Will looked over at Polly and smiled. "Don't you worry none, Miss Polly. If anybody, be it teacher or city punk, comes to bother you, we're gonna give 'em a reckonin' they won't soon ferget!" The young man's face seemed wild with confidence and determination.

Polly only shook her head. Her eyes were full of a sad doubt. "You would stand no chance," she half-whispered. "If my teacher finds me-"

"Then we'll finish this case before that happens!" Röger answered. He shared in Will's enthusiasm.

Polly looked over at Hindin. His crystalline eyes held the same promise. These men, or at least two of them, were men of their word. Her teacher had instructed her that such men were to be taken advantage of and exploited. It seemed only natural to use them as shields when the time came. They were strong, useful, and oh-so-trusting. Why not take them up on this offer of trust? They chose a life of danger. If she had to sacrifice them to save herself, why should she feel guilty? And why have this nagging feeling, this guilt? She looked over each one of them, still trying to smile. "You are all very kind, and you have my tanks. But I am starting to feel worn out from yesternight. So, if you don't mind--"

Just as she was about to retire, a civic policeman entered the tavern. "I'm here to retrieve Polly Gone, by orders of Chief Justice Taly," he stated in a calm, clear manner.

The three men at the table stood up.

"What for?" Röger asked, bothered by the announcement.

114

"What are the charges?" Hindin asked.

"You misunderstand," the officer explained. "I'm only retrieving her for questioning. The Chief Justice wants to see her."

"Is it all right if we come along?" Will asked, annoyed by the sudden intrusion.

"Of course," the officer replied. "But I'm riding a bileer, and he's awful spry. You won't be able to keep up."

Will grinned. "That sounds like a dare to me!"

◇

The bileer was a massive elk with antlers that curved back like the handle bars of a bicycle. The rider gripped the antlers and used them to steer the beast. The domesticated bileer was the only domesticated mount in all the Cluster that did not need bit nor bridle.

Polly held tight to the officer's waist as they rode through the busy street. Every few seconds, she would look back to catch a glance at her teammates. Will leapt, covering ground like a grasshopper, but with the agility of a rabbit. Off lamp posts, edges of fountains, business signs, and the tops of moving carriages, there was no telling where he was going to land next. Röger ran like the wind. Every once in a while, he would be lost from view. But now and again, he was able to catch back up. Hindin, however, was far, far, far behind. He opted to 'walk briskly', not wanting to risk plowing into someone.

Polly's stomach tightened as the Police Department came into view.

◇

The air grew thicker with every step. Even with the promise of three strong allies who offered to go with her, Polly Gone found no comfort. She was a fly trying to buzz in and then out of a spider's web and she knew it. She cursed herself for leaving herself so open, so known. The blood draining she did to Will yesternight was illegal. Hopefully, that was all this was about. She thought it odd that she had to fight a giant monster as punishment for using blood theurgy, and that to win her freedom she had to slay that monster with blood theurgy.

Her three teammates were instructed firmly to wait in the visitors lobby. She was led directly to the Chief's office. All around her were law men and women with strange and unusual weapons and gear. She did not want to find out how those 'tools of justice' worked.

The tall oak doors of Chief Justice Taly's office were already open. Inside, he sat at an exquisitely carved desk. He wore armor that seemed to be woven of thick strands of leather and steel cable. On his right hand was a golden gauntlet. On his left was a long black velvet glove. He appeared calm and professional, even courteous as he stood to greet her. "Please, come in," he said with a slight bow.

The girl's paranoia grew as she approached. She suddenly realized that they had let her keep her dagger. *Why didn't dey ask for it?* As she was busy with that thought, the two detectives from earlier, Rafe and Jana, stepped out from behind the doors.

"You may go now," the Chief told them. On the way out, they both gave Polly a studious glare that she didn't understand. Before she could react, they pulled the door shut. It made a loud knock as the lock fell into place. She turned back to Taly, who was sitting again. There was no chair for her, only a twenty foot gap of green carpet between the desk and the door.

"How old are you?" the Chief asked, cocking his head to the side.

"Eighteen," she answered. She kept her eyes on his hands.

The regal man smiled. "I know some women like to lie about their age."

"On my philocreed, it is true!" she answered, growing restless of his game.

"On your philocreed, eh?" The Chief Judge paused. "One of many things I know about theurges, is that if they swear on their philocreed, they lose all power if they lie. This even counts for the wicked ones."

"So?"

The man leaned forward with a half crazed grin. "So, I may have you swear by every answer you give me today."

Polly's eyes widened in fear. This man knew something, something she'd wished she could forget. Her insides churned.

"Seventeen years ago," he started. "There was a serial killer in this city. For five years previous, there were dozens of victims and no clues. Until one day, we discovered the killer's philocreed path: Crimson Theurgy or The Red River. It was a theurgy that worked differently with male and female practitioners. And all signs made it clear that this murderer was a female master. And you know what? We eventually found her. She lived in a mansion with many winding halls. Her physical aloofness made her hard to catch. There were twenty of us with the best equipment money can buy, and in less than two minutes, she cut us down to nine! Every time we shot her, she would hide and reappear to drain one of us just as you did to that tendikeye yesternight. Eventually, we must have overwhelmed her, for she was gone and didn't come back. But she did not leave us empty handed."

"In a red cradle, crying from all the gunfire, was a baby girl. I ruled that she be placed in the care of the Nyupe Shan Zahn orphanage. It was a mistake I regret to this day. Six years later, the shelter was attacked."

Polly was unnerved by the word. "Attacked?"

"Massacred, more like. Every sister-helper and every orphan were found dead. Some were slashed open. Some bled to death through their eyes. Some simply had hearts that stopped. And wouldn't you know it: the little girl we rescued was missing!"

Polly's body twitched and jerked as tears filled her eyes. Her tendikeye facade melted away as she broke down. The black wing quills fell off her back like leaves from a tree before fading to nothing. The purple hue came back to her skin and her white and blue eyes changed back to black and gold. "She didn't say anyting about killing dem!"

She let loose a scream that chilled Taly's heart. "She lied to me! She lied! She told me...she told me she just sneaked in dere and took me!" She covered her face with her hands and collapsed to her knees.

"So!" Taly exclaimed, rising up from his chair. "You *are* Veluora's daughter!"

Polly slowly pulled her hands from her face. In her eyes burned hatred deeper than love. Her teeth clenched hard behind her quivering lips. "Dat I am, sir! And now dat you have me, what is it you intend to do?" Her raspy breath clashed violently with her girlish tone.

The chief scoffed. "Why, ask more questions, of course. Is she back here in the city? Do you know where she can be found?"

117

Polly looked away. "I don't know. Her chateau is in Chume, but she is not dere. I am trying to escape her. If I stay too long in Embrenil, she will find me."

The Chief looked at her long and hard. "If she comes, will you try to let me know? I have long overdue justice to deal out to the crafty slag."

It was now Polly's turn to scoff. "She can't be stopped. You are a fool to tink such tings!"

"Be that as it may," Taly began. "I will not stand by and let her terrorize my city again. I need you to notify me if she comes. And I want you to swear by your philocreed that you will."

"And if I do?" she asked, suspiciously.

"Then I'll let you get back to the case you're on. By the way, I think you're doing a good job. Rafe and Jana just told me about your theories. I'm impressed, impressed enough to tolerate your *hemopathy*."

The girl's jaw almost dropped. "You would trust me to return to de task, even when you know who I am?"

"Why not?" he asked, crossing his arms. "Besides, if you can't make a good case-cracker, you'll make fine bait. Now swear."

Polly took a deep, contemplative breath. Once more, she found herself in a situation with no good solution. It was why she escaped her mother in the first place. She looked at the old stalwart man behind the desk, her enemy's enemy. Perhaps he too could be of use to her. "I swear on my philocreed dat I will help you in any way I can!" Her voice echoed with resentment.

The Chief smiled and made a strange gesture with his left hand. The velvet glove ignited with a bluish white flame. The room grew colder. Polly trembled, at first from the chill, and also from astonishment. "Winterfire!" she gasped with misty breath.

The Chief spoke. "And I swear on *my* philocreed to do the same for you."

❖

"I'm beginnin' to regret this deal!" Will grunted as he tossed an old, grime-covered kitchen sink into a steel dumpster.

As a way of saving money, Will and Röger agreed to clean out an old storage room for the innkeeper in exchange for three days lodging. To them, it seemed like a great way to beat the boredom of keeping a low profile. But as the day wore on, they wondered if the room actually had another wall on the other side of all that junk, and not just miles and miles of more junk.

It was high noon. The dumpster outside was three quarters full of centuries-old clutter. There were rusty spring skeletons of tattered mattresses, wooden bed frames covered in spider egg sacks, old pots and pans with the bottoms rusted out, two water damaged chests containing moldy curtains, a wardrobe containing the remnants of a stuffed beaver, printed paintings of various size and disrepair, a tattered wedding dress, stools and chairs not fit for burning, old NcRay beer bottles, a couple of rat infested couches, a love seat containing three grotz coins beneath the cushions, and a set of billiard balls.

"I got me an idea fer this eight ball." Will smirked, slipping it into his pocket before tossing the rest.

"You know," Röger started. "I hear that some theurges use those to tell the future."

Will shook his head and considered the notion. "Y'know, people think we tendikeye hate theurgy 'cause we're ignorant, or that we're jealous 'cause we can't use it. Truth is, Rög: You shouldn't cheat chance. And even if some can see what's around the bend, it dudn't mean you got a right to." He started stacking old window panes on the floor. He then peered up at his cleaning partner who yanked out another couch from a wall of debris. "Hey, Rög. There's somethin' I gotta ask you."

"Shoot, man," Röger returned.

"Well, yer sweatin' like a dog's nose under that helmet. I seen you take it off but once. That was to clean it an' yer head after that arena fight. Why keep it on all the time? You a wanted man 'round these parts?"

"Only by the ladies," Röger laughed. "Most people don't understand this. But I know you tendikeye value chance above all else. So, here it is: It's my good luck charm."

"Is that so?" Will remarked, lifting up the stack of window panes.

"Yep. It's kept me alive for a long time."

"You be careful with them good luck charms, now. They use up all yer good luck early. After that, you got nothin' left but bad."

Röger smiled. "If that's really how it works, then I used up all the bad luck when I was your age."

119

"How old are you?" Will asked, beginning to carry out his load.

"Old enough to want to keep it secret."

"Just like a woman!" Will taunted as he walked outside. Before stepping out, he caught a glimpse of Röger's middle finger.

The day was bright, and Will's eyes had not yet adjusted from working in the dark. Stepping into the alley way, he suddenly heard a loud screech beneath his large boot. "GAAAAH!!!" he yelled, leaping a good ten feet into the air. Before he landed, he saw a calico cat run off. Two pieces of glass he was hauling fell to the ground and broke, making a loud crash. "Dang fuzz-cougher!" he cursed as he landed.

Immediately, he heard Polly's voice from above. "Will?" she called. "Are you throwing dose away?"

Will looked up to see the girl looking down from her window. Her short purple locks hung down around her face. He smiled up at her with a glint in his blue-gray eyes. "It's nice to see you talkin' again. I was thinkin' Chief Taly struck you dumb yesterday."

"I need dat glass," she muttered through her teeth.

"Oh, really?" he asked playfully. "Well, come on down and git'em, little lady."

Polly sighed from impatience. "Can't you just toss dem up one at a time?" she pleaded.

Will was already a stubborn person by nature. He was also very curious and enjoyed teasing friend and foe alike. To him, the old panes were now a mysterious treasure desired by an aloof theurgess. "Why do you need 'em so bad?" he teased.

Polly slumped in frustration. "Please," she plainly replied.

Will regarded her a good long six seconds. "Are you sure you can catch 'em?"

"Of course. Just toss dem up high enough for me to reach."

Will smiled and sighed. "Fine, Miss Polly. If that's yer request."

He tossed the panes up one at a time. As they reached the height of her window, she clapped her hands to catch them as they spun for a second in mid air before they started to fall. After she caught fourteen panes,   Polly called out "Tank you! Dat's all I need!" before shutting her window and disappearing.

Will looked up with raised curiosity. Röger came outside, carrying a full-sized sofa on his shoulder. "She's a strange one, that Polly," Will remarked, tossing the rest of the panes in a dumpster.

Röger grunted as he heaved the sofa into the large wooden bin. He then walked back toward the doorway. As he passed Will, he whispered "I found something!"

As Will followed though the doorway, Röger whispered again "Close the door!"

"But it's dark in here. We need the light," Will disputed.

"Then use your matches," Röger answered almost angrily.

The tendikeye complied and shut the door. As he struck his match, a wavering light filled the room. Röger led him over to where he had removed the couch. As the human knelt down, he tugged at an old bed sheet. Then the match went out. "Gut snake!" Will grunted as he pulled another match from its paper box. He lit it and saw that Röger had removed the sheet to reveal an old leather covered wooden box. The box was small, and it looked like Röger already knocked off the latch. Röger opened it to expose what looked like six round coins the size of poker chips. He picked one out and held it to the light. It shined like a mirror and rendered a perfect reflection. Through its center was a small, flawless hole.

"That's a funny lookin' grotz coin," Will remarked.

"I don't think it's grotz. It's older than that. Here, feel the weight." He handed it to Will.

Will's eyes grew wide. He expected the gravity of silver or maybe platinum. But it had barely any weight at all. "Plastic?!" he gasped.

The two men shared a tense feeling of excitement. They shuffled through them, marveling at their flawless beauty. There it was! The most precious and rarest of all substances in their grasp!

The bukk trembled from awe. "These had to've come from before the Omni-War, before Slate laid his curse that ended the Age of Technology. I remember readin' about it in the schoolhouse."

"Me, too," Röger nodded. "These coins must be money that was used, what, three thousand years ago?"

"Somethin' like that since this year is 2848 A.T. (After Technology), accordin' to most calendars."

"I wonder how they got here."

Will shrugged. "Had to be before our time. I highly doubt the innkeeper knows about 'em."

"It's probably better that it stays that way," Röger smirked. "He won't miss what he doesn't know about!"

Will grinned back. "And he did say to toss everythin'!"

As they began to laugh, the second match went out, leaving them in darkness again.

"That's it!" Will huffed. "I'm gettin' me a lighter!"

◈

Upstairs in the room she and Hindin were sharing, Polly was trying to *cheat chance,* as Will would say. Hindin had gone out for a newspaper and a stroll, so she had the privacy she needed. A mirror that had once hung on the wall was now on her bed. It was smeared with dry blood. She placed the glass panes anywhere and everywhere. One on a chair, two on a dresser, six on the two beds, and the rest on the floor. She stood over each of them one at a time. Dipping the tip of her dagger into her palm, she held it over a glass plate. She studied the shape of each red drop, every nuance or notion of a pattern. She tried to clear her mind, and see an image take form in the crimson puddles. She took her finger and connected the pools, trying to help them take shape. Her eyes glowed faint red for several minutes as she meditated over that first pane. There was nothing to see.

After four more repetitions of the process, she grew frustrated and put her fist through the fourth pane. Feeling a sting, she drew back to see a slash on her fist from her knuckles to her wrist. She clenched her teeth as the blood flooded out from her torn veins. In a brief panic, she stifled a scream as she flailed her wounded limb. The motion left a curve of spatter on the glass on the floor. She then took a few seconds to tend her injury. Focusing her energy on and through her hand, the veins and skin began to weave back together, healing completely.

She cradled her brow in her hand and shook her head, looking over at the mess on the floor. The blood spatter reminded her of a rainbow. *"No"*, she thought. *"It looks more like the blade of a scythe."* Her eyes flashed red again, only much brighter than before. Drawn into a tremor-like trace, her mind's eye opened and beheld a vision.

A tall Drakeri man with a long white beard and wild hair knelt on a beach of black sand. He laughed madly as he watched a handful of the sand spill out between his fingers. He carried a great silver scythe that reflected pieces of eternity. On the end of his braided beard hung a heavy golden disk. As if by its own volition, it swayed back and forth like a pendulum in a grandfather clock.

Abruptly, the vision departed as Hindin opened the room door holding a newspaper. Polly gasped as he entered. She had hoped not to be discovered. Like a child caught disemboweling the family cat, she reached for something to say. "Hindin! I-I-I-I...!"

Hindin did a visual sweep of the room. His face grew both concerned and confused. "Polly," he started cautiously. "Why is there blood and glass strewn all over our room?"

Polly kept silent for the space of three breaths. "It is *my* blood, all of it, I swear!"

"All right," he laughed, smiling and nodding slowly. "That is a good start, Polly. Can you tell me why it is on these panes of glass?"

Polly smiled and giggled nervously. "It's nothing! Just a little, um, divination. I know it's foolish."

"Divination." He said the word as if it were the name of an old acquaintance. "So, let me guess. You are using your blood theurgy on glass, the enemy's theurgy, to access information on them through the mystical courses of existence?"

Polly's face went slack. "Hindin, you sound like a dictionary."

Hindin looked confused. "But dictionaries do not produce sound. They are merely books, Polly."

Polly's eyes widened. *"Is he really that thick-headed?!"* she thought.

Hindin laughed out loud. "I am only kidding!" he chuckled. "It is an old joke of mine."

The girl sighed. She was in no mood for jokes. "I had to do it," she insisted, pointing at the bloody panes. "I've only tried it a few times. But I tink it worked."

"Oh?" Hindin replied. "And what do you think you discovered?"

Polly paused with suspicion. "You are really open to dis, aren't you? I mean, even many mystics don't believe in divining

123

secrets. Most only believe in de maxims dey cast or people dey effect."

Hindin smiled warmly. "Have you ever heard of inward divination?"

"No."

"It is the same as meditation, only it is a personal theurgy. It does not affect the outside world that surrounds us, but rather, us ourselves. It helps we chimancers, or some call us bionomists, discover our potential powers without the further aid of an instructor. I have read that less subtle and less combative mystics can also learn it. Perhaps I could teach you this discipline?"

Polly nodded. "Maybe," she said. She looked down at the newspaper he held. "Was dere another victim?" she asked, worried.

"No. There was no mention of the case at all today. Even the attempt on your life was omitted. I suspect that the ECPD kept it out of the press to keep us safe. The gang may now believe that you are dead."

"I hope so," she said. She knelt down and began to clean up her mess, starting with the broken glass.

"So, what did you find out?" asked the malruka.

Polly seemed in a slight daze. "Find out? Oh! Yes! De Vision!" She proceeded to tell him what she had seen. She described every detail of the strange man with the tic-toc beard and the silver scythe who knelt on the shore of black sand. Afterward, she remarked "I hope dis vision is a literal one, and dat what I saw was not just a collection of metaphors. I hate metaphors."

Hindin remained silent during the entire description. There was something waking behind his emerald eyes. "Perhaps it is not so much literal, as it is *literary*." He stepped over to his bed, squatted down, and lifted the bed with one hand. Underneath it was his duffel bag full of books. He buried his hand into his horde of knowledge. There was no need to take them out and shuffle through them. He recognized each book by its size and feel. After a few brief moments, he yanked the book out like it was a newborn. "Here!" he proclaimed triumphantly. He set the bed down gently and showed the book cover to Polly.

She read it aloud. "*The Forgotten Texts of the Buresche by Mazil Whortshellean*." She frowned. "De writer's name is far
124

too long. He should have a pen name. So, who were de Buresche?"

"They were a tribe of Drakeri that existed before the Coming of Slate. It is said that they were beings of great power, still potent with the blood of archdrakes. Their language is virtually extinct now. The writer was a historian who translated some of their texts. It is this same book that also contains the *Four Winds-One Storm* poem." He flipped through the pages for the poem he was reminded of. "Ah, here!" He then read it aloud.

Xelor the Mad

Xelor the Mad of the Silver Scythe,
Raised his theurgy to spread his strife,
Secrets uncovered of temporal streams,
The cloth of time he cut and seamed,
The grains of sand fell out of place,
Into his grasp they fell from
grace, Melted with fire
and frozen to
make,
The shape
of an hour to remake
fate, The young became old
with no tales told, Black hairs turned
pale and the years would fold, Births
undone - his victims erased, Lost in time
and lost in space, An order of heroes did
seek this foe, After loosing many they brought him
low, They shattered his soul and shattered his hour, And
remade his scythe into trophies of power, pieces of time
with lids of glass, Always correct – Never slow nor fast.

As Hindin finished reading, he paused to see Polly's reaction. Although his eyes now held the answer, he wanted her to figure it out on her own.

Polly felt the secret bloom in her mind. Her face lit up with every shade of emotion. "Pieces of time...TIMEPIECES! Hindin, you were right at first! It was de silver watches dat were stolen. Dey must be de trophies from de poem. Dis Xelor dat I saw, he must have been a temporal theurge...a time traveler! But someone defeated him. Considering de source, it was probably members of dat Buresche tribe. Dey made silver watches from his weapon wit' glass face covers or 'lids', as it was translated. Dey must have some kind of hidden power. But if it's de silver dat contains de power, why does a glass mystic want it?"

Hindin listened to Polly like a proud father. "The glass might have come from the theurge's hourglass."

"Hourglass?" she asked.

"Look again." He held the book back up to her. "It says that he melted the sand with fire into the 'shape of an hour'. Even the poem's shape takes the form. Maybe the writer left it as a clue for lore seekers. The way you described your vision, it seemed that the sand itself contained some kind of influential potential over time. They could be the very Sands of Time that were scattered during the Ameliora, the start of Second Age of Existence."

"Dat's just a legend," Polly protested.

Hindin laughed a hearty and warm laugh. "And so too will be our victory!" he cried out, pointing his finger upward. "It appears that this glass master and his four ruffians may be attempting to collect these watches for some kind of time theurgy. Perhaps they seek to travel to the past or future." He paused for a moment to think. "Or maybe, just maybe, they seek to *steal time* from the victims!"

Polly jolted. "Dat would explain your theory of soul theft! By establishing a link wit' de blinding effect, de mystic could den siphon de life force out of de victim's to prolong deir own!"

"Time is literally of the essence!" Hindin exclaimed. "We must tell the police that the victims are in further danger!"

Will and Röger found Hindin and Polly's discovery hard to comprehend.

"You go on ahead an' tell Chief Taly. It don't take four people to deliver one message," Will told them. "Besides, me an' Rög still got work to do."

❖

When the two theurges arrived at the station house, they were informed that Chief Taly was too busy to see them. So, they sought and found Detectives Rafe and Jana in their office space. It was one of those open office spaces in the middle of a maze o cops' desks. After five minutes of explaining their discovery, they were rewarded only with skepticism.

"Let me get this clear," Jana started. "You, Ms. Gone, had a hallucination, and it reminded Mr. Revetz of a poem he read?"

"It wasn't a hallucination!" Polly argued, taking offense.

"It is not just a poem," Hindin returned calmly. He drew the book from his large pocket. "This is a historical document of an extinct culture. The writer was a wandering bard who compiled some of the stories he found into rhyming verses. It was a common practice in those days."

Detective Jana paid more attention to Polly. "And you, Ms. Gone, sustained substantial blood loss during your little experiment. Cutting yourself is a very unhealthy practice. You probably came in contact with a foreign substance as your wounds were open."

"Are you suggesting dat I used drugs?" Polly spat.

"Divination is an unproven method of research," Jana shot back. "even amongst the best theurges in the eight Huncells. It has been found to be unreliable and often just plain wrong. And behavior such as yours, while not illegal could get you put into an infirmary for the mentally unsound."

Hindin frowned at the detective's remarks. He looked over at her partner. "Detective Rafe, what is your opinion?"

Rafe's face was uncertain. He seemed very uncomfortable in his chair. "To be honest, Mr. Revetz, my expertise is better suited toward criminal psychology. My partner is the theurgy expert. But what I can tell you is that I do agree that many mystics try all kinds of ways to prolong their life spans. They develop a dependency on life, you could say. They spend so many years toiling behind books or meditating on top of mountains, that they develop varying degrees of social aloofness, inadequacies with personal relationships, and for some, the inevitable disconnection of society altogether. Such separations can lead to corrupt behavior like you suggest. But even if your ideas were true, how do you propose we find these perpetrators?"

Hindin's steel arms scraped sharply as he crossed them. His face was stern and decisive. "Question every theurge in the city, starting with the High Theurges, including those in public office."

Detective Jana scoffed and rolled her eyes. "Mr. Revetz, aren't you aware that many theurgy practitioners keep their art secret? They don't need to advertise because casting maxims for a customer is very expensive. It's not like they all walk around in robes and live in tall towers. And if a High Theurge *is* behind all this, he's probably the reclusive type, as well."

"But a High Theurge is behind dis!" Polly broke in. "Only a master can drain soul energy."

The female detective cocked her head and smiled. "Young lady, we're still not sure if that is what's really happening."

Polly gritted her teeth. "If you are such an expert on theurgy, den why aren't you a mystic?"

Jana raised her chin. "I need not answer that," the woman answered coldly.

Polly smiled with eyes full of gloating malice. "It's because you lack de gift, don't you? You spent so much time researching it. But researching and learning are two different tings."

"Polly, stop," Hindin ordered.

But Polly was far from done. The detective's insults and insinuations had gotten her fuming. "You probably tried your hand at several paths, hoping dat you had finally found de right one. You felt a calling dat you were destined to be a mystic. But den one day, you realized dat, like most people, it just wasn't in you! Because you believe in nothing, you faithless bitch!"

The long-chained pair of hand cuffs that coiled around Det. Jana's body sprung to life like a viper. She straightened her leg, letting it unravel in the blink of an eye. The loose cuff end enlarged and fastened around Polly's neck, making a clicking sound. Polly immediately raised her hand, sending out a jagged vein that weaved around the woman's long braided hair. Polly felt herself being tugged to the ground, but she managed to pull Jana down with her. Jana released the other end of her mystical shackles, latching it around Polly's wrist that used the veins. Polly used her free arm to fire out more veins to lasso around Jana's arms. The two women struggled on the floor as Detective Rafe and Hindin watched, dumbfounded.

"Let go of me, you little slag!" Jana yelled.

"It's only a theurgical weapon you use!" Polly hissed. "Dat doesn't make you a theurge!!" She yanked at Jana's braids, not caring if they came out of her scalp.

"Feline melee!" a nearby officer yelled.

In a rush of many loud footsteps, the mystical wrestling match between the two attractive drakeresses became an exciting event for a crowd of Embrenil's finest.

"Get her, Swarbule!" one cop yelled through several whistles and cat-calls.

Hindin at last felt the urge to break them up. Yet he did not want the cops to think he and Polly were resisting arrest or something similar. "Stop it!! Just stop it, both of you!!!" he pleaded.

Detective Rafe was still speechless. He looked lost.

Suddenly, Chief Taly pushed his way through the crowd. He stood over the two women, his face darkening with rage. Polly was the first to notice him. Without a word, she withdrew her veins and stopped struggling.

"Not so tough! Are you, you tweaky slag?!" Detective Jana cackled, thinking Polly had given up. Then out of the corner of her eye, she saw her boss. Her heart sank and her anger vanished. "Chief Justice!" she started.

"Not one word, any of you," the Chief ordered in a grave tone as a chilled mist escaped his lips.

The crowd of cops immediately dispersed, returning to their prior business. Those who weren't busy hurried to look like it.

The Chief glared at Polly and Hindin, then at his detectives. He fixed his stare on Rafe, who was shaking. "In your own words, Rafe: What happened?" he asked gruffly.

"W-Well, sir. Mr. Revetz and Ms. Gone arrived with more theories and ideas. We listened to what they said, but Detective Jana and I had our doubts. Then Ms. Gone became offended and insulted Jana. So, Jana...I don't know...attempted to arrest her, maybe? They ended up in a scuffle. Then you came. I'm so sorry for this, sir!"

"What do *you* have to be sorry about?" the Chief snapped. He looked back at Jana, who was still on the floor with Polly. "Swarbule, you've been warned about your temper. You aren't a mercenary anymore. You're a civic official. Act like it!"

The lady detective hid her face. It was a mixture of shame and resentment. "Yes, sir," she muttered.

"And as for you two!" the Chief addressed Hindin and Polly. "I don't want to see you back at my station house until you have hard evidence or a suspect ready to confess!"

"But what if there is another victim?" Hindin pleaded. "May we still retrieve their addresses and interview them?"

The Chief took a long deep breathe. "If and when it happens, I *might* send you a letter. Now get out!"

Chapter 5
The Cold Hard Facts

◈

Drakeri, despite their immense life spans, do not mature or grow wiser at the rate of humans or tendikeye. They are habitual creatures, and their points of view are slow to change. Once they are set in their ways, it could take centuries to sway them. Although they vary in moral points of view, there are few races as steadfast in their outlooks as the drakeri, especially the evil ones.

It was a simple, boring, bland apartment on the northeast side. They could have easily afforded a fancier suite somewhere, but the leader knew better. For the first time in their lives, they were making big money. It was easier than peddling drugs--no risk of getting shot by a competitor. It was steadier than common thuggery--a beating was always imminent. Better than flesh peddling, less wear and tear on the backs of their hands. In truth, they made for very poor gangsters. That's what always kept Drew, Zeni, Yelats, and Lertnac together; their mutual inefficiency.

Andrew Monitiz went by the alias Drew Blood, because of his penchant for stabbing people. In just over a century, he had stabbed over forty-two people for fun and profit. The fun and profits never lasted long enough, so it became a bit of a habit. He was a sneak, a murderer, and the oldest of the four ruffians known as the Mystic Mafia. He enjoyed the infamy and the money he was making, but once enough jobs were done, he knew he would feel a sad relief, like a high school student graduating. This would probably be the best job he ever pulled off.

Zeni was trying to read his pyrotheurgy book. His white dread locks hid the confusion in his eyes. He knew he had the gift. Fire theurgy was common amongst Drakeri. But as he skimmed over the text, he drowned in doubt. He hated book learning, and only comprehended one of the many *pyroglyphic* maxims; *A burnt child fears the fire*. The wise words rang clear in his mind and soul. He attained the correct thought that the

131

maxim could produce, and could in turn give that thought form, the form of a fearsome ball of flame. He had always maintained some level of pride from his meager talent, even though he was a novice theurge at best. But that pride abandoned him the day he encountered that blood theurge in the alley.

Lertnac was playing with his new pistol. He had always wanted one. Most firearms were crafted by hand and very expensive. He had used most of the money he had earned to buy it after getting his forearms shredded up by that blood mystic girl. But he no longer had worries about her. None of them did. He was confident with his aim that stormy night. The bullet he used was big enough to drop a bileer. Without her, those three hotshots she was with were hounds without a scent. His only concern was how their employer knew she would be at that particular window at that particular time. He did not care much why they were fetching silver watches, though. He got paid handsomely for that.

Yelats was the youngest, a year short of three decades. He was still sulking that a girl had broken his nose. Drew told him not to let it bother him, that it would add character to his thin face. He looked up to Drew and the others. He thought Drew was gutsy and tough, living his own legend. He admired Zeni for his wild personality and theurgy. Lertnac, although the shortest of them, he liked because he was strong and intimidating. They were older and they tolerated him. He knew they did bad things. But at least the bad things weren't happening to him like back home. To him, they were the best friends he ever had. He would have been mortified to know that they intended to kill him when he was no longer useful; greed outweighs loyalty amongst the lowdown.

They never knew exactly when their next assignment would come. Sometimes it would take a week, sometimes a few days. When it did come, the rule was that it would have to be done that very day. And so they would wait, all four of them growing stir crazy. Their mysterious employer insisted that all of them be available at all times. They hated being cooped up with growing fortunes in their own personal stash spaces. The promise of even more money braced their patience.

After an interminable wait, the familiar knock sounded at their door. They all stood up and Drew gave the sign that he would be the one to answer it. He went over and undid the vertical row of locks. The door opened wide enough for Mr. Shard and Mr. Crack to step in.

The two figures took their bowler hats off as they entered. The wood floor beneath them made uncomfortable creaking sounds as they walked. The cut of their fancy suits was identical, but the color combinations were opposite. Mr. Shard wore a brown suit, yellow shirt, and red tie and hat. Mr. Crack wore a red suit, brown shirt, and yellow tie and hat. Both Drakeri were unusually broad in the shoulders, with bulging arms and thick necks. Both were also bald with no facial hair. Upon close inspection, one could see that they wore a thick purple foundation, almost like paint, over every inch of their skin. The only thing about them that looked real was their eyes, only they made an eerie clicking noise when they blinked.

"Here is your next assignment," Mr. Shard said, handing Drew a yellow envelope. His voice seemed to come from his chest, rather than his mouth.

"Why don't you ever just tell us?" Drew asked, taking it.

"This is how the Master prefers to do business," Mr. Crack answered. "It is not for us to know, only you four."

Drew said nothing, but his face was wary. He did a good job of disguising his fear of the two men to make it look like suspicion.

"Did you kill the crimson theurge?" asked Mr. Shard.

"I did," boasted Lertnac from across the room. "She was right where you told us she'd be."

"And you are positive she is dead?" asked Mr. Crack. "The newspaper has yet to mention her passing."

Lertnac hesitated. "Unless she's bullet-proof, I'm sure of it. People die every day in this city and it don't get mentioned in the paper."

"It's true." Drew agreed with a grim smile. He pulled his hidden dagger from his long sleeve. "Half the pokebags who've felt this blade never even made it to the obituaries."

Mr. Shard reached out and flicked the knife with his finger. It made a slight *ping* sound as the blade flipped off the handle. It landed point-first between Drew's feet, sticking into the floor. Drew hopped back, his face growing in astonishment and rage.

"No more stabbings," Mr. Crack commanded.

"That was my favorite knife!" Drew yelled.

133

Mr. Shard took a fast step at him, poking him in the chest. Drew collapsed in pain, his purple face wincing into an almost black tangle of features. It felt like he was being jabbed with a broom handle. His friends stirred with worry and concern.

The two well dressed men knelt down to face him in unison.

"The master is still not happy about you killing your marks," said Mr. Crack.

"It is of the utmost importance that all the marks live through their ordeals," added Mr. Shard. "This is the second 'accident' you've had. As it is, you have five more marks to engage. It could have been three by now. You are wasting both the time of your crew, us, and the Master. One more death, and Mr. Crack and I will pull you apart like a roasted chicken."

Drew Blood did not need to answer. He could see his reflection perfectly in the glossy gleam of their eyes. It showed a face that was helpless and afraid, like so many of his victims had been. "What are you?" he asked.

Mr. Shard made a face that might have been a smirk. "We are *art* imitating *life*." The two men stood up and left the apartment.

Drew listened to their heavy footsteps clomping down the hall. As he stood up and looked at his friends, his face immediately went back to that of a cold-hearted miscreant. It was the first time he had been made to look weak in front of his boys. With wounded pride, he pondered which one of them he should bully first to feel better. Then he looked down at the envelope he had dropped on the floor, and decided to take it out on the next victim instead. He picked it up and opened it, took out the note, and read it aloud.

"You will find a Mr. Jonash Fluge leaving his home at 614 South 4ᵗʰ Street. Recognize him by his balding head, green suit, tortoise framed glasses, and brown leather briefcase. On his 63ʳᵈ step from his front door, he will be passing a stone flood trench that is about five feet deep. No one will be watching at this time. The mirror bearer must wait there hidden from view as the others push him in. This must occur at precisely 41 seconds after 4:12. Mr. Crack and Mr. Shard will be waiting in the alley between Yonoman's Barber shop and Binetti's Café.

They will be ready and willing to exchange your fee for the watch."

As soon as Drew finished reading, the letter burst into a loud flame. Before he could let go of it, the paper was completely consumed. He gasped through clenched teeth as the tips of his fingers were singed. "Every shunting time!" he yelled.

Down the hall, toward the building's stairwell, the two well dressed men had a conversation. Their lips did not move, and they made no sound--other than the unnatural thuds of their steps.

"They think the girl is dead."

"Let them. They must focus on their tasks."

"They make for poor assassins. Her blood belongs on our hands."

"After tonight's exchange with these fools, we will deliver the watch to the Master. Then we must deal her more trauma than a simple bullet."

The task was done and the exchange was made. The four ruffian thieves had left Mr. Fluge barely alive after taking his watch and money. They met up with Mr. Shard and Mr. Crack, who gave them each twenty five 100-grotz coins. From there, the four thieves scattered in separate directions.

It was becoming a custom of theirs to split up after a job well done. After spending so much time in that cramped apartment, they were glad to be rid of each other. They knew it would be at least another day before their next assignment. It was the time to enjoy the nightlife of the city.

Lertnac was a ruffian of simple tastes, but not because he enjoyed them. He honestly did not know how to have a good time. With the creativity of a wild dog, he resigned himself to uncomplicated procedures that most lost souls resort to. He decided to go to a bar alone.

On his way into the city's 3rd ward, he thought about his options.

"Should I go to Keever's? No, it's full of old people. How about the Rotten Cherry? They've got good beer prices. Naw, I'll

go to the Peanut, instead. The Cherry never has enough girls to choose from. The Peanut's closer anyway."

When he arrived, he found that the place was nearly packed. Here, there, and everywhere people were having a good time. The music from the house band wove a playful groove into the crowd. Feet moved and hips shook in all directions. There were tables with loud one-sided conversations. Women wore playfully trashy dresses that clung to their bodies for dear life. Bursts of laughter erupted from all around. The whole place smelled like a good time.

The ruffian found a stool empty at the bar. When the busy bartender finally paid him some attention, he slapped down one of his 100 grotz pieces saying "NcRay Select! And keep'em coming!" He had hoped that someone nearby would notice his impressive spending, but none did. The bartender took the coin, popped open a bottle of the expensive draught, and placed it in front of his customer.

Five beers later, Lertnac made three attempts at getting the attention of a pretty girl in a green dress. She was far across the room, dancing with two or three girlfriends. He tried to catch her eye with his own, but she wasn't looking his way. He tried to get the waitress' attention to send the woman a drink, but all the waitresses seemed too busy. He even tried smiling and waving, but the girl in the green dress didn't seem to notice. Frustrated, he began to down beer number six in a steady chug.

Just as he was about to swallow the last gulp, a familiar tendikeye bukk and large, helmet-wearing human entered the establishment. Lertac's eyes bugged out as he choked on the chilled beverage. *"It's them!"* he thought. *"It's those outsiders that blood slag was with at the arena!"* A fear rose inside him as he remembered what those two men did to that arena monster. But then he realized that they wouldn't recognize him. He was safe.

He watched out the corner of his eye as they moved deeper into the bar. Drakeri were good at watching without being noticed, thanks to the two extra pupils they had in each eye. He saw that the tendikeye wore his green scale trench coat. As the blonde-quilled bukk sat down at a nearby stool, Lertnac could spot the curved shape of a sword underneath it. The human that sat next to him had neither the huge sword nor huge ax he used

136

at the arena. They seemed to be having a heated discussion about something. Lertnac opened his ears and listened in.

"I'm telling you, Will: I'm gonna get you laid tonight!" the human boasted.

"It ain't necessary, Rög," the tendikeye dismissed.

"Neither is holding your breath, but you should breathe eventually! Come on! Look at all these girls. They're just waiting to be juiced and seduced. This is the best way to get used to the city, country boy."

The tendikeye scoffed and rolled his eyes.

The human continued. "Just think about it: You're missing nature and the woods and, um, exploring new terrain. Well, hey, man; How about you go explore one of these drakeresses?"

"I'm a foreigner, Rög. So are you," Will muttered.

"That's just it!" the human started with fervor and glee. "You're exotic. You're unique! You're forbidden! Nothing gets a girl juiced up better than breaking the rules!" The human paused. "Hey, wait. Are you a virgin?"

"No!" the tendikeye answered. "I've been 'thanked' by my share of village girls fer savin' their village an' what not. I'm up to six, if you must know."

"Only six and you're twenty-three?" the shocked human asked. "And a rare bukk at that? What gives, Will? You're a good looking dude, dude. Make use of it!"

"I just ain't tryin', is all. I'm a tad bit paranoid 'bout the prospect of accidental fatherhood. Don't wanna make another foundling orphan who's gonna wonder who his daddy was. It's a tough deal. Believe you me."

"So, withdraw and do some decorating when that magic moment arrives," the human responded with a shrug.

"I have. But a midwife once tol' me that there's still a risk. Sometimes the seed runs without you knowin' it."

"Well, tonight you are in luck, hayseed." The tall brute gave the tendikeye a jarring slap on the back. "You are in Doflend, land of the *Drakeri*. Your tendikeye seed will find no purchase in the soil of these fine, purple skinned beauties."

The tendikeye shook his head in protest. "I don't hunt fer sport, either. But if nature takes its course, I let it. I don't go out an' try to pick up on women. It happens often enough. And I prefer to be surprised when it does."

137

Röger nodded in understanding. "So, you like to let them come to you," he stated. Before Will could reply, Röger had already stepped onto the dance floor.

Lertnac watched in shock as the human approached the pretty girl in the green dress. Without shame, he brushed a bit of her hair behind her ear and whispered something in it. He then pointed at his friend, who was still sitting down. Lertnac spied in disbelief as the girl walked back with him to his pal.

"You're friend here says you wish to challenge me to a drinking contest," the girl said to the tendikeye. Her voice was amiable and full of life, and it made the insides of Will's ears turn to mush. Her cat-like eyes held a playful suspicion.

Will gave Röger a 'yer in trouble' glance. He smiled at the girl and stood up straight. "Well, Miss, I'll tell ya what: Since you look like a beginner, I'll take it easy on you. Does this place serve pepperwine?"

"Pepperwine?!" the girl exclaimed. "I heard that stuff tastes like fire! Mechjacks use it to clean the grease off of parts. How about you buy me a fizzing potga instead? It's a vodka made from sweet potatoes."

"You two have fun!" the human laughed before returning to the dance floor. He started dancing with the other girls. Badly.

"So, what's your name, stranger?" asked the belle in the green dress. Her expression was observant and studious, as if she were a lawyer giving a cross examination.

"Me? I'm Will. What do you go by?"

"Rhowshell," she answered. "I take it that you're not from here."

Her smile made Will forget how to talk. He paused for a few tense seconds. "Naw, I'm a Cloiherune native," he answered nodding absentmindedly.

"So, what are you doing in the city?" she inquired, never breaking eye contact.

"Lookin' fer the Mystic Mafia. We got a permit an' everythin'."

"Really?" she asked, impressed. "You're an Excursionist?"

"Yep!" he answered. "Me and Röger over there."

"That is so cool. But it's also too bad," she pouted sarcastically.

"Why's that?" Will inquired, raising a quilled eyebrow.

Rhowshell let out a small giggle. "Because, I don't usually go for Excursionists."

"Oh? That's good to hear," Will replied, fixing his stare with hers.

"Why is that *good* to hear?"

"Well", Will paused to clear his throat. "You said 'usually' and not 'ever'. It was quite a relief, fact be known."

The two smiled at each other, liking where the conversation was taking them.

Suddenly, Lertnac stumbled between them. "Hey! I know you!" he shouted into Will's face. "You're that tendikeye at the Red Dirt Battle Arena! You're the real deal, man!"

"Thanks," Will replied, smelling the beer on the stranger's breath.

Lertnac continued his drunken charade. "I saw you fight that big...what was it? That big Sizzagafiend!" He turned to look at the girl. "Man, can this man swing a sword around! You should've seen it!"

"Yes, I should have," she answered, struggling not to laugh at Will's growing embarrassment.

Will smiled at her with teeth bared. His eyes seemed to say '*I don't know this guy!*'.

"Say, friend!" Lertnac slurred. "Would you do me a small favor? My apartment is only a few blocks from here. I'm kind of drunk right now. Would you mind seeing me home safely?"

Will looked at the girl again. "Man, I don't know."

"I can pay you! Here's a hundred grotz piece. No, I'll make it two hundred." The thief pulled the money from his pocket. "Please, sir. The streets aren't safe anymore with that darn Mystic Mafia jumping people all the time."

Will looked at the new and interesting and fun girl in the eye and sighed. He then looked at the man asking for help. "Keep yer money, bud. Let's get you home real quick."

Rhowshell smiled. "Can I tag along?" she asked Will. "Someone needs to look after you."

"Sounds like a plan," Will answered with a wink.

"*RETAEH'S BREATH!*" Lertnac thought. "*I'm going have to kill her, too.*"

Will called over to Röger, who was by then surrounded by drunken dancing women. "Hey, Rög! I'm gonna help this guy home!"

139

The human kept dancing, giving Will the go-ahead with two thumbs up.

◈

The three of them stumbled out the door and into the street. Lertnac was indeed drunk, but he did not seem to himself as drunk as he really was. Nor was his inebriation as debilitating to the point that he did not know what he thought he was doing. To put it simply: He was a drunk who thought he was pretending to be drunk. The combination of the alcohol and the new pistol hidden in the back of his trousers gave him all the confidence he would have lacked otherwise. His chest swelled with pride as the tendikeye and pretty girl kept him steady. He was soon about to take out another member of Four Winds - One Storm. *"What a stupid name!"* he thought.

After a few minutes and several blocks of following the man's directions, Will asked "Are we almost there?"

"Almost," the ruffian answered. He looked around the block they were on, making sure there would be no witnesses. At last, the coast was clear!

"HA!!" the thug yelled stepping away from them and reaching for his gun. But to his drunken surprise, it wasn't there!

"Lose sumthin', shorty?" Will asked. He stood there, holding Lertnac's pistol by the trigger guard.

The thief's jaw dropped. "How did you..?" he strained to ask.

Will grinned a cocky grin. "Y'know, I don't consider myself the best pick pocket in the Cluster. You were too drunk to notice." Then the tendikeye's smile melted into a look most grave. It was a serious bearing that commanded both fear and respect. "I woulda given this back to you when we got to yer doorstep. But I'll wager yer doorstep ain't anywhere near here, is it?"

Rhowshell watched speechless as Lertnac began to tremble in his boots.

"This ain't no chance muggin'. It was you who shot Polly, wudn't it?!" Will yelled, his eyes blazed with a cold rage. "Did you think I'd be any easier, you sawed-off pissant?!" In a flash of manual maneuvering, Will unloaded the pistol and dismantled it

140

until it was nothing but a scattering of small parts on the ground. He then threw off his dust coat and unbuckled his weapons belt.

"What are you doing?" Lertnac asked.

"You made this too easy fer me!" Will growled as he tossed aside the belt with his sword and pistol. "I want a second try at catchin' you, boy. That first one didn't count!"

The thief's confidence rushed back to him with a surge of adrenaline. He'd been in enough street fights to measure his own prowess. This cocky, pretty boy tendikeye might be good with a weapon but he was certainly no match for a tough-as-nails street ruffian like Lertnac!

The thief bounced around with his dukes up, ready to stick and move like a prize fighter. He stepped at Will, preparing to jab. But the tendikeye squatted low and spun fast. His large boot swept in a hard, tight half circle. Lertnac's hopping feet were swept out from beneath him as the boot collided with his ankle. Before he knew it, he was sideways and vertical in the air. He crashed onto the pavement head and shoulder first. Stunned, he tried to get up. Then he realized he was being helped up by the scruff of his neck. Will pulled him to his feet. He reached back to throw a punch, but Will already intercepted his other arm. The tendikeye's grip was solid as he twisted the arm around behind the Drakeri's back. Lertnac felt his elbow being raised up behind him. The pain made him stand on his tip toes. Then once again he felt the sweep of Will's heavy boot. He landed hard again onto the ground, this time on his other side. He rolled slowly onto his stomach and began to push himself up. Half drunk and dazed, he looked around for his opponent. The last thing he saw was Will's boot before it crashed into his face. His body went limp, rolling three times before stopping.

Will stood over him unscathed, making sure the punk was still breathing. He then looked up at the belle in the green dress. "This here's one of the punks we been tryin' to track."

"You mean he's with the Mystic Mafia?" she asked. She trembled for a number of reasons.

Will nodded as he stepped toward her. "I reckon so, Miss Rhowshell. You must be a good luck charm."

The cat-eyed drakeress wrapped her arms around the tall bukk's neck. "I have a feeling your luck's not over!"

The two strangers kissed beneath the burning streetlight. As they pulled their faces away from each other, Will let out a sigh of disappointment. "I wish we could continue this. But I gotta drag this paper tiger to the police station. They'll probably have all kinds of questions."

The woman smiled and stroked his face. "I'm a witness. I'll go with you. No offense, but the scruples of your race do not translate like they should in this region. I should like to back your story and your word, if you permit me."

Will smiled in amazement. *"She just might be Lucky Seven,"* he thought.

He threw the unconscious ruffian over his shoulder, pretending that the burden was less than it was. Even after a victory, he couldn't help but show off. The two of them began their commute to the ECPD. It was in a different direction than the bar they had come from.

"What about your friend?" the belle in the green dress asked.

"Oh, he'll be fine. Don't be surprised if he hooks up with one of yer gal-pals."

Rhowshell laughed. It was a one of those melodious giggles that bubbled in a man's brain like sweet champagne.

The tendikeye was all too right, unfortunately. Neither he nor Röger would be returning to the Rotten Cherry that night. Not in time, anyhow.

It was a while past the usual supper time. Polly had worked up an appetite walking back from the police station (not to mention her little scuffle with Detective Jana). Hindin hungered merely for answers.

The two entered the tavern hall of the Rotten Cherry wearing long, discouraged faces. Hindin had just finished giving her a lecture on self control as they arrived. Even though Polly did not start the physical fight, she still felt responsible for provoking the detective's wrath. Hindin seemed to be waning in his disciplined luster. His usually perfect posture was now slightly slumped and broken.

The tavern hall seemed as empty as their hopes. There was a single table full of old men playing cards. The piano man meandered on the keys, improvising soulless melodies. Wickurdo the barkeep was building a pyramid of empty beer bottles on his bar to pass the time. A dusty, cobweb-laced wrought iron chandelier holding three and a half candles provided dismal atmosphere. But the many lanterns hanging on wall hooks provided most of the tavern's light.

The two tired theurges sat down at a table. The one waitress working that night carried a tray with two pitchers and a fat clay mug. "Beer or water?" she asked Polly.

"I'm not old enough to drink," Polly replied.

The waitress chuckled. "Beer or water?" she asked again, winking.

If Hindin was not there, Polly might have taken the beer. But she did not want to disappoint him further. "Just water, please," she answered. Her feet throbbed from walking and her back was sore.

As the waitress set the mug down and began to fill it, she said "Tonight's special is broiled chicken feet and mashed apples, served with your choice of bread or noodles."

"De noodles sound fine," Polly responded in almost a whisper. "Just de noodles."

The waitress smiled and left them. For a long awkward moment they said nothing before Polly broke the silence.

"Hindin, I really am sorry."

"I know," he replied, rubbing his head. He looked at her and managed to give an honest smile. "It is all right, Polly, seriously. We just had our hopes up about the divination, that is all. Even my ego took a blow when Det. Jana expressed her doubts. I am not angry. Nor should I be disappointed. You had a right to speak your mind."

She seemed so small in her chair sitting across from giant steel-skinned man. Polly crossed her arms and slumped in her chair, but her face started to brighten.

"But it was de tone of my voice dat pushed her."

"Perhaps," Hindin replied, shrugging one shoulder. "But......that was nothing compared to some of the taunts I have witnessed Will perform. He has developed a knack for angering people, particularly when he knows he's about to fight them."

Polly laughed and felt more at ease. "I bet it is quite a show." Two men entering the tavern caught her eye. They both wore identical suits, except the color schemes were opposite. It was none other than Mr. Shard and Mr. Crack. The two broad-chested Drakeri seemed annoyed, almost agitated by something in the room. Suddenly, they bolted toward their table. Then Polly realized it was she and Hindin who were the source of the men's disdain. As they dashed, they slammed aside entire tables and chairs with their great arms, clearing a path.

"Hindin!" Polly screamed.

Hindin was already on his feet, stepping between the men and Polly. However, he was late in his reaction, and Mr. Crack was ready to strike. The expressionless man grasped the end of a table with his left hand, and swung it hard at Hindin's head. Hindin managed to get his guard up, and the table shattered against his blocking arm. But just as his vision cleared from the scattering debris, Mr. Shard stepped in and landed a solid blow to the malruka's abdomen. To Hindin's surprise, the six foot tall man sent him flying over his own table and onto the next one over. The landing was neither solid nor soft. The malruka's weight made the table collapse.

Polly barely managed to dodge her friend as he flew back. Now within arm's reach of the two brutes, she made a desperate attempt to touch one of them. Her eyes flashed red as she lightly brushed the hand of Mr. Shard. To her utter shock, he did not bleed from the ears and pass out. Mr. Shard raised that same hand. The thick fingers seemed to melt together as the hand elongated into a single menacing point. The hand now resembled a giant serrated arrowhead ready to slash her brains out. As fast as fear would take her, she backed away. The two men almost matched her every step. She did not want to try using her jagged veins. These guys were beyond their strength. She focused her power into her eyes. For a second the world faded to black. She faced the direction of the two attackers, looking for two sets of circulatory systems and hearts to keep them going. But there was nothing like that in the two strangers, nothing at all.

Her vision returned just in time. Mr. Shard was about to impale her with his blade. She tried to dodge one way, but felt herself being pulled another. The blade found no mark save her gray cloak, which it split down the middle. Polly found herself being held by Hindin like a misbehaving kitten. Before she could thank him with a smile, he tossed her high into the air. She let out a squeak as he launched her at the iron chandelier. "Take hold and hang on!!" Hindin commanded as he parried the men's attacks with his hands.

Polly latched on like a cat thrown at a tree. Her veins popped out and coiled around the dusty light fixture, securing her there. She looked down and watched in amazement as Hindin fended off the two attackers. He did not move like some brute powerhouse, smashing and slamming like a grizzly. His steel covered body was like a silver sheet blowing in the wind. His arms coiled and bobbed like a pair of large vipers. His stance was always shifting and changing with no signs of a stumble. To watch him fight would have been hypnotic if he weren't so fast! After every other successful dodge or block, he would poke at the men with his fingers in specific places. But to his dismay, he had trouble finding the nerve zones he was aiming for. In a sudden leap backwards, he landed on one foot atop the bar. Wickurdo the barkeep ducked behind it.

With grace and poise to match any classical dancer, Hindin took a bold and menacing posture.

"Hindin!" Polly yelled. "Dey don't have blood! I don't tink dey are real!"

Mr. Crack looked up at her and sneered. "We are as real as he is!" he roared. His skin cracked and turned into a mass of sharp points. Then his eyes dropped out of his head, falling like shooter marbles onto the floor. The sockets wept small jets of red flame. Mr. Shard's eyes did the same as his other hand also formed into a blade.

"So," Hindin started "that is why you are immune to my chimancy techniques. I have been hitting the wrong spots!" He paused to look at them. "You are golems of fire and glass, no doubt the two paths of your master! I demand that you name him!"

"Only the master can make demands of us, malruka," Mr. Shard answered. "Your playful movements will only prolong your death...and hers!" He pointed up at Polly with a serrated finger.

Hindin glared at them and removed his hooded leather jacket. Polished steel skin rippled from the finely chiseled granite muscle sliding beneath it. The muscles on his back flared into a 'V' just behind ribs. His chest, shoulders, and stomach rippled with steel tendons and granite muscle. And his arms flexed like the legs of a tiger. His face blazed with fury as he spoke. "You are agents without wills of your own, so it is useless to offer you surrender. For that I ask your pardon."

The two golems seethed with fire and rage.

145

"I am Hindin Angledar Revetz!" the Chimancer declared. "108th generation successor of the Sacred Path of the Thorny Lotus! Keeper of the Secret Scorpion Fist and Tamer of the Seven Beasts! Master of my own fate and of those I name Enemy!"

"Mr. Shard and Mr. Crack, at your service!" the two golems returned in unison. Their suits started to smolder and smoke from within.

The old men who were playing cards had been near the exit, and were now long gone. The waitress ran out the backdoor in the kitchen, spilling noodles and chicken feet everywhere. The piano player still in his corner was trying to slip away unnoticed.

"Wait you!" Mr. Crack yelled at him, pointing with malicious authority. The golem reached in his inside pocket and pulled out three gold 100 grotz coins. He tossed them from a good twenty feet away at the musician's tip jar. Only one of them managed to land inside. "Peck out a dirge for this clay-spined whelp! Play, Play, PLAY! " His voice was now hot and hollow. The bug-eyed musician immediately sat back at his bench and began banging on the keys. The melody set the mood of tension and desperation. It was going to be a fight to the death the likes of which the Rotten Cherry had never seen!

Hindin leapt off the bar, aiming his iron palm square at Mr. Crack. The golem brought his guard up, absorbing the blow with his forearm. The limb was pushed hard and it crushed against his chest. Mr. Shard stepped in with a jabbing blade to the malruka's face. Hindin tilted his head, evading it, and landed an explosive kick just under Mr. Shard's out-stretched arm, into his ribs. Mr. Crack stepped behind, wrapping his good arm around Hindin's neck. Hindin answered the grapple with a backward elbow to the golem's torso, followed by a downward hammer fist to his glass groin. But Mr. Crack held fast as Mr. Shard prepared a second swing. Hindin still had all his limbs free, and the choke hold did nothing but hold him in place. As Mr. Crack came up with an upward slash, Hindin whipped out his leg, bringing his heel down on Shard's wrist. The blade snapped off the thick limb and onto the floor. An intense heat spewed out of the stump. As Hindin's foot reached back to the floor, he bowed quickly, flipping Mr. Crack onto his wounded partner. The two glass golems crumbled into a pile of burning clothes and shattered glass onto the stone floor. Hindin backed off from the pile, ever maintaining his gaze at it.

146

"Golems of glass!" Polly scoffed from above. "What theurge creates minions dat are so delicate?"

"Wait," Hindin warned.

Before their eyes the pile shifted, separating into two mounds of burning glass. The glass began to melt around the intense flames. The room's temperature rose. The two piles took on the shapes of fiendish crystal bipeds. Mr. Shard and Mr. Crack arose, no longer looking like muscle-bound Drakeri, but abominable monsters. They were nearly transparent with a fire inside them that illuminated their forms. They had two arms and legs, but the rest of them seemed insectoid and armor-like, covered in jutting blades and spikes.

"Brilliant!" Hindin exclaimed. "Your creator is a theurge to be admired *and* feared. To incorporate fire hot enough to melt glass and use it as a regenerative agent displays cunning and inventive thought on his part. I should like to know your master's name, that I may congratulate him!"

Mr. Shard laughed with a sharp toothy smile. "We are also impressed. Our blades are able to cleave through steel. No malruka has ever presented such a hassle! But no matter how skilled you are, you cannot slay us."

Mr. Crack continued. "It may take a few rounds, but you will run out of tricks eventually. Your end approaches, Mr. Revetz!"

The two golems charged with talons of enchanted glass, pouncing like hungry lions. Hindin bared his marble teeth and pounced back, but not *at* them; between them! Turning sideways in midair, he narrowly escaped their claws. His hands landed loudly on the stone floor as he sprang off them to his feet. Shard and Crack landed with their spine-covered backs to him. They turned to see him running to the bar, digging into his coin pouch. He slapped a few grotz pieces onto the counter. "Two pitchers of water, please!" he yelled to the cowering barkeep.

"All I have back here is beer!" Wickurdo answered.

"That will do! My two friends say it is very watered down!"

Shard and Crack spread out, preparing to flank their elusive foe.

"Why should I serve you at a time like this?!" Wickurdo screamed like a child.

"Because, you have an obligation to appease your customers!" Hindin returned. "Now pour me two tall pitchers! No head!!!"

The two golems approached once more from both sides. The chimancer was left with no choice but to fight. The claws came at him first. Even though he parried and dodged with matchless grace, a talon or two still managed to scrape into his left kidney area. Even though they are made of metal and stone, malruka still feel pain. Golems, however, only feel what their masters tell them to feel...

The injury in Hindin's side only strengthened his resolve. For the next few seconds, all the golems sensed were Hindin's two palms crashing into them like a volley of hand shaped bullets. Every time they put an arm out to defend, Hindin slapped it out of the way in some random direction. Pummeling hard and fast into them, he left behind palm sized craters from each impact. So concerned were they about his hands, they forgot about his feet. His kicks moved like whips of silk, but were as heavy as steel. Shard and Crack felt their legs break like thin vases beneath them at the knees and shins. But even as they fell to pieces, they began to reform, healing from the fires within them.

"Order up! Here's your beer!" the sweating barkeep yelled, placing the two pitchers on the bar.

Hindin turned immediately and grasped the handles. He turned back to see the two golems getting back up, their legs and bodies nearly healed. With urgency in his face, he poured the contents of the pitchers into their mouths and fiery eye sockets. A beer flavored steam erupted from their screaming faces. The flaming lights inside their glass bodies dimmed. Mr. Shard made one last swing with his clawed hand, tearing deep into Hindin's steel shoulder, exposing the granite muscle beneath.

Hindin growled in pain and responded with a side kick to Shard's neck. The menacing glass head broke off and shattered onto the floor. Mr. Crack became perfectly still, although a shuttering whimper still echoed deep inside him. The sound was like an old man shivering to death. Hindin looked down at the golem's transparent stomach and saw that the fire was not completely out. A dim light still remained, but it was fading fast. Out of the corner of his eye, Hindin saw the pyramid of NcRay Beer bottles on the bar. He took the highest one off the top. With a swift kick he put a hole in the golem's torso. Tearing off a tiny piece of fabric from his pant leg, he placed it inside the hole he had made. "If you do not wish to perish, take hold of this," he told the flame. Like a little bug, the candle-sized flame climbed onto the fabric. And as soon as it did, Hindin immediately stuffed the fabric into the glass bottle. "There," he said sternly. "This is your body from now on!"

Polly had watched in awe the whole time, but not just at the fighting. "Hindin", she called, "How did you know dat bottle trick would work?"

The Chimancer at first did not answer. He looked at the prisoner he now held in his hand. "I do not know. It just made sense that it would."

◎

It was now 7:46 (almost midnight). Will and Rhowshell were answering questions at the desk of Lieutenant Jetzpin. He, being the highest ranking officer there at that hour, sent two mounted messengers to retrieve Detectives Jana and Rafe from their homes. Lertnac the thief, still knocked out, was being held in a cell downstairs (ironically, it was the same cell that Will stayed in a few nights before).

The Lieutenant was a musty old Drakeri. He was younger than Chief Judge Taly, but looked much older. He seemed like just another piece of furniture in his office, unassuming and apropos. Like his desk, he was plain in his expression and bearing. But like his antique coat rack, he was old and thin. He asked the two young people to tell their story without leaving out a single detail. They told almost everything, leaving out the kiss under the lamplight. He kept up with every word as his spindly fingers pecked at a mechanical typewriter. When the two page report was finished, he had them both sign it before he started asking his questions.

"How can you be sure that this man is not just a common mugger?" he asked plainly. "According to your report, he never actually admitted to being a Mystic Mafia member."

Will reached into a hidden pocket in his dust coat. The overlapping scales made it almost impossible to notice. He pulled out a small piece of lead and placed it on the desk. "This here's the bullet that fell out of Polly's wound after she got shot. I found

149

it the next mornin' in a pool of dried blood in the room she stayed in at the Goose Egg. It's the same caliber as the pistol I took from him. A 7mm Havner circa 2814 to 2839, not that old of a gun. Only four of yer native handguns are found in 7mm: Dusckett, Sulaire, Phynt, and Havner. The latter o' which is the only smithmake you won't find in a museum or private collection."

"It was very common in its day," Jetzspin argued.

"But nowadays it's a bit expensive," Will returned. "The bullets are five grotz a piece, unless you repack 'em yerself. This guy I took in had over 3,000 grotz on him. Why try to mug a poor fella like me when he's got that much money?"

Rhowshell was quite amused with Will's knowledge. She watched eagerly for the Lieutenant's reply.

Even the old man smiled and gave a nod. "Son, have you ever considered a career in law enforcement?"

Will's face grew troubled, but only for an instant. Only Rhowshell noticed. "No, sir," he replied. "I prefer *justice-on-the-run,* you could say. There's still a whole lotta world to see yet. Besides, I'm a Foundling. We don't belong anywhere."

Suddenly there was a knock at the door. A young officer opened it and popped his head in. "Sorry to interrupt, Lieutenant. But it has to do with this same case. I have two people out here who need to see you."

"Thank you, Officer Ladue. Send them in." Jetzspin replied.

The door opened to reveal Polly and Hindin.

"Rev!" Will smiled with a child's excitement as he turned in his chair. "Guess what, Rev. I caught one of 'em!"

"Me, too!" Hindin matched with equal joy. "See?" He held up the beer bottle that held the small flame.

Will frowned and looked confused. "Rev," he started cautiously "that's only a beer bottle, not a criminal."

"Who is she?" Polly asked, looking at the woman in the low cut green dress.

"Oh, um," Will stammered. This here is Rhowshell Eknarf. She's a dentist, an actual tooth healer! She told me on the way here." He smiled with lost eyes, not knowing what else to say.

Rhowshell let out a small giggle. "I witnessed your friend apprehend, well, a very dangerous man."

Will stood up from his chair. "And he's the one who shot you, Polly. I'm sure of it!"

Lieutenant Jetzpin cut in. "But we will not know for sure until Detectives Jana and Rafe arrive to question the suspect." He then set his gaze on Hindin and Polly. "Now, you two also claim to have a suspect? Let me load another piece of paper into my typewriter."

Hindin and Polly (but mostly Hindin) gave a detailed account of the bar fight at the Rotten Cherry. Hindin also presented the bottle containing Mr. Crack's flame. The piece of fabric that he had fed it was gone. But the flame remained, sustained by nothing but itself. Hindin addressed it. "If you understand me, grow brighter." To everyone's astonishment, it did.

"Can it talk?" Will asked.

Hindin shook his head. "I do not think it is possible. The glass from his old body was enchanted by his master. It is greatly diminished in power, and doubt it can be of much help. Even if better communication were possible, I do not think it would be honest with us. Am I right?" he asked the bottle. The flame inside flashed and flickered angrily.

The Lieutenant placed the seven page manuscript on the edge of his desk. "If you and the young lady would sign this, please."

As Polly began to sign, Rhowshell asked her "So, how old are you?"

"Eighteen. How old are you?"

"I'm eighty-six," she answered. "I know. I don't look it, do I?"

"No," Polly agreed. "You look much older dan dat. It must be de light in here." She then swiftly handed the pen to Hindin.

Rhowshell wanted to laugh at the insult. *"Little girl,"* she thought *"you can have him when I'm done with him. You've got nothing on me, child."*

As Hindin signed, he noticed the manuscript for Will's encounter. "May I read this?" he asked the Lieutenant.

"Go ahead." Jetzpin answered, gesturing as if shewing a cat.

"It's all there, Rev," Will said in a sly boast.

Hindin's jewel eyes scanned back and forth over the two pages, finishing in the space of five breaths. When he was done, he shook his head in disapproval. "Sweep kicks, Will? More sweep kicks? When are you going to use those hand techniques I taught you?"

Will rolled his eyes and looked away like a boy being lectured.

Hindin continued. "I swear, Will. That's all you have: Kicks and childish grapples. You did not even *try* to out-box him!"

"Hey, Rev, you got yer way and I got mine."

"Wrong.' Hindin argued. "I have many ways and you only have one! Honestly, Will, if you intend to stay with one fighting style, you will lose miserably one day. You need to learn to use your hands to strike."

"I've already trained my hands fer my gun and sword. You try to tell me I haven't."

Hindin sighed. "But what if the day comes that you do not have them?"

Will grinned. "I'll still have you, big man." He pretended to be choked up and on the verge of tears.

Polly and Rhowshell started to laugh, but stopped as soon as they realized they were laughing together.

"That will be quite enough," the Lieutenant commanded with a tired sigh. "My office is too crowded. I have your statements. Detectives Jana and Rafe are being notified and should be here shortly to question the suspect. You may all go now. We will notify you if any further assistance is needed."

"We're not going back to dat inn!" Polly argued. "Dose glass men admitted to being servants of de Enemy. It was dat same mystic dat sent de four thieves to kill me."

"It was her they were after," Hindin concurred. "The Rotten Cherry was intended to be a *safe* house. But the Enemy found out we were there, somehow. It has ceased to be safe."

"I will wait for de detectives," Polly declared. She seemed to be keeping a secret behind her eyes. There was something going on. Something she did not like.

"I will wait, as well," Hindin agreed.

"Well, I can't wait," Rhowshell sighed, rubbing the back of her neck under her short hair. "I have work in the morning." She looked up at Will with a pleading shrug. "Do you mind walking me home?"

Deep down, Will wanted to stay with his team, help keep the facts straight, and hopefully find the next lead in the case. He felt obligated to see it through, no matter what. But there was also a matter of courtesy to be dealt with. "Sure thing," he answered warmly. He looked at his two teammates. "As soon as I drop her off, I'm goin' back to the Cherry to wait fer Röger. He needs to be filled in on all this. Give me yer room key. I'll get yer things packed and ready."

Hindin dipped in his pocket and handed Will the brass key. "Please, pay no mind to all the glass and blood that has been strewn about our room. It was just an experiment Polly and I were conducting." He then turned his head and gave Polly a knowing wink.

Polly did not respond. She was too busy thinking.

It was a stark white room with faded yellow drapes. Various plaques and photographs of honored officers cluttered the walls. Nothing passed for art. Hindin and Polly sat in silence on a marble bench. The pendulum driven clock displayed the time of 8:46 on its ten-numbered face. It was nearly morning. Hindin's face was calm and ponderous. On the floor by his feet was the bottle holding his captive.

Polly's eyes were bleary and restless. She sat on an egg of paranoia, having escaped death so many times this week. She felt that it could hatch at anytime, anywhere. Her childhood was stolen long ago. But that did not mean she was ready to deal with ruthless muggers, huge arena monsters, or hitmen made of jagged glass and fire. Not to mention her evil mentor could be hot on her trail. She had survived too many threats, and she decided to herself that the next one was about to come through the door of the very room she was in.

The waiting room door opened at last. Detectives Jana and Rafe entered. Polly stood up, glaring at the two of them with a maddening ire that pulsed through her brain. "You set us up!" she wailed at them. "Dey knew we were dere, you filthy pigs! What, you couldn't do de job yourselves?"

Hindin immediately stepped in front of her. "Polly, calm down!" he ordered.

153

Det. Jana's lips curled into a sneer. "How dare you?" she yelled. "You are in no position to make such claims, blood mystic!"

"Have you read the reports?" Hindin asked them.

"Yes, we did," answered Rafe, holding his large gauntlet-covered hands out in a 'keep your distance gesture'. "We even attempted to interrogate the mugger. But he was either too drunk or too clobbered. We're going to try again tomorrow."

The malruka's eyes grew stern. "The two of you are detectives, and therefore, expert deducers. Would you mind deducing why two glass and fire golems strong enough to tear my steel flesh, who openly admitted to having ties with the Mystic Mafia, attempted to kill us in the secret haven that you put us in?"

Polly was shocked. Not only was Hindin taking her side, but he had been thinking the same thing she had.

The two detectives were at a loss for words. They looked to each other for answers, but none came.

Just then, Officer Ladue popped his head into the room. "Detectives! There's been another victim!"

"Get in here, Ladue!" Jana ordered. "Tell us what you know."

The young officer stepped in. "The victim's name is Jonash Fluge. He was found beaten and blinded in a flood trench just off South 4th Street about an hour ago. He was taken to The 3rd Ward Temple of Health. From what I was told, they worked him over pretty good."

Det. Rafe sighed. "Tomorrow's going to be a busy day."

"Hey!" Polly shouted. "What about our questions? How did dose golems know we would be dere?"

"It is a good question to ask, Jana." Rafe told his partner.

The lady detective frowned and looked at Polly. "I don't know what to tell you. Maybe they used divination to find you."

Polly's face contorted with rage. "Earlier today, you said you did not believe in divination!"

"That's not what I said." Jana answered coldly. "I said it was unreliable. Especially with young, inexperienced, and emotionally disturbed mystics."

The veins under Polly's skin squirmed wildly. Her eyes glowed a shadowy dark red. Deep in her heart, she wanted to redecorate the white walls with Det. Jana's blood. She imagined painting a crimson mural of the woman in various states of torment.

Hindin placed a cool hand on Polly's shoulder. "Polly," he spoke softly. "Let's wait outside for Will and Röger. After that, we will find another place to stay," He then looked up at the detectives. "I will make no assumptions as to how the golems knew of our location. I favor proof over any probability. Added to that, I will take no chances with a known location in which to lodge. We will relocate to somewhere secret."

"You really shouldn't do that, Mr. Revetz." Rafe interjected. "Even though my partner comes off as a little thick skinned, you really should trust us. I for one think the case is going very well, thanks to your help. And I want you to know; I've been on the force for 112 years. This job is my life. It's my pain and my pride. Every time I hear that there's been another victim, I feel I have failed as a detective. I have faith in your team to continue to produce useful leads. I ask that you simply do the same for me and my partner. We need to be able to find you, or this isn't going to work."

Hindin sighed in doubt and frustration. He could see what looked like honor in Rafe's eyes. Jana's eyes held nothing but pride and contempt. "You will be able to find us," he answered.

"But Hindin!" Polly shouted.

"BUT," Hindin started loudly "we will not reveal Polly's or my whereabouts. We will scout for two locations. Will and Sir Röger will stay at one that you may visit as you please. The other shall keep Polly and myself hidden. If the situation arises where you must speak with one of us, send your message to Will or Röger, and they will let us know. I jump to no conclusions concerning either of you. But all the same, the mystic who created those golems will not be happy with me for destroying them. And Polly's safety is ever in jeopardy." He took a deep breath. "Now, at what times do you plan to interrogate the suspect, interview the latest victim, and look over the mess made in the Rotten Cherry's tavern?"

"We haven't decided yet," Det. Jana answered. Her face looked grim and tired. "Why don't the four of you join us tomorrow on all three ventures? We'll start with the suspect. Ms. Gone has yet to identify him."

"Fine by me," Polly answered.

"Very well," Hindin agreed. "At what hour?"

"How does four o'clock sound?" Rafe suggested. "It would give us all enough time to sleep, and plenty of time to conduct our investigation. And when I say that, I mean that it belongs to all of us. No secrets, no lies, no mistrust, and no fighting." He peered at Jana and Polly.

"Agreed," answered Hindin.

Rafe nodded in approval. "Excellent! Come back here first so we can start with the suspect. We won't start without you. I promise."

◈

Having spent most of their day on their tired feet. Polly and Hindin were obliged when they were offered a ride back to the Cherry in a department carriage.

"It's either her, him, or both of dem." Polly whispered to her companion as they swayed to and fro inside the bileer-drawn enclosure.

Hindin did not answer.

◈

It has been mentioned in passing that tendikeye hold chance and luck in high regard. It is, in fact, a pillar of their outlook. This does not mean that they leave everything to random fortune or that they easily succumb to the blind whim of fate. On the contrary, they believe that luck, like all forces in the world, is governed by laws. Every child is born with certain amounts of good luck and bad luck. Both must be constantly recognized and accounted for. In doing so, one can gain a better understanding of how life will turn out.

Take Will for instance. He made his way back to the Rotten Cherry, recalling his luck for the last 10 hours. Yesterday, he found a priceless treasure while cleaning a storage room (Good Luck). He met an interesting girl at a bar and got to kiss her without buying her a drink (Good Luck). He found and apprehended one of the punks that his team was looking for (Good Luck). He got to walk that same girl home, got a second kiss for his troubles. She told him that she wouldn't mind seeing him again, and that he still owed her a drink (Very Good Luck).

156

Other than needing a little shut-eye, his luck was going quite well. And that made him very nervous. Bad Luck was coming. He could feel it. In his mind, he recalled the old familiar sayings of his culture.

> *-When all goes well, nothing can go right.*
> *-7+7=13*
> *-Good Luck plus Good Luck equals Bad Luck.*
> *-Two generals of equal quality should not lead the same army. Both must have strengths that make up for the others faults.*
> *-Good Fortune clouds the foresight of impending*
Adversity.

He felt the three grotz coins he had jingle in his pocket. They were nothing compared to the rare plastic coins he split with Röger. He was willing to part with common money. All he had to do was find a gambling house and place a few bad bets. Hopefully, it would make up for the good luck he was having.

The soft glow of morning came at all sides from the Huncell walls. The Rotten Cherry came into view. As he reached the front, he looked up to see that his room's window shutter was slightly ajar. After walking all night, he felt rather lazy. He did not feel like climbing the stairs inside. After a few quick steps, he leapt and climbed to his window with relaxed agility. Squatting on its narrow ledge, he pulled open the shutters and hopped in.

A piercing scream filled the room, scratching at Will's brain. A leggy, big breasted drakeress had been curled up naked next to Röger on his bed. Röger, so startled by the intrusion, fell off the bed, landing helmet first. Yanking the bed sheet over herself, the woman continued to scream. Will felt like his eardrums were burning. "Whoa, whoa, whoa!" he exclaimed. "This is my room, too, lady!"

Röger stood up with his shame flopping around like a dead fish. The sheer sight of it scorched Will's eyes. The dark skinned, tattoo covered human covered the woman's mouth. "Lynda, its okay!" he told her. "This is Will, my roomie!"

She pushed the hand off her face and glared at the tendikeye. "Why, didn't you use the door and knock?!" she asked.

Will turned around and covered face. "I'm sorry, miss! I was only tryin' to use a short cut. Honest!"

The woman shook her head in anger and got up. Röger stood by defensively as she picked up her clothes and got dressed. Once she was semi-decent, she gave Will a hard shove, calling him an "Ignorant bumpkin prick!" before storming out.

As the door slammed shut, Röger jumped on the bed with his arms out. "Thank you so much!" he laughed. "That girl was talking about marriage right before you came!"

Will averted his weary eyes. "Rög, please cover yerself!"

Röger laughed again in his deep full voice. He picked up a pair of his jeans, jumped up, tucked in his legs, and kicked his feet into them, landing on the floor. "TAH-DAH!" he exclaimed as he buttoned his fly. "Nice trick, don't you think?" he asked with a cocky grin. "I bet you could do it, too, if your feet weren't so big!"

Will rolled his eyes and fell into his bed.

Röger chuckled as he stretched his back. "Well, you know how *my* night went. Tell me about yours. Did you find out that these Drakeri girls are grape flavored?"

Will reluctantly sat up. He suddenly felt exhausted as he looked at his roommate. He pulled the key that Hindin had given him from his pocket. "Have you been down to the tavern end of the inn yet?"

"No. Why?"

Will hunched his shoulders and let out a long yawn. "Some things went down yesternight. We need to relocate again. Take this key. It goes to Rev and Polly's room. Do them a favor and get their things packed. They should be gettin' here soon. Tell 'em I was too tired to explain things to ya. They'd be better at it anyway. Wake me up when yer all ready."

As he took the key, a dozen questions lined up in Röger's mind. "Is everything okay?" was the only one he let out.

Will yawned again and fell back on his pillow. "Fer now. Maybe," he answered. As he drifted to sleep, he was still keeping track of his luck. He had walked into his room to see a fabulous rack on an unknown woman (Good Luck). He did not have to stay up waiting for Röger (Good Luck). He had to see Röger wearing nothing but his helmet (Bad Luck). *"Looks like its finally changin'*," he thought.

❈

Will awoke with a start. Röger was now fully dressed and ready to go. On his broad back were his axe, his sword, and his backpack. Behind him stood Hindin carrying his duffel bag of books. Polly sat with her elbows on her knees in a chair by the door. A small red suitcase dangled from her fingers.

"You back already?" Will asked, feeling sore and stiff.

"It is 3:35 o'clock. Almost noon," Hindin replied. "I thought it best to let you and Polly sleep while Sir Röger and I kept watch."

Will rubbed his eyes and sat up. "Fair enough," he replied. "So, what's the plan? Did you fill Rög in?"

"Oh, they told me more than enough, Mr. Sweep Kick," Röger chuckled.

Hindin took a step forward. "We are to meet the detectives at the station at 4:00. There we will extract what information we can from the suspect you brought in. Afterwards, assuming we can get nothing out of him, we will visit the latest victim."

"There's been another?" the tendikeye asked.

Hindin nodded. "The police believe it happened shortly before we had our encounters."

Will sat up and took out his tobacco pouch and rolling papers. "This day's gonna wear my patience thinner than a dog with worms. I'd better roll me a double supply."

❁

After a late breakfast and many brisk steps, they arrived at the ECPD. Jana and Rafe were there waiting as promised. Everyone's mood seemed much lighter, if not still a little bit anxious.

The detectives led the team downstairs to the cell room. Röger had hoped to see Officer Feyna on duty, but remembered that she only worked nights. Before they entered the main cell room, Rafe asked everyone to stop. "Is everyone okay with approaching this man in one large group? Six people might make him feel overwhelmed."

"That's not such a bad thing," Will grinned.

"Actually, it could be," Rafe debated. "He might clam up, and we could get nothing from him."

"Are you suggesting dat you and your partner go first?" Polly asked suspiciously.

"Not at all," Rafe answered. There was a charming glint in his eye. "Normally, Jana and I would play 'good cop/bad cop'. I suggest that we all go in one at a time, each taking the roll of either a helpful and understanding benefactor or a hostile and cruel malefactor. We'll each get a turn of five to ten minutes. But please keep in mind that we can't touch or torture the suspect."

"Oooh! Oooh! I call good cop!" Röger announced. "I was always the good cop when I was oathbound to Karsely. For some reason, I'm able to make a real connection with criminals. It's like they see me as one of them!"

"Perfect!" Rafe replied with a cheerful laugh. "You can go first, unless anyone else objects." He looked around at the others, searching for contrary expressions. Everyone else looked as if they did not know what to think. Then at last, Hindin broke the silence.

"It is worth a try." And with that, the others reluctantly agreed.

Röger went into the main cell room where the thief was being kept. There were two guards keeping watch. "Uh, ease up, men!" he blurted nervously.

One of them looked at him. "Who are you with?" he asked.

"The detectives on the Mystic Mafia case, Rafe and Jana," he replied.

The two officers exchanged a look. The other guard asked "One at a time, right?"

"Um, yeah. How'd you know?"

"He told us. Have fun. The floor is yours." The two officers exited the way he had entered.

Röger looked around. All the cells were empty save one. Inside sat Lertnac on a cot. He stared at the brawny human as if he were a lion in a zoo exhibit. His face was expressionless, but his eyes glinted like dark amber. He tried to stare Röger down. Röger approached the bars and stared back, but for the sake of curiosity, not intimidation. The contest only lasted a few seconds. The thief immediately charged the bars, stopping just short of

160

them, and screamed in Röger's face. Röger blinked a few times as the Drakeri ran out of breath. A string of obscenities and insults leapt out of the thief's mouth. Röger slowly frowned in disappointment. He hung his head and began to walk away. "I guess you don't want my help," he sighed.

"How can you help me, you miserable round-eared mercenary lump of puss?" the thief replied with pride and doubt.

Röger turned. "Well, you know you're screwed, right? Can you safely say that *all* of your victims didn't see you before you blinded and jacked them? Did you know that they can still see out of the reflections in mirrors? It's pretty strange, but it works. I know at least two of them can identify you. So, you are going to get screwed, but you get to choose how hard."

"What do you mean?" the thief replied.

"All you got to do is hand over your buddies' names and where they live."

The thief scoffed and spat at him. "All I did was try to rob that prick friend of yours! I was drunk and feeling lucky. I figured I could make some money off those fancy weapons of his. I'm not with the Magic Mafia."

Röger nodded several times. "The story is that you told him you saw us fight at the battle arena."

"Yeah, so?"

"So it means you were there that night. An old man was shot and blinded in those stands. His wife saw the gunman. Come on. Give it up. You don't want to go down alone, do you?" Röger waited a long moment for a reply. He hoped that it was stubbornness, and not loyalty that stayed the thief's tongue. But to his dismay, no reply came.

"At least tell me who hired you to steal those watches," Röger urged.

Lertnac looked surprised, confused, and worried.

Röger smiled and pointed at him. "So, it *is* the watches you were after! And you *are* working for somebody! You don't have to say another word, sisterfister! You gave me enough to work with!"

Lertnac was speechless. He watched the human run out like it was the last day of school. He sat back down on his cot and thought of all the things he could say, any lie that would sound convincing. Two stomach churning minutes passed before the door opened for another visitor. His heart did a clumsy back flip when he saw her!

Polly strode in with a cruel smile on her lips. The droning rhythm of his quickening pulse was music to her supernatural senses. She made her eyes glow red for effect. When she spoke, his lips trembled. "You are a good shot for a coward," she hissed. She grinned with dark delight. Instinctively, her hips tilted, making a wicked, sensual pose. She giggled maniacally. "All I have to do is identify you as one of de nutless thieves I encountered in dat alley. I could swear by my philocreed dat you were dere. But I don't tink I will! I want you to lie and go free. Dat way I can have you all to myself!"

He felt the scratches she had made on his forearms tingle and itch. *"She's alive!"* he thought with wonder and terror. "Guards!" Lertnac yelled. "Guards!!! I want to confess! I want to confess!" His voice cracked as he screamed.

The detectives and the rest of the team rushed in. "Dang! That was quick!" Will exclaimed. "An' I had sumthin' planned, too."

"As did I," smiled Hindin. "But Polly has proven her quality yet again!"

Rafe and Jana reached the bars first. "Tell us everything!" Jana ordered. "Leave nothing out!"

Lertnac winced as his pride caved in. He did as he was told, telling all he knew. And as he did, he felt the torment and helplessness of failure. He knew his life was over. But there was still the elusive hope that some form of mercy might be granted. It was better to be on the lowest level of the winning side than the highest level of losers.

"My name is Lertnac Vondibitz. We were approached by these two guys. They call themselves Mr. Shard and Mr. Crack. They said they represented some pyrotheurge called The Master. They took Drew to meet him once somewhere secret to explain the deal. Every time we had a new mark, they'd give us a letter telling us where and when to find them. They paid us 2,500 grotz for every mark we jacked. We had to hit a total of ten. After we jacked number ten, we'd get a bonus of 50,000 grotz each. They gave Drew this mystic mirror to blind them with. We had to blind them, rough them up, then take their watch and give it to Shard and Crack. So far, we've had six successes and two shunt-ups."

"Two murders, ya mean," Will corrected.

Lertnac shook his head. "That was all Drew's fault! He stabbed that guy in the leg in the wrong place. That was an accident. And he only cut that kid's throat 'cause he was pissed that she jumped us!" He looked at Polly with a mixture of hatred and dread. "Drew's the leader. He's kills for fun! He's twisted!"

Det. Jana quickly grew agitated. "Just give us the names and locations of the scamps you run with!" The chain she wore started to writhe like a snake.

Lertnac hung his head and sighed. "Andrew Monitiz, but we call him Drew Blood. Zeni Ncaphry. And Yelats Norbenstoff. We all live in the same flat; 53087 Chipman Avenue #20B. But I don't know how to find Mr. Crack and Mr. Shard."

"There is no need," Hindin declared. "They are destroyed. Did you know that they were golems?"

The eyes of the thief became puzzled. "Golems? They looked...well...they didn't look normal, but..."

"Enough," Jana ordered the prisoner. "We'll send a scribe down to document and certify your cooperation. My partner and I will see to it that the Chief Justice goes easy on you." She turned to the others. "Are you all ready to bring this cloaca some company?"

"I second the lady's motion," Will agreed, lighting a cigarette.

Rafe smiled at his partner and looked at them. "Good! From this moment until these men are captured, you are all deputized to assist us. The goal here is apprehension. Are we all clear on that?"

Deep down, Polly had hoped to kill Drew the leader. But in spite of her disappointment, she was content with the plan. "It will be so," she muttered.

"Wait, wait, wait!" Röger interrupted. "Something doesn't feel right. These three ruffians are probably wondering where this man is--assuming they're not total idiots: What if they jumped ship and ran? What if they think he got caught and spilled the beans?"

Det. Rafe placed one of his huge gauntlet-covered hands on Röger's shoulder. "He hasn't been gone that long. But you do make a good point. So, we shouldn't dilly-dally. If they do decide to run, we must catch them before they do!"

❖

There was a protocol to follow for every bust in the Bone Brick City. The team was given clear and strict instructions on how to proceed. It was the first *urban ambush* Will, Hindin, or Polly had ever participated in. In any natural setting, the young tendikeye Bushwhacker would have insisted on leading the raid, law or no law. But he was content to hang back and learn the local procedures first.

It was a tall, thick apartment building full of unsuspecting residents. The outside walls were covered with *fostues*. These were statues that contained the bones of great extinct beasts. After careful chiseling and delicate reassembly, they became great partially skeletal artistic representations of what they might have looked like millions of years ago. In the case of these fostues, they bore a close resemblance to very large lions. Hence the building's name: *Lion's Dens*.

Too many cops would draw too much attention. The Detectives dressed in civilian clothes, but kept their mystical weapons. If the suspects were there, there would be no escape. There was only one way up or down: a square spiraling stairway in the building's core.

The police station had a copy of blueprints for every building in the city. In a dark alley two blocks away, Rafe and Jana unfolded the layout for the outsiders' eyes. Jana began to divvy up the commands.

"Their flat is the last door on the fifth level before reaching the next fight of steps. Apartment 20B. The four of you will act as barricade enforcers for each level before that. Rafe and I will make the arrests. You will all be there to prevent escapes. Polly on #1, Hindin on #2, Röger on #3, and Will on #4. Are there any questions?"

"I got a couple," Will said. "What if they decide to go up? This is an eight layer structure. Shouldn't one of us cover the sixth layer, at least?"

"Why would they run up?" she asked.

"Because they're idiots. Let's say they try to take a hostage up there. Shouldn't somebody be there to offset that chance?"

"It makes sense," Rafe agreed. "Are you volunteering for this position?"

"Might as well," Will answered with a shrug. "But it's still a bit of a downer; you not lettin' us help make the arrest by makin' us to hang back."

"Yeah," Röger jumped in. "It's a big rooster-block, if you ask me!"

Rafe laughed at the ground and raised his gauntlet covered hands. "Don't worry guys. I can assure you that your praises will be printed in the paper. Your glory will not go unsung."

"I don't care about glory," Polly muttered. She cast a distrustful eye at Rafe.

Det. Rafe returned a cold stare back at the young mystic. It was the first time she'd seen him make such a face. "Ms. Gone, if you can think of one unselfish reason why you should not go with this plan, let us all know. I've been doing this more than a century before your birth. Go ahead and 'wow' me with your expertise, if you can."

Polly bared her teeth. "How do we know you aren't just putting us in 'safe spots' like the Rotten Cherry was supposed to be? Dat was also *your* idea."

Rafe's eyes hardened. He opened is mouth to speak, but Hindin interrupted him.

"I must interject," Hindin started in a peacekeeping voice. "We have neglected two important details about these men. One is a pyrotheurge and the other possesses a mirror of blinding. Why are only the two of you entering the apartment? Should you not at least bring back up?"

The two detectives smiled at each other and looked back at him. "I wouldn't worry," Jana told Hindin. "We've alerted all the surrounding beat cops of our plans. They will surround the perimeter exactly three minutes after the raid begins." She held up the three sets of shackles. "But I don't think we'll need their help with these pretties. Catch!"

Hindin reacted with fumbling confusion as the three shackles flew at him. But before he could realize, they grew larger and clicked open on their own! In three fast clicks, the three handcuffs latched around the malruka's wrists! But to the dismay of the detectives, Hindin did not look shocked. He plainly looked down at them with disappointment in his face. "These are hexcuffs. Binding theurgy made these. Clever. But what if their hands are far apart from each other?"

Jana took out her keys and undid the cuffs. "Rest assured, Mr. Revetz: With my special cuffs and Rafe's heavy mitts, they won't have a hope to cling to."

Will raised an eyebrow to the woman's words. Something in her tone bothered him. He also did not cotton to the face that Rafe had made at Polly. "Hey, on second thought, I think I *will* keep watch on the fourth layer. You two seem to know what yer doin'. No need to over do it."

"Are you sure?" Rafe asked.

"Oh yeah," he smiled. "I ain't in no rush fer a scuffle anyway. I've done had my fun with that boy I brought in. You two've been workin' on this case longer'n us. So, you go on ahead an' bring it to a close."

Rafe smiled in surprise. "We appreciate your cooperation, Mr. Foundling." He responded with a nod of respect. "Not a lot of tendikeye display such trust."

Will grinned brightly and laughed. "Oh, I know, I know. We ain't without our faults."

Hindin cast a suspicious look at his friend. Will was never this agreeable, not even with him.

With tingling nerves they began the raid. The teammates hustled behind the two detectives up the building steps, one by one staying behind to guard their designated floor. Polly, the first to stay behind, felt more than a little betrayed and left out, but made no show of it.

"Be careful," Hindin told the rest of them as they cleared the second floor.

"Feel free to let one get by you. My axe is thirsty!" Röger joked as he was left to guard the third.

Will said nothing as Rafe and Jana continued up the steps without him. He had been puffing on a cigarette on his way up. He pinched the smoldering cherry out of the measly butt that was left. Wasting no time, he looked at the room numbers on all the doors. Using what little math he knew, he made an undereducated guess on where the thieves' apartment would be above him. There was a window a few steps down the hall. A gust of warm air rustled his sandy quills as he lifted it open. Once on the outside ledge, he found himself standing near a tall stone lion statue. *"They're even bigger up close,"* he thought to himself. The kingly beast seemed sturdy enough to climb. In seconds, Will brought himself up to the next level. The thieves' window was a few careful steps away, he was sure of it! Peeking carefully through the glass, he was startled by what he saw. Two young, nubile drakeresses were having a pillow fight in their underwear. The tendikeye shook his head, trying not to wonder if it was good luck or bad luck. He moved like the wind, peering unnoticed into every window around the towering structure. *"Finally!"* he thought.

He spied in through the glass with one eye, trying to keep from view. The apartment door had been smashed in. Jana had two men pinned face first to the wall with her long chained cuffs. Their hands were bound behind them with her smaller pairs of hexcuffs. Rafe held the third ruffian by his throat, keeping him on his knees. Beneath the oversized gauntlets the detective wore, a bit of yellow bandanna could be seen tied around the ruffian's neck. Rafe bent down, whispering something in the choking man's ear. Then with a free gauntlet, the detective grasped the thief by the thigh and picked him up over his head. Before Will could react, the thief came bursting through the window, shattering the glass like a soul! The man known by few as Drew Blood screamed his head off as he looked to see the sidewalk below. Will reached out to catch his ankle and succeeded, but at the cost of his footing.

Gravity was a harsh bitch indeed, accelerating her greedy pull on the hero and the villain. Three stories passed in the blink of a hummingbird's eye. Drew Blood saw the pavement growing beneath him, unaware of the large hand gripping his ankle. Will's other large hand aimed for its last chance. In a forest full of branches, many tendikeye would feel at home. But the stone ledges offered no salvation. They were just about to fall past another giant stone lion when Will saw his chance! The lion's mouth was opened in a majestic silent roar. Its massive petrified fangs were like the horns of a rhino. With a lightning fast death grip, Will seized one of the protruding stone teeth. There was a loud pop in his right shoulder with a rip in his pectoral muscle, but his grip held fast. His left arm, which held the thief, didn't feel much better. The muscles in his forearm blared in pain. As he grunted and strained, he noticed that the lion started to tip forward. Volleys of obscenities clashed in the bukk's mind. Then

167

the tooth broke off in Will's hand, and the beast tipped back in place.

It was times like these that Will wished he had wings like most tendikeye. Instead of speeding down helplessly he could have simply glided down. The fall was bad, but it could have been worse. Will's right arm (his sword arm) dangled loose at the shoulder. His gun arm was going numb from the elbow down. The wind had been knocked out of him. He gasped and gagged, trying to refill his lungs with precious air. The impact started a throbbing in his head. His quill covered scalp sprung a leak of warm blood. The thief lay prone beside him, showing no signs of life. There were a few onlookers in the area, but they were all too afraid to approach. His eye caught a shadow growing near him. Straining to look up, he saw Detective Rafe.

The concerned-faced Drakeri descended to the ground by aid of Jana's mystical chain, which seemed to shorten back to its original length once he let go of it. He stood over Will, clenching his large armored fists. "Why would you pull a stupid stunt like that?" he asked angrily.

Will stood up slowly, trying to keep from getting nauseous. "Don't we need this guy?" he asked. "This is the one with the bandanna. The one who met the mystic, right? Don't we need him?"

Rafe nodded. "Yes. We need him dead. He's a thief and a murderer, Mr. Foundling. Once he's dealt with, the 'Mystic Mafia' will be no more."

Will shook his head. The fall had clouded his reason. "But...but won't the mystic just find someone else to...?" His reply was cut short by Rafe's fist. He flew back first into a nearby wall. Many of the bricks behind him broke loose from their mortar. It felt like the fall all over again.

"You see, I knew it would come to this!" Rafe complained. "Now our cover is blown! Thanks a lot!" He thought he was talking to a fresh corpse.

"Don't mention it." Will stumbled, but would not fall. He glared at Rafe with focused clarity. "So, Pol was right. You an' that gal are a couple o' turncoats." As he grinned, blood mixed with drool dripped from his mouth.

Rafe's eyes widened. He took a deep breath and could smell something like garlic in the air. "That blow should have flattened you like a pancake!"

Will scoffed through the agony. "Obviously, yer a lousy cook!" It was times like these that he loathed his supernatural toughness. It made him live through things he'd rather not. Both his arms were nearly useless. His head pounded like a drum. Breathing became a hassle. The pain churned in his stomach. And the air around him was thick with the smell of chives. He looked at the detective's over-sized gauntlets. *"Strength enhancers,"* he thought. "So, what was yer price then?" he asked.

Rafe shook his head and scoffed. "That's a private matter, bushwhacker." He glanced over at Drew's body. "The Master needs this one dead. He's botched too many jobs already. We were hoping that catching these four pawns would sate your hunger for justice. There were always more punks out there willing to do the dirty work." He let out a sigh of frustration. "But now it seems Jana and I must carry out the remaining tasks. It's no big deal. The reward will still be worth it. But before I crush this punk's skull and take my leave, I should probably rip your guts out!" There was a ten foot gap between the cop and Will. Rafe closed it fast. But not fast enough.

Just as the detective slammed the wall with his mitts, Will leapt over to his left, landing a good twelve feet away. Rafe sneered in anger. There were mechanical clicking sounds coming from his gauntlets. The heavy mitts dropped to the ground, exposing two small pistols already in the detective's hands. There was no cover for Will to dive behind. But his own gun was drawn before Rafe could take aim. With fingers he could no longer feel Will squeezed the triggers. The two barrels of his Mark Twain Special reported their trademark stutter-shot. *KA-KRAK!* At the same instant, Rafe returned fire. The two bullets of the Harker's gun found their marks in the detective's throat and forehead. Rafe only managed to squeeze off a single shot before Will's rounds sank in. The bukk felt a cold graze slash across the side of his thigh, ripping his jeans. His leg was quickly losing feeling as the detective fell dead. *"Petra rounds!"* Will thought. He felt the skin on his thigh start to get stiff. In seconds, his hip locked up. But that was as far as it went. The petrifaction was minor due to it being a graze.

He stood there a moment in disbelief. He had just shot and killed a man of the law. A crooked cop, but a cop nonetheless. "How am I gonna explain this?" he thought aloud. A stinging thud came down on his wrist, knocking the pistol from

169

his hand. He tried to turn to see the new threat. He caught a glimpse of Drew Blood swinging the large stone lion tooth at his face. Something small and sharp hit the back of Will's throat. As he landed on his back, he felt with his tongue that it was a piece of his front tooth. He looked up to see the now conscious thief holding the giant lion tooth like a sacrificial dagger, ready to pin Will to the spot.

"Hey!" a female voice called out. It was now Drew Blood's turn to stare in disbelief.

Polly Gone had heard the falling screams from inside. She was already out the front entrance when she heard the shots. She stood there at the corner less than ten yards away. Her dagger was drawn, catching the glow of the day's light. Drew's reaction was not unlike Lertnac's, seeing that this young theurge had indeed cheated death. He backed away a few steps, readying the tooth like a club.

"What the shunt is going on?!" he yelled like a madman. It was the sum of all questions when someone is tangled in enough intrigue and/or bull droppings. He never met the detectives before a day in his life. Yet, only a minute ago, the newly made corpse nearby whispered to him "Change of plans: The Master wants you dead. We'll take it from here." before tossing him out of a window. He ached all over from the fall. He had landed flat, while the tendikeye landed head first. Now he was glaring defiantly at the young woman walking his way.

The crowd around them grew thicker.

Polly did not look concerned about the stone club he was holding. Nor did she appear concerned about her wounded teammate or the dead detective. Her eyes reflected no emotion whatsoever. She simply approached, holding her shiny little knife. She anticipated this moment ever since that bloody day in the alley. The thief looked too banged up to run. Perfect. She stalked closer. She walked around Will, paying him little mind.

"Be careful," the tendikeye coughed.

"I am in no danger," she responded.

"No. I mean be careful not to kill him. He knows where the Master is."

Polly considered the tendikeye's words. "All I'd have to do is slash his throat, take a few sips, and I could find dat out." Her flower petal lips curved together.

"We need him alive, Pol! Forget about that guilt trip he laid on you! Yer better'n that!"

She took a deep breath and let it out, watching Drew Blood shake like a leaf in fear. Will just made things more difficult. She was taught to kill and kill quickly, not apprehend. More importantly, it was a part of her philocreed; to shed blood and kill. Without such practices, her power would dwindle (as it had been since she entered the city). She would have to rely on her dagger.

"Fine," she answered, dashing forward!

Drew took a wild swing. She ducked and rolled between his legs, slicing his calf muscle instead of his femoral artery. More pissed off than in pain, Drew turned around for a downward swing. The tooth cracked the pavement inches from where Polly had dodged. She stood up fast, slicing deep from his chin to the top of his ear. Drew fell back in agony, dropping his improvised weapon. He writhed on the ground, screaming and holding his face. Tears flooded from his eyes, stinging the wound with salt. The blood stain left on that sidewalk would be there for weeks.

As Will slowly sat up, his keen ears caught the sound of Hindin and Röger's feet growing near. He turned to see them running up to the scene. Before they could ask what happened, he was already giving them orders. "Rafe and Jana were in on it!" he yelled. "You two run up and get her! Make sure she don't kill the thieves. Run like the biscuits are burnin'!"

"Biscuits?" Röger asked. "What biscuits?!"

"Let us not dally!" Hindin shouted as he guided him back around. The two sped back up the building.

The surrounding neighborhood (inside the building and out) was gathering, wondering why two men fell off a building, why people were getting arrested, shot, and cut with knives. The stairway became crowded with confused and frightened tenants. It was nearly two minutes before Röger and Hindin could reach the apartment. When they did, they found the two remaining thieves handcuffed, face down on the floor, and afraid.

"Where is the woman?" Hindin asked them.

"She ran away after the gun shots." Zeni the thief answered.

"Blind Bitch's Bane!" Röger exclaimed, kicking a wooden chair to pieces.

171

The two men went to the broken window that Drew had flown though. On the sidewalk below, Will, Polly, Drew Blood, and the mostly headless body of Detective Rafe Azell were surrounded by half a dozen civic guards. Those who still had heartbeats were being taken into custody at gun point. Will and Polly put up no resistance as the handcuffs were snapped on. Drew Blood with his gashed face froze at the sight of the policemen's carbine rifles.

"We can explain," Will told them.

An officer kicked the back of his knee, making him collapse. "Save it for the station house, outsider!" the cop responded. These were beat cops, block jockeys. They were given prior notice that there would be a bust in the building. But a high ranking fellow officer was made worm meat on their watch. Witnesses were saying the bukk was responsible. One of the block jockeys spotted Hindin and Röger through the broken glass. "You, there! Freeze!" he ordered.

Röger let out a half-hearted laugh. "Well, no need to find a place to stay after this. The police seem to have rooms open for us."

◈

At the Embrenil Civic Police Department, eight of its thirty-two cells held four heroes and four ruffian thieves. Four guards (in addition to the usual two) were placed between the cells, making sure that the prisoners remained silent. Every guard held a carbine rifle. Zeni the thief made the mistake of asking for a glass of water. Everyone found out what was loaded in those guns when the nearest officer fired into his cell. The barrel's report made the sound of a large bell chiming. No mark or hole appeared on the thirsty captive, but the officer's aim was true. Before Zeni could scream, his white-dreadlocked head froze with an expression of shock and terror. No sooner did the other prisoners wince and cover their ears, Zeni became nothing more than a sleeping stone statue.

Over the next hour, the guards took each prisoner individually into private rooms. Statements were taken, signed, and sent to the Chief Justice's desk. From those statements the truth would be distilled.

A doctor was allowed in to Drew Blood's cell to stitch his face and leg. Hindin asked if Will could also be treated. He was answered with many dirty looks.

Will, on his own, managed to fix his right shoulder back into place. There was a nasty cut on his scalp. It felt as deep as a coin is thick. He could not stop tonguing his broken front tooth. The feeling in his left hand was coming back, but it was an unwelcome feeling. *"Tendon damage,"* he thought. But all that paled in comparison to his petrified thigh and hip. He couldn't sit and it hurt to stand. It put a cramp in his back that made him wince and sigh like an overworked old man. He lay there on the cold cell floor, hoping the geotheurgic energy would not spread. Were he not a tendikeye, it would have worn off by now.

As the canopy of night swept over the city, a procession of higher ranking officers made their way down to the cell block. There were a total of ten led by none other than the venerable Lt. Jetzpin. The old Drakeri's face was stern in some places, relaxed in others. He spoke. "The prisoners known as Four Winds - One Storm are hereby summoned to trial in the office of the Chief Justice."

The guards who held the rifles stood down. The procession broke apart as the new officers unlocked the cell doors. They placed Will, Polly, and Röger in heavy chains. Hindin's wrists were bound by long strands of hemp paper. Polly had plenty of time this time to examine Hindin's paper bonds to see that they were normal strips of paper, not mystical in any way.

"How d dey use it to bind him?" she thought, really itching to know.

The four outsiders were led upstairs to the main department hall. The hall usually had only a third as many officers, but tonight the place was packed. Most of the cops were off duty, there only to witness the trial. Will felt the heat off their glaring golden eyes, but responded to none as he limped along. Röger spotted Officer Feyna in the crowd. His pleading eyes told her *"I DON'T KNOW WHAT HAPPENED!"* Her eyes glinted with doubt.

The huge double doors of the Chief's office were wide open for all to see. Just as he questioned Polly days before, he wore his grand suit of armor and the long black velvet glove. The walls were lined with even more cops. The various statements made earlier that day lay on his desk.

"I only need one of you for this," he said harshly. "Will Foundling, step forward."

The bukk did as commanded. Fear manifested in his stomach and bladder, but his mind and heart were rock steady. His expression toward the Chief was half reverent, half suspicious. Then a thought went through his mind like a thunderbolt. *What if the Chief was in on it, too?* He stopped walking.

"Here!" the Chief ordered, pointing at the spot right in front of him.

Will looked around and back at his friends. To his surprise, Hindin did not look worried. He gave Will an encouraging nod and slight grin.

"Hurry up, Will!" the malruka called for all to hear. "We have a goal to finish!"

Will smiled a broken-toothed grin. He turned back toward Chief Taly, and proceeded.

Taly's face was no less serious, no less arctic. He looked for a moment into the tendikeye's eyes before asking his first question. "Mr. Foundling, are you aware of the term *Cold Hard Facts*?"

"Yessir," Will answered plainly.

"Have you ever wondered where or how the term originated?"

Will thought for a moment. "Nossir."

The Chief raised his velvet covered hand. A white fire suddenly engulfed it, causing Will to feel a cold wind on his face. "This", the Chief began, "is *Winter Fire*. Like fire spreads through all that burns, so is Winter Fire attracted to that freezes. The mere touch of it can freeze over a lake in seconds. Imagine what it does to people, Mr. Foundling."

Will wanted to coil back. He did not want to imagine such a thing.

The Chief continued. "But there is a catch. A charm breaker, you might say. The fire has no effect on those who are truthful, those who are willing to admit the facts. No need for juries and certainly not lawyers. Just the Cold Hard Facts. In theurgical terms, this is nothing more than an interpersonal divination. Do you understand?"

Will nodded, only understanding the first part of it.

"Good," the Chief replied, placing the flaming hand on Will's shoulder.

Will gasped hard through his teeth, causing many officers to gloat and snicker.

"Relax! We haven't even started yet!" Taly yelled. "First question: Is Will Foundling your real name?"

"It's my given name!" Will answered with clenched teeth and unsure eyes.

"Don't worry. That will do. Next question: Why did you kill Detective Rafe?"

"'Cause he tried to kill me."

"Why would he try to do that? Because he tried to kill one Andrew Monitiz instead of take him alive?"

"Yessir! It wasn't the plan!"

"So, everything that I read in your statement is true?"

"Everythin'," Will told him.

Waltre Taly nodded. "Last question: Is it true that Detectives Rafe and Jana were in league with the mystic who employed the Mystic Mafia, the four ruffians downstairs?"

The tendikeye sneered. "That crooked bastard Rafe admitted it just before I dragged him to the brush pile."

The Chief Justice lifted his fiery hand upward. "There!" he yelled to the assembly. "Are you all satisfied?"

The gathered police force hung there heads in shame. Shame that two of their own had fallen to corruption. And shame that they been out-classed by Excursionist outsiders. They reluctantly took off their hats and saluted the four of them.

Officer Feyna ran to Röger, hugging him saying "I knew it!"

The office was soon cleared out.

Chains were undone and paper was unwrapped. The order was given to go fetch their weapons and gear.

"Get NcRuse in here!" Taly ordered. "This kid needs a healer!"

Chapter 6
Confrontation

The office quickly grew sparse as the crowd filed out. All that remained were the team of outsiders, the Chief Justice, Officer Feyna, and an unusually tall Drakeri man. His badge read *Coroner NcRuse*.

"How are you feeling?" Taly asked Will, his tone more cordial than before.

"Let's see:" Will began with a scoff "My head's busted, my arms're messed up, my hip is made of rock, an' my million grotz smile's been knocked down to 'bout twenty five."

"Your tooth and hip are your problem," NcRuse said, stepping toward the tendikeye. "The rest I will tend to." His face was thin and somber with groggy, peaceful eyes. His boney hands started to paw and examine Will's injuries.

"Who's this feller?" Will asked, slightly offended by the tall stranger touching him.

"This is Leal NcRuse, our coroner," the Chief answered.

Polly's eyes widened in apprehension. "Dis is him, de Necrotheurge who questioned de murder victim?"

The thin man's relaxed face seemed to fly toward her own face in one fast, fluid movement. "His name, young lady, was Davil Pert. You would be wise to honor it and not simply refer to him as 'the murder victim'. His turn in life was a tragically short one. Great was his potential, I assure you."

Polly hissed and stepped back. "Death fixation! Obsessing over anyone who dies unnaturally! You can sugarcoat it wit' good intentions. You can fool yourself, sir, but not me!"

The Coroner smiled down at the blood mystic, his face still as peaceful as a corpse. "I *do* use my powers for altruistic reasons, Miss Gone. And because of that, they are very limited. I live a very simple, boring life. I strive to gain the inner peace of the dead rather than animate corpses with the restlessness of the living. I do not command post-morts to gnaw on helpless villagers. I work in a quaint morgue and divine questions from the departed. That is all." He paused before adding "For the most part."

"He is also a skilled healer," Chief Taly added.

"How can dat be?" Polly asked. "Necrotheurges can only do harm wit' deir theurgy."

"It is not healing per se," NcRuse started to explain. "When a person is wounded, many of their cells are damaged and die by themselves. Damaged bones and tissue are an uncomfortable mixture of dead, dying, damaged, and living cells. What I do is partially convert and animate the dead and dying cells into undead matter. The only noticeable changes are that the pain is lifted and the *function* of the limb or organ is fully restored. The body still continues to heal itself naturally, provided the injury is not fatal. The only side effects are some numbness and a mild craving for brain matter."

"Brain matter?" Hindin gasped. "You turn your patients into bregenites?"

"Jest! I only jest!" the coroner laughed. He turned back to Will, reaching with his wormy digits. "Now, just relax and tell me where it hurts."

"Nuh-uh!" Will yelled, stumbling back, trying to stay balanced with his stone hip.

The coroner gave his best comforting smile. "There is no need to worry, my boy. Pieces of you are already dead. Itsy bitsy pieces. You will heal them away in time. Until then, please, accept my services."

"Thanks but no thanks, mister. I reckon I'll manage!" Will stood as defensively as he could, making his defiance plain for all to see.

Leal NcRuse frowned with disappointment. He looked like he wanted to help. He had heard many things about this team of heroes in the station house, some good, and some bad. He smiled sympathetically at the paranoid bukk. Then suddenly, his eyes darted past the tendikeye toward the entrance door. "Detective Jana!" he shrieked.

Immediately, Will spun around. He reached for his weapons by pure instinct, but then realized that the cops still had them. He looked for the rogue lady detective, but saw nothing! He then felt a hand touch his back and heard a voice say "*Death is rest from labor and misery. With the dead there can be no*
178

more suffering". He spun around once more to see the Coroner backing away from him. The tall Drakeri's eyes and left hand were illuminated with a brown smoky light. As fast as a constrictor snake, Will put the man into a complex arm lock from which there was no escape. Will held tight to the man's wrist, being careful not to touch the glowing hand.

"Discharge it now!" the tendikeye commanded. "Lose the effect or lose yer arm! It dudn't matter to me none!"

The light faded as NcRuse winced in pain. "Feeling better I see, Mr. Foundling?"

Will blinked for a few seconds. It occurred to him that his arms and head *did* feel better. He looked at the stoic face of the man he held helpless.

"Aw, let him go," Röger pleaded.

"Do it, Foundling!" the Chief commanded. "He was following my orders. Now, so should you."

A sense of pride and shame washed over the young man. He let the Necrotheurge go, not sure if he wanted to apologize or not. "I can't rely on theurgy. Y'all hear? There's already a curse I deal with that keeps me from achievin' my ends. I live with it every day. I don't need no more fast healin' treatments. My injuries are mine to learn from, got it? I won't take help from no witchworks."

"What kind of curse is it?" Polly asked, intrigued.

Will's face became grave. "The kind of curse that let me live after that fall. Makes me tougher than krilp jerky. The most a bullet's ever done to me was break a rib. And at odd times when a blade lands on me, it's never bad enough to need stitches. I'm willin' to talk more about it later with you, Pol. But now ain't the time."

"Indeed," the Chief interrupted, sighing as he sat down in his chair. He nodded to his ghastly cohort. "Good work, Leal. You may go now."

The Necrotheurge took a grand step back from everyone, bowing low. "I wish you well, Four Winds-One Storm! Thanks to Mr. Foundling, I have a fresh project to work on. I'll see what I can find out from Det. Rafe's soul husk." He backed away without stepping, but sliding as if on wheels. The great big office door opened for him as he left.

Röger waved cheerfully. "Later, creepy!"

"What about my hip?" Will asked the Chief.

The old man shrugged and shook his head. "Drink plenty of water. It should wear off soon."

"Great," Will pouted.

The office door opened again. Four officers entered, hauling the team's gear and a large wooden box. The biggest of the officers, a tall muscular man, had a hard time carrying Hindin's duffel bag of books.

"Thank you very much," the malruka said as he relieved the man of his burden.

Chief Taly picked up a piece of paper from his desk and held it up. "This is Drew Blood's statement. He refuses to give up the whereabouts of the mystic unless I cut him a deal and spare his life. I don't want to have to do that." He pointed to Hindin's bag. "Is your prisoner in there?" he asked the malruka.

"Oh, no, Your Honor. I would not have my collection jeopardized." He reached into the intricate folds of his black sash and pulled out the beer bottle containing Mr. Crack. In his large steel hand it looked no bigger than a medicine vial.

"I'm surprised my officers didn't find that when they arrested you." The Chief tweaked his mustache and glared at the bottle with disdain. "Please, set it on my desk."

"Very well," the malruka complied.

Taly gave a second order to one of the officers. "Officer Thritch. The mirror, please."

The officer pulled out a small envelope and opened it. One at a time, he removed three small shards of mirror and placed them on the desk. It was all that remained of Drew Blood's secret weapon after falling off a building. Had it not been in his jacket pocket, it might have been rendered to dust.

"And now, the head," the Chief commanded.

The officer carrying the wood box stepped forward. Will made an uneasy face as the officer opened the crate and reached in. Out came the severed glass head of Mr. Crack, recovered from the crime scene at the Rotten Cherry.

"Excellent. Now we can begin. Officers, you are excused."

As the men took their leave, Officer Feyna asked "Do I have to go, too?"

The Chief noticed that she stood unusually close to Röger.

"If you must," he sighed.

"Thanks!" She bounced like an excited teenager.

Hindin had an itch in his brain that he wanted Taly to scratch. "Your Honor, am I correct in labeling you a Cryotheurge?"

"I prefer the term *Frigorifist,* but yes. I am. I control the forces of cold."

Hindin made a confused smile. "But, if memory serves, is not Cold merely the absence of Heat, rather than an opposing force?"

"In scientific terms, you are right, Mr. Revetz. However, it is perceived, and therefore, real. It is an abstract theurgy, for it is based on cultural recognition. If it can be given a name, theurgy can react with it."

"But is it related in any way to Pyrotheurgy? I understand that fire theurgy is common among Drakeri."

"Any two theurgess can be related, if the application makes sense in the theurge's philocreed. '*All is relative*' a wise man once said. Such as, for example, heat and sand." He gestured toward the three pieces of evidence on his desk. He stepped over to them, examining them one by one.

-The severed head of a glass golem.
-A broken mirror.
-An emptied beer bottle containing a small flame.

"The key to finding the theurge behind this is in these clues." He turned to Will. "This flame burns within this bottle without fuel. What does that remind you of, Mr. Foundling?"

Will knew what he was getting at, any tendikeye would. "Fire's Flight." He pointed to a design on his belt buckle. It resembled a bird made of flame. "It's part of my people's outlook, or as you call it: *philocreed.* Legend has it that Pyrehawk, the spirit of Rebirth, taught us to farm and fight. In farmin' we do our best to deliver crops from birth. In fighting, we do our best to destroy. If a person's soul is raised to the proper level in life (we call it the Zenith Point) the soul continues on after death, like a fire without wood."

"And do you believe the legend?" the chief asked.

The young bukk shrugged. "I believe the legend inspired us to do great things an' get through harsh times. It's a symbol of
181

our resolve an' what not. The spiritual side of it ain't really fer me though."

"It may be as you get older," the Chief said. "Some men must live a life before they ponder it." He turned to Hindin, furrowing his brow. "Mr. Revetz, I'm a bit puzzled. You commanded this flame to reside in this bottle, yes?"

"Not exactly, Sir. I gave it an ultimatum: Get in the bottle or fade away. It must have some instinct of self preservation. Like fire, it desires to thrive."

"Maybe. But I have another hunch. Command it to leap onto your hand."

"My hand? Why?"

"Are you afraid of getting burned?" the Chief asked.

"Of course not."

"Then do it, and trust yourself."

Hindin did as he was asked. He picked the bottle up and pointed the neck toward the golden center of his open palm. "Crack, I command you to depart your prison and perch on my palm." In the shake of a lamb's tail, the small flame rolled out, doing as it was told. It flashed and hissed, but stayed put within the golden circle.

The Chief smiled and pointed his finger just inches away from Hindin's abdomen. "I'm surprised I did not sense it before. The many paths of power tend to cross from time to time...in certain individuals. Something in you has awakened, Mr. Revetz. At this point it is not even a spark. But your body is actually generating heat as if you were flesh and blood. I sensed it the moment you entered this room. Something in you has changed, evolved, since I saw you last."

Hindin arched an eyebrow. "Pardon?"

The Chief laughed in amazement. "How marvelous! To think: a Malruka capable of pyrotheurgy!"

Hindin's face lit. "Really? That...That is...wondrous news! I must write my parents! Mother is going to flip when she hears! No, really, she will!"

"Calm down, son," urged the Chief. "You have a ways to go before you can produce your own flame. But you've demonstrated that you do have some control over the one in your hand."

"What should I do with it? What *can* I do?"

The Chief smiled and patted the glass head on his desk. "Put it back where it came from. See if it will answer our questions."

Hindin looked for a moment at his friend's faces. Will appeared very concerned and uneasy. Röger was amused and quite anxious to see what would happen next. Polly beamed with joy for Hindin's gift. Hindin was now a mystic of two paths: Chi and Fire! Using his new found authority, he placed his flaming palm upon the head's jagged open mouth. "Go back," he rebuked.

The glass head lit up like a Jack o' Lantern and screamed "You gravel-balled, clay spined bastard! You may have the gift, but your will is no match for the Master's!"

"Who is your master?" the malruka asked.

"I'll never tell you!"

"Wrong!" Hindin yelled. "I AM YOUR MASTER NOW!" Everyone in the room except Will trembled at the sound of his voice. Only on rare occasions would Hindin raise it. But it was more than just loud. It was the kind of tone that made you say 'Yes Sir'.

Mr. Crack would have hid his face if he had hands. "I...I can't! I am bound by the laws of my creator not to tell his name or location. I swear it is true!"

Hindin looked at the mirror shards next to the talking head. "Then tell us about this mirror. How did it work? Not even its barer fully understood it."

Mr. Crack made a wretched face. "It's a maxim carrier. The master knew the exact time it would be flashed at the targets. He waited, watching through his own mystic mirror to see the target's face. When he did, he would cast his maxim through his mirror, and it would shoot out of this one. Other than the benefit of distance, it also keeps the words of the maxim from being heard while still creating the effect."

"I see," said the malruka. "Is it possible to communicate through it?"

"The Master can see and hear through it whenever *he* chooses."

"Is that so?" grinned Officer Feyna. "In that case!" She reached over and picked up the largest shard. Looking into it she yelled "Hey, you in there! You'd better clean your ass, 'cause we're shining our boots!"

"No! Wait!" Polly yelled.

But it was too late. The shard flashed as a ray of black energy leaped into the lady cop's eyes. As they went black, she swooned and collapsed.

"FEYNA!" Röger screamed. He caught her as she fell. "Feyna? Feyna, snap out of it!" But she was stuck in a dream.

A mad, sick cackle came from the pieces of mirror. The shards were now as black as jet.

Röger turned his head to them. "It's him," he growled. "He's in the mirror."

The cackling continued. "Foolish slag-cop! Such pride and ignorance only Embrenil's Finest would have!"

"Who are you?" the Chief demanded. "Why are you doing this?"

"Ah, ah! Crawl back behind your desk, Snowflake. My business is with Four Winds-One Storm."

"Izzat so?" Will asked, facing away from the shards. "I hope it involves a confrontation. We're overdue fer one, don'tcha think?"

"Indeed!" the voice answered. "In fact, I am making an open challenge to the four of you meddling children!"

"It won't be just the four of them," Chief Taly declared.

"Oh, yes it will, Chief Justice. I will not have my abode crawling with your cronies. I want the band of Excursionists. They are the real threat to my plans. Once they are dead, you will have lost your advantage."

"What makes you so sure?" the Chief asked.

The voice paused to gloat. "Hindin Revetz, Hatchling of the Sacred Flame, take up the head of my creation. He will lead you and your companions and no one else to my hidden domain. There we shall do battle and resolve this matter. If anyone tries to follow you, I will know. And the flame of Mr. Crack will be extinguished, leaving you guessing again! Death will come from all sides if you refuse me!"

Hindin Revetz paused in thought. "To your misfortune, Enemy, we accept your challenge."

❖

They argued with the Chief for almost an hour. During that time, Will drank a gallon of water, Röger took Feyna to the station infirmary, and Polly polished her pretty little knife. After much reluctance, Chief Taly finally gave them permission to go alone. However, there were a few conditions. He made Will take a dozen petrifaction bullets to try to take the mystic alive. Will put them in a hidden pocket in his dust coat, but made no promises about using them. Polly received a brown leather poncho to replace her shredded cloak. It was what the local Fire Department used to resist intense heat and burns. Taly crafted it for himself years ago using his cryotheurgy. He offered Röger a gun, but the Black Vest refused to take it. To Hindin he gave a set of handcuffs covered with an unmelting layer of frost.

"They neutralize pyrotheurgy," the Chief explained. "I've apprehended plenty of fire theurges over the years. I crafted these cuffs for that purpose. Put them on any pryotheurge and it will create a void in their hearts that will nullify their casting." He let out a weary sigh. He hated that these four young people might be marching to their deaths.

"But do what must be done if he's too powerful to be taken alive. You all have until morning before I make a deal with that punk downstairs."

And so, the team embarked. Hindin carried the head of Mr. Crack, who guided them through the night. As Will limped along, he could feel that his hip was almost back to normal. Röger was unusually quiet, making no jokes or wisecracks. Polly felt her power slowly fading into nothingness. How could she explain to her new companions that she needs to kill in order to use her powers?

"How far is it?" Hindin asked Crack.

"Just outside the city."

❂

The glowing head led them far out from the ancient metropolis. To the northwest, there were no small neighboring towns or way stations. There was barely even a road. Many leagues yonder were the Fossil Mountains from which the city first harvested its famous stone. But the team would not venture so far.

They came to a valley of black smoke and blazing fire. The air reeked of rot and filth. But the valley range was not volcanic or sulfurous.

"This must be the city's hell," Hindin spoke.

185

Hell in the common tongue simply meant *'place where garbage is burned'.* Embrenil produced enough waste and refuse to fill the valley many times over. The blaze was tended daily by a miserable crew of city employees.

"They must use theurgy to keep it burning like this," Röger uttered, mildly interested in the sight.

"Look here," Will uttered. He knelt and pulled something off the ground. "Sandstone," he said, picking up a brown rock. His large fingers tensed around it, making it crumble. He shook his head. "Whole valley's made of it. This is definitely the theurge's turf."

"Sand and Fire!" Hindin exclaimed with wonder as his emerald eyes reflected the billowing inferno.

"And garbage," Polly added before spitting on the ground. "Dat is all dis mystic represents."

The glass head laughed. "All that the city dwellers wish to forget about comes here, from broken furniture to corpses made in secret deeds. That which the fire consumes the Master claims for his own. He has fastened his spirit to this sacred place. His heart and mind are like this grand inferno: claiming forever what it destroys. When you meet him, your bodies and souls will be elevated by his flame such as crude sand elevates to glass!"

"That sounds pretty spooky," Röger responded sarcastically. "Where's the entrance, shot glass? Not in the fire, I hope."

The head lead them down a winding flight of brick steps onto an immense stone platform. Just off the platform's edge rose a wall of rising smoke and ash. It was one of many 'tossing zones' in the valley. They then came to the foot of a tall cliff at the far end of the rocky plateau.

"Here!" said the head with a jagged smile. And just as he did, a tall door of opaque glass appeared and opened on the cliff's side. Within the doorway, a lavishly lit hallway seemed to beckon them. Its light fixtures resembled big glass daffodils.

Hindin brought the head to his face. "Is this the only way in?" he asked.

"The only way you will find," the head returned with pride glinting in its sharp face.

"I see," the malruka replied. Then without warning, he smashed the head into the stony ground, making it shatter like a wine bottle full of glowing cinders.

"Why did you do dat?" Polly asked, shocked by Hindin's sudden action.

Before the chimancer could answer, the massive door slammed shut and disappeared into the rocky wall.

Hindin smiled darkly. "To show the theurge within that we will not fight on his terms. We will find another way in."

"Besides," Will added, "This guy might be trap-happy. Delvin' into unfamiliar territory and fightin' a strange enemy got one thing in common: never take the first openin'. Might be a trick."

Röger shook his head, not in doubt, but reluctance. He was about to let another side of himself be seen. He had grown lax in the aspect of a lecherous oaf. Now was the time to show why he earned the vest he wore. "There has to be another way in," he insisted, pointing around with his finger. "Most likely there are multiple places."

"How ya figure?" Will asked.

"Fire, mystical or not, is fed by open air. If the theurge's domain is underground, he must have some kind of vent system to allow his pyrotheurgy. I say we head back up those steps and walk to the top of that cliff. I'll bet there are holes up there that can get us in."

The others complied, and followed the human's lead. Sure enough, they found a hole. It was an old brick well that looked deeper than the cliff was tall. Still, it was somewhat in line with where the great door had been.

Röger continued with his analysis. "This probably serves as two things; the mystic's water supply and a natural cooling vent for any heat that escapes. If you listen, you can hear water echoing."

Will ran his hands over the hewn bricks the well was made of. "These bricks ain't native sandstone. Probably from them mountains."

"Do you think they'll hold if we climb down?" Röger asked.

"Should," Will answered. "But not all of us." He nodded toward Hindin.

Hindin sighed. "After this venture, I am going to invest in a spool of paper rope. My weight and strength are not substantial to such material."

"Why is dat?" Polly asked with bothered curiosity. "I noticed de police bound your hands with paper earlier. Why can't you tear it?"

"I will be delighted to explain it later," he returned before hopping effortlessly into the well. With his long arms and limber legs, he pushed hard against the sides of the vertical tunnel. His bright eyes shined up at them. "I do not think I will be the rotten egg today!" he smiled as he slowly climbed down.

Röger turned his back to Polly. "Hop on, Milady."

Polly resented the offer, but her power grew weaker by the minute. She doubted that her veins would be strong enough to help her descend. She jumped onto the human's back in the piggyback fashion. Röger took a long deep breath before telling her that her hair smelled nice. "Just go, you idiot!" she hissed. Röger's hands were like steel vices on the way down. He climbed with such ease, that Polly noticed the muscles in his arms barely tensed at all. And right before the dark enclosed around them, her eye caught something etched into his helmet. Amidst the swirling lines and decorative shapes that were caked with black tarnish, nestled and perfectly hidden in plain sight, she saw a small symbol that made sense to her. Just behind his left ear hole there was a small hoop enclosing a hexagon. It was the seal of imprisonment, containment. "*How strange,*" she thought. "*Dis man seems to be so free-spirited. What can a hex seal mean to him?*"

Will shook his head in shame. "A Harker without rope," he muttered to himself. He wasn't willing to climb down in Röger's fashion. His large hands were meant for climbing bough and branch. Their thick finger tips wouldn't fit between the bricks. Nor could he reach out his arms to touch both sides of the interior as Hindin did. He leapt in belly-first, pushing his arms and legs out strong and straight, tensing his body as stiff as a plank. He stopped, still facing down, supported by his palms and boot soles pushing against the walls. Not wasting anytime, he began a fast pace down, walking on his arms and legs. Before long, he was gaining on Röger and Polly.

Polly looked up in astonishment. To her, Will looked like a spider crawling down the hard way. "Go faster," she told Röger.

"I thought I was going faster!" he answered.

The deeper they went, the darker it became.

"How do we know dis is safe?" Polly asked.

"Rev's got it covered," Will grunted.

"Why did we not tink to make a torch?" Polly wondered aloud.

"More fun this way," laughed Röger.

"I got matches though," Will said with playful sympathy.

Polly took no comfort. Still, she was thankful for the darkness. Looking down was a little less terrifying.

"I found a foothold!" Hindin's voice called up. "It seems to be a rung ladder transfixed into the rock. They are very rusty. I count about nine of them. Be careful. They go all the way down to the river below." There was a brief pause and the sound of metal scraping metal. "All right. I am down to the last rung. Now, I'm hanging from it. Oh! There are more rungs along the ceiling. They lead over the river onto a creek bed. Hurry, everyone! But hurry carefully!"

Röger quickened his pace, pawing at the wall on the way down. His boot found an old piece of steel rebar. "Got it."

Will and Röger took their time on the rungs. Polly maintained a death grip around Röger the whole time. Hindin guided them with his words and helping hands to the rocky creek bed.

They had reached far down below surface, even lower than the burning valley. Will lit a match to have a look-see. The cavern they were in still had the tracings of the men who had worked in it. The walls were rough hewn and plastered over in places. Broken rocks had been gathered into scattered piles. Just before the match went out, he noticed an old wooden support beam.

"Hey, Rev, you reckon we can use a piece o' that beam to make a torch?"

Hindin examined it. It was an old dusty archway for the opening of a small room. He took a look inside. "There is no need," he said, walking in.

The others could hear him picking things up. Will lit another match as Hindin came out carrying two rusty mining picks.

"These must have belonged to the well diggers. Forgotten, no doubt." The Chimancer slapped the rusted pick heads off the handles, leaving the wood undamaged. "Will, your flask please."

189

"Waste of good liquor," the tendikeye groaned. He removed a canteen-sized flask from one of his coat's many hidden pockets. The elixir carried the scent of pepper sprouts and grain alcohol. He drenched the ends of the handles with it until the flask was empty. "So much fer a victory swig later on." After two slight touches with the match, they then had two very functional, very bright torches.

They followed the river upstream. It seemed to whisper at them as they went.

Polly's power waned. She could feel it in her heart. It had been weeks since her last sacrifice, her last kill. The Sizzagafiend was too animalistic to count. She needed something that could think, reason, and feel. She had a little bit of power left in her. It was enough for one more casting. After that, she would have to rely on her knife. But as she walked alongside the three seemingly fearless men, she felt that she could rely on them, as well. To depend on others at that point didn't seem so bad.

They came to see a large pipe rising out of the river. It was about as thick as a man's thigh. It led straight up about forty feet before bending into a brick wall. Just above where the pipe went in, there was a large air vent.

"Sir Röger," Hindin beamed. "You were right! This must be the main water line. And there is the air vent. Well done!"

The human shrugged. "It was rudimentary, Hindin. That's my big word for the day."

Will eyeballed the structure. The river was about forty-five feet across. The pipe was in the middle. He could make the jump to the pipe. If they could climb up the pipe, they might be able to break in through the vent. The pipe was the solution, but it was also the problem. "There ain't no getting' up that pipe," he declared as he shook his head. "It's covered in moss and grime. Too slick to climb or stand on up top."

"Well, we still have to get up there," Röger insisted. "Unless we want to go back to the front entrance and hack our way in."

Polly studied the pipe and Röger's large weapons. "Hindin? How thick would you say dat pipe is?"

190

"Hmm. I would guess three-quarter inch thick walls and, oh, about eleven inches in diameter."

"Can your axe cut dat, Röger?" she asked, turning her head to the human. "I mean, if Will were to jump out dere and use it?"

Röger took a step back and seemed offended. "He is not allowed to use my axe. Plus, I could make the jump myself. But I'm not gonna! This axe is for windpipes, not water pipes!"

"Why do you want to cut the pipe?" Hindin asked.

"If we separate it from de water by only a few inches, I can swim to it, use a maxim to get inside de pipe, go up, come out of a tap or spigot, find the vent, break it open, and hopefully send a rope down if I can find one."

"How you gonna do that?" Will asked. "Shrink yerself? Change into a varmint?"

The young woman looked embarrassed. "I...I am going to alter my form into a completely liquid state. I'm going to turn into blood. So, I need you to...to watch my clothes for me."

Röger's eyes grew large as he erupted with laughter. "On second thought, Polly, I would be happy to cut the pipe! I would see this!"

Polly sneered and kicked him in the shin. "You will not see anyting, you dungtongue! As soon as you make dat cut, you will swim back and put your silly helmet on backwards! All of you had better avert your eyes, or I'll stab dem out!"

"Of course," Hindin replied.

Will let out a slight chuckle, but also swore not to look.

Röger readied his axe and backed up against the wall. He had eight steps to build a running start. Leaping off over the murky water, he choked up on the handle for a huge swing. With a guttural shout he swung his weapon in a cleaving half circle. As he splashed into the water, the section came off!

Hindin cheered, clapping his steel hands in ear-piercing clangs.

Will was silent. He never met or heard of a human that could jump like a tendikeye and hit with the strength of an ox. There was more to Röger than the Fevärian let on.

The drenched human laughed as he swam back. "Piece of pie! Easy as cake!"

He climbed out of the water, gave Polly a wink, and promptly spun his helmet around. "Hurry up, doll face. I'm freezing my stones off!"

All eyes were averted as Polly disrobed. Parting with her clothing was one thing, but leaving her dagger behind bothered her even more. She dived into the nameless river, taking the shock of the cold wetness that swallowed her. Once she was under the severed supply line, she looked up into the narrow dark tube. She could hear it sucking air. She had to hurry before the Master noticed that his water supply had been literally cut off. Reaching up, she was able to get her hand inside. She proclaimed the maxim *"A house's pipeline is its bloodline."* She felt her body stretching, yet becoming very relaxed. Instantly, the pipe made a loud slurp and Polly was gone!

Like blood through a giant straw, she flowed through a vast network of plumbing. Unable to see, hear, or feel, she was better able to concentrate. She had to be careful not to let herself be split up when the pipes divided. The passages grew narrower with every pass. After many twists and turns she finally sensed an exit.

At last, she sensed herself emptying into something large. Slowly, she reverted back to her shapely young form. With her senses returned, she found that she was in a bathtub made of clear glass. The spacious bathroom she found herself in was like a dream of crystal and mirrors. Everything sparkled and shined as if it had never been touched. The room was illuminated by a single oil lamp, its light reflected and magnified by the many mirrors and sculpted glass. She felt the vulnerability of her nakedness multiplied as she was surrounded by her many reflections. A feeling of dread crept over her. What if the Master could see her through them?

"Breathe and move, you silly bitch!" she told herself in a rough whisper.

There was a towel closet nearby. Inside she found a fluffy white robe and it put on.

In a cabinet by the sink she found a small straight razor.

She looked all around for an air vent to crawl in, but the only one she found was on the ceiling and too small. As quietly as she could, she turned the latch on the entry door and pulled. Peeking out, she saw a well lit narrow hallway full of mirrors and doors. At the right end of the hall, there was a large vent at floor level. Without hesitating, she dashed toward it! It was bolted into the wall. She needed a flat head screwdriver. She knelt down and tried to use the flat end of the straight razor. After a single hasty turn, the blade snapped off the handle. "Cheap lump of junk!" she exclaimed.

Suddenly, her ears twitched. The sound of footsteps and chains were behind her. Something cold and hard clasped around Polly's neck, yanking her into the air. Before she knew it, she was slammed into one of the hall's grand mirrors. The impact would have knocked the wind out of her if her windpipe wasn't clenched so tight. She turned her head to see her attacker. It was Detective Jana Swarbule.

"You had this coming, little girl!" the rogue detective roared with vicious delight. Her face was contorted with hatred.

Polly struggled and squirmed, kicking wildly at Jana's head. But the crooked cop kept her at a safe distance. Polly's power was depleted. She couldn't even summon her vein tendrils to counter-grapple Jana's prehensile shackles. The cuff around Polly's neck tightened like a vice as she was slammed into another mirror. She would have lost consciousness if it weren't for the many glass shards grinding into her back. Her hand felt a large shard still inside the frame on the wall. Without even looking, she pulled the shard loose and threw it with an upward flick of her wrist. The whirling projectile slashed deep into Jana's left breast, splitting the nipple in half. The detective screamed like a wounded animal and lost control of her chain. Polly dropped to her bare feet onto a pile of broken glass. A large shard impaled her foot, filling her head with blinding pain. The cuff around her neck loosened enough for her to scream, but she was unable to. She was too busy trying to breathe again. Feeling the glass slash and dig into her feet, she lost her balance and fell to the floor. She was barely alert, loosing blood and air and taking the sting of a dozen glass fragments. She picked up another glass shard, intending to use it like a knife. Jana's chain latched onto her wrist, squeezing nerves against bone. The shard fell, shattering against the floor.

"Die! Just die!" Jana yelled. The other end of her chain bashed into Polly's forehead. Polly's free hand grasped it before Jana could land another hit.

"Let go!" Jana screamed, yanking back on the chain.

193

Polly didn't let go, but she let herself be yanked with it, closer to the chain's wielder. In that brief moment Polly was close enough, she raised her shard-impaled foot and landed a solid kick into Jana's throat!

Jana's eyes widened in terror as the broken glass sank into her neck like the fangs of a giant serpent. Her chain went limp as she and Polly both fell to the floor. She gasped for air through the new hole in her esophagus. Her left jugular was severed. A pool of dark red began to form on the floor by her head.

Polly climbed onto her prey with a fearsomeness magnified by her striking looks. Her eyes shown like pools reflecting an unforgivable wisdom. Her rose petal lips were lax and neutral. She placed her fingertips into the expanding blood puddle and commenced her chant.

Jana could make no sense of the incantation. It did not even sound like a language. It was a series of jittering consonants and morphic vowels. Not just words were spoken as Jana Swarbule lay dying. Fear seized her heart, making it beat faster. Her blood gushed out, replaced by the cold emptiness of death.

◈

The boys were still by the river, impatiently waiting. Hindin paced back and forth, fraught with worry. Röger morosely watched the whispering water pass them by. Will's mind was choking on doubts of Polly's success.

"She ain't comin' back," Will said, gritting his teeth. "Even if she's just lost up there, it's only a matter of time 'fore she get's caught powerless. An' WE were the ones who let her go!"

Before Hindin and Röger could respond, the large vent cover came crashing down, splashing into the water. Polly stood, leaning against the vent wall.

"Polly!" Hindin called, raising his arms as if for a hug.

"You are one crafty fox!" Röger cheered.

Will looked up in a mixture of relief and guilt. He was glad to be wrong for once.

Polly said nothing as she lowered down a particularly long length of chain. Hindin was the first to recognize it as Jana's extendable wrist shackles. It was wet with blood in places. He

194

looked up with a face of concern. Polly kept most of her weight on one foot. She was deathly pale.

"I do not care who comes up first," she bitched. "Just make sure dey bring my red bra wit' dem!"

The three men were each hoisted to the opening by the mystical chain. They all voiced concerns for her injuries.

"I will feel much better once I am clothed," she laughed lightly.

She led them through the cramped vent, limping. The three warriors stood in shock as they reached the hallway opening. The hall was decked with blood and glass. Jana's body still lay where she fell. Polly had her clothes and dagger tucked under her arm, tip-toeing her way to the bathroom.

"Watch for de glass," she said, stepping over the corpse.

The three men waited for her to close the door before talking to each other.

"What a waste," Hindin said, frowning at the woman's body.

"She wasn't *that* hot," Röger responded.

"That is not what I meant. What cause drove this woman to cater to such harmful deeds? What was the price paid for her to turn her head and let innocent people be blinded, beaten, and killed? Was it because others more desperate than her were doing the dirty work? The most evil of deed is sometimes doing nothing at all."

"Aw, piss on her!" Will scoffed. "A criminal's a criminal no matter who they are or how they get started. Its how they *end* that's important." He drew back his scaly dust coat, exposing his pistol and gun. He took a deep breath and exhaled as he looked about the place. "Gettin' to be that time." he said with a dark smile.

Röger smiled back with unsure eyes. He had heard a lot of young men talk tough like that over the years, that stubborn confidence fueled by a vendetta of justice. They did not act so tough when he had to shovel dirt on their faces. He started to envy Hindin, who seemed like a big brother to the young bukk. He decided that if it came down to it, he would be a big brother to the both of them. He cleared his throat, getting their attention.

"Um, I just wanted you two to know that we *are* in fact going to beat this theurge. You have nothing to worry about, any of you."

195

Hindin smiled. "Thank you, Sir Röger. You too can rest assured that I have your back, as well."

Will grew suspicious at the human's words. "Somethin' buggin ya, Rög?"

The Fevärian laughed nervously and looked at the floor. "Just don't judge me if my fighting gets...gets a little unorthodox."

That was a word Will had to digest slowly. He nodded in response, but made a mental note to later ask Hindin what its meaning.

Polly entered the hallway once more, no longer limping or pale. She was fully dressed and never looked healthier. "My power has returned," she smiled awkwardly. Picking up one of the blood-soaked shards off the floor. She examined it and her eyes glowed red. She whispered "He knows dat we are inside. And he is not happy about it."

✧

They continued down the hall of mirrors and doors. The walls were a khaki color with red and yellow trim. The glass doorknobs sparkled like large diamonds. Whenever they passed between two mirrors, their reflections reflected infinitely.

"Hey, Will, I bet you ten grotz one these reflections comes to life and tries to kill us." Röger teased.

"Please, do not make him paranoid. Sir Röger," Hindin groaned.

The tendikeye's eyes shifted left to right. He felt the growing urge to pistol-whip the mirrors into teeny tiny pieces, but resisted. "Any o' you reckon this mystic could cast his blinding maxim through one o' these here mirrors?" he asked.

"Maybe," Polly answered. "Probably more maxims dan just dat one. But he *is* watching us through dem."

"Maybe we should bust them up." Röger suggested, holding his huge axe.

Polly shook her head. "He would still be able to see through de shards, I tink. Save your energy."

"Or maybe we could take 'em off an' turn 'em around?" Will offered.

"We have no time to deal with all these mirrors," Hindin argued. "There are too many. But perhaps we should check these doors, or rather, behind them."

The others agreed. They also agreed to check each door one at a time. There were six total in that particular hallway. There was a billiard room with colored glass pool balls (Will pocketed the eight ball). There was a study with many old and rare books (Hindin almost had to be pulled out by force). There was, of course, the bathroom. After that, there was a meditation room. Then there a was walk-in closet. And finally, there was a bedroom with a kitchenette (from the look of it, Jana had been using it). But there was no evil theurge to be found. At the end they reached a "T" section with another hall. Hindin recognized the daffodil light fixtures that illuminated it. Down to their left was the great entrance door that they had refused to walk through earlier. At the other end was a stairway. They all agreed that the stairs were the next best choice.

"We must be more careful from here on," Hindin warned. "Our host did not expect us to enter this way." He pulled the bedroom door off its hinges and tossed it into the new hall. A series of burning rays shot out of the flowery fixtures, blasting the door to cinders. The malruka turned to Will. "So, my friend, how are your trigger fingers?"

Will grinned. "Itchy."

With an exhilarated jolt Will leapt into the hall, the ends of his dusk coat flapping in the air. No one saw him draw his gun, but there it was in his hand. His forefinger and pinky wrapped around the triggers like arms around a lover. Each barrel took its turn, waiting patiently between shots. Will ricocheted so fast between the walls, ceiling, and the floor, that gravity had to wait until he finished. He dodged the flaming rays as he shot with uncanny ease. Each leap, flip and mid-air twist led to safety for him and doom for the fire spitting flowers. Eight of his twelve bullets were fired as all eight mystical light fixtures shattered to pieces. The hall, now shrouded in darkness, had only one light left in it: a lit match kissing the tip of a cigarette.

Polly became very, very, very angry. "You pig-molesting hotshot!"

"What?" Will asked, confused and losing his cool.

She clenched her teeth and glared at all of them. Each man took a step back.

197

"What is it, Polly?" Hindin asked with a look of worry.

Polly was so pissed she could barely talk. "I...You...STUPID ASSES!!! We did not have to take de way we took, did we? No! We could have just gone through de front door, and DEN Mr. Hotshot could have shot de lights out wit' his fancy hopping around and BANG BANG BANG! But no! You are all EXPERTS, aren't you? Find another way in, you say! And what happens? We end up in some stupid well and I have to fix de problem by getting naked and almost killed!"

The three men looked at each other, not knowing what to say or too afraid to say anything at all.

Polly ran her fingers through her short hair and let out a hoarse sigh. "Forget it. Let's just do dis." She pulled up the hood of her leather poncho and started toward the stairs.

"But, uh..." Will stammered.

"I DON'T WANT TO TALK ABOUT IT!"

Will frowned and reloaded his gun.

✧

Somewhere in a dark, yet to be discovered room, an old man toiled with his newest creation.

"What are we doing, Master?" the creation asked.

"We are making *Prince Idvard's Tears,* Mr. Pane. And I require your assistance."

"What shall I do?"

"Do you see that bag of white sand in the corner? Pick it up and bring it over here by this brass basin."

The creation did as it was told and picked up the three hundred pound bag as if it were a feathered pillow. It carried the load and set it down between the bathtub-sized basin and the old man.

"Thank you, Mr. Pane."

The creation nodded. "Master, what are *Prince Idvard's Tears?"*

"They are a very special mystic weapon. First I will levitate large portions of the sand over the basin after we fill it with cold water. I will then use my pyrotheurgy to melt the sand into hot globules of molten glass. I will then drop the globules into the water. They will instantly take the shape of large glass teardrops. These teardrops will be completely indestructible except for the tapered tail ends. I will make as many as I can and use my will to control them if the four intruders reach us. Then I will make the tears fly at our visitors with killing force. And if perchance they manage to hit one of the tear's tails, the entire thing will explode into many shards, cutting them into bloody ribbons."

The creation smiled. "You are truly brilliant, Master."

"Thank you, Mr. Pane. Now, let's get started, shall we?"

The old man reached down to a faucet that aimed down into the basin. He turned the handle marked *COLD* and waited. And waited. And waited. No water came out. So, he turned the *HOT* handle. Nothing.

"What the hell?" the old man muttered, confused and dismayed.

"Why isn't the water coming out, Master?" the creation asked.

A look of utter puzzlement formed on the Master's face.

◇

The ceiling was tall, so the stairs were many. The team moved slowly with the utmost caution, not for stealth, but to be ready for any possible danger. Hindin could not help but remark on the design of the stairway.

"See how it glitters!" he exclaimed in a soft whisper. "It seems that it was carved out of the sandstone mountain itself. The mystic must have used his pyrotheurgy to smooth them out into rough glass. The result makes it appear as white icing on a many layered cake."

"All it needs is candles," Röger replied with either wariness or weariness. "Look, everybody. If you all don't mind: Let me take the lead for a while. I've been on a few 'theurge raids' in my time. If this man's a master pyro, expect to be burned, expect it to get so hot you can't breathe. A theurge's domain is his weapon. Trust nothing, not even the ground you stand on."

Will became amused at the human's sudden seriousness. "Is this speakin' from yer Black Vest experience? Hey, just what is a Black Vest, anyway?"

"Depends," Röger smiled. "We were many things. One squad usually consisted of one Flicker, a Scribe, a Banger, a Tipper, and a Slugger (that was my job). I've had formal training

199

as a policeman and as a fireman. That's why my weapons both have big hooks on them. They're great for pulling shingles. At the academy I majored in archaic weaponry and minored in criminal psychology. But what really makes a Black Vest is his loyalty to his country. Or in my case: What they believe in."

Will did not dare to reply. They were very far from either of their countries. And neither one seemed in the mood to discuss loyalty.

When they reached the top there was a large red door with brass handles. Röger placed his palm on it in various places, feeling for heat.

"It's not hot. But that doesn't mean its safe."

Hindin took a peek inside. "Odd," he remarked, pulling the door open.

Their eyes beheld a lavish dining hall. The lengthy table was surrounded by finely crafted chairs. In fact, they more resembled large wooden thrones. The table was the epitome of master carpentry. Various geometric designs had been hand carved into the wood. They swirled and beamed in many directions on the table's surface. It was a grand pattern of pure wonder. The hall itself was tall and grand. On the two side walls were a total of eight stained glass windows. A huge chandelier of wrought iron was suspended high above the table. It was covered in white candles and dripping with shimmering crystal. Far on the other side of the room, there was another large door.

"What's so odd, Rev?" Will asked.

"It is odd that we are inside a small mountain, and there are windows. Perhaps the Master wanted to create the illusion of being above the surface."

Slowly, Polly ambled toward the table. She studied the windows with a curious suspicion. The stained glass works of art depicted the eight signs of the Draybairian Zodiac.

> The Understanding Dog
> The Wary Owl
> The Speaking Raven
> The Acting Monkey
> The Working Mule
> The Exerting Tortoise
> The Thinking Man
> The Concentrating Spider

The images were twisted, abstract, and horrific. These were creative interpretations of a malign imagination. Any serious zodiologist would find them to be offensive, grossly obscene, unfitting representations.

"So, what's your sign, Will?" Röger asked, trying to stifle the suspense.

"If I knew my birthday, I'd let you know."

The brute shrugged. "I'm the Monkey sign, if anyone cares."

Hindin's worried gaze shifted from one window to the next. "I am the Dog of Understanding, Sir Röger. These signs each represent a specific virtue, laws of truth. Such irreverence! These aberrant depictions paint a clear picture of the artist's lack of morality."

"NONSENSE!" came a loud voice from all around them. "They represent all that I have sacrificed to fuel my soul, you walking mockery of life!"

"Reveal yourself, recluse!" Hindin demanded. "Test your *philocreed* against mine!"

"In time, hatchling," the voice answered. "I have foreseen your deaths on the whispering embers of time. It is almost over."

"Why are you blinding innocent people?" Polly asked with a challenging grin. "Is it to steal deir souls? Are you Xelor de Mad Reborn, or do you merely seek what was his?"

There was lingering pause as silence claimed the air. Polly looked around wearing taunting pride on her face. The voice spoke again.

"Do not mistake me for some sadistic power hungry lunatic. I am a lover of life. My soul is an inferno of a passion you could never understand. So many of us waste our lives without trying to achieve some purpose, some goal. When all of this is over, I will give ten souls true meaning! They will not shatter. They will not die! They will live on in me forever, as one with the sands of time!"

Polly laughed and bit her bottom lip with a smile. "Immortality? Lifespan elongation? Pathetic! No doubt dat's what you offered de Detectives. Dose two were your narrow-minded *rooks*. The four ruffians were your *pawns*. Hindin destroyed your *knights* at de tavern! How many more pieces must be taken before we take de *King?!*"

"More than you can handle, child!"

The eight windows became wreathed in angry flames. The twisted images sprung to life and leapt onto the floor and into the air. They looked just as they did when frozen in glass and iron, only closer to being real.

Will leapt onto the center of the grand table. His sword and pistol were dawn, catching light on their polished steel. It was enough to make half of the stained glass entities take notice and try to swarm him. The Thinking Man caught two hot lead nuggets in its chest, making it crumble to jagged bits. The Acting Monkey fell in two shattering halves from the sword's flashing cleave. The Understanding Dog's jaw busted off from a kick that seemed to come from nowhere. The onyx wings of the Talking Raven were broken off by the next pair of bullets. The glass bird had just enough time to scream "Oh Shunt!" before splintering on the table top. The yashinin sword flashed once more, finishing the Dog off.

Polly's show of confidence was not in vain. As the Wary Owl descended upon her, she quickly summoned her veins. They squirmed from her forearms like long thorny worms. Catching the screeching fowl in a supernatural grasp, the young blood mystic took a long deep step and spun around as hard as she could. The large bird crashed into the side of a dinner chair, leaving a broken pile of wood and glass.

Sir Röger barely dodged the hind hooves of the Working Mule. Quickly switching to his huge greatsword, he took a few steps back to ready a swing. The hooked-end Billblade was designed to take down live thick-legged bileers. A glass ass would be fast out-classed. The Mule let loose another set of kicking hooves. Röger evaded to the side and swung down as the hind legs came up. The beast's limbs broke off with ease. A hasty follow-up swing knocked most of its head off.

Hindin was amazed by the speed of the Exerting Tortoise. Not because the Tortoise was too fast to deal with, but he knew that real tortoises were much slower. He needed only to jump onto its big shell and deliver one good hard stomp, and the fight was over.

"Yeah!" Will celebrated. "We're gonna eat this boy's lunch!"

"You *are* Dasaru trained!" Röger cheered. "Not bad. Not bad at all, Willy-boy!"

Hindin looked down at the pile of shards he stood in. "It was a tortoise, for Slate's sake! It should have been designed for durability, not speed!"

Polly looked very nervous all of a sudden. "De Spider! De Concentrating Spider! Where did it go? Did one of you destroy it?"

The three men looked at each other. Heads shook and shoulders shrugged.

Right above them came the sound of metal bending and crystal tinkling. The grand chandelier descended on its chain like an arachnid on a strand of web. Its long crystal and candle-covered limbs were spread like spindly fingers on a giant hand. As it lowered, its shadow eclipsed the four intruders.

"Move!" Will called. "Spread out!"

What none on them noticed was that the Concentrating Spider had leapt onto the chandelier. The first seven signs were only meant as distractions in the Master's design. As the intruders destroyed them, the stained glass Spider had melded with the hanging wheel of lights. What the team faced now was not unlike the Sizzagafiend in size and shape. But this threat had no throat to cut or blood to spill.

It crashed down upon the table, sending wooden debris everywhere. All were knocked prone. One of its heavy legs crashed onto Röger's back. Luckily, his axe was strapped behind him, absorbing most of the hit. He managed to roll out from under the heavy iron leg. He saw his teammates get up and scatter. He did the same. They were each backed into their own corners now. The huge animated light fixture creaked with loud shrill noises as it flailed its many legs. The team was perfectly divided, unable to hear or see each other clearly. Everyone was on their own.

Polly could not believe what she was dealing with. Her theurgy was at its full strength. But it meant nothing against such a threat. She had two or three of the spider's legs to contend with. Their alien movements confused her. She had been instructed to dodge men and animals, not mystical constructs. Suddenly a leg whipped down at her so fast that she felt frozen in place. There was no time and no choice.

Meanwhile, Will emptied all twelve rounds of his Mark Twain Special into the Spider's core with no results. The Spider answered with an arched leg that slammed down hard and fast.

The stone corner where Will had stood was pulverized into gravel and dust. It was a narrow evasion, even for him. Another leg arched and came down like a scorpion's tail. Will dodged again, avoiding becoming part of a crater.

Hindin had less to worry about. Being a construct himself, he had zen-like awareness for the Spider's movements. As a leg came down at him, he deflected it to the ground at his side. Before the leg could come back up, his canvas pants flapped like a flag in the wind. He kicked the wrought iron leg with such speed and explosive force, that the giant leg bent like a paperclip. It was a small victory, though. There were seven more legs to contend with.

Röger had dropped his billblade by the table when the Spider descended. He pulled his axe, not noticing the thin fracture in its wooden haft. Opting for offense over defense, he dashed for the nearest leg. With true aim he swung with all his might. The blade bit half way through before the handle snapped. The human gritted his teeth, too pissed off to efficiently use profanity.

Will had no time to reload. He weaved his way between the crashing legs, slashing at them with little effect. He tried to find a pattern to the Spider's attacks. Its reach extended throughout the room. Its core never strayed from the center. Its legs attacked sporadically. They were all on the offensive, arching and slamming the floor to pieces. But if all the legs were busy attacking, how was it being supported?

"The chain!" he thought. *"The chain is still holdin' it up so it can hit with all its legs!"*

The bukk's yashinin machete was not just a close-quarter melee weapon. It was also designed to be thrown. He leapt as high as he could between two of the massive glass covered appendages. The chain was now in clear sight. With a fast wave of his arm he slung the razor edged blade. It spun through the air like a glimmering boomerang until its deadly rotation was stopped by the thick chain. The sword cut a chink in a link before clanging onto the floor. The link, now weakened, stretched and pulled apart. As the chain broke, the Spider only fell a few feet, landing on all of its legs.

Hindin seized the opportunity. He began a barrage of kicks and open handed strikes, crippling the giant walking chandelier. Two more legs were knocked crooked by his loud, explosive blows.

Röger dashed for his fallen sword. But as he did, he caught a glimpse of a bloody crater where Polly had stood. His eyes darted around, looking for her. But when they returned to the crater, he could see pieces of her blood soaked clothes inside the rock-strewn hole.

Something deep within his helmet snapped like the hinges on a door best left shut. An all too familiar sensation burned in the back of his skull. His silver helm did what it could to keep his mind from total collapse. But the rage had already surfaced. He pounced to his billblade and gripped its long handle like it was the throat of an old enemy. He shifted quickly from kneeling on the floor to leaping into the Spider's core. The entire room trembled at the sound of his primal roar mixed with the tearing of metal through metal. The huge construct split in two! The Spider's limbs froze in place as its two halves came crashing down into the already demolished table and chairs.

Will and Hindin watched in disbelief as their human companion climbed out of the wreckage unscathed. He dragged his sword and breathed heavy. But it was not from exhaustion. He was still angry. The muscles in his arms and neck flexed and twitched as if they each had minds of their own. He seemed taller, broader, and more hunched. The whites of his big brown eyes were now the darkest shade of green. Letting his sword clang to the stone floor, he shambled like a madman to the bloody crater.

"Oh, no..!" Hindin mouthed in a hoarse whisper.

Will clenched his fists and hung his head in shame.

Röger convulsed with rage and grief. Slowly, he cleared away the blood-splattered rocks.

The three bereft men stood in utter confusion at what they saw in the hole where Polly had stood. There were her clothes and blood everywhere, but no body! Then they saw all the surrounding blood flowed back and filled the crater as if a hidden will commanded it. It seemed to soak *through* the clothing, rather than into it, making it take on a familiar shape.

Polly lay in the crater like a fetus in its womb. Her eyes were closed and she shook with a chill.

"Get her out of there!" Will ordered.

205

Hindin reached in and scooped her out gently. She groaned as her eyes snapped open.

"Put me down!" she demanded. "I'm going to...!"

Hindin put her down just in time as she started to throw up. A flood of blood and small rocks spilled onto the floor. Then another. And another. She spat out the last piece of gravel like it was a broken tooth.

"Polly, you are alive!" Hindin exclaimed.

"Lucky me," she muttered. She carefully got up, not wanting any help.

Röger started to calm down. There was something in his voice that made it deeper, bigger. "You turned into blood again, didn't you? Before it could hit you."

She looked at him queerly. "Yes. I had to. But I can't do it all de time. If I am in a place dat is too dirty, den dat will happen." She pointed to the mess of rocks, glass, and wood on the floor.

"Are you going to be all right?" Hindin asked.

"I tink so."

Will shook his head. "I swear, Pol. You must be part cat with the way you keep almost dyin'. Do us all a favor and knock it off, all right?" He turned to Röger and narrowed his stare. "An' you. What's yer deal, stranger? There's more to you than you been lettin' on. We've all been quiet about it until now. But you jump like a tendikeye an' yer stronger than an ox. No amount o' training can put a human up to that level without theurgy. So, you'd better start talkin'."

The Black Vest only shook his head and turned away. "There's no time for explanations, kid. We got a mystic to take out of business. Don't push me for things you don't need to know. I need to calm down and cool off. Just...please....let me cool off, okay?" He paced around, taking deep, relaxing breaths.

Hindin could tell that the breathing was a habitual routine by the slow but steady rhythm of his breaths.

Polly sensed something new in Röger that she did not pick up beforehand. Something not right. Like a secret kept hidden in his blood.

◈

Röger had calmed down, and looked as if he had shrunk back to normal. He picked up his sundered axe. The blade was undamaged, but the haft was half gone. He gripped it with one hand like it was a huge, awkward tomahawk. "Good for one throw," he thought aloud. There was doubt in his voice.

Polly looked pale from vomiting so much blood. She felt weak, but her spirit was still strong. But she was no fool. She knew that things would only get worse.

Hindin was concerned for the both of them. He wanted to offer sympathy and encouragement. But there was little time. The more time a theurge had to prepare, the deadlier they became.

Will reloaded his gun for the second time. As he did, a thought bloomed in his mind. He turned to the Black Vest and the blood mystic. "I got me an idear. Me an' Rev were in this fer the long haul from the start. You two volunteered to give us a helpin' hand, and it's been just that. No need to risk yer well-bein' any further. Turn back. Go tell that Chief Justice how to get here. Tell him what went down. Have him assemble a witch huntin' posse to clean this place out. Me an' Rev'll stay here an' keep the theurge in check."

There was a long pause before Hindin spoke up. "It is not a bad plan. We shall not think less of you both."

"But what if he kills you both and gets away?" Röger argued.

"Then he only kills two of us," Will answered. "If he get's away, it mean's he loses his base of operation. He'll be a spider without a web." The tendikeye's face was stern, his eyes reflecting his resolve.

Polly did not know what to say. She was given a chance to leave and live. No doubt the Master was still watching them. The Spider was not the limit of his power. She could feel it in her veins. He was a Master Pyrotheurge. Attacks such as his could not be nullified by simply turning into blood.

For Röger Yamus, the answer was a simple "No". But he looked at the young Drakeri girl standing beside him. She was young, full of life, smart, and beautiful. And she would remain so for many centuries thanks to her heritage. Should he let his pride put her at risk? His instincts told him that if he decided to leave, she might feel inclined as well.

But before any decision could be made, the voice of the theurge echoed once more throughout the hall. "That was not our deal! The four of you were to do battle with me!"

Will smiled at the air. "Then you shoulda met us outside 'steada hidin' in here grippin' yer twig!"

The wreckage of the chandelier stirred, creaking and scraping the floor. Everyone instantly stood on the defensive. But the wreckage slid and tumbled away from them, blockading the door from where they had entered. The doors on the other side of the hall flung open by a sweltering current of heated air.

As the four teammates looked inside, they only saw reflections of themselves, as if an entire mirror took up the entry way. The only thing that it reflected was them. A strange darkness surrounded the reflections. Strange shapes and images appeared on and around them.

Hindin's chest and abdomen seemed to be illuminated by spheres of flame. The Master's voice spoke to him first. "I see, I see. Two of your torso chakras have been reborn. Whatever it is that allows you to channel chi also allows fire. Perhaps it is because you were born of fire, no? You have two paths, hatchling. One is well on its way to being mastered. The other could use some ...instruction. Perhaps I could help if we grant each other mercy."

A strange aura surrounded Will, like it was composed of crystal clear liquid. The Master's voice cackled. "Oh, this is strange indeed. You carry heavy burdens, don't you, sir bukk? You keep in your heart a profound hatred! Such fire fuels you, does it not? But that is not the only wickedness that keeps you alive. That theurgy. Do you know where it comes from? No. But you would like to. With my flawless divination skills, I could find out for you for a price."

Polly saw herself in the mirror with a face as sinister as the woman who raised her. She wore a flowing gown of scarlet and crimson. Her eyes blazed with passionate malice. The Master sighed with admiration. "You my lady, kill to fuel your theurgy. Is it not a requirement of your philocreed's doctrine? You took joy in killing Detective Jana, didn't you? You are a red rose who has yet to bloom. I am burning pieces of spirit for the sake of a goal. Those who have been blinded will have a part of themselves live on through me. Surely, you would not judge me on this procedure, would you? We are both hunters, Miss Gone."

Hindin's ears burned at the sound of the theurge's words. He looked at Polly, hoping it was not true.

The dark shadow of a great horned beast stood behind the human. Its hulking body was shaped like a great ape or an upright jungle cat. The Master said nothing of it. The fact was: he had no clue what to make of it. All he knew was that it brought on a feeling of dread.

He then spoke to the group as a whole. "Temptation is my next weapon. For I swear upon my philocreed that I will give you whatever it is you need to complete your life goals. All I ask is that you let me do the same for myself. I can only sense the fires inside you, your inner spirits. They all yearn for something. Knowledge, power, the means to an end. I could grant you immortality when my work is finished. Or if money is an issue, I have access to that, too. Not all of you need to agree. But you should decide quickly."

A shot rang out and the mirror shattered. Will peered forward as the glass fell in huge shards. "General Tidsla Childoon once said: *If a merciless tyrant is ever willing to negotiate, then he must surely be afraid!*"

Polly could not help but smile. She drew her dagger and put faith in her poncho. The veins in her face and arms wriggled with anticipation.

Hindin cleared his mind and felt the air on his steel skin. It was hot and dry like a desert wind. He focused his chi to run like hundreds of rivers of energy throughout his body.

"For Love of the Blind Bitch, Lady Justice!" Röger bellowed. "And for all of those you have wronged in this city!"

The Four Winds rushed in together as One Storm, not knowing what to expect, but ready for it all the same. The space they entered was the inside of a sixty foot tall by sixty foot wide three-sided pyramid. The walls and floor were enormous triangular mirrors. At the far end stood two Drakeri men. One was very old and shriveled. White had invaded and conquered his thin hair. His skin drooped wearily over a rickety old frame. He wore spectacles and a robe of red and light brown. Polly instantly recognized him as the sweet-faced elderly customer from her father's barber shop. *"The mystic picture glass!"* she thought with wonder. *"Papa said it was a gift from him!"* She winced in regret for forgetting about that mystic picture glass's origin. *"I was too distracted to remember!"*

209

The other man was nearly identical to Mr. Crack and Mr. Shard, wearing a yellow suit, red shirt, and brown hat and tie.

Will fired three more shots at the gruesome twosome. The paths of the bullets seemed to bend and curve harmlessly around them. *"Gut snake!"* Will thought. *"Some kinda barrier."*

"Mr. Pane!" the old one commanded. "Focus on the round-ear wearing the helmet. I will deal with the rest of them!" He then pointed a finger at Will, who had closed in the fastest. *"You are your own worst enemy!"* he declared.

Will had trained to dodge bullets and maxim effects by the angle of the barrel or the finger. But nothing came out of the spindly digit. He paid little mind to the perfectly polished sword he wielded. Little did he know or understand that within the Master's sanctum, any reflective surface was his to manipulate. Another blade seemed to grow out of its polished steel. Without warning, an arm identical to Will's arm came out the side of the sword. It held an identical yashinin sword and it aimed straight for Will's skull. Will gasped at what he saw. This gun arm jerked to the blades path. He caught the blade in the heart-shaped notch between the barrels, for such was the notch's purpose. The blade was trapped, but the mystical arm was strong. That, and now both his weapons were tied up for the moment.

The elderly mystic spat into his hand and aimed his wet palm at Hindin. *"Better to die in action, than sitting still!"* A cone of mystical steam burst forth, enveloping the malruka. Hindin wailed in agony and crashed onto the floor. The pain came not from the heat of the steam, but the thick layer of rust that instantly covered his entire body.

Polly Gone dashed forward like an autumn wind, cold and smooth. The poncho of the *Frigorifist* flapped with blue light as she dashed.

The old man held up his hands as if holding a ball. *"A burnt child fears the fire!"* he yelled as a massive ball of spiraling flame appeared above him. He hurled the ball at her. The sphere of flame was too fast and large to dodge or douse with blood. It completely enveloped her in its blazing light. The old man reveled with laughter as she disappeared inside his fire.

Then from out of the burning ball, a cherry-red dagger flew at the cackling theurge. The blade sank into his right thigh and sizzled in his flesh. As he screamed in pain and pulled the dagger out, the huge fireball dispersed. Polly was still running at him. She was covered in soot but unharmed thanks to the fireproof poncho she wore. Her jagged veins were out. But the Master proved too cunning. Before she could get within ten feet of him, he raised his arm and clenched his fist. *"Beauty breeds arrogance!"* he said. Her own reflection beneath her came to life and ensnared her with its veins. She fell to the floor, pinned in place.

Röger threw his broken axe at Mr. Pane. But the golem henchman deflected it with his hand. The billblade sword proved much more useful. Röger was able to keep his distance from the glass man's devastating blows while blocking with his heavy blade.

Will's luck got worse. Out from of the other side of his sword came another arm. And it held a Mark Twain Special identical to his. He shook his cursed blade, trying to shake the effect loose from it like it was a burning stick. A familiar shape spilled out of the steel and fell to the floor. Will backed off, abhorring what lay before him. It was a creature identical to him, yet twisted like the stained glass images in the dining hall. It sprung up to its sharply pointed feet, clutching weapons like Will's. Its crooked face warped into a wicked grimace.

"Who the ...?!" Will gasped, pointing his pistol at it.

"If you are Will, then call me *Won't*," replied the creature. It licked the edge of its jagged machete, the tongue making a smooth, scraping sound. "I'm gonna gut you like a gut snake-eatin' carp!" It tried to raise its gun arm, but Will already tugged his triggers. Two pieces of lead exploded out of the barrels, blasting the doppelganger's arm off. The limb fell to the floor, shattering like ice.

The creature laughed madly and raised its blade. It darted at Will with a forward thrust, stabbing into Will's extended wrist. The point of the blade wedged hard and fast along the arm's tendons. Will's fingers loosened on his gun, letting it drop to the floor. Will and *Won't* now fought blade to blade. The creature matched him stroke for stroke, smiling the whole time. Whenever Will threw a kick, *Won't* would dodge or counter it, and vice versa. They seemed evenly matched until the doppelganger's blade snapped in two while trying to block. Will's yashinin sang through its glass imitation and bit halfway into the creature's neck. The creature stiffened, its gaze fixed on Will. It laughed as steaming cracks ran throughout its face and body.

211

Will peered at him, trying to yank his weapon free. Then a loud boom and a thousand shards of glass flew at him. He shut is eyes just in time as a dozen points dug into his face. Hundreds of other points collided into his body, knocking him back several yards. He landed hard on his back. Reeling in pain from his face to his thighs, he rolled onto his side. He looked down at the mirrored floor. The flabbergasted face looking back was full of tiny cuts. The air around him suddenly smelled of fresh cut chives.

Hindin could see everything that was happening, but he was unable to move.

Röger, however, could move just fine. He finally saw an opening in Mr. Pane's defense. With a mighty diagonal cleave, he bust the golem into a pile of flaming broken glass. He then glared at the elderly mystic. "You!" he roared like a rabid lion. He began to charge. But as he did, the pile of burning glass reformed into the golem's true form: a spike-covered, talon handed monster with a fiery core.

"Röger! Look out!" Polly called. The golem began to charge from behind him.

Röger turned for an instant and threw his sword wildly at the golem, missing terribly. He just kept sprinting at the theurge. He was unarmed, unafraid, and screaming like a lunatic.

"You are a fool to charge me, human!" the theurge yelled.

Röger scoffed with a grim growl. "I haven't been *human* for a long time!" He dived forward and began to run on all fours. Polly and Hindin could not believe what they were seeing. Muscles expanded and became coated with layers of thick striped fur. His body grew longer with every pouncing stride. Clothing shredded. The form of a human was replaced by something like a charging cat or pouncing bull. A tail sprouted. Everything changed except for his head and helmet, which now seemed too small for his body.

The old man froze in horror. "A Werekrilp!" He raised his hands again and threw another fire ball. The charging beast leapt over it, scorching only a few hairs. The old man became eclipsed by the shadow of the pouncing monster. He fell onto his back as the Werekrilp pinned him to the floor. The glass golem hopped on its furry back and tore at it with its talons. The beast reached behind with its massive clawed hand, grabbed the golem by the arm, and smashed the creature onto the floor beside him. The

212

impact was so extreme, that the fire inside it went out. Just as he turned back to face the old man, a black light surrounded the theurge's hand. His old lips stuttered as he tried to speak. He was about to cast the blinding maxim.

The thought of what happened to Officer Feyna shot through Röger's rage-addled mind. With a vicious swipe of his claw, he broke off and shredded the glowing limb. But it did not stop there. The beast kept rending and tearing flesh and bone long after the old man had no throat or lungs left to scream with. Spurting wet popping sounds could be heard from under the beast. Pieces of viscera plopped this way and that. The Werekrilp raised its blood-spattered head and let out a roar of victory, and the enormous mirror walls around him cracked in answer.

Will hopped up from the floor, brushing pieces of glass off his dust coat. Regaining his composure, he looked at the nine foot tall monster that had Röger's head for a head. He picked up his sword and stood perfectly still, watching and waiting.

Polly stood up, as well. The theurge's effects were broken. Even Hindin was back to his normal shiny self.

The Werekrilp turned to face them. Röger's big brown eyes looked worried from inside his silver helmet. The face within was still human! It spoke in a big deep voice that shook their ribs. "First rule of Theurge-Hunting: A theurge's true power comes from doing the unexpected, to load up their sleeves with tricks."

Hindin tilted his head in baffled astonishment. "And so, it would only be prudent to keep a trick of your own hidden, as well."

The silver helmet nodded.

Will gritted his teeth. "So, that's what you meant when you said yer headgear was a good luck charm." He watched the beast's every move and reaction. He did not put his blade away just yet.

The beast slumped, looking weary and dejected. "This helmet was forged by Grandmaster Thiadric Jameel, the last great High Theurge of the Sfotanhai Dynasty. Over a century ago before the civil war broke out, I was part of a squadron of Black Vests. We were on the trail of a murderous werekrilp who had already slaughtered over four hundred people. We tracked it back to its lair, an abandoned steel mill on the city's outskirts. But the cursed bastard was ready for us! He killed all of my

213

teammates, friends I'd known for years. Thanks to my dumb luck, I was able to take it out. But not before it bit me...and passed on the monster into my blood. There was no way to break the curse, but even the Grand Duke himself, Nostaw of Kromm, insisted on finding a way to let me keep living. But I lost everyone I cared about. And when the old autocrat died heirless and his Wemloc cousins took over, I lost my freedom, too. All non-humans were banished. I was counted as a monster according to the new regime, so I left the motherland. So, now I wander alone from place to place and help whoever I can. I'll admit that I'm no saint. But I'm no murderer, either. I only kill when it's necessary, like just now. But before any of you settle on a judgment," he took a deep, sad breath. "I want you to all to know that it was an honor and a lot of fun working with you all."

There was an unsure silence in the air. Will took a few steps toward him, still clutching his blade. "You mean it *is* an honor to be workin' with us."

"What are you saying?" Hindin asked his partner.

"What I'm sayin' is that it dudn't hafta end here. Sure, we got a hokey team name an' we get on each other's nerves a little. But we might just be able to take this show on the road, so to speak. Plus, if I'm gonna let a werekrilp an' a blood mystic wander about, I think it best that me an' you tag along with 'em. Make sure that if they do kill somebody, it's somebody worth killin'."

Hindin looked at Polly and frowned. "Polly, is it true that you must kill in order to maintain your power?"

Polly heaved an uneasy sigh. She could not bare to look the kind-eyed malruka in the face. Her voice trembled. It annoyed her to show such weakness. "Well...um, since Röger has revealed so much. Perhaps you might be lenient wit' me, as well. But I doubt it. I am a killer, a murderer trained for assassinations. I have killed innocents and evil people. But none of it was ever by choice. My teacher, my mother, would catch people of all kinds for me to fight for de sake of my training. She would false-promise dem liberation if dey could kill me. Some seemed to succeed at first. But she would always heal me before I could die and be free of her. I even tried to kill myself once. But her powers of healing were too great.

Over time, de fighting became easier. I learned to deliver killing cuts wit' little effort. De more I killed, de more my own

214

powers grew. And every time I killed someone quickly, it meant dat dey would not be imprisoned and tortured for weeks. My mother adheres completely to de Philocreed of Crimson Theurgy, De Red River; to shed de blood of your target as joy floods your heart. Our power is tied to it, you see. But I took no joy in killing innocent people, only de ones in which I sensed evil. But often, I could not tell which was which. Dat is why I ran away. And dat is why I am still running. I do not wish to be like her. Though I must admit; a part of her is still a part of me. I enjoyed slashing dat bastard Drew Blood's face open. I relished watching Jana bleed to death. It is like a reflex of my heart and soul."

"Do you feel you must continue this path?" Hindin asked plainly.

"If I must keep running from her, den I will always be on it. Not all places have laws against it like in dis city. I traveled here on foot from Chume. On de way, two bandits tried to rape and kill me. Dey are probably still rotting under de tree where I left dem. I am what I am, Hindin. You cannot change me."

"Then I will guide you," he replied. "We all will. We will guide each other, in fact. We will be like...like radishes and carrots."

The three looked up at the man-shaped mountain as if his proverbial lid had just flipped.

"Radishes an' carrots? How ya figure?" Will asked.

"You are the expert planter, Will," Hindin smiled. Did you not tell me once that radishes and carrots are planted together in order to protect each other from weeds? We can and should rely on each other for a similar purpose." He turned to Polly. "Polly, become an Excursionist with us. You, too, Sir Röger. We can all rely on each other, learn from each other. We all have skills to share and problems to deal with. For instance, Will is supernaturally resilient to injury. We do not know why. But perhaps we could stumble upon the answer together someday."

"Perhaps," Polly returned. She looked at the bukk with a studious smile. "I should like to know what theurgical crafting it is he *relies* on."

"Don't know. Don't care," Will replied. "I just want it off me."

Röger slowly shrank down to normal size. His clothes were in tatters, but he did not seem to mind. "It all sounds like a great idea, a group of three wild cards and a wise-spouting rock

215

man. But let's all discuss it later in private. We have to get the police down here. That and we have to get our story straight. Some things might need to be edited out, if you catch my drift."

◈

Coroner Leal NcRuse had his work cut out for him, literally. While all the other officers collected evidence and searched for clues, he had two on-the-spot rituals to perform. He started with Jana's corpse, since it was more intact than the other. The proper candles and incense were lit. The right words were whispered.

Communing with the dead is very tricky-especially in this world-for when anything dies, its soul shatters and disperses in every direction throughout the Huncells. The fragments join with other fragments wherever life begins anew. It is called the Soul Cycle, the natural process of spirits in the Draybair Cluster. Think of it as reincarnation, only the souls are broken up, mixed, and reformed in new vessels.

However, there is a sort of shell left behind. Not the body itself, but a hollow husk composed of spiritual energy called the Anima Husk. If a person dies naturally and peacefully, the husk breaks apart and eventually dissipates. But in the event of an unnatural, violent death, the husk could stay intact for a long time. And in some cases, it retains memory.

The Coroner commenced his questioning.

"Who are you?"

"Jana Swarbule," a voice whispered in his mind.

"Very good. How did you die? Who killed you?"

"The blood mystic. We fought. She...cut me with her...with her foot?"

"That will do. Tell me why you served the Master here?"

"To live forever. Young. Healthy. Forever."

"How? How would he accomplish this?"

"The watches are special. Only need a few more. He swore on his philocreed. Rafe and I will get them. We will."

"Good luck with that. Who is he? What is the Master's name?"

"Lurcree. But it...it isn't..."

216

"Isn't his real name. Just his mystic alias. I understand. We are almost done, Jana. I can tell that you're getting confused and uncomfortable. Do you know who I am?"

"That creepy necrotheurge who works downstairs."

"That's right. And how is it do you think I am getting these answers from you? You are a detective. Figure it out."

The voice inside his head began to breathe heavy and whimper.

"Good bye, Jana." He then blew out the candles.

Upstairs in the Pyramid Room, Detectives Sirron and Emmad interviewed the team. Sirron was a middle-aged Drakeri with thick knuckles and a short trimmed beard. Emmad was centuries younger. His dark wavy hair was tied back into a short ponytail.

"So, explain once more how he died, Miss Gone." Det. Sirron had a hard time understanding her explanation.

"It was an act of desperation," she started. "De mystic's powers were too great for us to take him alive. De maxim dat I used was our only option. It works by commanding de victim's blood, I mean *enemy's* blood inside him to rip out and make it look like an animal attack. Blood mystics in de past would use it to throw de law off deir trail. But I would never do such a ting. I am willing to tell you men de truth."

"But his guts and limbs are everywhere," Det. Emmad argued. "Can blood alone do that?"

"Yes, it can," Polly cheerfully returned. "Like liquid rock destroys a mountain in a volcanic eruption. All it takes is de right kind of pressure."

"Don't volcanoes only erupt from the top? That would mean that just his head would explode, wouldn't it?" Det. Sirron asked.

"True! But de skull is very strong. Dat is why de viscera are used instead. It is a much easier area to work wit'. Nice and squishy." Polly explained gutting maxims like other woman explain cooking recipes. The Detectives grew uneasy.

"But volcanoes do not just explode up top," Hindin interrupted. "They are known to explode in multip--!" His words were cut short as he felt Röger's elbow strike his side.

217

Polly giggled and shrugged a cute shrug. "I am no good at analogies. Explaining theurgy to dose who are not mystics is like...is like...well, like I say; I am no good at analogies." She smiled brightly as she passed a nervous hand through her short hair.

Coroner NcRuse entered the room, stepping over the broken glass in the entry way. He carried a briefcase containing his candles, incense, and other tools of his trade. "A most curious way of dispatching your foe, Miss Gone," his voice echoed far from across the room.

"You have good ears," she hissed with a slight sneer.

"I listen to dead people for a living. Compared to them, we living are as loud as elephants." The solemn Drakeri proceeded to the theurge's gutted corpse, ignoring everyone else. "Hmm. I see there is no need for an autopsy. Oh, Look. He was dying of cirrhosis. Just look at that liver! That explains his desperation." He knelt over where most of the body was. All that was left was a head, spine, one and a half arms, and shriveled little legs.

The entire team, the two Detectives, and the few other officers in the room were unsettled by the Coroner's presence. It was not just his reputation as a necrotheurge. It was more than him being very odd. His awareness was far different than theirs. It was as if some of his emotions had been replaced by others that they had never felt.

He placed candles and incense around the body. He then took a specially prepared piece of parchment, rolled it up, and lit it with a match. Black smoke slithered from the burning paper. One by one, he used it to light the candles and incense. When all were lit, he began to chant. There was a reverence in the words, yet no one could make them out. The incense gave off the scent of fresh flowers on a rainy day. After a minute or two of chanting, he started what sounded like a one-sided conversation.

"Lurcree? Lurcree? Is that not a name you answer to? (Pause) No, you are not dreaming. Why were, I mean, why *are* you stealing watches and blinding people? (Pause) Immorality and eternal youth? Do you think it will really work? (Pause) How will it work? How will you go about such a task? (Pause) Who I am is not important. What was your plan? (Pause) My, but you are a stubborn one, aren't you? (Pause) Because you are dead, sir. Therefore, keeping it secret no longer matters. (Pause) Oh, for about an hour now. (Pause) Yes, they are still here. Do you have something you wish to tell them? (Long pause) But how could you have foreseen them burning in your fire if they have killed you? Perhaps their collective *medicine* was stronger than yours. Destiny is a bileer with many horns, sir. (Pause) Yes, it *is* over, sir. Justice has been done upon you. (Pause) And how do you still plan to kill them in your state? Come back as a ghost? It is part of my job to insure that that does not happen. Not that it could. Your Anima Husk is already starting to crumble. Do you have any final words?"

There was a long pause of listening before he blew out his candles.

"What did he say?" asked Det. Sirron.

"Many things, Detective. Many, many things. However, he would not divulge his method for stealing souls to gain life eternal. It is for the best, I suppose. Such knowledge should stay unknown."

"Did he say anything about how he died?" the detective asked.

"He mentioned it in passing," he laughed in a sudden giddy manner. "Get it? In *passing*?"

"Well, how did he die, then?" Detective Sirron pressed.

The tall necrotheurge smiled with narrow teeth at the team. "It happened just as the young lady said it happened. Now, if you all will excuse me. I have a report to fill out." He took a deep, relaxing breath and looked at the team's baffled faces. "I love making house calls," he said with a happy sigh. With that, he took his leave.

"He lied for me," Röger whispered in astonishment.

◈

For the remainder of the night, the four Excursionists gave a detailed account of their raid. Many of the officers congratulated them on a job well done. They were given a lift to the station house, this time as heroes, not suspects. They were greeted by a proud Chief Justice and crowd of policemen who treated them with honor and respect.

Will tried to return the unused petra bullets, but the Chief insisted that he keep them as a gift. The Chief did, however, take back his mystical poncho from Polly and the shackles from Hindin. He gifted Polly with a gold and ruby brooch. "We have a huge pile of confiscated jewelry in the back," he told her. "Keep it on and you will always have some red on." For Röger, he had the station's weaponsmith repair his axe. The new haft was fashioned from maple.

"This is the least thanks we can offer you, so far," he told them. "But tomorrow I will contact the local Gazette and the Mayor himself. And I will see to it that you will be recognized for your bravery and selflessness. I am happy to say that this case is at its closing point!"

They were given beds for the night in the station barracks. And all seemed well and good.

Chapter 7
The Council Banquet

✧

It was officially confirmed that the hermit known only as Lurcree was indeed the theurge behind the assaults. The prisoner known as Drew Blood identified the remains. Coroner NcRuse reinforced the confirmation with his reports made from communing with the corpses of the mystic and the two dead detectives. The pieces of the three golems known as Mr. Crack, Mr. Shard, and Mr. Pane were ground down and turned sent to the NcRay Brewery to be turned into beer bottles. The four ruffian thieves were given the choice of three sentences: Execution, 900 years in a prisoner colony, or almost certain death in the Red Dirt Battle Arena. All but one chose the second choice. Drew Blood was willing to try his luck in a fight or at least go down in a blaze of glory. All money and possessions of the conspirators were counted up to be put into a special city administered account. It would be used to ease the sufferings of the victims and their families.

The Excursionists known as Four Winds-One Storm received no monetary reward. The law of the city prohibited the local police from employing mercenaries and vigilantes. The Chief Justice, however, promised them to pull some strings to find them "gainful work opportunities".

The stolen silver watches were never recovered. Bileer riding officer's returned with news that none of the blinded victims regained their sight. This roused great suspicion, since most effects break when the caster dies. But the Department was still glad it was over. The Gazette was happy to be getting a resolution to their ongoing story. The public would soon feel safe again.

Röger asked around about Officer Feyna. He found out where she lived and immediately left to visit her. The Coroner's reply from yesternight was still on his mind. He was normally a man without any cares. Now he had two to deal with; his dark secret being exposed and the woman he felt protective of.

Polly stayed in bed. Her mind and body were exhausted.

Hindin received a package from the Chief containing two books and a pair of spectacles. The thin book was entitled *The Basic Principles of Pyrotheurgy*. The older, much thicker book was called *The Tome of the Sacred Flame*. The spectacles he had seen the night before when they rested on the nose of Lurcree.

Will looked and felt like a stomped turd. After falling off a building, being bashed in the mouth with a stone club, and getting showered by exploding glass all in the same day, he could have looked worse. All he wanted was to be left alone to rest and relax. But when an officer mentioned that the press would want to take a photograph of the team later in the day, he started to grow self-conscious. He had a huge bruise on his forehead, a face full of scratches, and a broken front tooth. He disappeared from the station, telling no one where he went.

"So, let me straighten this out: Your tooth was knocked out by another tooth?"

"Well, actually it was a big stone fang."

Will sat back nervously in Rhowshell's dentist chair. He had never been to a "tooth healer" before. That, and her short, hip-hugging white skirt, her shy-yet-sly smile, and her whimsical voice did not help him maintain his cool.

She leaned over a sink to wash her hands. Will's large rough hands clenched the arms of the chair. The air was heavy with lilac perfume and exotic herbs.

"So," she started, turning around. "How is the case coming?"

Will stared at her, at first not knowing what she was talking about. "The case? Oh, yeah! The Mystic Mafia! Well, I am happy to say, Miss Rhowshell, that yer city is a bit safer now. That punk I caught spilled the beans. An' when we caught more of'em, they spilled more beans. It was all one big avalanche o' beans, I tell ya. Anyway, we got'em all. We took out the leader yesternight."

"Took out? As in *killed*?"

222

"'Fraid so. He was a master mystic who didn't want to go peacefully. We had to resort to lethal procedures."

The lady nodded and crossed her arms. "So, have you killed a lot of people in your time?"

"Why?"

"You seem very comfortable with it. That's all."

"It had to be done. There was no other way around it."

"Oh, I believe you on that. You did what you had to do. But why do you seem so at peace about doing it?"

Will thought deep and hard for a moment. Then he raised an eyebrow and smiled as if he just discovered some great secret. "Why, Miss Rhowshell, I am flattered."

"Flattered? Why?"

"That you'd be so interested to go as far as ask such a personal question." His grey eyes glinted as his smile widened into a grin.

It was now the dentist's turn to be nervous. She did not know how to respond, not that she had to.

Will kept talking. "Since that's how it is, I'll give you an answer: You ever been attacked by a wild dog, or worse, a pack of 'em? Where I come from, the whole countryside's full of 'em. An' I killed more'n my share of 'em growin' up. It was natural. It was necessary. They'd tear a sweet thing like you to pieces. That don't make 'em evil. They're just animals. But if a grown person makes a conscious decision to be like those dogs, then that *is* evil. They become worse than them dogs, in fact. So, killin' them becomes natural, necessary, and very easy on the conscience. Sure, it's okay to feel bad fer a misguided fool who's turned to wicked ways. But I don't feel sorry fer'em when they hurt other people. I'll also admit that combat holds a thrill. But that ain't why I do what I do."

"Help people you don't know?" she asked.

"It's what I live fer, Miss Rhow. You don't mind if I call you that, do ya?"

The belle dentist answered with a bright smile. "Okay, well, let's have a look at that tooth." The professional in her took over. Now was not the time to let herself be impressed. In the time it took to give the broken bit of tooth a quick examination, she thought "*It has to be his accent, that's all. That unrefined charm probably works on other girls. Wow, his hands are huge! They could cover a lot area in a short time. Stop! He probably*

223

has girlfriends all over this huncell and maybe a few others. But he doesn't have one here...What's that smell on him? Is that tobacco? No, it's too sweet, like caramelized onions. Maybe if I lay my head on his chest, I'll get a deeper whiff. Yeah, that would be smart."

"Well, I hate to tell you this," she started flatly. "But the rest of your tooth needs to be removed. It could get infected if we leave it in."

"Great," Will groaned. "I'm s'posed to show up fer this photograph meetin' fer the newspaper later. I guess I'll just not smile then. Or maybe I could, just not with my mouth open. What do you think?"

"I think I can replace it before you have to make such a tough decision," she laughed.

"Really? Yer sayin' you can just hammer in a whole new tooth before then?"

"Sure. Which would you prefer; gold, silver, or porcelain?"

He pondered his choices. Metal teeth were usually for pirates and sleazy tradesman. And if he had one, future enemies might think of it as a weakness, that he lost a fight or something. Plus, he viewed it as a way of showing wealth. But a porcelain tooth looked real. "Porcelain," he answered proudly.

"Okay. But it's more expensive."

"What? Like, how much more?"

She gave him an estimate. And it turned out being a bit out of his price range. He then considered one of the plastic coins he secretly kept. But before he could decide...

"But don't worry," she teased. "You're a big hero now. It's on the house."

"Really? Aw, yer a doll, Miss Rhow! I'm in yer debt."

"And the city is in yours, Mr. Foundling." Her tri-irised eyes were lit with a playful glow.

Will could taste the air between them. He could hear her breath and smell her hair. Every curve of her face, the shape of her scythe-shaped eyebrows, the natural flare of her upper lip, and the upward turn of her nose: each feature distracting in its own way. Whether it was in a city or the wilderness, some things never changed.

The procedure went smoothly with little whining on the patient's part. There were more patients waiting, and little time for interpersonal explorations.

◊

The nation of Doflend was as a Confederated Capitalist Democracy. It was a union of seven city-states each governed by its own citizens. There was no one capital. And no one person was in charge of any one thing except The Mayor, The Chief Justice, and The Grandmaster. Freedom was earned by paying taxes, keeping the economy flowing, and not breaking the local laws and regulations.

The City-State of Embrenil's Gazette newspaper was not a free press publication. It was owned and regulated by the city administration. While it was the Mayor and Grandmaster's people who gathered the daily facts, it was the Chief Justice's job to confirm them with theurgic divining. Because of this, no lies were ever printed. However, just because the news always printed the truth, it did not always say the whole truth.

"Aw, come on, agave. Why don't you want to be in the picture?" the reporter asked the antisocial blood mystic.

Three of the four teammates had arrived at a conference room at the prestigious city hall. Röger was 16 minutes late, so far. The reporter, Wice Threberjh, was a short, stocky Drakeri in his middle years. He had a face that made expressions like a bowling ball; excited, confused, and overwhelmed. Accompanying him was a tall, nerdy young Drakeress with a large elaborate magnesium camera. She too seemed a bit dense until she started setting up the bulky photography equipment. Her job seemed a lot harder than the reporter's.

"I do not owe you an excuse!" Polly hissed back.

"Well, you're the mystic of the group, aren't you? Maybe you could tell us about your theurgy. What's your philocreed?"

"It is not for de public to know, you annoying worm!"

The reporter made another face like a bowling ball, only with a slight frown.

"Please, sir!" Hindin interrupted with a nervous laugh. "Our young lady friend hides her shyness with anger."

225

"She gets kinda fussy at times, that's fer sure!" Will teased with his freshly fixed grin.

Polly made a sour face and crossed her arms. "Where is dat idiot round-ear at? I will not suffer dis much longer."

"Perhaps it is best that we do the interview without him," Hindin suggested.

"That's fine with me, Mr. Revetz," the reporter agreed. "We'll start with you. Are you the group's leader?"

"This group has no leader. We all possess our own strengths. And we take turns leading based upon our areas of expertise."

"I see. And what exactly are *your* strengths?"

"Oh, I really should not brag."

"Oh, but you should! The public deserves to know who saved them and how they were saved. So, what's your area of expertise, son? Don't be modest."

Hindin nodded with a sigh of agreement. "Very well. I am an intermediate practitioner of the South-Western internal style known as Thorny Lotus. It is a style of meridian based chimancy similar to Kiew Sho. I have studied the seven animal styles known as Heron, Copperhead, Lynx, Owl, Puma, Fox, and Dragon. There are other odd techniques that I have learned in my travels, but too many to name."

"Oh, that's fine," said the reporter. He scribbled on his notepad *Hindan Revitz-Malrukan chimancer-Thorn Lotus technique-Fights like an animal*. "And what made you decide to take this case?"

"My partner, Will, and I were roving the countryside when we caught wind of the city's plight. It seemed like an unusual case. And we, being unusual excursionists, decided to take it on."

"And what makes you so unusual?"

"We are on a general mission of goodwill, not for wealth or necessarily thrills. Wherever there is need, we go and help as best we can."

"Got it. Good stuff," the reporter replied. "And how about you, Mr. Foundling? Did you become an excursionist to escape the tyranny of Cloiherune?"

"Excuse me? Tyranny?" Will glared at the man. "You'd better get yer words straight, bud."

"But aren't your people oppressed by their empire by not being provided proper educational opportunities to the general public? Or what about entire families getting massacred if they have just one criminal among them? Would you not say that Doflend is a better place to be? Here, you are free to wander from place to place."

Will darted at the man like a gust of wind. Luckily, Hindin's arm was fast enough to catch him. "Will! Whatever you say to this man will be printed tomorrow for a many eyes to read! Remember your goal!"

The reporter was still making that gutter-ball face, only now it was condescending.

Will glared at the little man. "Sir, your luck at attacking my country with words is no different than the luck of anyone who has ever tried to invade it. In my country everyone is born with the right to fight fer what they believe in. And I carry that right with me wherever I go. I am free to walk whatever road I'm on because of the spirit I share with every tendikeye who's worth their salt. I came here to save yer people from being blinded. But it seems that it's to late too save you!" Will half-expected the man to make a mean face and storm out. But instead, the reporter seemed to shrink in shame.

"I'm sorry for rousing you so, Mr. Foundling. It's just that you must admit: Emperor227 Necluke is a bit extreme when it comes to your...harsher ways."

Will shook his head. "He's a dud-of-a-shot-caller. But many of the officers who elected him ended up dead by his order. They reaped what they'd sown, as far as I'm concerned. Whole country's payin' fer it now. But guess what? It was the common folk who put the officers in power! Ain't that a pain in the foot! But why you askin' me all this? Why not ask one of our diplomats? Let's get this flash-picture over with so I can go out an' smoke!"

"But aren't there supposed to be four of you?" the photographer asked.

Before anyone could reply, the doors to the conference room swung open. Röger entered with clenched fists and a hanging head.

"How is she?" Will asked.

"Taking it pretty bad," the human replied. "She's got her whole family over, taking care of her. It was hard to feel useful around all that support."

"Are you Röger Yamus?" the reporter asked, extending his hand for a shake.

Röger reluctantly shook it, not currently caring for pleasantries. "That's SIR Röger Yamus. Make sure you put that in your article. I hope you got enough info from these guys. I'm in no mood to talk right now."

"Oh, that's certainly all right," the reporter replied nervously. "I'll just hand you all over to Nod here. Then we can be on our way. She's quite the photographer, Nod. Not cheap either. People have been known to pay great sums for her work."

In Nod's heart, she was more than just a press photographer, more than just an artist. She was a hunter who captured moments in time. Many of the moments she had taken were planned trappings, as this one would be. She was able to convey to the four teammates how she imagined them standing. She even convinced Polly to participate. Nod told her that she was a mystery not meant to be solved. She said that even though Polly had a lovely face, it was not meant to be fully exposed. She made her stand sideways to the camera with her hair covering her eye and most of her cheek. Polly complied not out of flattery, but because she felt strangely understood by the photographer. After her, the other three were a cinch to pose. Will proudly displayed his repaired grin and held up his Mark Twain pistol. Röger removed his helmet and cradled it like a rugby ball. Hindin's expression was reserved, yet pleasant.

The flash stick popped loudly as the moment was ensnared. The room became foggy with the smell of sulfur. It reminded Will and Hindin of how they first met. After the session was over, the press man and lady photographer departed. It was the first time the team was alone together since the raid. Polly turned just in time to see Röger putting his helmet back on.

She bit her lip. *"I was hoping he'd keep dat helmet off after de picture!"* she thought, hiding her disappointment. *"But he put it on before I could see his face!"*

"How long can you go without your helmet, Röger?" Hindin asked.

"Only for ten minutes or so at a time. These last fifty years or so, I've learned to stay in human form as long as I keep my cool. Before that, I'd have to hide while in my krilp form."

"So, how old are you?" Will asked.

"161. It happened when I was 27."

Polly eyed the helmet curiously. "So, it helps you maintain your will over de beast. Dat explains why it is silver. De metal is a charm breaker to de dark forces in your blood. Curses are strange tings. De stronger de curse, de more powerful de cursed person can become."

"How's that?" Will asked.

"Theurgy is almost always give and take. If someone is permanently afflicted by an effect or a curse, den de person's spiritual being may eventually compensate by manifesting powers to balance out the deficiencies of de affliction. In Röger's case, he gains all de benefits of de beast's physical aspects, but de madness is neutralized by de helmet. He will also live forever, but...but..."

"But I'll never lead a normal life." Röger finished the sentence for her. He smiled at them all sadly. "It's okay. I've gotten used to it. On the night I was bit and turned, six other Black Vests lost their lives. The way I see it, I'm living out the time that they lost. That's why I always try to enjoy life the best I can."

As Röger finished speaking, a sudden idea jolted Hindin to change the subject. "I am sorry, but I must interrupt. My thoughts are still bent on the blinded victims. Consider this: What if it was more than an ordinary effect? What if it was a curse that blinded them?"

Polly shook her head. "Curse energy is a more emotional theurgy, while maxims are more analytical. Lurcree would have needed a catalyst or personal vendetta in order to curse dem."

"But I think he did. They had something he wanted. Is that not motive enough for an evil mystic's vendetta?"

"No," she answered. "A vendetta is an all-consuming desire. His desire was youth and eternal life. Blinding people was just a means to dat end."

Hindin sighed in frustration. "It just does not sit well with me!" He paced throughout the room. His usually light footsteps now pounded with his full weight.

"Rev, let it go," Will pleaded. "There ain't gonna be no more victims. Ain't that enough?"

Hindin would not listen. "Maybe there were other conspirators. They may know something."

"We've done all we can, Rev!" the bukk argued. "Unless anything turns up real soon, I say we move on and move out. This town can go back to normal. Let the cops deal with the loose ends. We eliminated the main threat."

Hindin did not respond to his friend. He turned to Röger. "Sir Röger, don't you feel that if there is some way to restore Officer Feyna's sight that it should be worth looking into?"

The Black Vest said nothing. He only turned his head away.

Polly placed a calming hand on Hindin's arm. "Hindin, please. My mother is no doubt on my trail. If I am to walk wit' de three of you, den we must leave soon. We are in danger if we do not keep moving."

Will looked at her with doubtful curiosity. "So, yer mother is the teacher yer runnin' from, eh? You said the same thing yesternight. Is that the truth about you then?"

"Yes," she answered gravely. "Dere is more to why I came here. But dat is no one else's concern."

"Is she *that* powerful?" Röger asked. "Like, more than Lurcree was?"

Polly scoffed and gave the human a worried smile that seemed to say *"You have no idea, you fool."*

Hindin was still pacing and rubbing his temples. "Splendid," he sighed. "Then how much longer could we stay? The Chief Justice booked us three days at a new inn. He insists on finding a legal way to reward us. Three days. That is all I ask. If nothing happens after that, we can depart."

The three reluctantly agreed. Deep down, the city was starting to grow on the wild Will Foundling. Polly grew more paranoid with every hour. Röger had the most to lose: his life, if his secret was revealed.

Only Time would tell.

The Evening in Westpear was lit with a thousand lights. It was the main entertainment district of the city. The cool air was full of the sweet smells of exotic foods. There was live music booming on every block. The theatre houses erupted with laughter and tears. Groups of friends hopped from pub to tavern and bar to ale house. Couples walked hand in hand.

"It's a circus 'round here!" Will exclaimed. "Yer tellin' me it's like this every night? It's like a nonstop holiday or somethin'."

Rhowshell the belle laughed. "I keep forgetting this is your first time in a big city. This is just how people here wind down. Didn't you enjoy music and good food back home?"

"After a hard day o' plantin' or reapin', sure. But everybody'd bring their own food an' instruments. An' almost everybody knew each other. We call it a Shin Dig."

"Sounds painful," she smirked.

"It was only painful the next day after too much pepperwine."

"Oh!" She jumped like an excited teenager. "That reminds me! We were supposed to try some of that!"

Will rolled his eyes. "Good luck findin' the good stuff in this town."

"I think I know just the place!"

It was called The Bloody Plow, a genuine tendikeye owned and operated restaurant. It displayed a large sign depicting a winged tendikeye farmer using a farm plow to slay a great beast. As Will and his date walked in, he felt a strange *at-home-but-not-home* feeling. Parts of the interior resembled a tacky plantation house. Other parts looked like the inside of a new barn. It was a mixture of rich and poor aspects of his culture. Only the poor parts looked too pricey to be authentic. And the rich parts looked too cheap to be real. The customers consisted mainly of other tendikeye. But they were all dressed in the local garb and spoke with watered-down accents.

"Welcome! Welcome!" blasted the hostess. She was a fresh-faced woman with long sandy quills tied into a spiky bunch behind her head. Her matching wings were full and well groomed. "Dinner for two?" she asked politely.

"Ya got pepperwine?" Will asked.

"We certainly do! You won't find better in the whole city!"

"Then dinner fer two it is! Lead the way, ma'am!"

The hostess sat them down in a cozy booth lit with a single candle in a large mason jar. The tablecloth was a thin quilt with many colors and patterns. She made a gesture to a large bulletin sign on the wall. "This is our menu. I'm pleased to say that we are fully stocked, so order what you like. Shall I have your waitress bring two pepperwines when she comes?"

"Sure!" he answered, impressed with the friendly service. "An' have her bring a tall glass o' water fer the lady. Maybe two."

"I understand. sir," she answered with a wink. She then left the two alone.

The tendikeye and the drakeress smiled warmly at each other. She wore silver earrings that spiraled like sea shells and a strapless lavender dress that hugged her down to her knees. Around her neck was a silk collar that matched her black high heels. Will wore a white cotton long sleeved button down shirt in place of his green dust coat and t-shirt. Like his dust coat, the right flap of his collar was flared. His feather-adorned dog tags were out, dangling as he leaned on the table. He still wore his gun and sword. But the belt, sheathe, and holster were very well crafted, and gave his simple outfit a flare of panache.

"So, how is your new tooth?" she asked.

"Still kinda tender. Good thing boiled vegetables are easy to chew."

"Oh, are you a vegetarian?"

"Naw. I just don't eat meat that ain't *tuntrum*. That means wild and hunted. We Cloiherunians got reserves about eatin' domesticated animals."

"But this is a tendikeye restaurant. Maybe they...I don't know...serve *tuntrum* meat. Here, let's ask them before we order."

Will waved away the idea. "No need. Don't bother. Me an' Rev been walkin' Doflend roads for a while now. No tendikeye restaurant we've encountered serves it. An' I can't really blame 'em. Most of 'em don't own enough land to hunt on fer supplyin' an' what not. An' this bein' a city; it's a safe bet the meat here ain't legit. An' the last thing I wanna be is jerk an' give these people a hard time fer not havin' *tuntrum* cutlets."

Rhowshell did not know whether to frown at her date's lack of dietary options or smile at his personal convictions. "So you haven't eaten meat since leaving your homeland?"

232

Will grinned. "Naw, I hunt my own whenever I find a thick enough patch of woods. I tell ya; my innards have been itchin' fer some striped elm boar."

Nearby, a lone *ruan* player picked allegro in some minor key. It was a familiar tune to Will's ear, though he did not know its name.

"So, tell me more about this banquet tomorrow night," she playfully inquired.

"Well, me an' the crew've been stayin' at this inn the last two days. We were s'posed to leave town tomorrow. But we got this letter this mornin' from the Chief Justice. Said we were wanted to attend this Council Banquet. S'posed to be a real fancy affair it said. Well, at first, Röger thinks it might be a party thrown in our honor. I'm thinkin' it's just a friendly invite. Well, turns out ol' Chief Taly booked us a job working security fer the city's high society elite. That's our big reward fer takin' out the Mystic Mafia. But I can't complain. The pay from the job's gonna carry us awhile once we head out."

She smiled and nodded with a bittersweet understanding. "So, this is our first and last date, then? That's too bad. I don't suppose there's anything I can do to make you stay longer."

"Miss Rhow, I'm sure there's plenty o' things, yer smile bein' one of 'em. But some of my crew are itchin' to leave. We're a team now an', well, we gotta move as one unit, y'know?"

"Don't worry about it," she whispered, reaching for his hand. "I'm having a good time right now, and nothing's going to spoil it."

"I knew I recognized you!" yelled an approaching waitress carrying glasses of pepperwine and water. "You were on the front page yesterday! What was your name? No, don't tell me. Will Foundling!"

Other tendikeye in the restaurant, staff and customer alike, took notice. He had been the main topic of discussion all day yesterday. And now he was there with them! A crowd of a dozen regulars and workers surrounded the booth. They told him that it made them proud that one of their own as a local hero. A few of them even recognized him from the Red Dirt battle. He was bombarded with words of respect and praise. Even his drinks and dinner were comped by the manager. All the while, Rhowshell the belle sat patiently as the last of them finished chewing his ear.

"Sorry 'bout that," he told her.

"No worries," the belle replied. She raised her shot glass of pepperwine. "To you, Mr. Foundling. And your band of merry heroes."

The bukk laughed and clanged his glass against hers. In the space of a second, he gulped down the shot and slammed the glass upside down on the table. For a brief moment, his handsome face twisted and contorted into a monstrous visage of anguish and agony.

The belle looked down at her drink timidly. "What's in this?" she asked.

Will let out a loud exhale before answering. "Drink first. Then I'll tell ya."

She was too nervous now to shoot it fast. It took two gulps to get half of it down. The third gulp was an utter disaster. From the tip of her tongue to the bottom of her esophagus, a violent burning tingle buzzed in her throat and mouth. All her years of shooting vodka and whiskey could not have prepared her for suffering her first taste of pepperwine. It was immediate helplessness and panic. She tried to look over at her date, but her eyes blurred with the rush of tears. She tried to scream *Help me! Make it stop!* But her throat and tongue tensed with horrid coughing. The few swallows that made it to her stomach turned her digestive juices into a raging sea. She had no idea where the bathroom was, so she ran to the front door. But not three steps from the table, Will had already maneuvered in her way. He held up both glasses of water.

"Drink it slow!" he ordered. "It only gets worse if you puke it up!"

She grasped one of the glasses with both hands and started to drink. At first, the water did nothing. But after the second glass, she was able to calm down.

"It still hurts!" she cried.

Their waitress reacted quickly. "This is what she needs!" She handed the belle a huge mug of goat milk.

Slowly, the fury of the tendikeye liquor subsided. Will was able to get his date to sit back down and relax.

"Never again," she sighed gravely.

Will couldn't help but feel a little guilty. Still, he had to let out a chuckle. "What we do is take the raw juice of a pepper sprout, add in a few secret ingredients, then ferment and distill it. When it's done, it has all the old heat and spice with the added burn of grain alcohol."

"It was horrible!" she pouted. "I hate you!"

Will laughed and gave her a sly stare. "No you don't. C'mon, let's eat."

The dinner and conversation that followed was a mutual delight. Rhowshell discovered that the pepperwine enhanced the flavor of her food. They sat and talked until closing time. Afterward, they walked the streets and talked some more. They traded odd facts about each other's culture. But for the most part, Will let her do most of the talking. She was intelligent, open-minded, classy, and fun to be around. The sound of her voice was both relaxing and exciting at the same time. He knew that there were wonders and treasures about her that no man could find in just one night, or in his case; a life time. She was almost four times his age, but her mind and body suggested a girl slightly younger than himself, full of life and curiosity. They took the longest route back to her apartment building. There they kissed for a long time on stone steps that were full of fossilized seashells.

"I want you," she breathed, looking up at him. "But I don't know you. How can I want something I don't understand?"

"I reckon we want things we don't have *because* we don't understand'em. An' that's why some people stop wanting somethin' after they get it."

She wrapped her arms around the back of his neck. Her body was soft, warm, and strong. "So, as soon as I have you, I'll understand you better, and then I'll stop wanting you?" She had a playful gleam in her eyes.

He felt the small of her back with his large hands. His fingertips slid the material of her dress against the smooth curve of her indigo skin. The scent of her hair messed with his balance. "I think that things like this happen, not just 'cause we want to know people better. But, like, we try to figure ourselves out, too, you know?"

She pulled his head down and breathed in his quill-covered ear. "Come inside."

Whatever else happened that night is their business.

❖

The City Council of Embrenil consisted of three Primary members and eight Secondary members. The Primary members were the Grandmaster, who was the head spiritual, philosophical, and moral leader of the city, who attains their position by how their theurgy and wisdom have benefited the people. The Mayor is a publicly elected official who presides over the city Legislature. And the Chief Justice is the head of law enforcement and punishing the guilty. The first represents Morality, the second represents Law based upon that Morality, and the third represents Consequence based upon the Law based upon the Morality. The eight secondary members are the highest grossing business owners in the city. While they all acquired their positions in different ways, they still represent the people and their various livelihoods. In the event that the Legislature tries to pass a new law, the Secondary members have the power to veto it. That veto can only be overridden if all three Primary members vote in opposition of the Secondary members. In times of war or cataclysm, the three primary council members assume temporary total powers and rally forces to counter the threat. This Confederated Capitalist Democracy has been the system of government for the seven city-states of Doflend since the last dynasty of the old monarchy had been overthrown.

All this and more Hindin explained to his companions on their way to the City Hall building.

They were all dressed in their best attire, but that wasn't saying much. The few changes of clothes they all had were weather-worn and faded. None of Röger's shirts had sleeves. Hindin had only one outfit, and his one pair of pants were starting to fray. Will wore his button up shirt from the night before, but also his green dust coat. Polly cleaned up the best. She took a ratty old t-shirt, shredded it just right, and made a strapless top that complimented her new ruby brooch.

"Now, ain't that a sight!" Will said of the structure they were approaching. His cigarette bounced in his mouth as he spoke.

City Hall towered high above them like a mountain of stone and bone. It was formerly a palace for royalty, taller, grander, and older than any other structure in the city. The fossilized bones of a great winged dragon had been cut from a stone floor and reassembled brick by brick to form the building's main tower. The long dead beast seemed to spiral up through the brickwork. Its gargantuan wings hugged around the colossal stone cylinder. On the very top was a reconstructing area of some sort. There were massive white sheets and scaffolds hanging on ropes and pulleys. Reaching high into the night's darkness, it was hard telling what kind of work was being done up there.

"Hey, Polly! Look! It's your great grandpa!" Röger teased, pointing at the dragon.

"Dat is not funny," she replied, eying the tower with a measure of unease.

There was a line of sophisticates filing into the main entrance. Three malruka checked names and ushered people in. The hulking doormen wore matching suits of shimmering red silk, black velvet, and fine white lace. The four teammates walked straight up to the List-checker. Before any of them could spout a word, the well dressed brute raised an unpleasant expression. "If your name's on the list, get in line! The wait won't be long."

"We are fellow staff, sir," Hindin explained. "We are Four Winds-One Storm, the hired security for this evening."

The List-checker looked at them all as if the very sight of them was offensive. He had eyes of solid gold with many topaz stones incrusted to form sparkling irises. He used them to look down at Hindin. "A bit under-dressed for the festivities, aren't we, poor-forged? That weather-beaten jacket just won't do for tonight's gathering."

"I was under the impression that only shoes were required for our kind," Hindin replied with a stern voice.

"Ha! This is a more formal affair. But not to worry. We have a spare jacket you can put on. May be a bit big on you, though!"

It was at this point that Polly noticed that Hindin was only two thirds the height of most malruka, now that she was able to compare them. She had met a few malruka before Hindin when she lived in Chume. But when she first met him, he seemed as big as any.

The List-checker sent one of the ushers to fetch a jacket. He returned a minute later and helped Hindin put it on. He looked like a child playing dress-up in his father's clothes.

"There," Hindin sighed, a little embarrassed. "May we enter now?"

"Almost done," the List-checker answered. "Have the tendikeye approach."

Will stepped up to the ten-foot-tall walking boulder, unafraid with a too-cool-for-you look in his eyes.

The malruka reached out with a huge stone hand and pinched out the smoldering cigarette in Will's lips. "No smoking or drinking on the job. Also, do not start or end a conversation if you find yourself in one. There are important people in here. If they want to talk with you, let them. If not, keep your yaps in a trap, understood?"

Will took a step back and glared up at the List-checker. For a brief instant he forgot where he was, who he was with, and whoever else was watching. He only saw a potential enemy. His glare changed into a malicious smile. "What's yer name, dirt baby?"

"Who are you calling a dirt baby?!" the List-checker roared.

Hindin stepped in, stammering. "Will, that was very...very...it, was uncalled for!"

"But he called you poor-forged, Rcv!"

Hindin shook his head and pushed Will through the entrance. He spoke to the List-checker with a nervous laugh. "So sorry, sir! His pride is without armor!"

"Aw, c'mon, Rev! I call you dirt baby all the time and it dudn't bother you!"

"It is *Children of the Ground,* Will! You know that!"

Röger and Polly followed after them. She shook her head from embarrassment. Röger shook his head in disappointment. "No drinking?! I was hoping to get sloshed."

Nothing could have prepared them for what came at the end of the corridor.

All at once, their senses were dazzled by the grandeur and spectacle of the immense ballroom. Dozens of tables were draped in white and crowned with shining cutlery and round disks of porcelain. Hundreds of Drakeri were dressed in the finest garb money could buy. Waiters and waitresses served various meals that caught the eye and seduced the nose. A sixteen piece ensemble was sending an elegant melody through the ears and hearts of the young and old. On a stage, overseeing the vast enclosure, sat and dined the Primary and Secondary Council members.

A regal Drakeri man armed with two pistols and well-trimmed muttonchops approached them. "Four Winds-One Storm, I presume?"

"We are, sir," Hindin answered, bowing formally.

"You are early. That's good. I am Marshall Stake, head of security for the night. We are pleased to have you all. Do you have any questions before I place you in your areas?"

"Yeah," Will answered. "Is Marshall yer first name or is it a title?"

"It is a title, Mr. Foundling. My first name is James. I'm what you call a Reserve Commander." He looked down at Will's gun and his face lit up. "So, that's the Mark Twain Special I've been hearing about. I've never actually seen one up close. Tell me: Did a tendikeye named Mark Twain invent it?"

"Nossir. No one knows who originally designed it since it was meant fer secret scouting agents. They had to keep it secret so enemies couldn't make their own. It's called a Mark Twain simply 'cause it hits two marks at the same time."

"Impressive," the man nodded. "I'll have to tell you about my guns later."

"You won't really have to, Marshall. What you got there are two Sulaire P10s. A tried and true gun, I must say. Are those tortoise shell hand grips you got on 'em?"

"Why, yes they are!" the man replied, astonished.

Will tilted his head as he looked at them. "Let me guess: *Indigelli Donetellis,* the North-Eastern Flatbox Turtle, am I right?"

The man looked down at his guns. "Um, I honestly couldn't tell you. I bought them off a local merchant."

"Oh," Will shrugged and hesitated. "Well, they're real nice, sir."

For an instant the Marshall's eyes reflected a humbled amazement. Then his expression changed into a face of playful challenge. "All right, young man. But can you guess what ammunition I've loaded?"

"There's only one way to find out without lookin' inside," Will joked. "But if I had to guess, I'd say they're fulla them petra rounds the cops use."

The man let out a light laugh and gave the tendikeye a pat on the shoulder. "I'm no cop. C'mon, let's put you all in position."

There were eight pillars that held up the distant ceiling of the room. The four teammates were each placed at one of them, far apart from each other. They were instructed to keep watch from all sides of their pillars. They were asked to be courteous, polite, and reasonably helpful. The teammates could see other security guards standing at the remaining pillars. Like Marshall Stake, they each wore a matching pair of pistols. Each one of them looked bored out of their minds, as if they had done this a hundred times before. It was expected to be a very tame night.

The sound of a silver spoon pinging against a crystal wineglass rang throughout the crowded hall. Some theurgical working carried the sound to everyone's ear. Conversations stopped, seats were taken, and eating utensils were licked clean and placed down. All eyes were aimed at a man standing in front of the Council's table. He ceased the mystical chiming and spoke in a clear, strong voice. "Sons and Daughters of Doflend. The Council will now address you. I present to you first our most beloved teacher, the Supreme High Theurge of Embrenil, Grandmaster GoLightly."

As the announcer took his leave, all eyes shifted to a man standing up from the table. He was a well preserved handsome old man with dark green irises and long dark hair. A well trimmed mustache curved with his capricious happy smile. He greeted the applauding crowd with a flamboyant bow. They loved him, and that love was reflected.

"Thank you, friends." His voice was nasally, yet warm and lively. "Another year has passed since our last gathering. Little has changed, yet our way of life is preserved. Let this remind us that while little has been gained, there is still much we can lose. My mentor's mentor was there when the decadent tyranny of the old empire collapsed under the weight of revolution. We have not forgotten the things that our ancestors fought for: Equality, Freedom, and the right to pursue life affirming goals.

Let us not forget that not all parts of the world know such peace. We must not only be glad for our fortune- but understand it, as well. For when the good things in life are understood, they are easier to grasp and maintain. Bless you all and enjoy this bountiful evening."

The people applauded with reverence and admiration.

"I wonder what his philocreed path is," Polly thought.

As the Grandmaster sat, the Mayor Roi Krouslin stood. He was a tall bearded man with short white hair and a deep hollow voice.

"Thank you, Grandmaster, for those encouraging words."

"My fellow citizens, I am pleased to announce that the construction of the building's new clock tower will be completed on schedule. The generous contributions of four of our Secondary Council members have enabled us to build the structure without drawing from our city treasury. Tonight I wish to honor these four chairpersons. Thim Growno of the Naveh Steel Firm, Elai NcRay of the NcRay Brewery, Maymee Ritcherdcin of the Mason's Union, and Loary Lechkanton of the Embrenil Railway Company."

As the Mayor spoke each name, the four council members rose from their seats. The crowd clapped politely as they smiled and waved.

The Mayor then began to wrap up his speech. "There is still, however some debate on what the clock will be called. Maybe I'll let these four fight it out."

The audience let out a chuckle. Röger sighed from boredom and mild disgust. He hated big wigs.

"I will now hand you over to the Chief Justice," the Mayor ended, taking his seat.

As Chief Taly stood, he did not receive the same response as the first two. Everyone seemed to applaud out a forced respect or cautious politeness. Faces were lax and neutral. Will swore that some of them looked like poker faces.

"Thank you, Mister Mayor. As many of you all know, two high ranking officers under my command were recently discovered to be part of a criminal conspiracy. To make matters worse, I was the one responsible for assigning these officer's to investigate the very case that they were criminally involved with. And even though the threat they posed has been neutralized, the E.C.P.D. has been marked with disgrace. And it is for this...failure that I will be resigning my position as Chief Justice."

A wave of shock went throughout crowd. Voices began to whisper and murmur.

The Chief continued in a steady voice. "This city deserves a reliable police department. They need a Chief Justice who is not only true to his word, but dependable. Without the trust of the people I cannot continue.

But," he continued. "if it were not for four brave young individuals who put the city's needs before their own, the threat would still be alive and well. Corruption would continue to thrive. These outsiders were able to sniff out the corruption that had been right under my nose. Furthermore, they helped bring the case to an end by using unconventional methods that I never would have let my officers use. It is clearly time to hand the reigns of justice to the younger generation. I will not be appointing a replacement. I will let the civic officers elect a new leader."

He looked around and gave a tweak to his mustache.

"Before I sit back down and finish my plate, there is one last act as Chief Justice I wish to perform. Would the team of heroes known as Four Winds-One storm please approach?"

The four Excursionists were startled by the request. As they walked toward the stage, they felt the many eyes of the crowd follow them. Polly absolutely hated the attention. Will and Hindin were speechless and suspicious. *"He's callin' it quits over this?"* Will thought. As they reached the stage they were made to face the crowd.

The Chief spoke. "My fellow Drakeri, you may have read about these people in the Gazette. You may recall that they started out as minor law-breakers. Well, let it be known henceforth that I am extending their Permit of Criminal Investigation and Apprehension to Lifetime status. As long as they draw breath, they will have full rights to assist the law in any case in the Seven Cities of Doflend. It is my privilege to present them with this honor. We the people of Embrenil are in their debt."

He reached into his suit pocket and pulled out a rolled up piece of paper tied with a black velvet band. As he handed it to an astonished Hindin, the crowd stood and applauded.

The four teammates were caught between a wave of cheers and the nagging question of why the Chief gave up so easily. In the short time they knew him; he seemed an immovable figure, a man fully committed to what he stood for. On the other hand, the sudden show of approval and praise from so many made them swell with a great yet humble pride.

"If anyone can keep me alive, they can," someone thought nearby.

◈

Elai NcRay was the youngest and least experienced member of the Secondary Council, but a member nonetheless. Only two years after his father bequeathed him the family-owned brewery, he was able to generate just enough revenue to qualify for a Council seat. Now a decade later, his business has overtaken half of its competitors as his political agendas help sway the way the city is run. He was young, yet distinguished. He stood and smiled as if he were always posing for a family photograph. He preferred to remain aloof in mixed company. But he had a certain charm that made his opinions catch and spread like wildfire. But all these attributes would not help him when the time came.

He watched the four heroes return to their positions. After the Chief Justice spoke, they were each swarmed by other well-dressed aristocrats. NcRay waited nearly half an hour before he saw that one of them was alone. It was the girl, Polly Gone.

"She's pretty. And very powerful, too, from what I've heard," he thought as he approached her. *"But she's just a child! I must remain calm and approach her without appearing nervous. Her body language suggests a withdrawn demeanor. She's clearly not the leader, too young, too cold. But I have no choice. It's a matter of life and..."*

"May I help you wit' something?" she asked the approaching man.

"I believe you can, Ms. Gone. My name is Elai NcRay, Council Member and owner of the NcRay Brewery. I have a business proposal for you and your associates."

She squinted up at him. "Is dat so? What kind of proposal?"

"For a discrete service, Ms. Gone. One that I cannot speak of here. I need to discuss it with all of you alone, if it is possible. Please, tell me that it's possible."

She hesitated, not knowing what to say. His eyes were too piercing, unreadable. There was something perplexing about them.

243

"What makes us so worthy of dis dire task?" She made sure she sounded very sarcastic.

"It is a...an unusual problem. Something that police or common bodyguards could not handle properly."

"Are you in some kind of trouble?"

A melodious tune started up from the orchestra. Elai appeared to become distracted.

"Dance with me. Stay close to me, and I will explain it to you."

"No," she answered harshly.

"Why? Don't you like the music?" His smile brightened. It was a well practiced smile.

"No. De piano player here is awful. Dat and I don't want to."

"Very well," he replied cheerfully. "Win some, lose some. But you could have said that you couldn't because you were on duty. You might have spared my feelings." He bowed respectfully, before turning to walk away. "Please, consider my offer. You just might be saving a life." He turned and hurried his way to the tendikeye, not waiting to see Polly's last reaction. He had planted one seed. On to the next.

His thoughts stirred again. *"Look at that. He's schmoozing with the good Chief Justice. No, not schmoozing. It's a serious discussion. The tendikeye looks frustrated, or is that his constant attitude? It wouldn't surprise me, either way."*

"Chief Justice!" NcRay cried out with open arms. "I was saddened to hear the news. You could have simply retired to save face. Resignation does not become you."

Taly frowned irritably. "I have explained my reasons, Councilman. You and everyone else will have to accept them," he cast a knowing eye at Will as he finished talking.

The Secondary Councilman grinned. "I'm sure that when I reach your age, I will be able to understand your wisdom. But until then, I will find no solace in your departure." Elai's words poured out like boiling honey.

Will could see that the Chief had no love for the man. There seemed to be a longstanding dislike between the two. And it was more than just political.

The Chief turned to Will. "Remember what I said." He gave Elai a nod. "Enjoy your evening, Councilman." He left the two of them alone.

NcRay smiled as Taly walked away. "He's an admirable man, despite our differences."

"What differences might those be?" Will asked.

"Different philocreeds, mostly. He is a moral and just man who could get nothing done. And I am a selfish rakish man who gets everything done. It's really not fair; to be more efficient than a man who is your better. Sad. Very sad."

Will raised an eyebrow. "What do you want, Mister...NcRay, right? Yer the one who runs the beer factory, if I'm not mistaken."

"You aren't, Mr. Foundling. I require the talents of you and your comrades for a short while. It is nothing illegal. But I must ask that we keep it confidential from start to finish."

"When does it start?"

"Right now. In fact, if you tell anyone of this offer, the deal is off. It is a very private matter that requires discreet rectification."

"Is that so?" Will replied as if he understood that last word. "Legal, but secret, eh? I gotta hear this."

"Then bring your team to my Brewery tomorrow morning at 2 o'clock. If anyone asks you why you went there, say it was to take a complementary tour. You'll get a free case of our premium select beer whether you take the job or not. This is all the time I can spend with you for now. So, please consider it."

"We'll see," the tendikeye replied.

Elai gave a respectful bow to the wary-eyed bukk. As he did, his eyes caught the sight of Will's pistol and sword. A chill flowed up the Councilman's spine. He then arose and walked away. *"He is a good judge of character,"* NcRay thought while trying not to tremble. *"But it appears to be more intuitive than trained. Just to be safe, I will not waste my façade of righteousness on him. He is no sucker for charm. He has enough of his own to know how it can work. He will grow to detest me, but at least he will feel he understands me."*

Next was Röger. He was surrounded by three elegant, slightly tipsy debutantes.

"Ah, a fellow ladies man," he thought with a grin. *"The role of the teddy bear-bad-boy seems to work on these boozy floozies. My, my. He could have his pick tonight. Out of respect for this well-rehearsed womanizer, I will be brief."* He approached with his head respectfully lowered.

245

"Sir Röger, I do not mean to interrupt you, but..."

"You're the beer man!" Röger clapped his hands together with a sudden sparkle in his eyes. The sound of the clap caused Elai's spine to stiffen for a fleeting instant.

"It is an honor to meet you, sir! Your beer is the best in town!" Röger proclaimed.

"Thanks. We try our best to please. Say, how about you and your team come to the brewery tomorrow. I'll give you a tour, show you around the place. Nothing too formal, just hanging out."

"Will there be free beer?"

"Of course. But try to bring everyone, yes?"

"Polly isn't old enough to drink, though," Röger warned.

"Don't worry. I don't supply minors."

"She's not a minor," the brute replied with a randy tone. "She's eighteen."

"Oh? Is she taken or available?"

"Neither, pal. I've already called dibbs."

The two men laughed as the three debutantes scattered.

"Elai NcRay," the Councilman said, putting out his hand.

The human gripped the smooth purple hand and gave it a hardy shake. "Sir Röger Yamus, at your service."

"That is what I'm hoping for; your service."

"Huh?"

"Your friends will explain it to you later. I must go now. Please, enjoy this fantastic night." Before Röger could squeeze out another word, Elai was already seven paces away.

That was easy, he thought. *I like him best so far. Round-ears are so self absorbed. That's probably why we get along so well. Now for the malruka, Hindin Revetz. Funny. His name means Lava Stirrer in Malrukan. Hmm. He who stirs lava.*

When Elai reached Hindin, he saw that the malruka was already engaged in conversation with two professors from Embrenil College. For a long while, he overheard them talk about the murdered student, Davil Pert. It turned out he had attended one of the professor's classes. For some time, the three of them talked about any and every subject that would come up. And as they did, NcRay was learning.

"Astounding is the heart and brain of this man of iron and stone! His mind is a sponge, soaking up anything and

246

everything. He is moral and honorable, yet I do not detect the judgmental nature that often dampens such resolute character. Surely, he could understand the situation. He would not leave me to die the death that some might think I deserve. He has the heart of a child and the mind of a scholar. Incorruptible. I will keep it all the simpler."

He stepped between the two professors to shake Hindin's hand, beaming with respect and admiration. "Congratulations on your Permit License, Mr. Revetz. I hope you will feel more free to act when others are in need of you."

"Thank you, Councilman," Hindin happily returned.

With that; the fourth seed was planted. Elai NcRay bowed and left the party.

It was impossible to find a taxi-cart when the party was over. It was well after midnight. The team's legs were tired from standing and their bellies were full from all the leftover food. It had been a successful night. There was a little extra jingle in their pockets and most of the people at the banquet had been very kind. But with the unexpected departure of their former benefactor and the emergence of a mysterious possible new one, it would be a long walk and talk to the inn that night.

"I think Chief Taly was forced out of the job," Röger shared as they walked the dim-lit streets. "There must have been someone, maybe more than one, who wanted him to step down."

"It certainly does not sit well with me," Hindin admitted.

"It's gut snake's what it is!" Will added. "I saw it in his face. He ain't quittin' 'cause he wants to or he think's he's gotta. Somethin's up."

"Maybe we don't understand him as well as we tink," Polly offered. "He might very well have his own reasons. He does not strike me as de type who ends tings so easily."

"He ended the Lurcree case too easily," Hindin muttered.

"What about that NcRay feller?" Will asked, wanting to change the subject. "He basically offered us a job."

"We can't," Polly protested. "I must keep moving to escape my mother."

"But maybe it's important."

247

"Or maybe you're just hoping to get another tooth knocked out," she teased.

Will jolted, not believing what he just heard. But Röger spoke up before he could reply. "I agree with Polly that we should go. But I also think we should at least hear the man out. He *did* offer us a case of free b---!"

Röger could no longer talk. A large knife appeared sticking in his throat.

"Gut snake!" Will yelled angrily. He looked into the darkness, searching for the threat.

The human fell onto his back, wheezing and clutching at the blade's handle.

Polly immediately knelt beside him. "No, Röger, don't pull it out! Let me do it!"

But he did. And a spring of blood shot into the air. The wounded man clutched his neck, gagging and coughing.

The memory of Davil Pert dying flashed in Polly's mind. "Röger, move your hands! I can heal it!"

Will had his gun and sword out and stood in front of them. Hindin stood at his side. "Show yerself, assassin!" the tendikeye yelled.

The sound of light footsteps and blades hissing through the air was the only reply.

Will spun around with surprising inertia as three more blades grazed off the scales of his dust coat. The knives clanged against the pavement. "You throw like a girl, assassin!"

A lithe shape stepped out from the shadows. It was a human woman in a tight black leather suit with a matching purse. Her long blonde hair was done up with two pointed metal sticks. Her entire outfit was covered with projectile daggers. In her right hand was a short sword with a blade shaped like a holly leaf. In her left hand was another throwing knife. Her fine face was distorted from her crazed mouth and eyes. Eyes that were wide open, unblinking, and as steady as a rock.

"Run away," she offered in a sleepy raspy voice. "We needn't kill all of you."

Will already had his pistol trained on her. "Whatchaya mean 'we'?"

"I mean he and me make we." She laughed and took a fencer's stance. "The late Lurcree Katlemay really had it in for you. So, he hired us to help you die. He sent us half the money up

248

front. The other half would have been paid when the job was finished. No such luck. He grew impatient waiting for us and challenged you outright, the fool. That's why you should always leave a serious job like this to professionals! Oh well. We have half the money, so half of you must die. Any volunteers?"

Röger's blood spilled through his fingers onto the ground.

"Move your hands!" Polly yelled.

She slipped her small hand under his meaty mitts. The blood flowed like warm milk against her palm. She felt the wet slit in his thick neck and began to chant. *"Good healing always tastes bitter!"* The slit mended as the spilt blood flowed back in it. He was healed, but still gagging and gasping.

The female assassin threw her knife as she dashed for Will. Without blinking, he deflected the projectile and steadied his aim. Before she was thirty paces away, he fired his first pair of rounds into her throat and heart. As she fell, he rotated his wrist and put two more bullets through her lungs. She landed still and lifeless on the cobblestone street. Will Foundling preferred to match blades to blades and bullets to bullets. But he didn't shunt around when it came to assassins.

"She said there was another!" Hindin shouted. His emerald eyes surveyed the location. Rather than look for someone he thought of how a *follow-up killer* might attack in their situation.

Suddenly, Will dropped his gun and gasped through clenched teeth. "What the...?!"

Hindin saw though the darkness that Will's wrist was bleeding. "What just happened?" he asked.

Will did not answer. His eyes barely caught something hopping around close by. It was very small and fast. The thin glint of blue metal was all he could make out from the dashing blur.

"It's some kinda little man!" Will yelled. The blur flew past him, opening another gash on his thigh. He leapt high into the air, trying to get a better view of the threat. Right beneath him he could see it jumping up. It resembled a Drakeri infant only half a foot tall. It was garbed in loose black silk and held a small curved blade in both its tiny hands.

Will still had his sword. He aimed its point directly in the path of the tiny assassin.

The tiny thing slapped the side of it's blade against the point of Will's weapon, deflecting itself from the path of danger. The assassin and hero landed back on the sidewalk, not seven strides apart. The tiny thing now stood as still as a stone, no longer hiding.

It began to rain.

As Polly helped Röger up to his feet, Hindin and Will stood in disbelief of what they were facing.

"Is that a...a...?" Hindin could not get the word out.

"Fetus," Will uttered with trembling eyes. "Some sick witch of a theurge animated an unborn! It's a *post mort!*"

"Be careful how you speak of my lord!" the fetus warned in a raspy whisper.

As the four of them looked down in shock at the unliving atrocity, the female assassin that Will had fired upon reached into her purse. She pulled out a steel ball covered in spiky protrusions. Using her thumb, she clicked a small button on it.

Will's ears twitched at the sound of the click. He turned to see her rise to her feet, ready to throw what she had. "She's one, too! She's got a hand mine!"

The woman grinned and tossed it at them.

Immediately, Will dropped his sword and dive-tackled Röger and Polly. As the three of them crashed onto the ground, Hindin stepped between them and the flying projectile. He planted his feet just before it hit his chest. Lying on the ground the three flesh and blood heroes watched as their friend was engulfed in a bright, deafening explosion. The wind and the rain grew stronger. Lightning and thunder filled the atmosphere above them. The smoke cleared and Hindin still stood. They watched, frozen in fear as his knees started to buckle.

"Rev!" Will called out.

But there was no answer. Hindin's torso was caved inward. His green crystal eyes stared blankly as he fell face forward. The sidewalk crumbled beneath him.

"Now, Shiver!" the fetus ordered.

"Right!" the woman answered.

The two assassins rushed in with their blades.

Will sprang up to get his sword, his eyes blazing with rage.

Röger stood up and drew both of his large weapons as if they were each meant for one hand. His muscles expanded and

250

sprouted fur. He screamed though his helm in a monstrous growl. "Die a second death!" he screamed.

As Will reached down for his sword, the assassin called Shiver could have stabbed his wrist. But that would have left her open to Röger's massive blades. Instead, she cut her charge short, letting the tendikeye pick up his toy. She now had two very differently skilled warriors to deal with. *"No worries,"* she thought.

Polly could see the blade wielding fetus darting at her. She had never seen any thing so horrifically adorable or hideously cute before. And it aimed to kill her. Without thinking, she shrieked and pulled her knife. "Get away from me!" she screamed, throwing her only weapon in a panic.

The miniature assassin leapt just inches to the side, twisting like a corkscrew. The knife passed by, blunting its tip on the stone ground. After a hop, skip, and a very fast jump, the fetus landed on her shoulder and cleaved into its target!

Polly felt the side of her neck open up like a toothless mouth. Her eyes flashed red and the wound closed, becoming nothing more than a thin red line. Still on her shoulder, the assassin grabbed a lock of her hair in one hand. Holding the small, long handled sword like a javelin, he readied a thrust for her temple.

"Try healing a pierced brain!" it whispered.

But Polly's hands were already moving. She grasped the mummified fetus, sword and all. The thin blade cut into her palm, but she didn't care. She had it!

Will and Röger used very different weapons in very different ways. They were not used to fighting side by side so closely in such a way. Neither one could really cut loose without worrying what the other man might do. The assassin called Shiver took full advantage of this. She fought with a defensive grace that was tough to outwit. It was as if she had limitless flexibility, dodging and parrying in bizarre, uncanny ways, like her every joint could move in any direction. And it did not help that the enraged Will and Röger still knew so little about each other's attack methods. They were more in each other's way than helping each other.

Shiver finally solved the pattern in their strikes. Now was the time to fight back. Faster than a blink, she arched her back as if about to do a back flip, but her feet stayed planted. Her lower

251

back bent so far that it touched her tight round ass. For a fraction of an instant, she was completely bent in half the wrong way. Her head and arms scooped up from between her legs. With sword in hand, she jabbed its serrated point straight into Röger's groin, then flipped away as he screamed. Will swung his sword in a fast upward arch, missing her by a hair's breath. Shiver drew another knife with her free hand. She sprung in, aiming her holly leaf sword at Will's heart. He instinctively turned his body, letting the weapon pass within inches of his chest. But as he did, Shiver jabbed upward with the knife into his ribs. Will writhed from the pain, his face just inches away from hers. At first she smiled with an *I gotcha* look on her face. Then she sensed that something was wrong. The tendikeye was still angry, but in a different way; colder, more focused. She jumped back, avoiding a decapitating strike. She looked down at her dagger. It had only the tiniest bit of blood in the tip. Her sword looked about the same. She looked back up at the two warriors. Their wounds had hardly affected them.

Röger was growing bigger now. His large axe and sword began to look small. His neck was all but healed, and his crotch only stung a bit. But his rage flourished as he changed form, sprouting striped fur that rose on his back like a pissed off cat.

"Lycanthrope!" Shiver gasped. "Chepsu! We must retreat! Lurcree said nothing of this in the letter!"

"Right!" the fetus called back. He looked at Polly, who still held him tight with both hands. "Farewell, Red Witch." He let go of his sword and grappled her thumb. He was small and, therefore, weak. But he could out-wrestle a hand or two. He twisted the digit fast and hard, snapping it like a neck. Polly yelped as he slipped out and landed on the ground. He darted toward his partner. He scurried up the lycanthrope's massive back and leapt off the top of his helmet, landing into Shiver's open purse. He poked his head out like he was an aristocrat's tiny pet dog. "I'm ready!" he shouted.

The female assassin yelled at the three heroes "We can keep dancing or you can check on your friend! He might still be alive!" Then she dashed away into the night.

"I can catch her!" Röger roared.

"Rög! No!" Will yelled. "We gotta get Rev some help! See if you can roll him over!"

252

The beast looked back and forth at his two choices, the rage clouding his reason.

"Röger! You need to calm down!" Polly urged, holding her thumb. "Hindin needs us!"

The beast looked around and thought *"People will come soon. I have to change back!"* He went over to Hindin and gently rolled him over. Lightning cracked and flashed high above them. As it lit the area for a brief moment, they could see Hindin's eyes blink ever so slowly, catching the cold rain.

Chapter 8
The Proposition of Elai NcRay

Malruka did not heal naturally. Occasionally, they need repairs. Most practiced good hygiene, such as rust removal and eye shining. But when serious injuries occurred, a specialist was needed.

Doctor Toney was a full-sized malruka, eleven feet tall and weighing nearly three tons. The kind of work he did required a vast amount of strength, and he had plenty to spare. He was broad of shoulder with brass skin and a face like a peaceful lion. Dark onyx eyes looked out thoughtfully over his wide featured face. He had long lengths of thick chain for hair tied back tight behind his huge head in a jingling ponytail.

It was very late when he heard the loud knock on his door, long past business hours. One of his own kind had been loaded into a bileer pulled taxi-wagon and sped to his shop. A few of the bomb victim's friends stood outside the door, dripping with rain and pleading for help. He picked up the wounded malruka and carried him inside. For the rest of the night, he made them wait in the lobby as he toiled away on his patient behind closed doors.

Polly shivered and rocked back and forth. Her nibbling teeth tore away at her nails. She was thinking about the long trip it took to get here. For half the length of the city, she sat by her wounded friend. He was incoherent for most of the trip. It terrified her to see him so feeble and negated.

Röger had seen it before. He knew that a malruka's mind wasn't just in their head. It was in their entire body. The better built they were, the more intelligent. But if they lost a limb or had their chest caved in by a hand grenade, they were lucky to remember their own name.

As for Will, the worry for his partner of the last few months tormented his heart while the slits in his wrist and leg throbbed like cannons in the distance. A thin sliver of razor-edged metal had succeeded where other blades had failed. For the first time in his life, he was cut bad enough to need stitches. He refused Polly's offer to heal them mystically. He had let the cold rain cleanse his wounds as he ran, looking for a taxi. When a taxi was found and Hindin was loaded up, he tore the sleeves off his nice white shirt and bound his injuries. Now, in that cold waiting room, those white rags were soaked in red.

Polly could see the anguish in his face. In a way, she felt glad that she wasn't so close to Hindin, that she didn't know him that long. She got up and walked over to the distraught bukk. He hardly noticed her as he leaned against a plaster wall. She reached up and touched his face tenderly, platonically, methodically.

"Good healing always tastes bitter," she said, gazing into his eyes.

"What's that mean?" But Will wised up fast as he felt the throbbing cuts tingle and close shut. He made a face of disapproval, but before he could get a word out, she backed away and looked at him coldly.

"I never asked for your help either!" she hissed. "I would heal Hindin, too, if I could! But dat is not possible. So, I heal you for your own good. If you don't want it, den tough! Be more careful in de future!"

Will wanted to argue, but fatigue and worry had worked its way through him. He had little inclination to defend his creed. "Let me see that blade, the one the fetus used on me" he demanded. "You still have it, right?"

"I gave it to Röger," she said.

Will turned his head. He saw the big man sitting grimly on a stone bench. His silver covered head hung low in shadow. His hands were clasped between his knees. "You don't wanna see it, Will," he warned.

"Why not?"

Röger only shook his head. He reached into his leather vest and pulled out the miniature sword. It was a variation of a nagamaki with a four inch handle and four inch blade. If it were full size, it would have rivaled Röger's billblade in cutting power. He handed it grudgingly to Will.

The bukk's eyes widened as they beheld the blue sheen of the polished blade. It was not a mystical glowing hue or a light-within type of color, but it was *metallic blue*. "Charm-cutter steel.

256

Cobalt some call it," he whispered as if telling a dark secret. His body trembled and his eyes welled up with tears of rage and disgust. He dashed to the entrance door, yanked it open, and wretched his dinner onto the rain drenched sidewalk.

Röger shot up to his feet. "Don't jump to conclusions, man!"

"It all makes sense now!" Will thought as he wiped his mouth. "I don't wanna talk about it! Not now!"

"Let me see de blade," Polly said, putting out her hand to Will. He gave it without hesitation. She paced around the room, examining it. "It isn't supernaturally sharp. I'd feel an invisible edge on it. And the assassin who used it wasn't very strong."

"It was able to break your thumb," Röger disputed.

"It was only dislocated. I popped it back on de way here. No, de blade is special, maybe?" Her eyes glowed bright red. "Or maybe not. It is just a blue metal, from what I see."

Will screamed and kicked the frame of the doorway. "It...happens to be...the most coveted an' sought after substance in Cloiherune next to the iron it's mixed in with, 'though it can only be mined in the Great bowl itself, Ses Lemuert. There walks, crawls, flies, and swims the enemies of my people."

"My people, too," Röger added.

"Yeah, but we're the ones who hafta deal with' em. Anyway, the best way to put a quick hurt on these monsters is *cobalt-steel* from their own Huncell. It ain't mystical, but it works the same way silver does on lycanthropes like Röger. It's a charm breaker, or charm cutter dependin' on the weapon. I heard tell that every major monster has a weakness to particular types of metal or substances mixed with steel. That blade right there was made to kill Lemuertians."

Polly's face was as concerned as it was curious. "I have read about dese beings, seen illustrations. Dey rule de realm from which de Sizzagafiend was taken. If dis metal is meant to cut through deir preternatural hides, den how would it hurt yours as well?"

Will stared at her as if every hope he ever clung to was lost to him. "It also works on their half breeds, Polly."

The large steel door to the Doctor's workshop/emergency room opened. Doctor Toney walked out, rattling their teeth with every step. "He's alive, but out cold," he said. "But they messed him up pr'ee bad. Ya'll told th' police?"

257

They shook their heads.

"Ya'll unt to or don't, makes no diff'n'ce to me. Business i' business, here in Emby, same as anywhere else."

"We have money," Will offered, forgetting his own problem.

"You goan need it, Buh. 'Cos I'm goan need it to fix'im. He needs a new chest. The steel skin plate is shot t' hell. The granite underneeth been busted t' gravel. All kinds o' *gold* wires and cords goan all through him. 'Lot of tedious fixin' that's goan be. Replacin' that *gold* is what's goan hurt yuh wallits, though."

"How much?" Röger asked warily.

" I'll make enough jus' bein' honest. 8,000 to get him tip-top."

"8,000 grotz!!!" Röger exclaimed. "We don't even have half that!"

The Doctor hung his massive head and shook it. "Shame. It'll take 'least half that much to pay for the *gold*. He had at leas' fourteen yards of it destroyed. Add a week of solid work, an' there you go."

Röger and Will looked at each other, both waiting for the other man to cough up a solution. Instead, Polly spoke up.

"Elai NcRay," she muttered bitterly. "How much longer will this city keep us?" she wondered out loud.

When day broke, Röger, Will, and Polly made their way across the city on foot. They were still damp from the rain the night before. They had slept with little comfort in the Body Shoppe lobby. On their way to the NcRay Brewery, the Police Station came into view.

"Think we outta fill out a report about yesternight?" Will asked.

"No," both Polly and Röger answered.

He was shocked by their reply. "Why not? Rev would want us to."

"I'm tired of dealing wit' dem," Polly answered. "Besides, I need to get out of dis city as soon as possible. De sooner we can help Hindin and leave, de better."

Will's eyes shifted to the Black Vest. "An' you, Rög?"

The tall brute hung his head so the shadow of his helm hid his eyes. "What are we going to tell them, Will? That we were attacked and the assassins didn't run away until I let the beast out? I doubt that the ECPD would be tolerant of a werekrilp in their midst. And you should know by now that the only reason they put up with a Crimson Theurge is because of Chief Taly being extremely lenient with her. And now he's out of the picture."

"So, we'll leave some things out," Will offered. "Just like when we took out that Master Pyrotheurge."

Röger shook his head. Polly looked away.

Will began to lose patience. "We are bein' hunted fer cryin' out loud! A couple of post-mort assassins are out to get us! The cops should at least be made aware of it."

Röger stopped and raised his head. "Should they? Would you honestly feel more at ease if that cop-shop got involved?"

Will hesitated. "I don't know. But our belongings are still at the police station house. We didn't get around to picking them up yesternight on account o' bein' ambushed. I figure while we're there we could at least..."

Röger raised his hand, interrupting Will. "I'll go," he said in a stern tone. He let out a weary sigh and scratched his neck. "I'll pick our things up. And if it'll make you happy; I'll fill out a report. It would be better if only one of us did. They might find inconsistencies in our stories. I'll keep it nice and simple."

"Thanks, Röger," Will said. "Yer a real pal."

Röger raised his index finger. "But let me go on record by saying: *If* those assassins weren't scared off for good, or *if* they decide to try us out again, it would be better that we destroy them outright without the police's help. Those two post-morts know my secret. Are we all understood?"

Will and Polly nodded.

"Don't forget my little red suitcase," Polly said with a hint of a smile. "I just bought it."

Röger chuckled. "No problem. I'll meet you all back at the Body Shoppe then."

When Röger arrived at the station house he found it in a state of chaos. Anywhere and everywhere, officers of various rank carried boxes of papers, arguing with each other, wandering around, and looking various shades of confused. He looked around for a moment until he saw someone he somewhat recognized.

"Officer, uh, Ladue! Officer Ladue!"

The young policeman turned. "Mister Yamus? Where are the others? We have all your things ready to go."

Röger approached the man close enough to whisper. "What's going on in this place? Why is everyone so on-edge?"

"It's because of Chief Taly's sudden departure. He didn't appoint a replacement before he stepped down. And he's been the Chief Justice for so long that we all are having trouble seeing who the new Chief Justice should be. A lot of sides are being taken. It's a political mess, if you ask me."

Röger nodded in understanding. He leaned in closer, still whispering. "Officer Ladue, is there any way I could fill out a report? We were attacked yesternight by assassins."

"Attacked? Is everyone okay?"

"That's a good question that I can't answer just yet. Is there any way I could just fill out the report, collect our belongings, and leave without drawing too much attention?"

"Certainly," came another man's voice from behind them.

Slightly startled, they turned around. There stood Leal NcRuse the Coroner.

"I would be more than happy to take Sir Yamus' report," the Necrotheurge grinned.

Officer Ladue showed immediate discomfort from the man's presence. "You, Coroner?" he stammered. "You, um, aren't too busy?"

The Coroner shook his head. "No. All my slabs are empty for the present time." His sleepy eyes shifted to Röger. "And even if they were all full, I don't think the cadavers would get up and leave."

"Unless you told them to," Röger scoffed with wary eyes.

The Necrotheurge did not respond. He merely gestured with his arm politely. "Please, follow me. There is an empty office we can use."

Röger gave Officer Ladue a friendly, yet rather hard, pat on the back as a way of saying thanks. He then followed the gangly Coroner down a long hallway. They came to a room that looked like it had just been cleaned out. All that remained was a small writing desk and a couple of chairs. The two men took their seats.

Röger watched as the Coroner NcRuse took ink, pen, and paper from the desk drawer and gingerly placed them on the desk top. The Coroner began to scribble on the yellow parchment, making it into an official form. Without looking up, he raised his boney hand and made a 'come hither' gesture. Röger heard the door slam behind him.

The human twisted in his seat to see the door closed. His face slowly turned back to the Coroner who was still preparing the form.

"How did you do that?"

NcRuse did not reply.

"How did you do that?" Röger asked again with some anger. "You're a dead head, a necrotheurge. How is it you can command doors?"

NcRuse raised his face as if slightly annoyed. "The door is composed of deceased wood. You should see want I can do with an old barn. Now, please let me finish this form."

After a minute or so of more scribbling NcRuse gave Röger a thankful nod and said "Now we may begin. Tell me everything that happened. Rush nothing. Explain all."

The burly man adjusted himself in his seat. He gave the Coroner a full account of how he and his teammates were attacked by two post-mort assassins, how the action went, and who got hurt and how bad. He took great care to leave out himself transforming into a hulking cursed beast.

"So, the two post-morts ran away after you decided to display your 'superior axe swinging skills'?" NcRuse asked with doubtful eyebrows.

"Well, yeah," Röger replied with a shrug. "After they hit Hindin with that eagle-egg, I was through messing around. Blind Bitch's Bane! If Will hadn't have been in the way when we fought that dead slag together, I would have finished her off right quick. So, I pulled out a few combat maneuvers that I save for rainy days (or in this case; rainy nights) and I showed them just what a Black Vest like me is made of."

NcRuse smiled, his big grin full of narrow teeth. "And just *what* are you made of, Sir Yamus? Whatever it is, it's not exactly human, is it?"

Röger's heart began to race. "*He knows!*" he thought. "So, what exactly did that theurge's corpse tell you the night we took him out?"

The Necrotheurge steepled his fingers. "That you turned into a big, scary werekrilp and gutted him mercilessly with your big sharp claws." The room slowly filled with a cold despair. Röger could feel it prickle his skin and creep into his heart.

"Oh, yeah?" Röger snarled as he hunched forward. "Well, I think it's weird that a necrotheurge like you works as a police officer. I also find it kind of odd that two *post-morts* would attack us after recently making *your* acquaintance! So, tell me, dirt-napper: did that theurge's corpse tell you some great secret before his soul shattered? Is that why you sent your two post-mort minions to kill us? I doubt there's many Necrotheurges in Embrenil, let alone Doflend!"

The coldest of scowls appeared on the Coroner's face. "How dare you! I find your childish speculation to be nothing more than a defensive reflex of your own shame! If I wanted to do you harm, I would have revealed your...your condition to my fellow officers."

"So, why didn't you?"

"Why? Simple. Because I sense good in you. There is good in both of us, Sir Yamus. The world is very critical of men like us."

Röger scoffed. "Aw, don't give me that bullpie and keep your lips off my ass! Hindin was right! This whole Mystic Mafia thing isn't over, is it?"

The Coroner's face did not change. And the fact that it remained perfectly still was good enough for Röger. "I knew it. You're hiding something. You and Taly both, probably. If this case were finished, all of the victims would be getting their sight back, including Officer Feyna! Now, it makes sense why Taly 'retired'."

NcRuse took a long breath and sighed. "My, but you are a creatively paranoid individual. I admire your imagination. I really do. But, for what it's worth: Waltre Taly and I *are* still working on the case, secretly. You of all people should understand the value of secrets."

Röger was mildly relieved by the Coroner's change of tone. "So, what should I do? What about Hindin? What if the post-morts come back?"

"I wager they will. From the way you explained them, they sound like minions of Oroga."

"Oroga? Who's he?"

NcRuse let out a soft chuckle. "*That* is the question. No one knows. But rumors are that he is one of the most powerful Necrotheurges in the Cluster. It is said that he has many talented assassins under his dark wings, all post-mortum and 'made from scratch'. I have heard that it takes powerful divination theurgy to even contact him. That is probably how Lurcree communicated with him to contract the assassins. An arrangement could have been made. And if these assassins *are* agents of Oroga, then I think that you have not heard the last of them. They said that they were obligated to kill only two of you, right? Since only half the payment was made?"

"Yeah," Röger replied. A shiver went up his spine.

NcRuse shrugged. "Well, there it is. Get out of the city while you still can."

The Black Vest shook his head and growled. "This is bullpie! How do I know we can trust you? How do I know that *you* aren't an agent of this Oroga or the Mystic Mafia or both? Why don't I just go find some other cop in this building and tell them everything I know plus everything you've told me?"

NcRuse grinned. "Because, Sir Yamus, causing such chaos and confusion in this already chaotic building might force me to reveal you to be a terrible monster hiding beneath a deceptive layer of human skin. I'm sorry we must part so bitterly. Now leave."

"No," Röger replied, his voice dropping an octave. "What did you and that theurge's ghost talk about before it shattered? How do I know you're not just getting us out of the way?"

NcRuse sat back in his chair. "I *am* getting you out of the way...of harm."

Röger felt it just then, that dreadful buzzing in his skull. For an instant, his eyes flashed green and a flood of rage washed down his arms. He watched NcRuse straighten in his chair, alarmed. His sleepy eyes, now shocked wide open, stared down at the desk. Röger looked down and saw that his fingernails had lengthened into sharp points, and there were ten deep gouge marks on the wooden desk top. His head snapped back up to see the Coroner, who was now out of his chair, shaking something in his hand. It was a small stick with a gourd fixed to the end with leather straps. A few ratty old feathers dangled from it. Gently, the Necrotheurge shook his wand, making a soft, rattling rhythm. And slowly, Röger calmed down. His anger passed away like a leaf in a strong breeze.

"There," NcRuse said, sighing with relief. "I have temporarily stifled your desire to cause death. Yet, I know that this desire stems from your tainted blood, not your heart. Now go."

Röger stood up. He took a deep breath. He felt ashamed and embarrassed for losing control, but no less suspicious. "You're a theurge. Can you at least swear on your philocreed that--?"

"No," NcRuse interrupted firmly. "I only take *that* sacred oath with other theurges who can do the same. Furthermore, I am an officer of the law. I cannot make any promises about anything until I have all the facts I need."

Röger regarded the Drakeri man behind the desk. He knew no matter what he said or asked, he would not get a straight answer. The Necrotheurge was a man of many secrets. *"But then again,"* Röger thought, *"so am I."* He turned and walked out.

Coroner Leal NcRuse waited a solid five minutes. He then reached into his pocket and pulled out a dead white moth. He held the moth up to his lips and began to whisper.

"Waltre, the Four Winds are on to us. I need you to follow my instructions immediately. Go down to Doctor Toney's Boddy Shoppe. There you will find Mr. Revetz alone. I understand he is also quite injured and helpless...."

He went on giving the dead insect his instructions. When he finished, the moth fluttered out of his hand and out the window. The message was delivered in only a few minutes.

❁

As Polly and Will arrived at the site where two thirds of the city's beer was brewed and bottled, they couldn't help but marvel at the colossal structure. It took up four city blocks in a series of monumental buildings and steaming towers. The structures were not made of the normal fossil-filled bricks like the city's other prominent structures. It was mainly composed of plain kiln-baked red brick. The most prominent of these buildings displayed an enormous painting of an ornate carriage being pulled by a team of strong bileers. At its main gate, Will and Polly needed only to state their names before a guard led them directly to Elai NcRay's office. There they waited for him in comfortable chairs while sipping the finest coffee Will had ever tasted. Framed certificates, plaques, and ancient photographs dignified the room. Two portraits stuck out more than the others. The first was of Haon NcRay, the Founder. Next to it was a picture of two grown male twins, Elai and Arnu NcRay.

As the last of the hot liquid they had been served went down Polly's hatch, the entry door behind them sprang ajar.

"I'm glad you came," Elai NcRay greeted as he walked in. He wasn't looking at any of them as he marched toward his desk. It wasn't until he sat down, facing them, that he noticed something missing. "Where is Mr. Revetz and Sir Yamus?"

"Laid up," Will answered flatly. "We got bushwhacked yesternight. Ol' Rev took the brunt of the punishment. It seems that assassins hired by the mystic we took down came to us a bit late. But they bit off more'n they could gnaw an' ran. But not before hittin' our friend with an Eagleton Sphere. He's gettin' a fix-up now. Sir Yamus is off runnin' an errand. So, all you got is the two of us."

Elai took a moment to consider this news. "What kind of assassins could they have been? Were there many?"

"There were only two," Will divulged. "Post Morts."

"I see. And do you think they may attack you again?" NcRay pinched the tip of his chin.

"Hard tellin'," Will replied, frowning.

"I see," Elai repeated with a slight laugh. "Then we have the same problem. Different assassins, mind you. But the same...same problem..." He became distracted by something internal. A thought? A memory? An idea? All three.

"Who an' why?" Will inquired with peering eyes.

Elai grinned. "To understand your employment, you must first understand your employer. As a businessman, I am a success. As a person, I am an utter disgrace. But I am not paying you to like me, only to protect me. I did not enter the world alone. My twin brother, Arnu," he sighed, gesturing to the portrait on the wall. "I ruined his life. So, he is going to take mine if you don't help."

"Why us?" Will asked. "Why not cops or bodyguards?"

"Chief Justice Taly has it in for me. Even with his recent departure I doubt any of his loyal officers would come until after the crime had transpired. As for bodyguards, I grew up with quite a collection. Unfortunately, my brother grew up with them, as well. And, with him being the better brother, I fear they would do nothing to protect me from him. Instead, I decided to hire impartial, unbiased help: a team of outsider Excursionists. But I am getting ahead of myself. Please, allow me to start from the beginning."

Polly and Will sat in their comfortable chairs, silent and intrigued. As the handsome, well groomed brewery owner and council member unfolded his tale, those same chairs grew harder to sit in.

"I am the evil twin. Remember that. After you hear my story, you will understand.

My brother and I were raised to take the company by the horns when our father died. When that sad day came, we did just that. Our innovations brought forth a revolution in production and distribution. Our father would have been proud.

We became Aces in the aristocracy. Oh, the glorious parties we attended! Women fawned over us, swooning over our matching outfits and charm. What conquests we had in those days!

Sadly, Arnu fell in love. True love, I believe. Her name was Misa. She was not the most enticing girl. She was prudish and wholesome, conservative and well learned. Only in true love could he tolerate something like that. They became engaged. I began to attend the parties alone. It just wasn't the same anymore. I grew jealous. Not just of her taking him from me. But of him for having her. But I suppose envy is a better word for it.

As twins, we had always been given the same things, from our matching toys to this great company. It wasn't fair that he had something that I could not. I longed for that experience. To be loved. Extravagant sport-shunting grew a bore. I wanted *her*. And I would have her.

Imitating my brother came naturally. It was a twisted deceit, I will admit. That was probably the only thing that made it exciting. So, I had my way with her. He walked in on us, unfortunately. I shouldn't have been so surprised. It was his bedroom, after all.

He did not believe me when I claimed that *she* was the seducer. But he did not believe that I had fooled her either. The engagement was broken, as was my nose. She ran out, sobbing. He hated us both, thinking that we both deliberately betrayed him. But I was convinced that he would forgive me someday. We were family, after all.

Then, later that night, she killed herself. Hung herself with the train of her wedding dress. After that, of course, he believed her. He then tried to kill me. He, being the better fighter, thrashed me within inches of my life. But what little theurgy I knew saved me."

"What theurgy is dat?" Polly asked.

"Pyrotheurgy."

"Other *flame tamer*," *Will* thought aloud. "What gives, NcRay? Why do so many Drakeri have the fire path? So far, we've run into three pissants who cast that element, you bein' number three. This ain't a volcanic region, nor is it very hot. Must be in the blood."

"Quite right," NcRay laughed. "Have you heard the legend of how the Indigo Race came to be?"

"Dragons an' fey rollin' in the hay," Will recited. It was an old rhyme to him. "I hear that's why the ol' fashioned term fer Drakeri is *Draco-Erie*. It also explains yer politics a bit. Dragon's bein' the epitome of greed, chokin' the flow of money. An' as fer fey; they naturally cotton to self leadership. So it only leads to reason that the union o' these two critters could add up to a Capitalist Democracy in which a merchant man like you can get a shot-caller's seat."

Elai raised a curious eyebrow. "You certainly have a way with words for a slack-jawed thicket-sneak."

Will just grinned and tilted his head and thought of Hindin. "It comes from runnin' with a word-mongerin' nerd fer the last few months."

"Now is not de time to discuss legends *or* turns-of-phrase!" Polly shouted. She looked at NcRay with a disgusted morbid curiosity. "Go on wit' your story."

NcRay smiled gingerly. "I burned half of my brother's face off. It was self defense, of course. There was no choice. It was the first and only time I ever produced a flame that hot that

267

quickly. It must have been fear. I had never been so afraid. He ran out cursing and swearing revenge. Many of our house servants saw this to confirm my reports to the police.

Anyway, that was four years ago. No one has heard from him since...until two days ago." He pulled a drawer in his desk and pulled out a piece of parchment. He read it aloud before passing it around.

Dear Elai,

You will die in five days. I had hoped that in these long years, you would learn to love someone as I did. But I fear that may never happen. So, I must content myself with your blood alone.

-Arnu

"Bitter," NcRay remarked with a shrug. He regarded his visitors thoughtfully. "All I ask is that you protect me these three days hence. Have at least one of you stay near me from now until then. On the last day, I will need all three of you around for the whole day and night. I am willing to pay you each 5,000 grotz, 10,000 if you catch him in the act."

"And how much if we kill him?" Polly asked.

NcRay laughed. It was a nervous laugh. "Oh, is that an option, too? 20,000 a piece, then if it is legal defense."

The young theurgess looked down shamefully and scoffed. "If we didn't need the money..."

"I understand," NcRay replied with sympathy.

Polly whispered over to Will. "Hindin's treatment..."

"I know," he replied, never taking his eyes off NcRay. "Sir, is there anythin' yer not tellin' us?"

"I told you everything that I've wanted to tell you, which is all you will need to know. Nothing about this deal will be illegal and there is no need for a contract. Keep me safe for the next three days and you will be paid handsomely. As a show of good faith, you may be my house guests. I will even cook for you if you wish. How about some new clothes? I'll hire the best tailors in

268

Embrenil to make new outfits for you all. Please, I insist. Let's face it: you are all looking a bit rag-tag."

"You're a real sleazy lump of puss, you know dat?" Polly hissed.

"I know," NcRay replied calmly. "I work hard and I play hard, Miss Gone. I killed my mother on the way out of the canal. Arnu had to be cut out. I suppose that is why I treat women so badly. I never had one to set me right."

"Lucky bastard," she thought.

"Still," he continued. "I have a business and a city to help run. I've taken the next three days off. Also, take this under consideration: The assassins who hunt you won't know where you're at. I must insist that we keep this deal private, of course, for both our sakes. So, please. Let us help each other. What say you?"

It was Noon. Hindin woke with the gentle tap of a large bronze finger on his brow. He looked up to see the morning light show on the kingly face of Doctor Toney. "Slate be praised," the face said.

"Slate be praised," Hindin answered. "Where am I?"

The Doctor filled him in on how his friends had brought him in yesternight, how he had almost died, and that his friends were out to find a way to pay for the bill. "But the reason I woke you," he admitted, "is because you have a visitor. Are you feeling up to it?"

"I do not know," Hindin replied. "My mind seems a bit foggy."

"Well, as your doctor, I would advise you to take a test. Jus' some questions to measure your reason. Are you ready?"

Hindin looked down at the thick sheet of canvas covering his chest, afraid to peek under it. "I hope so," he replied timidly.

The Doctor smiled. "Okay, relax, little brother. We'll start wi' somethin' easy: What is the leader of a clan called?"

"A Keystone."

"Good. What is the Capital of Tomfeerdon?"

"Sahaukkey."

"Good. Why do we only live for two hundred years?"

"Because...Because that was the average age of the ones who lived before us. In reverence to them..."

"That'll do. What is 8 times 4?"

"32. Eight represents infinity. Four are the basic directions."

"Okay," the Doctor replied, raising a curious eyebrow. "You seem fine to me, in spite of your damage. I'll go get your visitor."

"Who is it?"

"Didn't say. But he looks like a reporter."

"Wonderful," Hindin sighed. The reporter with the bowling ball face came to mind.

The doctor got up and left the room. It was a massive workshop full of tools and assorted scraps of stone and steel. Here and there, malrukan limbs, some used and some new, were scattered on large tables. It certainly was a body shoppe.

A moment later, the great steel door opened, letting in a spry old Drakeri man. He was dressed in a plain brown suit with a matching fedora hat. His face was now clean-shaven, but still unmistakable to Hindin's eyes.

"Chief Justice Taly?"

"Waltre," the old man corrected. "I resigned yesternight, remember?" His eyes sparkled like glaciers under a bright night. "I am not here on official business. Coroner NcRuse notified me about a report your teammate made this morning. The station house is a bit too preoccupied to send someone down. So, I just thought I'd just stop by." He smiled like a grandfather who was visiting a sick grandchild. "No one but NcRuse knew that I was going to make that announcement yesternight. The department's in total chaos for the time being. Nothing major. Just enough confusion to keep whoever they are distracted." He took off his hat and sat down by the massive bed/slab.

"Whoever *who* are?" Hindin asked.

"The remainder of Mystic Mafia," Waltre frowned. "You and your team may have killed the leader. But that doesn't mean a new one couldn't emerge. It may take a while, years even. But there are too many inconsistencies in the case. I plan on finding them out on my own. Leal NcRuse will be my man on the inside. With me now being 'retired', the Mystic Mafia won't see me coming."

"How can you be sure they are still a threat?" Hindin asked.

"NcRuse found out a few juicy details off Detective Rafe's corpse. Things he hasn't shared with anyone but me. And now, two assassins have come to kill you all. This case isn't quite over yet, Mr. Revetz."

"Indeed," the astonished malruka replied. His head swam with questions. "Then why did you relinquish control? Why did you make it seem like the case was over?"

"It's a feint," Waltre replied. "I want the existing members, whoever they are, to think that they are safe from me. I'm investigating from the outside in secret. I'm sorry for lying to you. But I knew that Polly had to leave as soon as possible."

"I think I understand," Hindin said guardedly. "But now that the Master is dead, it will prove difficult to find the assassins he employed. And the stolen glass was never recovered."

"Not all of it, but some of it." Waltre replied slyly. "I gave it to you with those books."

He thought for a moment. "The spectacles!" he exclaimed. "I left them in my duffel bag. But why just let me take them? Are they not evidence?"

The old man shrugged. "Yes. But I got what I needed from them. I had the Coroner do a minor necrotheurgic divination on both lenses. One belonged to Davil Pert, the other belonged to Dahms Capgully."

Hindin nodded, trying to understand. "They were the only two victims who were killed, yet their watches were still taken. Lurcree needed the victims alive to complete his ritual. Nonetheless...the glass could have still been useful to him. Maybe...perhaps..." He looked at the old man. "I need to study those glasses. My bag is at the station house."

"No worries," the ex-chief replied. "I heard that Yamus picked it up. But you're on the right track, though. What other reason do you think I gave them to you?"

"Because I'm a pyroactive?"

"Exactly. That's also why I gave you those books. Those glasses were crafted by a master flame mystic for some optical purpose. Maybe you could find a use for them."

"I see," said Hindin ponderously. "Then what should we do in the meantime?"

The old man sighed. "Nothing. You've all done plenty, so far. Leave as heroes, Mr. Revetz. I'll tie up all the loose ends."

"But..."

Waltre shook his head. "Polly Gone must not stay long in this city. If she does, she will bring a bloody terror that I doubt even the Grandmaster could contend with. Her teacher and mother, Veluora the Red Witch of Chume, is that threat." He turned his head. "Where are Polly and Will, anyway?"

Hindin looked once more at his broken body. "They must be off to talk to Councilman NcRay."

"Elai NcRay? Why would they go see that cloaca?"

"I presume to discuss a job of some sort, though he would not tell us directly. He approached each of us yesternight at the banquet. At first, we all agreed to decline whatever offer he made. But now, with my present condition requiring expensive treatment; I would guess that that is what they are doing."

Waltre Taly slumped and hung his head. "How much will it be?" he asked.

"8,000 grotz."

Taly winced and shook his head. "Too rich even for me. Shunting cop's pay. I wonder what NcRay wants..."

"What can you tell me about him?" Hindin asked.

"I have good reasons not to like him. But the only one I can disclose is that he's power-hungry. He has a selfish ambition rarely seen amongst us Drakeri. But I recognize it. He had a brother that owned half his company. When that brother ran away and went missing, Elai became the primary share holder. When that went into effect, he was qualified to become a Secondary Council Member. He hasn't done anything politically drastic, yet. He's a bit of a mug-wump."

"Mug-Wump?"

"He has his *mug* on one side of the fence and his *wump* on the other. He's a crippled mallard. But I can tell he revels in the prestige of his position." Waltre sighed distressingly. "Maybe I can gather donations at the station house, pass a hat around. If not, there must be a better way than dealing with that scoundrel. What could he want from you?" A thought popped into the old man's brain. A quick blink in his eyes made it apparent.

"What are you thinking, sir?" Hindin asked with a touch of concern.

Waltre shook his head. He stood up and put his hat back on. "If he pays them to do anything illegal, of course, refuse him. If he asks for any kind of protection, take it from me: he doesn't deserve it. Goodbye, Hindin Revetz. And good luck."

"Peace be with you," the malruka replied. He did not know what else to say as the old man took his leave. But just as Waltre was about to make his exit, he turned.

"Oh, one more thing! Just curious. The report your teammates made at the station house mentioned that the assassins said why they were attacking you. I haven't had the chance to read the report firsthand, just hearsay from the Coroner. But what *did* those post mort assassins tell you?"

"They told us that they had only received half their payment from the Master before he died. So, they decided that they would only kill half of us. It is a twisted logic, I must say."

"Indeed," agreed Waltre. "I suppose I'll keep an eye out for them for their ties to the Mystic Mafia. If they're still in the city, of course." He pinched the brim of his hat. "Wish me luck, Hindin."

"Good luck, Waltre, *Frigorifist* of Embrenil." Hindin watched sadly as the old man left.

Röger, Will, and Polly had arrived at the body shoppe at roughly the same time. There was much excitement and relief that Hindin was awake. Will had been holding in the stress and worry all day. He released it all in the form of crude jokes and a thicker accent. The four teammates exchanged their stories of who they had spoken with and what about.

"So, the old buzzard wants to tackle the stray pawns on his own," Will scoffed. "He thinks he can solve the rest of the case by himself. Maybe find the missin' glass an' cure the victims' blindness. I wish him luck an' all, but he didn't get far without us before."

"That is because the two detectives he had on the case were corrupt," Hindin defended. "But I have faith in Waltre Taly."

"But why quit his position to do it?" Röger asked. "He said he *wanted* to cause confusion at his own police station. Why? So that any surviving members of the Mystic Mafia

273

wouldn't notice him? Or to make the department think that there was no more case to solve so that he could tackle it without other cops getting in the way? I just don't like it. None of it makes sense."

"Enough," Polly interrupted. "We have something new to speculate on. Elai NcRay has hired us to protect him from an assassin. We must ensure dat he remains safe long enough to pay us de money to fix Hindin. Protect de Councilman. Get money. Fix Hindin. Leave de city. Dat is the plan and dat should be de only ting in our heads."

Röger gave her an intrigued smile. "You know, Polly, you sound an awful lot like my old rugby coach."

❖

A common phrase for Excursionists is *Arrive, Alter, Amscray.* Taking out the leader of the organization would have to be enough for Polly, Will, and Röger.

As for Hindin, he buzzed with excitement. For the first time ever, he was able to examine the inner workings of his own complex structure. With his chest removed, he could see just how intricate he was.

"My mother is a Chimancer, too," he explained. "She is *Jawdrim,* a tendikeye/human half breed, thus incapable of having children. She and my father are husband and wife. They are both also quite learned. Her knowledge of nerves and chi flow combined with my father's skill with the forge and chisel led to my creation." He pointed at the network of golden threads weaving in and out of his granite muscle. "These cords are gold, the metal of life. It conducts life energy the way copper and steel used to conduct lightning. It is woven all through me, mimicking a nervous system. Many of the cords have been severed, making me a near invalid."

"It also must have cost your parents a fortune," Röger surmised.

"It did. In fact, their original plan was to make me ten feet tall like most of my race. But because they could aquire only so much gold, they were forced to scale me down to seven feet. And now, thanks to my own knowledge of chi and nerves, I am confident that I can assist Doctor Toney with my own repairs, lowering the cost and shortening the amount of time and labor."

"Ya think so?" Will asked.

"He and I have already discussed it," Hindin declared proudly.

Everyone smiled but Polly. "Den we won't have to work for NcRay?" she asked.

Hindin frowned at her, knowing her distress. "We only have 1,280 grotz among us. I am confident that I can do another 1,000 worth of work. That leaves about 6,000 left that we do not have. Doctor Toney and I should be finished in three or four days. By then you will have completed your dealings with the Councilman. I am sorry, Polly. I can see no way around it."

"Wait!" Will ordered, recalling what he had kept hidden. Röger knew what he was thinking of. He watched as Will dug into a hidden pocket in his dust coat. The bukk pulled out his three flawless plastic coins he and Röger discovered in the Rotten Cherry. "One o' these alone should pay for it! Plastic coins, Rev! Can you believe it?! I'll go get the Doc!"

"Will! Wait!" Hindin ordered. "Where in the Cluster did you get those?"

"Rög and I found them when we cleaned out the Rotten Cherry. He's got the other three. If we can find the right buyer, then our money troubles are over!"

"Let me see one," Hindin requested, holding out his hand.

Will flipped one to him with his thumb. Hindin caught it easily. He looked at the thin circle of mirror plastic for a long moment. "Plastic money," he mused, thinking. "Yes, I have read of such a thing. Only it was usually in the shape of a playing card with brail numbers and letters. Debt Cards, I believe they were called. These however are not currency. They are compact discs."

"Of course they are!" Will responded. "They fit right in my pocket."

"They are not money, Will," Hindin corrected, annoyed.

"Oh......Well, they're still plastic. We could still get a good payoff from 'em."

"True," Hindin agreed, nodding. "But their value may depend on what information they contain. Let me explain. These discs contain microscopic etchings produced by concentrated beams of fire. These etchings are a code that can only be understood and read by a Seer Box of some kind."

"But a Seer Box runs on lighting," Polly argued. "No one has been able to start one in three millennia."

275

"Still," Hindin fought, "there may be other ways of accessing the information, perhaps a divination of some sort. All the same, I have a hunch that these discs are worth more than a paltry 8,000 grotz. I appreciate the thought to use them. But, please, now is not the time." He flipped the disc back to Will, who caught it and pocketed it back with the other two.

Polly shook her head and sneered at the bed ridden malruka. "But didn't Taly tell you dat NcRay does not deserve protection? Don't you tink dat he has it coming to him?"

"I am not Waltre Taly," Hindin answered. "My philocreed differs from his. In fact, I have no opinion of Elai NcRay. I only know that he is in danger and that he has requested our help." He turned his eyes to Will. "It is yet another chance at heroism."

Will nodded. "You can sit this one out, Pol. Keep Rev comp'ny. Röger an' I can deal with it." He turned to the Black Vest. "Whudya say, Rög?"

"I say after we save his lily ass and we make him give us a keg of his finest beer. Then we make Hindin carry it for us on the trip out."

"I will agree to that," Hindin smiled.

Polly ran her fingers through her hair and sighed. "No. I should stay close to NcRay on de day it's supposed to happen. If he gets wounded, he will need a healer. But de two of you better not let dat happen. I hate de thought of touching him."

❖

Lanigiro Grove was the area where the oldest and richest families lived. The mansions were of the same fossil rock construction as the city's other historic buildings. Here and there, a skull or a claw of some extinct monster faced out as if giving warning. How like gargoyles they were, stripped of their stone flesh and frozen in the hewn bricks that were stacked and mortared with careful planning. Sometimes a large chunk of fossil was left uncut and simply had the rest of the wall built around it. Even the gates to the estates were bone brick. Their archway openings almost always had a crowning piece of petrified skeleton to welcome those who passed beneath them.

The strangest part, however, was that none of it was really that scary. Moss and flowered vines grew happily over, under, and around the deathly decorum. The mansion windows were stained glass of many brilliant colors. The sound of children playing and laughing came from behind tall hedges. Majestic trees (some local, some from foreign lands) stood tall and elegant. Although it was the final resting place of beasts that would never be seen again, the bones seemed at peace.

Will, Polly, and Röger rode in an open-air taxi wagon (Malrukan pulled, of course). The cobbled street was so smooth and level, that they hardly shook or swayed as they rode. The sight of the mansions they passed almost made them forget that they were hungry, tired, and various shades of perturbed. Will's mind bounced from Hindin to that small blue sword that cut him. He felt selfish for worrying why the blade was able to hurt him, thinking about what it could mean. Then he would think of his dear friend, and how they had been taken by surprise. In the wild woods or even a rural area, he thought they might have stood a better chance against those post-morts. Maybe.

Polly put aside the concerns about her mother. *"It's no use fretting over,"* she thought. If Veluora were to find her, this excursion would be over. Her new friends would be dead. She would be hauled back to continue her malign training. She would be grieved and her heart would continue to darken. That was what would happen. She would not be surprised when it did. For now, she merely humored the hope of fixing Hindin and fleeing this miserable city.

Röger was contemplating the night before. It was twice now that he and his companions depended on his lycanthropy to save them. But each time he used it, it also put himself at risk. Were it not for his helmet, he would be a nigh unstoppable monster bent on devastation and death. He was more than what children spoke of to give each other nightmares. Werekrilps were rightfully killed by anyone wishing to preserve their loved ones and territory. In his past, whenever any authority discovered his secret, it would then be time to run, no matter who he made friends with. But these people he rode with now were cool with it. But would they stay cool with it once the law was after them? *"Perhaps,"* he thought, smiling.

The NcRay mansion was actually very similar to the Brewery. It would not surprise them to know that the two structures had the same architect. It was a large, yet plainly conservative, red brick mansion, in contrast to all the more ornate homes around. Were they to ask about it (although they never would), Elai would have told them that it was from his late father's taste for mediocrity. It was a new mansion, anyway. And all the precious bonebrick had long ago been quarried.

Evening came. Their stomachs squirmed from a day's neglect.

The property's surrounding wall opened in the front in a tall archway. Two thick wooden doors stood invitingly ajar. Within lay a neatly tended front yard with a path of flat stones leading to the front door. Hindin would have known what mineral they were, but they looked expensive. The entry looked pleasant and serene until they walked in. With the gateway now behind them, they now saw the entire front yard.

On either side of the path of stones were two immense skulls. They were both almost as large as a train car. They were adorned with huge pairs of tusks and horns, chalk white protrusions that seemed to reach out for whoever dared to walk the path. The eye sockets were filled with soil. From them red roses grew, exactly one dozen per eye. But it gave the skulls a sinister look that was hardly romantic. The three Excursionists were caught between their fearsome, lifeless stares. Fear, fascination, awe: it all meant the same.

"What were dey?" Polly asked in a half whisper.

"Tree Chompers of some kind" Will replied, snapping out of his gaze. "Herbivores. Just lookit them teeth! Not the tusks, mind ye, but the side-chewers. They got one solid tooth on the top an' bottom 'steada a line o'teeth. No space fer splinters to wedge between, jus' like a Bashle River Rat. 'Cept them're beaver-kin. These two're kin to none. Monsters." He then thought of the winsome dentist he'd known for too short a time, and smiled wistfully.

Then his ear caught the sound of the front door opening. Elai stepped out waving and smiling. "Don't worry! They'll only bite if I tell them to!"

They all looked back and forth at him and the skulls a few times before realizing he was joking.

"What were dey?" Polly asked, feeling a bit silly for repeating herself.

Elai sighed and approached. No doubt he had answered this question too many times. "They were a present from my father, for Arnu's and my coming of age. They were twins, too, in a way. They came from the same beast of yore: The Dreaded

278

Two-Headed Prongmateinas. Lovely, aren't they? Would you care to sniff the flowers?"

No one answered.

"Come on then," Elai beckoned with a lazy gesture. He turned back toward the house. They followed with wary eyes. "I have given my entire staff the next three days off. It will provide better security, since some of them may be in league with my brother."

"Why not keep your enemies closer?" Röger asked as they went through the front door.

Elai stopped to ponder the question. "Hmmm...keeping enemies close... You are right, sir. I loathe admitting it. But the three of you may have found some tactical advantage if they had stayed. Pardon me, for I have acted out of turn. It must be the paranoia of impending doom that clouds my judgment." He said no more and continued to walk.

The entrance hall was indeed entrancing. Two staircases curved down from the upper level like the jagged mandibles of some colossal vermin. Waterfall-sized drapes cascaded over enormous windows of colored glass and iron. Paintings both tall and wide were of people and places they had never met or seen. The floor was a dizzying design of circles and crisscrossing lines. And resting on a column not even four feet tall, under a dome of clearest crystal, was an old unopened bottle of beer. It was the first of many bottles of beer that would amplify emotions both apparent and hidden throughout the city for centuries.

"How did you know we were comin'?" Will asked curtly. "And how were you so sure we'd agree to yer offer, sendin' away the help an' such?"

Elai smiled and pulled out a lighter. He woke a small flame with his thumb. He looked at it for a moment, as if he were double checking a note. "We are having lemon pepper salmon tonight. Along with mashed potatoes with the skins left in. Semi lumpy. Broccoli, bamboo chutes, and yellow onions sauteed together in a pan of grape seed oil. Afterword, we will have pepperwine and banana pudding for desert. It has all been prepared in the dining hall."

Will's face lengthened in shock. His blue-gray eyes grew confused and strangely intrigued.

NcRay made a wry grin. "I assume that is *your* favorite dish, Mr. Foundling. And I can assure you that the salmon was caught wild. Tomorrow and the next day, Ms. Gone ands Mr. Yamus will have their favorite meals, as well. But we shan't find out what they are 'til then." He looked at them all with half-hidden smugness.

"Cooking, next to brewing, is my passion, you see. And fire is my gift, the heat aspect more than the flame and light. I never know what to cook, though. So, I ask the nearest flame. After you left my office this morning, I checked my lighter. It told me what I just told you, what to cook this day. The bamboo chutes and pepperwine suggested that a tendikeye would be dining here this night. That was answer enough for me."

"I've never seen divination used in such a way," Polly remarked. She looked a freshened shade of nervous.

"You are still young, Ms. Gone. I'm sure there is much you haven't been shown." There was a playful seduction in his tone.

She wasn't impressed.

"That IS my favorite dish," Will half-whispered, still amazed.

"Of course it is!" Elai shouted with sudden manic glee, his arms raised in a V. "For you are guests of Elai NcRay! Welcome, Keepers of my Salvation!" Then his arms dropped, slapping against his sides. His face went neutral again. Morose, almost. "Would that I had the power to wield fire to do battle. I would not need help in this endeavor. Nonetheless, this is the least I can do in the meantime to show my appreciation for you all being here." He looked once more at his lighter, waking another flame. He looked at it curiously, then at Will. He flipped it shut and tossed it to him. "Keep it."

"Why?" the bukk asked, examining the shiny piece of metal.

"You've been meaning to get one, right? Sick of matches, yes? Well, there you go. A gift."

Röger tilted his head. "Not many pyrotheurges are so...practical in their craft."

"I do not consider myself a true pyrotheurge, Sir Yamus," Elai replied, closing his eyes and shaking his head. "I am pyropathic. You see, there is a difference between a pryotheurge and a pyropath. The philocreed is basically the same. But a pryotheurge is someone who is good at what they do. A pyropath is someone who *knows* what they are doing.

Believe it or not, fire and heat has a mind. A very simple mind, but it is still vaguely aware how it relates to other aspects of reality. I can read that mind, see what it sees, and touch what it touches. And with the right concentration, I can control that mind and make it do something extraordinary: cook food to perfection! I love to cook! My philocreed is tied to my own desires, making me a master chef. Fire reveals many things—including delicious flavors hidden within the things we eat." The councilman laughed almost madly. "If you think that carrots can be boiled in the same manner as potatoes, you are direly mistaken!"

It was at that moment that Röger, Polly, and Will could not ignore that they were indeed very hungry.

Far, far beneath the streets of the city, below the sewer systems, in a network of nearly forgotten catacombs, a man of the law carried a lantern in his hand and dread in his heart. He has walked all day through countless twists and turns, ancient broken steps and water worn ramps, through places few people know about. He was covered in grime and spiderwebs and his boots were soaked. He was not happy.

He reached into his jacket to look at a map covered in old blood stains. "Almost there," he told himself. Before he took another step, something flew from the darkness. He was too slow to react. His lantern shattered and the light goes out. There was only darkness and the sound of his breath.

"Wait!" he yelled. "I come bearing a message!"

The sound of a woman's laughter echoed around him. "From who?" the voice asked.

"From the Master."

"Master Lurcree of the Sacred Flame is dead," the voice responded.

"There is a new Master!" the man of the law declared. "One who is willing to take over Lurcree's goal, and also pay you the rest of Lurcree's debt."

There was a long silence. "Continue," she invited.

"The outsiders, the ones you failed to assassinate. We know where they're at, where they'll be staying. They made some kind of deal with Elai NcRay, the Secondary Councilman. But we of the Mystic Mafia have a plan to get them. We need your help still."

"I should say you do!" the voice condescended. "The human turned out to be a werekrilp!"

The man of the law paused in thought. "I come bearing instructions and the other half of your payment." He reached into his jacket and took out an envelope. He suddenly felt something small scurry up his body and snatch it from him. "What the..!?"

"Relax," urged the female voice. "That was just my partner."

The man of the law could hear the packet being opened. He waited for what seemed like minutes for a response.

Finally, she spoke. "This all seems a bit tricky. But if that's how the new Master wants it done, then so be it. I only have one question for you: Why are men of the law like you and your partner mixed in this?"

"Eternal life," the man replied. "Besides, I've earned it by doing good deeds while being paid a cop's measly salary for too long. We're just going to use the old Master's plan. New Master, same plan."

"Very well," a new voice answered. It was a small voice, like that of a raspy child. "By Lord Oroga's hollow heart, we will aid you in your hour of need."

Will would never admit it. The food they were eating tasted better than any other version of it he ever had. Even the woman he had called *Momma* couldn't measure up. It was dern good grub. He was so in love with it, that he paid little mind to Elai and Röger's argument on dining etiquette.

"But, Mr. Yamus, it is irrelevant that you can still eat while wearing that thing. It is only polite that you remove your helmet during dinner and under this roof."

The large man rolled his big brown eyes. "I have my reasons for keeping it on, pal."

"*Sir* Yamus. It is not my intention to boss you around. But I did go through the trouble of cooking for you all and-"

"All right, all right! Just quit whining about it! But only for dinner though!"

Polly watched attentively as he doffed his silver helm. It was her first time seeing his face. Secretly, she was very curious about what he looked like. She would never admit to it, of course. It would open up a flood of unwanted vulgar flirtation. His face revealed what she had suspected: He was of mixed variety, most likely a *quadroon*. The term *human* was first keyed by tendikeye. Literally, it meant *men of many HUES: Humans*. The term stuck and spread. Röger was a light olive brown. His nose was both wide and thick at the bridge. His lips pouted and flared naturally. His hair was a well-trimmed field of curls and waves. The gleam of his brown eyes seemed to sparkle even more without his helmet. His face was so manly, in fact, he made Will look like almost pretty in comparison.

"Thank you," Elai told him, and continued to eat.

Röger hunched over his plate and began to shovel and chew. He could control his changes enough when the helmet was off, but only in the least stressful situations. As long as Elai's brother did not attack during a meal, things would go smoothly. Hopefully.

Polly took her glass of pepperwine, sniffed it, grimaced, and put it back down. The rest of the food was to her liking, simple as it was.

Will had already cleaned his plate.

"Would you care for seconds?" Elai asked him.

Will smiled politely, playfully twiddling his large thumbs. "Naw, that should hold me. By the way; we ain't gonna kill him, yer brother I mean. Ain't no amount you could pay. We're gonna try to take him alive an' turn him over to the police."

Elai wiped his mouth with a napkin and gave a tiny laugh. "You had no trouble killing that Sizzagafiend. Or those two corrupt police officers. Or even that old theurge by the burning pits. I read the papers, Mr. Foundling. And I can see it in your eyes, all of you. You are all killers."

"Only when there's a need," Will replied, still smiling.

"There may be. My brother is no slouch with a pistol. He knows the lay of the house quite well, since he grew up here."

Will took out a cigarette and his new lighter. He lit up and admired the contraption briefly. Then he locked eyes with his host. "Y'ever kill anybody, rich boy?"

"No."

"Well, just keep this in mind: them cops an' that mad hermit of a mystic had it comin'. Yer brother don't. You caused him to lose the love of his life and burned half his face off. I'd wanna kill you to. But luckily, I ain't the one after ye. I wouldn't write a note. I wouldn't..." He paused, recalling the wrong memory at the wrong time. "I would've done it diff'ernt."

Elai nodded respectfully. "Pardon my misjudgment then. Handle it however you want. Just remember: If I die you won't get paid. By the way, how *is* your friend Hindin doing?"

"Rev? He'll pull through."

"Oh? Good."

Will finished off the last glug of pepperwine from his glass.

Watching this, Röger winced and shook his head. "How can you drink that? Peppers are meant for corn chips and beefalo burgers, not to help tie one on!"

Will smiled. "It's a man's drink, son. But seriously, I hear ya. We tendikeye got stomachs lined with lead. Thousands o' years o' practice."

NcRay grew cheerful and leaned back in his seat. "But nothing beats a cool bottle of NcRay, am I right, gentlemen? Would you care for some?"

The two friends exchanged a fast, slightly suspicious glance, not knowing what to think or say.

"Um, sure," Röger answered cautiously. "By the way, after this job is done, we'd like a barrel of your finest to take with us. Is that fine by you?"

"Certainly. But on one condition: Tell me about this case you just solved."

"Why?" Polly asked, stabbing at her salmon.

"Because I am going to bed after dinner, and I want to hear a story," he answered. "Now if you will excuse me, I must get this man's beer." He hopped up and began to leave.

Will stood up, shaking his head. "Hold up there, pard. Ain't gonna be no story tellin'." He looked at Röger. "Ain't none of his business, Rög. Everythin' he needs to know, he's already read in the paper."

284

"I wasn't going to tell him everything," Röger offered.

Will aimed his fierce eyes at Elai. "Just what is it you wanna know? Who killed who with what an' how? Z'at what yer after? Somethin' to share with yer socialite friends, that it?"

Elai only shrugged and grinned. His expression was cheerfully pleasant.

Will sneered and took a step toward him. "I had to blow the head off a corrupt detective after fallin' off a three story ledge. Little Polly here cut the throat of another while getting' choked by a mystical chain. And as fer that lousy old fart of a theurge-!" He stopped and hesitated, looking back at his partners. Polly had her mouth open, but could say nothing.

Instead, Röger spoke up. "Polly, took him out, too! With her theurgy! He never stood a chance!"

"Really?" Elai asked, sliding his gaze over to the pretty young lady. "You, a girl of eighteen years were able to slay an elderly archmystic?"

She met his stare, all timidity washed away. Lies were easier than truth. "My companions managed to distract him. I was able to get in close to cast my maxim. I made his blood and veins rebel against de rest of his body. He was torn apart like a stray cat amongst wolves. His maxims may have been powerful, but he used dem poorly. Strong faith is what is needed to cast giant fireballs. But old age must have robbed him of his guile."

"I see," Elai sighed and yawned. "My, but it is late." He clapped his hands together. "All right then, I am now a bit more convinced that you are all capable of protecting me. That is all I really wanted to know, fact be known. I can sleep easier now. Just let me get this man his beer, and I'll show you all to your rooms."

"Nuh-uh," Will contested. "One of us is standin' watch outside yer door."

Elai NcRay laughed and dared to place a hand on the tendikeye's shoulder. "Mr. Foundling, we have two more days!"

The crimson theurge was shown to her room first. She was glad to be rid of her host. Outwardly, he was restrained and civil. But she could practically feel the fear emanating from him all evening. It was the way his blood ran, rushed and unsteady.

For her, it was more than just intuition. Ever since her first blood cycle, she was able to sense when men were afraid. The Councilman was masking his fear with a pretention. He may have been an upper-crust aristocrat, but he seemed to be amplifying his personality to disguise his discomfort. His own brother was coming to kill him. His own brother gave him three days to wait for death.

"Why?" Polly thought. "Why give Elai time to prepare? Is Arnu NcRay indeed so confident?"

She looked around her room. It was definitely a guest's quarters. The furniture was elegant, but slightly mismatched. The art on the walls was pleasant, but had nothing in common. A single large window displayed a nice view of the mansion next door. The vanity was equipped with a spotless oval mirror. She was still wearing what she wore at the banquet. "You look like a used up whore," she told her reflection.

She shucked off her boots and crawled into the big soft bed. For a while she admired her new gold and ruby brooch before placing by her bedside. She slept easy for over an hour. Then she opened her eyes, realizing that she wasn't alone.

"Who are you and why are you in my house?" a creaky voice asked.

Polly sat up. Her eyes saw nothing in the velvet darkness. "Who's dere?" she asked.

"I asked you first," the voice replied.

She clenched her knife beneath the pillow. Whoever was there with her saw the veins in her chest and arms glow a bright shade of red from beneath her pale indigo skin. The flowing rivers of mystical light fed into her eyes, making them glow like beacons.

The voice chuckled sickly. "Ah, a mystic of some sort. Good thing I'm prepared."

She set her sights on the drapes in front of her window. "I see you," she said pertly. "I see your heart. It's working a bit too hard, don't you tink?"

Her's was, too. She watched the illuminated circulatory system of a man step from behind the curtain. It lifted its arm, as if pointing at her. She heard a familiar metallic click, and her hopes sank. She blinked her eyes and the mystical vision was gone. In its place was a Drakeri man holding a fancy flintlock pistol shaped like a roaring dragon. At first, she thought it was

Elai. But as her eyes adjusted in the natural darkness, she could make out a porcelain mask covering half his face. His clothes were dull colored and rustic with worn-out boots and a tattered cape.

"I'll ask you once more. Who are you? And who are your well armed friends?" His voice was as worn out as his garments. But his eyes meant business.

"Arnu," she said, nodding to herself. She tried to stay calm. "We are excursionists hired by your brother to protect him from...you." She recalled the stormy night she was shot at her windowsill. There would be no close calls this time, though. The huge hand cannon was aimed at her face.

"Your name," he demanded.

"Polly Gone."

"Do you think my brother is worth protecting?" he asked.

"No. He told us why you hunt him. I don't blame you." She trembled slightly.

"Then why do you help him? Is it the money?"

She looked back and forth at his eyes and his gun. "We have a friend who is...injured. We need 8,000 grotz to save him." Her fear surrounded her like an aura. "We planned on taking you alive," she added nervously.

"Is that all?" he laughed. "I can triple that this very night. I know where the family safe is hidden. The combination is still fresh in my mind. Do you think you can convince your friends to walk away from this? It's obviously beyond you, anyway." His face (well, half of it) was a stone cold portrait of uncaring.

She thought hard. What *would* they think? It sounded like a good idea. Who were they to deny another person his revenge? But deep down, she knew the others would not comply. Stupid honor, always getting in the way.

"Shoot me!" she dared him, breaking through her fear.

Arnu raised an eyebrow (the only visible one).

"Kill me if you want. But you won't be so lucky wit' my comrades. And when dey see me dead, dey'll know who did it. So when you make your move to kill Elai, dey will show you no mercy!"

The gunman frowned and shrugged. "What if I kill them, too? Pay them a visit when I'm done here?"

Polly cackled. "You will need more dan dat rat-shooter. Dey are more dan what dey seem, Arnu NcRay. Run away and disappear. Learn to let go of your hatred. And, when you do, let me know how you did it, for I harbor my own!" Her defiant eyes blazed. She was ready for anything.

The masked man slowly lowered his weapon. "This is our compromise then, Polly Gone: In two days, I will try to end Elai's life. When I make my move, I will trust in your mercy if I fail. You will have my avoidance until then. Goodnight." He turned and dashed toward the window.

For a split second, Polly fought the urge to toss her hidden dagger into the base of the man's skull. When he jumped through the closed glass window without breaking it, she began to regret her restraint.

Chapter 9
Parting Clouds

After an exquisite breakfast and Polly's disconcerting report of her nocturnal visitor, Elai NcRay seemed vexed. "He jumped through a window without breaking it? How?"

Polly had no answers, not even theories. At least, not for him.

He sighed and rubbed his face. "He was able to get the drop on someone I hired to stop him. He's showing off and shunting with me, I know it!"

Will and Röger offered no words of comfort. They were more concerned for Polly.

Elai balled his fist and hammered the breakfast table, knocking over his glass of jubube juice. "This cannot work. I need to think."

The Councilman tapped his finger on the table, his eyes wide open and glancing about aimlessly. After a long moment, he looked at Will.

"Mr. Foundling, you are a capable warrior in the wilderness. Am I correct?"

Will shrugged and nodded humbly.

"But in this city, you are out of your element. You claim to be a Bushwhacker, but bushwhacking is different than, say, a hit. Am I correct?"

Will frowned in slight confusion. "Ya mean like a hitman type o' hit?"

Elai nodded.

Will shrugged again. "We'll jus' hafta see, I guess."

"That answer is not good enough!" Elai barked. "Arnu plans on getting the drop on me. But first, he must get the drop on you. How do you think he would go about that?"

Will made a confused smile. "Uh. He'd hafta be purdy darn good. His only chance would be to kill me with one hit. 'Cause once I know he's there, it'll be over." The tendikeye drew his gun in the blink of an eye as a demonstration.

289

Elai twitched from the motion. He could not help but marvel at the firearm's construction. "Is the caliber 10mm?" he asked.

"Yep," replied Will. "Exactly."

Elai's eyes looked up, as if recalling a piece of information. "370 degrees," he mumbled to himself.

"Huh?" Will uttered.

Elai ignored him and looked at Röger. "And you, Mr. Yamus. I've always wondered: What exactly is a *Black Vest*?"

Röger straightened in his chair. "Imagine someone who graduates from both the Police and Fire Fighting Academies. Imagine this person receiving top marks in athletics and paranormal psychology. Now teach this person to fight with a thirty pound, razor sharp hunk of steel. My role in the Black Vest Squad was 'Slugger'. My job was to cut something or someone in half when bullets, brains, or theurgy failed to beat it. We handled the things regular cops couldn't." The man paused and smiled. "Just like now."

Elai attempted to smile. "But what are your weaknesses, do you think?"

"I have none!" the Black Vest declared triumphantly. "I'm an independent Fevärian Black Vest with more notches on my belt than a Lemuertian's sword! I get more ass than an outhouse! I've saved countless people in countless places from certain disaster. I am the quixotic, erotic, neurotic, gin and tonic, super sonic, don't-touch—my-chronic master of bloody justice!"

"Yeah!" Will responded with boyish enthusiasm. He rose from his chair and gave Röger a loud, smacking high-five.

Polly rolled her eyes and sank in her seat. *"Idiots,"* she thought.

Elai frowned in disgust and looked at Polly. "Miss Gone, was there nothing you could have done to catch him yesternight? Surely, your theurgy could have helped you in some way, yes? You were able to kill that hermit mystic."

Polly frowned. "I'm not like most mystics. I must be close to my marks in order to affect dem. Arnu kept his distance wit' a gun. I was helpless."

Elai gazed at her, his eyes firmly neutral. "The three of you may not be enough it seems. Perhaps I should ask the police for additional support. Yes, I think so. Taly isn't there anymore.

Maybe now I can get some trustworthy assistance." He looked at them all. His eyes seemed to ask "What do you think?"

"Couldn't hurt," Röger shrugged. "We were gonna turn your brother in to them, anyway."

Elai turned his face to the Black Vest. His face looked like it had aged from a century of worry. "Would you accompany me to the Police Station, Sir Röger? I would feel safer."

"Not a bad idea," Will nodded. "You two go on. Me an' Pol should stick around an' get used to the layout. If bullets are gonna fly here tomorrow, we best get settled in the groove o' things."

"I agree," Polly said, crossing her arms and hunching in her seat.

Röger nodded to them and looked at Elai. "Let's go, boss."

Elai led Röger down to the western hall until they came to a large pair of double doors. Röger expected they would open up to reveal a stable with a team of well-bred bileers and a carriage worthy of an emperor. But deep down, he should have known better. Men of Elai's wealth and station preferred more advanced means of travel.

Elai pushed the double doors to reveal a large dark room made entirely of concrete. The Councilman flicked his wrist and spoke a word known only to other pyrotheurges. Wall mounted oil lamps awoke, shining their light on something that made the human mad with envy.

It resembled an amalgam of the front of a train and a carriage without steeds. It was made of many pieces of steel, each one different and fitted perfectly together. It was hollow on the inside where two finely upholstered seats sat facing forward through a window of thick glass. In front of one seat was a mounted rim of metal with leather laced around it. And jutting out of the back of the four wheeled machine was a large pipe almost as wide as a man's waist.

"You have a steam car!" the human exclaimed. His whole body twinged with boyish excitement. "You have a shunting steam car! A Clary J82!"

"J84," Elai corrected with a smirk. "This model originally came with solid rubber tires, but they rotted away centuries ago.

291

I commissioned a woodcutter to fashion these from hard oak, heat-treated by me later, of course. I then had a leathersmith make coverings for the treads for traction. They hold out rather well, considering they're made of *hurklyone* hide."

"Where did *you* get *hurklyone* hide from?" Röger asked, flabbergasted.

"Why, the Red Dirt Battle Arena, of course. I purchased the remains of one that died there."

"Someone actually managed to kill it?"

"No. It died of old age. Bootrose was his name. He was a fan favorite monster for many years. The kids loved him."

Röger could not help but marvel at the leather clad tires. "Well, ain't that something!"

Elai grinned. "Oh, no. What is *something* is the engine." He pulled a small lever near the back which triggered a sideways hatch door to pop open.

Röger's eyes widened and blinked.

The 'guts' of the steam car engine were composed of many interweaving steel parts. They tangled into one another in aesthetic and scientific perfection. Some of the parts gleamed like tube shaped mirrors.

Before Röger could utter more words of astonishment, Elai slammed the hatch door shut. "It's not *that* old, really. Only four hundred years. But that's still quite a while for you. Isn't it, Fevärian?"

Röger did not respond.

NcRay smiled and opened the driverside door. "Shall we?" he asked.

◎

The city streets were busy and pleasant. The air was friendly and cool. Many people waved at them, recognizing the esteemed councilman in his steam-spouting ride as it puttered down the lanes. Elai waved back joyfully, as if he were a one man parade. Occasionally, a random man would call up to him "Hullo, Boss!" He was loved and respected by many. Ladies swooned. Children ran along side them until their parents called them back. Many men asked for free beer half-jokingly. To be celebrated was nothing new to the Brewmaster of Embrenil.

They halted directly in front of the E.C.P.D. building. He asked two officers who happened to be outside to watch over his transport. They were all too willing to oblige. He walked into the station as if it were his own house. As he entered, everyone wearing a uniform took special notice. Gestures of respect came from all around. He asked one of them at random "Would you please take us to see Detectives Sirron and Emmad?"

"Right this way, Mr. Councilman," the officer nodded. It was the young Officer Ladue. He smiled and nodded at Röger, who did the same.

They were led to an office in a long hallway. The door was closed.

"They should be in there," Ladue said, giving the door a swift knocking.

"Come in," a voice called out.

"Thank you, sir," Elai told Ladue. "That will be all."

The officer smiled again at them both and went away.

Elai grasped the knob, twisted, and pushed as if it were his own door.

The cramped office contained two small desks. Two Drakeri men sat behind them. Röger recognized them as being the detectives who asked the questions at Lurcree's hidden lair. The older of the two, Det. Sirron, had a well trimmed beard and thick knuckles. Resting on his desk was a wide brimmed hat. Det. Emmad was well built and handsome, but not in a strikingly unique way. His semi long hair was tied back into a three inch ponytail. They both stood up, spines straight as Elai and Röger entered.

"Hullo, Detectives," Elai sighed tiredly. "Please, sit down. I have something very dire to report."

They slowly took their seats. "Go on," Sirron said. His voice sounded like a bassy hiccup.

Elai closed the door and hung his head, half in shame, and half in dread. "You were the ones who investigated the...incident...between my brother and I four years ago. You told me that if anything else should happen, I should report it to you."

"What happened?" Sirron asked, casting a glance at Röger.

Elai raised his chin. "My brother, Arnu, has returned."

"Returned?" Emmad asked, blinking hard. "How?"

293

"He sent me this letter." Elai pulled out an envelope and handed it to Sirron. "It contains a threat on my life planned for tomorrow. I have recruited three of the Four Winds-One Storm to be my bodyguards. But yesternight, Arnu paid an unexpected visit to one of them. It was probably to display his ability to get past their defenses. He has also picked up the ability to leap though glass without breaking it. If he can do the same with walls, then I fear my life will soon be over. I apologize for telling you all this on such short notice. But...events have transpired in unexpected ways. My plan for a long happy life has been compromised. So, gentlemen, now that you know the threat, will you help me?"

Det. Sirron took out the piece of paper and read it thoroughly. After a long moment the detective furrowed his brow and nodded in understanding. "Of course, Councilman. We'll be there tomorrow morning. It's a good thing you brought this to us. It will be a relief to have this case finished."

"Thank you," Elai replied with a bow.

"We want to take him alive," Röger added, not knowing what else to say.

The two Detectives exchanged a glance. "We hope you can, Sir Röger," Sirron returned. "By the way, how is the rest of your team doing? Word got around that your malruka was injured."

"He was. But he's getting fixed up as we speak. In the mean time, me and the others are watching over the councilman, here."

Sirron nodded, grinning proudly. "You have already done so much for this city and this department. And yet you do more. It will be an honor to work with you, sir."

"Likewise, Detective," Röger returned. But something was on his mind. "Say, have they made any progress on curing the victims that were blinded? Your fellow officer, Feyna, I mean. Do you know if she's doing any better?"

Det. Emmad shook his head. "From what I've heard, there's been no change."

The burly human dropped his shoulders.

"It could have been worse, big man," Sirron said, trying to sound sympathetic.

"Yeah," Röger agreed, looking at the floor. "Could have been worse."

"Could ya please try to remember what it looked like a little better? Are you sure it was a matchlock pistol? What brand did it look like most?"

Polly was trying not to lash out at Will. But he was making it very difficult.

"Well, if you couldn't see it that well in the dark, I understand. But what kinda sound did it make when he cocked the hammer? Was it a sharp clicking sound, or was it kinda dull, like *CLUK* or *CLAK*. Or was it more of a *tick* than a *click?*"

They had been meandering through the mansion all morning. No door they tried had been locked. And Elai had given them permission to explore the house freely.

"But yer sure it was a matchlock, though, right?"

"Yes," she answered through clenched teeth.

Will shook his head in disbelief. "He must be one heckuva shot, 'cause he's only gonna get one chance. Reloadin' them things is a pain. But you did say it looked fancy. Maybe it's one o' them duelin' pistols. Then he might have a spare tucked away hidden. What do you think, Polly?"

She only shrugged. Her eyes were half open from lack of sleep.

Will looked at one of the large stained glass windows. "Are ya sure that the window was closed when he jumped through it?"

"Yes. He jumped through the glass wit' out breaking it."

Will lowered his eyes and nodded. "More theurgy an' glass. Y'think, maybe, Arnu had a connection with Lurcree?"

"It is very possible," she said gravely. "I'm glad you said it first. Arnu was gone for four years. He could have made an alliance. But it might be unreasonable to speculate any more dan dat. Dere are dozens of other ways a person can jump through solid matter or a closed portal. I, for instance, could just turn into blood and flow under de windowsill."

"But can ya do it as fast as jumpin' through it?"

"My mother can." She pinched her tattoo, and wanted to change the subject. "How good are your ears?" she asked.

"Sharp as a scorpion's ass. Why?"

She smiled and looked around, as if checking to make sure no one was watching. "Let's play a little game. You go to de west wing of de house, I'll go to de east. We must try to find each other wit' out being found."

"Like hide an' seek?"

"Yes. Only, we both hide and we both seek. "Dis way, we can better prepare for Arnu's sneaky attack."

Will's face lit up. He loved training games. "You don't stand a chance, missy!"

"Dis isn't de woods, bumpkin!" she fired back with a playful tilt in her hips.

"Yer on!" he shouted. He turned and dashed away toward the far west wing. Deep down he started to admit that he was growing fond of her. To him, her voice sounded like a little chipmunk with a scratchy throat. *"Cute,"* he thought. *"But naive."*

Polly Gone just smiled and shook her head. *"Cute. But dumb, too,"* she thought. Turning on her heel, she sauntered with perfect silence and grace not to the east wing, but up to her room. She went in, closed the door, locked it, and crawled into bed.

"Dat should keep him busy," she whispered before taking a pleasant nap.

◈

Lightly breaded plantain slices fried in fish oil. Ground lamb loaf seasoned with red and green bell peppers. A spinach leaf salad drowned in Ten Century Isle dressing. Banana bread and fresh jububes for desert. Tall glasses of whole milk. Polly never knew such bliss could be found at the end of a dinner fork.

Elai and his three protectors sat at the dinner table once more. He noticed that Röger had barely touched his food. "Cheer up, Sir Röger. If all goes well tomorrow and I survive, I will make for you *your* favorite dish."

The sullen human did not look up from his plate. "Yeah? And what might that be, NcRay?" He was still thinking of Feyna.

"I won't know until then. But, please, do not give me any hints! I want us both to be surprised!" Elai laughed.

Röger just smiled and nodded, still not looking up.

Will took a slice of plantain off his plate and flipped it like a coin. "Say, Elai. What if you die tomorrow? You thought of that?"

Elai nodded. "Truthfully, I am terrified of dying. Nothing scares me more. But I have no regrets in spite of all my wrong doing. If I live, I will continue to live as I always have. If I die, then that means Arnu's *medicine,* his ability to steer the mad bileer that is destiny, is stronger than mine. His vengeance will be wrought. I will die only a seducing trickster, while he will live as a lowdown killer. Almost all fires eventually go out, anyway. We poor souls are like droplets of rain. Some of us will fall and dry up when we hit the bottom. Others will join with collections of water to either move or stay still. Some will freeze for a time. But we will all eventually make it back to the clouds, and lose what we were." He stood up and raised his glass of milk. "If I die tomorrow, let it be said that I did not run and hide like a guilty house cat! But that I faced what came with dignity and grace." He drank the whole glass.

No one drank with him but Will. And it was only a sip. "We're takin' turns watchin' you tonight, whether you like it're not," he insisted, flexing his eyebrows.

"Oh, I might like that." NcRay grinned, sneaking a glance at Polly.

"We'll be sittin' in a chair in yer bedroom. An hour per watch-stander," Will added.

"Oh, really?" He was blatantly staring at Polly now. "Would you be prepared for an intruder, Ms. Gone?"

"I'd be prepared for anyting." As soon as she said it, she regretted it.

Elai's eyes were laughing now.

Will saw and recognized that look, and didn't cotton to it one bit. "This is how it's gonna go." He spoke gruffly to get the man's attention. "I'll take the first watch. Röger'll go second. The last third of the night, him an' Pol are gonna switch out. We'll try not to wake you during the switches."

"You're too kind," Elai muttered.

Will continued. "When yer awake, the three of us're gonna stick to you like gum under a desk. We're even gonna be around when you empty yer ass on the pot. Now, I've scouted every room and all over the outside. We're gonna wait it out in the main entrance hall."

"Are you sure? It's the biggest room in the house."

"Sure, I'm sure. Plenty o' open space. Less room to hide an' sneak in. Plenty o' room fer us to hop, chop, scoot, an' shoot. Real echoey, too. Good fer listenin' fer footfalls. You just wait an' see, son. An' after the confrontation, yer gonna cook up what ever it is Röger wants most an' pay us what you owe."

"You make it all sound so simple," Elai sighed with doubt in his voice.

"Well, it's gonna hafta be fer now. What we're facin' is a pre-warned assassination. Yer brother has four years of hate to guide, fine tune, an' sharpen his mind. I'm sure he's got a doozy of a plan. When he makes his move, we're gotta be ready to counter it right off the bat, keep them dominos from fallin'."

And so, the plan went. As night fell, Will cleaned his gun as he puffed on a cigarette. He kept his eyes on the large windows in Elai's room. Meanwhile, the Drakeri man slept lightly. Elai stirred, but did not wake when Röger came in to change places. He woke up fully when Polly's turn came. He sat up when they were finally alone.

"Good morning," he said with a wry, drowsy grin. He rubbed his eyes and put on his spectacles.

"Go back to sleep," she replied dismissively. She sat slumping in the chair like a child in time out.

"I'm rested," he assured. "Being a workaholic makes sleep less important." He waited for a response. There wasn't one. He smiled at her. "I truly am grateful for your help."

No response.

"Do you think I'm evil?"

No response.

"Because, I think that *you* are evil, Polly Gone."

She looked at him.

"I can tell, you know. The rag-tag life of an Excursionist is not for you. You are obviously of some noble class. There are three types of evil: those that neglect, those that destroy, and those that consume. We are both consumers, Polly. The blood of Retaeh runs strongly through us. Not that I think that good and evil are primary forces in the world, that's all hogwash. But they do exist in the abstract sense."

"You tink too much. And you talk too much," she told him. "You are a tangled mess of deception and bullpie and fear. You speak in broad terms to sound wise. But you know nothing of evil. You are merely a boring man wit' too many options. But I am not one of dem. Now shut your eyes and mouth. I don't care if you sleep."

"I apologize," he said, lying back down. "You are still just a teenager, anyway. And what little maturity you might have had has been..."

"Shut up," she ordered harshly.

He did so until dawn with a smile on his lips.

The fateful day came. After a small breakfast of diced fruit, the three protectors took their positions.

The entrance hall had six towering stained glass windows, each one five and a half feet wide by twenty feet tall. They were all nearly identical, with depictions of rose vines snaking around gray columns. There were three on either side of the front door. They all rose to the second level of the building where the stairs lead. Six iron and glass light fixtures dangled from the high domed ceiling like sleeping bats. With the morning light shining through the ominous windows, they remained unlit. The three Excursionists and their charge waited patiently in the center of the hall floor, right in front of the pedestal that held the first bottle of NcRay beer.

"I feel like a squatting mallard," Elai groaned nervously.

"Oh, yer bait, all right," Will agreed. "It's how we gotta bring him out."

At first, Elai grew furious, but quickly calmed himself. He warily looked at the blade and gun on Will's belt and the leather case strapped to his back. "What's in the case?" he asked.

"Falcona. We won't need her fer this job." The bukk gave no further explanation.

The front doorbell rang. Elai grew tense. "I hope it's the detectives," he said in a cracked whisper.

Polly looked at him with mild disgust, and then walked to the door. Her steps were careful and silent, taken with gentle ease. As she drew closer to the large red door, she pulled out her knife. She placed her free hand on the polished crimson wood.

299

She could feel the lust for blood on the other side. It was not as strong as the psychopath, Drew Blood's, but it was there.

"Who is it?" she called out.

"E.C.P.D. Detective Maxwell Sirron," answered a man's voice.

"And Detective Charlz Emmad," a younger man's voice added.

She gripped the knob and pulled open the door. The two well groomed Drakeri stood just outside the door. They wore fine cut suits of dark brown and burnt orange with polished badges pinned to their lapels. The older of the two, Sirron, wore his black wide brimmed hat. He bowed to the pretty young woman standing before him.

"Well met, Miss Gone. It's nice to get a chance to see you again." He grinned like a thirsty wolf.

Pretty Polly peered at the policeman. "What are you planning?" she asked with suspicion.

The two men's smiles melted. Det. Emmad noticed the knife in her hand.

"What do you mean?" Sirron asked, taking a step back. "We came to protect the councilman."

She scoffed and shook her head. "To what extent? His brother does not deserve to die. But you are here to kill. I can sense it in your blood."

The two men looked at each other. At first, they seemed confused, and then they laughed.

"Little girl," Sirron chuckled. "all I know is that the councilman's life is in danger. It is my duty to protect him no matter what. I have no respect for assassins, no matter what their cause may be. You need to grow up. Killing is necessary sometimes. You as a crimson theurge should understand that."

The two men entered, brushing past her before she could respond. *"I hate this!"* she thought as she slammed the door shut.

"Welcome, gentleman!" Elai called with a relieved smile. "It is good to see you both. Are you well prepared?"

"We are," Sirron responded. The detectives approached Will and Röger, and bowed to them respectfully. The two excursionists returned the bow.

As Will raised his head, he locked eyes with Sirron. "Pleasure to meet you two again."

"Likewise," Sirron returned.

Will took a cautious breath. "Sir, I understand that this is yer city, and that you like to do things yer way. But I really think it best that we take Arnu NcRay alive."

"How?" Sirron asked, amused by the tendikeye's politeness.

Will drew his gun within the blink of a humming bird's eye, startling both men. "I'm sorry. Was that too fast? Force o' habit. Anyway, the moment I see his gun, It's gonna fly out of his hand."

"And what if you don't see the gun in time?" Sirron asked.

Will sighed and nodded. "Then you two do what you hafta, I suppose. Better on yer conscience than mine."

Suddenly, one of the glass roses on the windows exploded with a loud bang.

"Everyone! Make a circle around the councilman!" Sirron shouted.

"It's Arnu!" Elai cried in terror.

Will, Polly, and Röger followed the command. It was the obvious thing to do, anyway.

Another glass rose exploded out of a different window.

The two detectives joined the circle. Reaching into his shoulder holster, Det. Sirron stood between Röger and Will. Röger gave the detective a friendly nod. Sirron looked at him nervously, not liking the look of the giant axe the human held. Det. Emmad stood between Will and Polly, also reaching into his jacket. She could feel his urge to commit violence grow stronger.

Another glass rose blew out of another window.

"That ain't no matchlock he's got!" the tendikeye yelled. He drew his sword. "No way he can reload one that fast!"

Elai NcRay looked at the warrior bukk who stood right in front of him. He felt a deep appreciation for the circumstances, no matter how risky they seemed. He swallowed his fear. Reaching into his jacket, he pulled out a matchlock pistol that looked like a roaring dragon. He pointed the barrel just inches behind Will's quill covered head. Then he yelled three words that only the detectives and whoever was outside would fully understand.

"SMOKE AND MIRRORS!!!"

It was a signal.

301

In that instant, Elai pulled the trigger, Det. Emmad gripped something in his jacket, and Det. Sirron pulled out a hammer that shown too brightly to be steel.

Will saw only the windows before seeing nothing at all. His head jerked forward in an explosion of blood and smoke, and he fell limply to the ground.

Before Röger had time to understand what happened, Det. Sirron swung his silver hammer in a horizontal arch into the human's ribs. As the brute curled from the shock of pain, Sirron swung down hard on Röger's wrist, shattering bone. As Röger's giant axe clanged to the floor, he felt another vicious blow on the center of his back. He collapsed, howling in mad agony.

Glaring at Polly, Det. Emmad pulled out a sap full of powdered lead. He swung it with full force at her face. But by some stroke of luck, she saw it coming and dodged. He growled angrily and took another swing. She stepped back and slashed open the flailing bag. A cloud of gray powder flew out and engulfed her. Emmad dropped the rent piece of canvas and took a bouncing fighter stance. He threw a fast thrusting sidekick into the gray cloud. Polly flew out the other side, landing and sliding ten feet away. Emmad dropped to the floor screaming. His calf was sliced open from knee to ankle.

Polly, still clutching her knife, got up. Her guts felt smashed, but she gave no sign of injury. Her eyes grew wide as she witnessed Röger getting pounded by Sirron's hammer. Will was motionless, laying face down in an expanding puddle of blood. And Elai NcRay held the very same pistol that "Arnu" held the night before.

"You..." she gasped. "It was you. IT WAS YOU THAT NIGHT!" Overwhelmed by rage, terror, and confusion, Polly trembled as her belly felt sick.

Elai glared at her with bared teeth. "The dream has subsided, my dear. Let the nightmare begin!" He hunkered down next to Will, and took back the lighter from his pocket. He looked over at Sirron. "Detective, I said that I wanted that human alive. It said so in the letter I gave you. Ease up a little!"

Sirron took one more swing, crushing Röger's shoulder. The Black Vest lay broken before his feet, breathing hard and partly conscious. The detective was also breathing heavy, not from exhaustion, but fear. "I'm sorry, Councilman. I wasn't going to take any chances. The post-morts told me he was a werekrilp. That's also why they failed to make the hit."

Elai's eyes widened. "It's a good thing they did fail. A werekrilp, you say?" He had a look of confusion that turned into furious curiosity. He looked over at Polly. "Did you know you worked with a werekrilp, Miss Gone?"

She gritted her teeth. They had been played. They had all been played. Will and Röger were bloody and broken. It had all been a lie.

"What about Arnu?" she asked in a cracking voice.

Elai's face flooded with sarcastic sympathy. "Arnu died last year. I hunted him down and reduced him to ashes. Now, *you* answer *my* question. Who really killed Lurcree Katlemay? Was it you or your round-ear monster here?"

"Why is it so important to you?" she asked, her head spinning.

Elai raised his chin in sinister pride. "Because I was the Master's apprentice. And I am bound by the Philocreed of the Sacred Flame to avenge him. Only then may I attain the power he had lost in death. And with that power I will provide life eternal for myself and my helpers."

"Why?!" she screamed, baring her teeth. "Why play dis game wit' us? Why wait three days to..to..."

"To kill you?" he asked, breathing hoarsely. "Because I was afraid of you. All of you. You killed the most powerful theurge I have ever known. I had to be careful. I had to learn about you all. My master and I were both born under the Concentrating Spider, you see. I took the utmost care in weaving this web of deceit!"

Polly's eyes passed over Röger. His eyes were half-closed, but his unsteady breathing continued. A single tear escaped her eye. She looked at Will who lay lifeless on the floor. Then she looked back at NcRay and the two detectives. Emmad was still on the floor wincing in pain. A rage rose inside her, tempered by icy cold discipline.

She raised her dagger, pointing it at NcRay. "One down, two to go!" she laughed with a smile as beautiful as it was twisted.

Elai's face filled with concern. "Hold her off!" he ordered Sirron. "Take her alive no matter what! I'll get the others from outside!" He made a mad dash for the front door.

Polly threw her knife at Elai.

Sirron threw his hammer at Polly.

Only one of them hit their target.

Elai fell face first fifteen feet from the front door. The knife stuck out of his back, four inches from his heart. Dodging the hammer had caused Polly to miss. Elai now crawled on all fours.

Sirron threw off his hat and charged her. She summoned her jagged veins. They sprouted from her wrists like thorny vines, snaking for something to latch on to.

The detective halted and dodged one of the swiping tendrils. For an older Drakeri, he was spry. He was able to evade, flip, and jump with dizzying agility. He laughed as he avoided her. "Two time Embrenil Martial Arts Champion," he declared with pride.

"Oh?" she asked. She took three fast leaping steps to where Emmad still sat. She wrapped a barbed red tendril around his neck. "Did you teach him, I wonder?"

"Wait!" Sirron demanded.

Polly grinned with malicious glee. "Take me alive no matter what, remember?"

Poor young Emmad would have yelled "NO" if his throat wasn't tied shut. He felt a strange feeling in his chest. Certain arteries closed off as others expanded. In the blink of an eye, all of Emmad's blood spewed out of his wounded leg. It made a huge red triangular spray trail across the marble floor. Thus perished Detective Charlz Emmad.

"You slag!" Sirron howled. He went in with reckless abandon. The force of his kicks knocked her veins to the side. She tried to dodge, but his thick knuckled fist caught her in the left shoulder. She spun to the floor, landing on her back hard against the marble floor. Her shoulder was going numb. She looked up to see Sirron raising up his leg for a devastating heel stomp. A stray vein coiled around his ankle, keeping his foot high in the air. Struggling to get up, she settled onto one knee. The Detective was stuck doing the standing splits right in front of her. The opportunity presented itself. She sprang up swift and straight, bringing her upper cutting elbow right into his groin. A dreadful sensation flooded Sirron's abdomen. The leg he stood on gave out, and he fell into the fetal position. Polly loomed over him with hate in her eyes. She steadied her veins for a finishing strike. But before she could, her double-pointed ears caught the growing sound of running footsteps.

She looked to her left. Elai managed to crawl to the front door and unlock it. Running to her now were two figures she had hoped to never see again: Shiver and Chepsu, the post-mort assassins. The grim faced blonde woman carried the small fetus on her shoulder. She tossed a smoking pistol to the floor and drew throwing knives from her form-fitting outfit, three blades per hand. She let them fly as soon as she and Polly made eye contact. For a fraction of a second, Polly could see the flying formation of the blades. The formation changed three times before they reached her, each blade curving like an arrow in a strong wind.

"How do I dodge that?" was her last thought before all six knifes violated her flesh.

Will Foundling, do you hear me? Do you hear me, Will Foundling?

"Yeah."

Good. Will Foundling, you have bled your last drop. You are dead, Will Foundling.

"...aw...Gut snake......"

Do you wish to come back? If you come back, you may be able to save yourself and your friends. Do you wish to comeback?

"Fer what price?"

Um, you have to buy Waltre and myself a beer? Is that fair?

"Fair enough. Do it."

Will opened his eyes. Above him stood the Ex-Chief Waltre Taly and the lanky Coroner Leal NcRuse. They helped him to his feet.

"How are you feeling?" NcRuse asked.

305

"Fine, I guess. What just happened? Where are the others?" He looked around and saw the body of Detective Emmad and the floor covered in blood.

NcRuse shook his head. "There is little time to explain everything. Taly and I scarcely knew the facts until I just now questioned Emmad's corpse. But this is all that matters: Elai NcRay lied to you. He is part of the Mystic Mafia. So were Detectives Sirron and Emmad. Waltre and I tailed them here to confirm our suspicions. Arnu NcRay has been dead a while now. It was all a scheme to learn your weaknesses and ambush you. Sir Röger and Ms. Gone have been taken somewhere in this mansion. They are not dead. I'd be able to sense if they were. It is up to the three of us to find them."

Will followed every word the Coroner spoke. There was something about the Necrotheurge's voice that made him accept the information as if it were the most obvious truth to be told. There was no doubt, no suspicion, no sense of surprise. He just knew for some odd reason that the man was not steering him wrong. "Right," Will replied, nodding. "Is there anything else I should know?"

NcRuse hesitated and looked at Taly.

"Tell him," Taly ordered.

The Coroner smiled nervously. "Um, well, you didn't exactly...survive the shot to your head. In fact, most of your blood is on the floor over there. But don't worry! Waltre froze it before it could lose oxygen and coagulate!"

"I also froze your brain," Taly added cheerfully.

Will's mouth gaped in horror. He grabbed NcRuse by the collar. "JUST WHAT ARE YOU SAYIN'?!"

NcRuse shriveled fearfully. "You are dead, Mr. Foundling. So, I raised you as a post-mort. But do not despair. You still have free will, and most of your *anima* is still intact. You would have probably become a ghost had I not shown up in time. You must harbor some deep animosity, young man. Further more, if we can rescue Polly in time, Waltre can thaw your blood--"

"And your brain," Taly added.

"And then she can put your blood back in you and revive you!" NcRuse smiled with bugged eyes and narrow teeth.

Will's eye twitched. He let go of NcRuse and grabbed Taly. "Why did you freeze my brain? Why don't it feel froze?"

NcRuse placed a hand on his shoulder. "Because you aren't breathing. Your brain needs air to survive. Waltre froze it to preserve it. Further more, you are incapable of feeling physical pain. Now, are you through worrying for yourself, and ready to help your friends?"

Will frowned and hung his head slightly. He rubbed the back of his neck and felt the hole in it. It wasn't that big, but it was enough to sever an artery. It was a point blank shot just to the left of his spine. A sloppy shot, but it did the trick.

Twenty-three years of memories flashed before his eyes. All that he had experienced and all that he had hoped to make happen ceased to matter. He was dead, on his way to the brush pile. His best friend lay crippled half way across the city. Two new friends were missing and at the mercy of the man behind it all. Elai NcRay, a suave politician who had played them like fools.

Will folded the right side of his collar down, making both sides lay flat. "If Polly or either one of you dies down there, I got no chance of comin' back, right?"

"Right," they both answered.

Will gritted his teeth. "Well, then if that comes to be: I'd better be a still corpse after this."

"So be it," NcRuse answered. "On my philocreed, I will not allow you to stay a walking dead."

Taly nodded at them, grunting in agreement. "Good. Glad to see that settled. But where do we search?" He seemed to be asking himself more than them. He looked around, studying, deducing with centuries of detective experience. The smear-trails of blood told him that Emmad and Will's bodies had been dragged to the stair cases. "But why?" he asked aloud.

Will and NcRuse noticed it, too. Will walked over to one of the puddles of blood. It was round except for one part that was perfectly straight. It had settled on a part of the vast design of circles and lines in the marble. He dropped to his stomach and placed his ear to the floor. He drew his gun and tapped one of the barrels against the marble. "Here!" he called.

"Are you sure?" NcRuse asked. "What about the rest of the house?"

"They're under here," Will insisted. "I've combed this dive over three or four times. Look. The blood was leakin' down through that crack. Quite a bit of it. It's gotta go somewhere."

The Coroner knelt down, touched the floor, and closed his eyes. "Hmm, yes. I do sense the presence of life down there." He paused for a moment. "But there is also the presence of death. There are one, maybe two post-morts down there."

"An' I'll bet a pack o' smokes who they are." Will took out a cigarette.

"Don't bother." NcRuse told him. "You're lungs aren't functioning, remember?"

Will shuffled his hand in his pocket. *"Shunter musta took his lighter back!"* he thought. He placed the cigarette in his lips anyway.

"Watch your step, Will!" Taly called. "I believe I've found the triggering mechanism." He stood next to the pedestal that displayed the first bottle of NcRay beer. He removed the glass dome that covered it. He carefully wrapped his fingers around the bottleneck, pulled, then pushed. There was a loud click beneath the floor.

A hole opened up by Will's feet, revealing a dark stairway. He looked back up at Taly and NcRuse. "Whatchu boys got fer weapons?" he asked.

Waltre Taly wore his fireproofed poncho. Under that he wore his steel and leather cord armor. On his left hand was a black velvet glove. He made a fist with it, and it ignited with white flames.

Leal NcRuse held up an old dry gourd that looked like a deformed maraca. It was crested with tattered black feathers and white beads. "This is my death-rattle. Get it?" he giggled with a coy smile.

Will blinked twice. "No guns?" he asked. "Swords, even?"

"The more faith you put in a weapon, the less faith you have in your theurgy," the two men spoke together seamlessly.

The tendikeye rolled his eyes. "Theurges," he muttered.

Röger had been hammered before, but never like this. The treacherous detective had hit him square on all four limbs. A few pieces of rib had broken off, and were suspended in swelling flesh. And thanks to the blow to his back, his lower half was completely numb. In his 161 years of life, he had survived much worse. His lycanthropic curse allowed him to recuperate from any wound. Unless those wounds were caused by silver weapons.

But alas, the armory at the Embrenil Civic Police Dept. was smartly stocked. When the post-mort assassin informed Det. Maxwell Sirron of the human's hidden power, he went straight back to the station house to find the perfect weapon. The armory had silver bullets and a silver plated bastard sword. But in the end, he had decided upon a one-handed silver sledge hammer. It was small, easy to conceal, and great for subduing unsuspecting lycanthropes. Röger wouldn't heal these injuries anytime soon. The hurting pounded through him like a boiling poison. His mind was clouded in sickening torment.

But his ears still worked fine. He had overheard Elai's confession to Polly. Will had been shot. Polly had fought back and lost. He had been picked up and carried down some stairs. They chained him down to a bed made of iron bars. Someone took off his helmet and threatened to smash his skull if he moved. He opened his eyes, seeing a brick wall to his left. He slowly turned his face up, and saw Det. Sirron standing over him with his hammer raised. Then he looked left. Polly had also been chained down on a bed made of iron bars. A pile of chopped wood and straw lay beneath it.

They were in some kind of huge underground wine cellar (or beer cellar, more likely) that had been converted into a dungeon.

Elai NcRay winced in pain as he put on a brown and red robe. The knife wound in his back was not deep (it had imbedded in his right shoulder blade), but he was not accustomed to injury.

"What should I do with these?" Shiver asked him. She held Röger's sword and axe in her arms.

"Toss them underneath him. They should share his fate in the fire," the Councilman replied.

The dead-eyed blonde examined the superior quality of the weapons. "Pity to waste such fine instruments of death," she said. "It is against my philocreed to destroy lethal weapons."

Elai's eyes flashed like flickering candles. "Do as you are paid, assassin. This is no necrotheurgic ritual."

Shiver showed no sign of concern. She merely shrugged and tossed the weapons as she was told. "Your will, not mine, sir."

Chepsu was still on her shoulder. He was happy to have his tiny blue bladed sword back. *"I'm glad they did not sell it,"* he thought. He turned his dried-out cherub face to his employer. "Master NcRay, we offer our most sincere apologies for not checking in with you before we attacked them. Your late teacher, Lurcree, said he wanted it done as soon as possible."

"I understand. But the circumstances have changed." NcRay replied. "The old Master is dead. I am the still-glowing embers beneath his ashes. The glory his flame failed to reach I must achieve. And if I am to inherit his power and complete his ritual, I must kill his killer." He turned, looking at Polly and Röger. "But *who* is it? Who killed him? The official police report was that Miss Gone had made the fatal move. Isn't that right, Detective?"

"That's correct, Councilman," Sirron replied. "I wrote the report myself." He watched as Elai walked over to Polly. "Um, Mr. Councilman? Why do you need to know who specifically? Aren't you going to kill them both, anyway?"

Elai did not answer at first. He reached out and caressed Polly's cheek and mouth. He scanned his gaze over her limp body, ignoring the six unlethal knife wounds. "It will take all my power to sacrifice him or her in the correct and proper way; by sacred rite. I can only attempt this once. That is why I did not waste a single maxim upstairs." He heard a strained laugh behind him. He turned to see Röger smiling.

"You cook up more than just food, don'tcha, fancy-pants? Schemes, too." The Black Vest coughed up blood as he laughed again.

Elai stepped over to him, his eyes cold. "It was you, wasn't it? It was you who killed my mentor. Ms. Polly may be a crafty little theurgeling. Nonetheless, my master would have easily resisted her powers. But a monster like you could have taken my mentor by surprise."

Röger laughed through his agony. "If that old coot was something you aspire to be like, then you're just as shunted as he was. He died wailing like a dog as I pulled his guts out, for what it's worth."

Elai smiled. "You make a good point. He *was* my mentor for awhile. But we grew apart. He was a brash old drunk who wanted to keep living, but not enjoy life. His soul was a

310

smoldering bitter flame. Why stay a hermit for all eternity? The immortality he sought would be better enjoyed by me."

"And me," Sirron added.

"Yes, and you, Detective." Elai concurred. "It is a shame your partner could not join in our spoils."

Sirron made a sour face. His fierce eyes shifted over to Polly. "Since we know who did it now, can I kill her? Emmad was more than a partner, he was a-"

"Rump-Buddy!" Röger interrupted, coughing up blood.

Sirron looked down at him and sneered. He was about smack him with the hammer again.

"Stay your hand," Elai ordered. "You may not kill either of them. You need only keep the peace while I complete the sacrificial vengeance." He raised his hands over Röger. "This is really going to hurt, Sir Röger!"

"Wait," Röger grunted weakly. "If you want to be immortal, how about I just chew your face off? Werecreatures live forever, you know."

"I'll pass," Elai returned.

"Well, at least tell me how a two-faced politician, corporate shunt-off, aristocrat playboy can learn an obscure secret to eternal life!"

"You really want to know?" NcRay laughed. "It's simple. Even a wretched round-ear like you can understand. Time has been measured in increments of ten in the entire Cluster since the first histories were written. This caused the universal flow of existence to adapt to this spiritual/social rhythm. The faces of clocks were looked upon with more devotion than parents, loved ones, heroes, heads of state, and teachers. Long ago, a theurge discovered the mystical path of time. He taught his secrets to no one, and did as he wished. He crafted an hour glass that allowed him to stop, reverse and travel to past and future events. He also wielded a scythe of pure silver. One day the theurge was slain by a group of fifteen excursionists. They took the sand from the broken hourglass and the shards of the broken scythe and made matching mementos for themselves: pocket watches. This was when the Drakeri race was young, mind you.

Five hundred years ago, my master learned via divination that all fifteen of the watches would find their way here in this very year, mainly because the clock tower was destroyed and people had need of such devices. And so, Lurcree Katlemay made a place for himself by the city hell. Sensing my potential, he became my private tutor, secretly teaching me the intricacies of pyrotheurgy and sand-based geotheurgy. I learned well, but played myself off to the public as a self-taught novice. Together, we composed a maxim that would slowly siphon a small piece of soul out from someone's eyes. A side effect is blindness, for fire and sand make glass, glass makes mirror reflections, reflections are an aspect of sight. It's a stretch, I know. But theurgy thrives on how well your faith stretches with what you imagine possible. We used the glass from the watches as a focus point for the soul fragments to filter into. But the big part of the plan was the new clock tower being rebuilt on top of City Hall.

The restoration was my idea. I proposed it to the rest of the Council. We all voted. It got passed. The glass from the watches will be mixed secretly in with recycled beer bottles from my company. All that glass will be used to create four giant faces for the colossal clock. Two, I have made thus far. And when it is completed next year, all who look upon it will lose ten years from their lifespan. And it will be added to my own! Is that such a crime? Ten years for a Drakeri is nothing! And as for humans, most of them just waste their short lives anyway. No one needed to die as a result of this plan. All that the "Mystic Mafia" really wanted was surplus time to be put to better use! There may be no time like the present, but there is certainly no present like time! It was a gift to be shared with four of Embrenil's finest policemen. Rafe, Jana, Emmad; they understood that the prospect of eternal life outweighed what was socially acceptable. They saw the light and clarity of the Sacred Flame!

But you, Sir Röger Yamus! You and your cohorts became nosy and curious and thirsty for some superficial form of justice. How am I different from any other politician who sneaks and schemes to make his life more comfortable? How am I worse than any other company owner who milks his workers for that extra bit of energy to compensate for my lack of creativity? *'If you can't be creative like your brother, be productive.'* my father used to say."

Elai wiped the sweat from his indigo brow. The room was getting hot, muggy. It was because of his growing excitement.

Röger looked up at the man with cold eyes. "You're no different from them, Elai. Only, you have the means to take what they want. And now, before you burn me alive, I want you to take out your lighter and tell me what my favorite meal is."

Elai paused, laughed with amusement, and shrugged a shoulder. "Oh, all right!" He took out his lighter, woke the flame, and looked in it. His smiling face melted to one of disgust and terror. He shouted at Sirron. "Hit him again, you fool! Hit him!"

Det. Sirron glanced down at Röger before swinging his hammer, and hesitated from a paralyzing fright. Röger grimaced with green glowing eyes and a mouth overflowing with drool covered fangs. A roar erupted from that terrible mouth that made the two captors tremble. The sound caused Polly to wake.

"I said hit him!" Elai cried, backing away quickly.

The chains that held Röger down began to stretch and expand.

Det. Sirron raised his hammer, ready to bring it down. A loud *KA-KRAKK* came from the dungeon's entry way. Sirron's hand exploded and the head of the hammer broke off.

Elai NcRay turned his head to where the shots had come from. "YOU!"

Will stood in the stone doorway with his sword and gun drawn. Two trails of smoke snaked upward out of the pistol's barrels. On both sides of him were Waltre and NcRuse. The tendikeye had no words of righteousness for NcRay, just the next two bullets. He fired another two rounds, aiming for the chest and throat. The hot pieces of lead were turned off course by the Pyrotheurge's will. They both exploded into the brick wall behind him.

"Gut snake!" Will thought. *"Just like Lurcree!"*

Polly looked around and saw that she was held by chains. She looked around for the lock and found it. A subtle vein slithered out her wrist and poked around inside the keyhole.

Det. Sirron wailed at the top of lungs, looking at the mangled, squirting stump at the end of his wrist.

Röger's chains popped. He grew bigger and hairier. He could smell the fresh blood from Sirron's injury, and his mind melted away into a blissful rage. With his massive arms, he snatched Sirron down onto the grill-bed with him. Sirron choked on his own screams as the crippled Werekrilp chewed random pieces off of him.

"Elai NcRay!" Waltre Taly yelled. "Surrender or die. The Department knows about Sirron and Emmad. Furthermore, they

313

now know of your involvement. This place will be crawling with cops in minutes. It's over, Councilman. By tomorrow, all of Embrenil will know of your involvement."

Elai's eyes widened in a disappointment that few could fathom. He clenched his teeth and fists, and shook his head madly. "You will all share in my ruin, Taly!" The wood beneath Polly and Röger's grill-beds ignited. Det. Sirron began to burn to death while being eaten. The Werekrilp was too mad with hunger to care about his fur getting singed. Polly managed to pop the chain's lock, and rolled off the bed with only minor burns.

"Shiver! Chepsu!" Elai called. "Assist me!"

The post-mort assassins drew their swords and leaped passed NcRay, charging the three men at the doorway.

Waltre Taly raised his glove-covered hand. "*Sharp winter is now loosened!*" he yelled. A burst of light blue energy exploded from his palm. Three log-sized icicles appeared and flew at the post morts. They dodged them easily. But they were not the target!

Elai saw the thick spears of ice darting toward him. He stood between the two beds of fire. "*Neglected fires are wont to gather strength!*" he yelled, raising his arms. A wall of flame rose up from between the beds. The flying icicles turned to vapor.

Shiver and Chepsu were closing in. Will fired four rounds into the dead-eyed blonde. None of them mattered. Coroner NcRuse raised his gourd-wand and rattled it in a chanting rhythm. "*May your bodies rest free from evil!*" he called to them. Chepsu stopped, entranced by the rattling. Shiver pressed on.

With a scraping, high pitched ring, Shiver and Will's swords met. Taly and NcRuse stepped away, giving them plenty of room.

"You were dead!" she hissed, thrusting her blade at him.

He side-stepped. "Still am," he replied grimly. He dashed in closer, knocking her blade to the side whenever she tried to aim it for a thrust. As she started to slash at him, he side stepped again and slashed at the ribs under her arm. She backed away quickly, pulling herself off his blade. "*This one's a linear fighter,*" Will thought. "*She goes straight in for an attack and backs straight out to evade.*" He started circling her as they fenced. She tried her fancy contortionist attacks, but he always managed to evade the tip of her piercing blade. Growing frustrated, she swung wildly at Will's neck. Between the barrels of the

314

tendikeye's Mark Twain Special was a steel plate with a heart shaped notch cut in the center. It was more than just for show. Will caught the holly leaf-shaped blade in that heart-shaped notch and twisted his wrist. Shiver's sword became trapped. But she didn't have the sense to let go of it in time. Will closed in fast, spinning like a dervish wind, and sliced her head from her shoulders. Before the screaming head could fall to the floor, Will spun around again, leaping and raising his heavy boot. Like a soccer ball into a goal, he kicked the head of Shiver into one of Elai's barbeque inferno beds. The body dropped limp as the head was consumed.

Waltre ran through Elai's wall of flame unburned (thanks to his poncho). His velvet glove burned with *Winter Fire*. Elai stood on the other side with his dragon pistol drawn. "Afraid to debate with me maxim to maxim, you spineless novice?" Taly asked in a taunting tone.

"Oh, I *am* being fair here, *Frigorifist*. I forged these bullets using my own theurgy. They are stronger than steel. Good Day!" A burst of flame shot out of the barrel. Taly crashed onto his back, clutching his chest.

NcRay turned around and ran to the back wall. He raised his hand. *"A blazing fire makes a house look more pleasant on a winter's day!!"* he cursed. A door appeared in a wreath of flame. Before he could run through, something sharp coiled around his ankle. He was pulled face first onto the floor. His nose broke, and he went blind from the impact. He felt something crawl onto his back. His arms wouldn't move. They were pinned. He felt teeth sink into his neck. At first, he thought it was the Werekrilp wanting a second helping of living flesh. But he could feel her nubile young curves pressed against him. Polly had lost a lot of blood from Shiver's throwing knives. She needed to restock.

As she drank him away, she could hear him talking to her in her head.

"I never enjoyed killing anyone. I just wanted to live young forever. But you, my dear. You kill because it feeds your power, because you enjoy it. You're enjoying it right now. It's going beyond the ecstasy of winning. I was wrong about you. You are not an evil consumer like I was. You are a destroyer! Perhaps...that is a better way to be..."

Polly's eyes widened as she realized that the blood in her mouth was boiling. She jerked her teeth out of his neck, screaming and spitting and grasping her face. She rolled off of Elai, roiling in agony. The heat of his blood went all through her. She saw him rise up to his hands and knees. He looked like a skeleton with pale purple skin. His sunken eyes shifted to her. At first, the eyes looked weak and tired, but then they lit up with fire and rage. In utter terror, Polly watched as his eyeballs boiled and popped away like fat in a skillet. The holes left behind wept away the fluids and blazed with smoke and fire. Like some terribly wounded animal, Elai turned away from her and ran into the fiery passage he had opened, disappearing with the flames.

❖

Chepsu's mind went blank the second he heard the Coroner's words. Leal NcRuse looked down at the tiny figure. The undead unborn looked like a little doll holding a toy sword. Leal felt a fracture in his heart as he reached down to pick it up. "You poor unfortunate child. Never you fear. You are with me now." He put the diminutive post mort in his inside pocket, and looked around.

Waltre was badly wounded.

The post mort female known only as Shiver was a foot shorter and not moving.

Polly was slowly getting up off the ground.

Elai NcRay was missing.

And Will was okay, sort of.

Will and Polly helped Waltre to his feet.

"I can heal you," Polly offered.

"No," replied Taly. "You must save your power for him." He nodded his head to Will. "I'll be just fine."

Polly looked at Will. "Save you? What's wrong?"

Will ignored her. The flames of the barbeque beds began to grow. In a dark corner of the dungeon room, a great striped beast was huddled, battered, broken and burned. It was moaning and whimpering in a deep timbered voice. Its large head was crowned with two long horns like that of a bull. It held something shiny in its good paw. Its other limbs didn't seem to work.

"Hey, Rög!" Will called.

The monster turned around and snarled. It held the silver helmet.

"We need to get outta here, Rög," Will muttered sadly. "I don't think that helmet's gonna fit over them horns."

The beast growled and dropped the helmet. It began to drag itself to them.

Will took aim. "I'm so sorry, Rög," he said, his throat dry and cracking. He pulled the triggers until the gun was empty.

The beast screamed, but kept coming, slowly.

Will's eyes filled with tears. "We can't jus' leave 'im like this!" he yelled. He looked over at Polly. She was already crying. The stress of the last week was finally coming down on her.

"There," Taly said, pointing at the silver hammer head on the floor. "Use that."

Will jumped over and picked it up. With all his might he threw it at the beast. A gash opened up on its hairy brow as the hunk of metal bounced off. The hateful expression went blank, and the beast collapsed. Within seconds, the hairy, bulky body shrunk down to its human shape.

NcRuse timidly walked over and felt Röger's neck. "He's still alive. Barely."

"Good!" Will cried. "Put that helmet back on him. He needs it to keep a lid on the beast. Now, let's amscray!"

Waltre scoffed. "So, he's a werekrilp. And it got past me? Good thing I retired!" But in Watre's mind he thought *"That explains why he bribed me to let him keep his helm on when I locked him up."*

NcRuse and Polly helped Waltre out. Will threw Röger over his shoulder.

As they all reached the top of the steps, they saw that the mansion around them was burning.

"How'd all this catch fire?!" Will exclaimed, setting Röger down.

Waltre raised his head. "It was that last maxim NcRay casted. He tried to use it to escape and leave us to burn."

"Ms. Gone, listen to me!" NcRuse ordered. "Will died when NcRay shot him. He bled to death. I managed to preserve his soul and make him a post mort. Waltre froze his brain and blood. That puddle over there is his." He pointed down at the small lake of crimson. It was not frozen anymore thanks to the surrounding blaze. "Do you think you can save him, Ms. Gone?"

Polly looked confused and unsure for a moment. Then she looked at Will.

"I don't mind just this one time," he told her with a cocky grin and worried eyes.

She smiled back. "Lay down den."

Will lay down on his back near the blood puddle.

Waltre hunkered beside him and grabbed his forehead. *"Spring follows Winter! After this season will come another!"* he whispered like a cold wind. "There. Your brain is thawed."

"Treat him as you would any dying person," NcRuse told her.

Everything around them was burning. If not for the hall's high ceiling, they would be choking in a cloud of hot black smoke.

Polly placed a hand on Will's chest and another in the puddle. She closed her eyes and whispered something no one could hear over the fire. The puddle seemed to come to life as it flowed back in the hole in Will's neck. She jabbed her finger in the hole and picked out the bullet. Placing her palm over the wound, she said *"Good healing always tastes bitter!"*. She then placed her hands on his sternum and began to pump it up and down. Will's eyes grew wide as she pinched his nose shut and breathed air into his mouth. She pumped his chest again, and then switched back to mouth to mouth.

She looked him in the eyes with innocent concern. "Are you starting to feel alive yet?"

"Um..." Will blushed, but it could have just been from the heat from the fire.

"Dis isn't working," she cried. She put her hand over his heart. "Will, I need you to work wit' me on dis. You need to tink of your reason for living. Whatever it is dat's in your heart dat keeps you going--use it now!"

Will frowned "I got more to die fer than live fer, Polly. And today may be the day."

Polly shook her head. "I felt someting in your heart when I first touched you! Someting strong dat won't give up!"

Will looked at her with hollow eyes. "It was hate, Polly. Nothin' more." His eyes closed and he breathed out a long gentle sigh.

Leal NeCruse raised his chin. "He feels the pull of death, and is yielding to it. Goodbye, Will Foundling. Your sacrifice will not be—"

"Shut up!" Polly glared at the Necrotheurge and then back at Will. Her eyes blazed blood red and said *"I call upon you by de meaning of your name. Will. A name dat means stubborn. Reverse your defiance from life to death."* She used her will to command his blood to flow throughout his body. She kept every drop of it moving. *"Wake up and LIVE! You can find a reason to later."*

Will felt an eerie sensation. His heart started to beat again. Throughout his body, organs began to function as if waking from a nightmare. He was being brought back to life, but was conscious through it all. His brain woke up. It felt like barbwire being pulled behind his eyes. He started coughing and convulsing. Polly kept his heartbeat at a steady rate. He felt sick and stiff all over, like having the flu during a hangover. But he was alive.

"OooaaAAGHHUUUUUGH!" he screamed as he puked all over the floor.

"Hurry!" NcRuse ordered. "The front door! The wood has burned away!" He pointed at the flame filled doorway.

Polly looked at the blazing opening and shook her head. "We won't make it through! De wall of fire in front of it is too hot!"

"Not for me," Waltre protested, standing up slowly and wincing. "I can go through, then I'll toss my poncho back inside. We can all take turns wearing it on the way out."

"Let's give it a go," Will said, wiping his mouth.

Taly stumbled to the doorway and walked into the blinding flames. A moment later, his poncho came flying back in. NcRuse went next. But before he could take it off and throw it back though, the archway support gave out. Thousands of bricks fell and closed off the doorway.

The two law men outside could do nothing for them now. Taly tried to use his theurgy to cool the blaze, but the fire was too strong. The entire outside crawled with police men and women. They pulled the two men away, telling them it was too dangerous to go back inside.

Will and Polly dragged Röger back from the fire. The air grew dark with smoke. Their lungs felt hot. They looked around

319

for some kind of escape. There was none. Even the hole in the floor they had come out of had a long tongue of flame blazing out of it.

Will shook his head and laughed. It was a sad laugh. "Miss Polly. Please, help me drag Röger under that staircase."

"Why?"

"You'll see. Just...I said please. That's all there is to it."

She looked at him with soft eyes. "Okay."

They went underneath one of the blazing staircases. Burning debris started to fall.

The smoke in the air got thicker.

Will reached into one of his hidden pockets. He pulled out three bullets and showed them to her. "I don't wanna burn to death. Do you?"

She looked at them for a long moment. "I understand," she smiled. "It was good...and fun...and irritating working wit' you, Will Foundling of Cloiherune."

Will gave her a cocky wink and loaded the rounds. He took aim at Röger lying on the floor and fired. He pointed the barrel at Polly point blank and fired. Then he put it under his chin. "I'll never live this down," he sighed, and fired.

Grandmaster GoLightly was the most prized and celebrated theurge in all of Embrenil. His path was weather. It was because of him that most of the surrounding farmland was plentiful, making the city an ideal place for trade. Those who did not love him still felt some semblance of gratitude and respect.

On this day, he had *heard* that one of his fellow council members perished in a house fire. Without asking why or how, he sat on a carpet and rode a current of wind to the blazing estate. The police and fire department had their hands full just keeping the fire from spreading to other houses. He landed atop one of the massive monster skulls in the front yard. Everyone stopped what they were doing to watch him. He pulled a fiddle and bow from his large sleeve while gazing sadly at the house. Everyone quieted down as he started to play. The notes were sweet and joyous, but the melody was wise and ancient. He dipped and swayed with a thousand years of emotion beaming from his face. Dark clouds formed above the smoking building.

The rain began to fall in time to the beat of the music. With each beat came a sheet of raindrops. He played faster and with more feeling. The sheets of rain fell and fell at a faster rate. The tired people outside felt invigorated with every splash. The blaze of the building died down. After a few minutes of sonic ecstasy, it wasn't even smoking anymore.

The people rejoiced and showered him with praise. The Grandmaster bowed and smiled graciously. Then he sat back down on his carpet, and the wind carried him away.

The fire department went in to investigate. There were no survivors. All the art was destroyed except for three odd looking statues beneath one of the staircases.

"It's them!" an officer shouted. "They must have used petra rounds to survive the blaze!"

◈

An hour later, the three soot covered statues turned back into flesh inside the 3rd Ward Temple of Health. They were given the best treatments the staff could offer. Will, who still had the flu/hangover feeling of being brought back to life, also had to contend with that itchy stiff feeling of converting from stone to flesh. Barely conscious and robbed of reason, he was all too willing to let the Sisters there use any theurgy they wanted, for his pain out-weighed his pride.

Röger required the most care. The Sisters were given special instructions by the former Chief to not remove his helmet. The top Healer, Sister Julya, was called in to treat him. She offered no promises for how he would turn out.

Waltre Taly was in the midst of a delicate surgery to remove the bullet from his chest. Polly required little to no attention. She sat in her recovery bed as she explained the events that lead up to the fire to high ranking police officials. Leal NcRuse sat in a nearby chair, filling in the gaps and confirming her story.

"It was I who found out about Emmad and Sirron," the Coroner explained. "The dwindling spirit of Detective Rafe informed me that the Mystic Mafia had two more cops in their pocket. We suspected it was Emmad and Sirron since they all but begged to document the dead theurge's lair by the hell pits. Rafe and Jana showed similar enthusiasm when the case started. Some people will go to any extreme if it means the promise of eternal life, no matter who they hurt along the way. Waltre was hoping to flush them out eventually. But when Waltre and I found out that they were going to 'assist' Four Winds-One Storm in a protection gig, things went from fishy to down right rank. I'm just glad we made it there in time."

Polly gave a detailed account of the Mystic Mafia's every activity, who their every member was, what deals were made amongst them, and what plans were made by them. It was as if she knew everything about it that Elai NcRay knew. Times, dates, every victim's name, the legend of Xelor the Mad, the nefarious Clock tower plot, everything. All was revealed and everything matched up.

"One more ting:" she asked. "Elai NcRay is not dead. His *philocreed*...changed slightly as I had him down. He became a different kind of theurge when on the brink of death. Beware of him." She took a deep breath and smiled slightly. "On a better note: I tink I know a way to undo some de damage he has caused. Contact every victim who has been blinded."

Just then, the entry door swung open. The young Officer Ladue stumbled in, out of breath. His violet skin was paled to a sickly shade of lavender. "The NcRay Brewery! It's burning! Every Officer needs to get down there!"

Polly gritted her teeth. Her tongue was still raw from being burned by NcRay's blood. "He's dere!"

The Coroner rose from his seat. For once, he actually looked worried. "The Fire Department already had one fire to deal with today. There is little doubt they will be late in arriving. Officer Ladue, were you told how bad the blaze is?

The Officer frowned. "One crew of firefighters already managed to get there, sir. They tried to rescue the brewery employees. But Councilman NcRay was inside and attacked them. Nearly the whole crew was roasted alive! The nearby buildings are already catching. If the fire continues to grow, it could spread throughout the city!"

Polly leapt out of bed and started lacing up her boots.

NcRuse put a hand on her shoulder. "No," he answered firmly. "You've done enough, been through enough. You may be fine, but your friends need healing. Stay with them, Miss Gone."

By the time he finished talking, she had finished tying. She ran out of the room never showing any sign that she heard his words.

✦

In the early evening, Will awoke once more in a hospital bed. Nearby, on a stone bench sat an old friend.

"Rev!" The tendikeye attempted to jump out of his bed, but quickly found that his body was sore and his legs were weak. Still, he was overjoyed to see his partner. "Rev! Are you okay?"

Hindin rose to his feet uneasily. "Almost. I am well enough to pay a visit. Doctor Toney still needs to make a few adjustments."

Will frowned through his joy. "Rev, I don't think we'll be able to afford yer fixin' bill now."

The malruka made a dismissing gesture with his hand. "All has been paid for by our many, many friends at the E.C.P.D. Your and Sir Röger's treatment has been comped, as well."

"Rög," Will gasped. "How's he doin'? Do you know?"

Hindin shook his head. "I heard it was serious."

"Well, I'm feelin' right as rain in mid-winter. Let's go check on him."

They asked around and went to the room where the Black Vest was being treated. As they approached the room with worried minds and heavy hearts, the door burst open. Out came a beautiful woman running and screaming.

"He's changed again!" Will exclaimed.

Out came Röger wearing nothing but a smile and his helmet, looking all too human. "But Sister Julya! You must let me properly thank you for saving my life!" He started chasing her down the hall with his bare ass for all to see.

"Hey, Rög!" Will called, starting to chuckle. "How ya feelin'?"

Röger turned around, brown eyes sparkling with a devious grin. "Like a new man, my bukk brother! Like a new man!" He raised his hand and waved. "Hey, Hindin!"

"Hello!" Hindin waved back.

Röger gave them a brief nod, turned around, and continued his chase. "Oh, Sister Julya!"

At that moment, Polly came running around the corner and collided with the naked man. It wasn't until her butt hit the floor did she realize what she ran into.

"Polly-pop!" Röger exclaimed joyously. "Glad to see you're okay!"

She squeezed her eyes shut in disgust. "Put a towel on, you shameless ass, before I cut you!"

Hindin and Will rushed over to help her up. Polly looked up at Hindin, smiling. "Are you alright, Hindin?"

"For the most part," the malruka answered, looking unsure.

Polly bared her teeth and grinned. "Good. I'm glad for dat. Because de four of us still have blood to spill!"

In little time, they were all dressed and ready. They left the Temple of Health, and flagged down a taxi to pull them through the busy traffic of the Bone Brick City. Will, Polly, Röger, and Hindin sat in the back, discussing what might go down.

"From what you have told me of Elai NcRay," Hindin began "he is an exceptional tactician and a reasonably dangerous pyrotheurge. While not as powerful as his master was, he is younger and better adept at planning. Added to that, he is once again in his own territory. No matter how efficient we think we may be, he still holds the advantage. He knows the layout of the brewery better than anyone. So, even if we use stealth against him, there will still be the need to explore the terrain with the high risk of being caught."

"I could scout it 'fore the rest of you come in," Will offered.

Hindin shook his head. "There will be no time. He holds hostages."

"Dere is also no need to scout," Polly added. "I drank de bastard's blood, remember? I can lead us through."

"Do you know the entire layout?" Hindin asked.

"For de most part. It's hard to explain how it works. Just trust me."

"Getting Elai should be our last concern though," Röger added. "We have to get to those people, even if they're already dead. We still need to check for survivors."

"Agreed," Hindin replied. "However, Elai may be using them as bait, or worse some malign sacrifice. We must keep a wary eye, lest he take our flank."

"Then I'll keep us covered," Will said.

Hindin looked at Will and then the other two before frowning. "You three are flesh and blood. You breathe. The complex is filled with smoke and flame. I would be the safest in such a place."

"You ain't goin' alone, Rev!" Will shouted.

Hindin raised a hand up. "No, but I will stay in there until we know every hostage is out. And I will stay in there, alone, until Elai NcRay is dead. I hereby name him Enemy, and by doing so I will master his fate. Now that his plans for eternal life are dissolved, he cares only for death and destruction. And I will give them to him."

Röger shook his head in doubt. "You don't have to do this, big man."

Hindin squared his shoulders, his eyes sad but certain. "If not I, then who?"

❖

They could smell the rank smoke long before they saw *the cloud*. It was a great mass of churning darkness that rose high into the atmosphere like a colossal flower or tree blooming tall above the city. The rays of day failed to pierce it. It replaced the dim evening's light with sinewy shadows that slithered over hundreds of rooftops. And blazing at the roots of that swelling cloud of ash and cider was the NcRay Brewery.

The surrounding streets were choked with police and fire wagons. Any and every last civic guard and firefighter had their backs turned to the burning brewery. Other buildings had caught fire from the falling cinders. Drakeri firefighters worked swiftly, trying to pull burning shingles off roofs with their long reaching hooks while others evacuated residents from their homes. Malrukan firemen labored tirelessly, pumping hydraulic levers on massive water tanks while others wielded great hoses that spouted jets of water.

The bitter air stank with the smell of ruined beer and broken dreams. With the spreading fire came spreading fear. People were burning in their own homes. The city was wounded, and the wound was growing. And unlike the secretive methods of the Mystic Mafia that kept everyone guessing, word had spread quickly about who was behind it.

When The Four arrived at the scene, every officer they confronted was either too busy or uninformed to tell them anything more than what Polly had heard.

Will hopped to the top of a lamp post, landing with perfect balance. He looked and listened through the chaos and panic. Somewhere, he harked the distinct sound of a child screaming in agony. His eyes followed his ears, and he saw a man he knew by name.

"NcRuse!" he yelled. In little time, he slid down the post and led the others to the Coroner.

Leal NcRuse knelt on a sidewalk by a little Drakeri boy and his parents. The child's arm and face had been hideously burned nearly to the bone. The mother was bawling uncontrollably. The father's face shook with restrained outrage.

Polly covered her mouth at the sight of the boy. Roger shut his eyes and looked away. Hindin bowed his head. Will's eyes were wide and alert, and they reflected the fires nearby.

Leal NcRuse looked sullenly at the boy's parents and said, "His suffering is over. I'm sorry. This was the best I could do."

Just as the mother inhaled to scream for the loss of her child, the boy's good eye opened. He sat up, looked at his distraught parents, looked at his charred arm, then back at his parents. "It doesn't hurt anymore, Mommy," he laughed with an amazed half-smile.

The mother cried out and grasped her son in a tight embrace. The father looked at that NcRuse with a mixture of awe and fear. "You are the necrotheurge from the ECPD, aren't you?"

NcRuse nodded.

The father swallowed hard. "What did you *do* to my son?"

NcRuse frowned. "I killed the nerves in his arm and face. They are forever paralyzed, unfortunately. But he will not die from the shock of pain." He glanced over at The Four before finishing. "He still needs serious medical attention. Take him and leave. Now."

The couple complied without thanking or condemning him. As the family disappeared into the escaping crowd, NcRuse turned to address The Four. "This is getting to be a habit, I'm afraid. Would you not agree?"

Will glowered. "Where's Taly an' that Grandmaster fiddle player fella at? Why ain't they here to combat this fire with cold an' rain?"

NcRuse sighed. "Waltre is still bedridden from NcRay's bullet. And the Grandmaster is three counties away making rain for crops."

"We heard there are hostages in the brewery," Hindin said.

"Are or *were,*" NcRuse replied. "I doubt they could still be alive now. Even a pyrotheurge such as NcRay could not stand up to such destruction for long."

Polly looked at the towering inferno. "No. NcRay has changed into something horrible. His ambition of eternal life was ruined. He said we would all share in dat ruin."

"Has there been any sight of him?" Röger asked. "Or any contact or demands?"

NcRuse looked at the burning complex. "It started not half an hour ago. NcRay appeared among the employees there. Then he started murdering some of them in order to corral the others into some part of the complex. But the problem is we don't know where that place is. The few employees that escaped don't know either. A rescue crew of firefighters and civic guards was sent in when the blaze was not so dire."

Will took out a cigarette and lit it. "Yeah, heard that didn't work out so good. So, here's the new deal: Hostages or no, I owe that little pissant a bullet. We're goin' in. Care to tag along?"

The Coroner shook his head. "Thank you. But I am needed out here. There is much more suffering I must ease."

"Suit yerself then," Will said, giving a slight nod of respect.

"I do every morning," the Necrotheurge replied, smirking.

◈

Polly led the way in through a huge archway in one of the side walls. It opened into an outside area full of burning wagons

327

baring the NcRay Beer logo. Dozens of docking doors belched out rising blankets of black smoke.

"Dis is where de beer is shipped out," Polly said. "If we go to de last dock door on de left, keep against de wall until we reach de cave-hatch –"

"What's the cave-hatch?" Will asked.

"It's a door dat leads to de caves beneath de complex. Dat's where de beer is stored to keep it cool until shipment. And dat's where NcRay took de hostages."

"You know all this from drinking his blood?" Roger questioned doubtfully.

Yes and no," she replied. "Dere's no time to explain."

Just as she turned to walk away Will put his hand on her shoulder. "Pol, we're about to walk into a burnin' buildin', bein' led by a little theurge gal. I'd feel a whole lot better if you'd tell us just how you know what NcRay knows. How does drinkin' blood outta a poor guy's neck allow you to do that?"

"I would like to know, as well," Hindin added.

Polly looked at Hindin, hoping that he of all people would be more compliant.

But Hindin only frowned and explained "It is not that we, or rather *I*, do not trust you, Polly. But –"

"Fine!" she spat. "But I'll explain it on de way. Come on, you scaredy-pusses! Dis way!"

As they followed, she educated them.

"Dere is an old maxim: *Fill a teapot wit' water and it becomes de teapot.*"

"I have heard this saying," Hindin replied, raising up his hand.

Polly shot him an annoyed look. "Don't interrupt me!"

Hindin frowned and ducked his head.

Polly continued. "De water assumes de shape of anyting it fills or engulfs. Blood does de same thing, but more so. Every drop of blood in our bodies has been through every part of our bodies, even our brains. It encompasses de body as well as the mind. And as it passes throughout you, it records everything about you. By drinking de blood, I can learn past memories, present knowledge, or my body can become like de source and take its form."

They entered into the dock door.

"I do not *know* so much as *remember* de layout of dis complex. Elai knows de layout like de front and back of his hand."

"An' how you sure he's down where the beer's kept?" Will asked. "He had too've made this plan *after* you sucked his heart-juice out."

Polly walked over to the left wall and signaled them to follow her along it. "De Necrotheurge said dat Elai tried to corral de employees and herd dem somewhere. If he wanted dem dead right away den he would have made it so. So, it only stands to reason dat he would usher dem to de safest part of de complex for some purpose. He might have been trying some kind of sacrificial ritual like he attempted with me and Röger." She paused, and her eyes widened with fear. "He might have already done it. He views his employees as *his* cattle, *his* property. By sacrificing dem he may hope to achieve something."

Will shook his head as he unstrapped the narrow, rawhide pack he wore. "None o' that makes sense to me, quite honestly. But thanks fer explainin' anyhow. Maybe Rev an' Rög can make sense of it. But my main concern is how the pissant is still alive. You said you drained at least half his blood before it started boiling. An' then his eyeballs burned outta his head. Yet, he was able to escape. How?"

No one had an answer.

Röger looked down at his hands. They were trembling. "Guys, I can't beast-out in front of all those people. And my weapons were destroyed in that fire."

Without any hesitation, Will pulled out his pistol and sword. "Here,' he offered. "Take yer pick. Heck, you can borrow'em both. Jus' try not to hurt yerself with'em."

Röger slowly accepted the yashinin sword. "Just the blade, thanks. You're not gonna use them?"

"Nope," the tendikeye replied. "It's time I broke out *Falcona*. Poor gal's been missin' out." Will holstered his pistol, and took off the slender, rawhide pack he wore. From it, he produced his secret weapon! It was a mechanical device folded into three long sections. With a whipping jerk of his arm the hinges of the mechanism clicked and locked into their proper places. It had turned into a bolt action rifle that made Polly and Röger's eyes bulge in amazement. The wood stock was darkly stained with several chips and burns beneath a fresh, lacquered

329

finish. The bolt and barrel gleamed like mercury beneath a clear night sky. And mounted under the barrel's mouth was a polished bayonet in the form of a reaping scythe. Two handles protruded from the barrel and the wood stock, revealing the rifle's secondary function: to cut down men as easily as stems of barley.

"Will," Röger started. "Why did you wait until now to pull that out?"

Will did not look at the awe-struck human as he caressed his wicked toy. "*Falcona* is a long range gal. She an' me are gonna keep our distance an' try to find a hidin' spot to roost in. NcRay an' his Master were able to move my bullets because they were hot. But they also had to know that bullets were comin' at 'em. With *Falcona,* a bit of confusion by the ruckus y'all'll cause, and a few shadows ; that rich boy won't know what hit him."

He stuffed a clip of five rounds into the breach. "Now let's have us an ol' fashioned witch-hunt!"

✦

They reached the cave-hatch. It was a huge steel plate on sliding tracks on the floor. On either side of the plate were two chains meant for pulling the plate to expose the opening.

"Two grown adults can easily slide de plate back," Polly explained. "But it's loud when it slides. De noise will echo throughout de caves below."

"We'll lose the ambush," Will argued, shaking his head. "There's gotta be another way in."

"Dere isn't," Polly returned. "And if dere were, dere is still no time."

Hindin paced around the plate, examining it. "It does not look *too* heavy...and the track wheels are not fixed in place...perhaps...." He looked up at Röger. "Sir Röger, I sensed from our first handshake that your strength is comparable to my own when in your present form. This plate is not locked to the tracks; it merely slides on them. Would you assist me in lifting it off as quietly as possible?"

Röger took a deep, slow breath before nodding. "Let's do it."

Each man took a side and began to lift. The plate was surprisingly light to them, but it was very large and awkward.

330

"Don't let a corner bang on the floor!" Will ordered in a hoarse whisper.

An eye-watering wave of heat escaped the opening. Polly cringed because she expected cool, cave air.

Hindin and Röger stepped carefully to the back of the room. With utmost caution, they bent their knees and lowered the plate to the floor. It made a slight scraping sound, but nothing more.

They all looked down the long ramp that led into the caverns below.

"Will," Polly whispered. "You can survive bullets and blades. What about fire?"

"It burns me the same as you," he answered. "And it ain't a fun way to die."

Polly gulped and lowered her head. "What's de plan?"

Hindin placed a hand on her shoulder, gently. "I will face him head on. The rest of you will catch him off guard. We must deliver a killing blow, and then help the hostages escape." He then regarded them all. "I have faith in each one of us."

The caverns were dimly lit with methane gas powered lamps fixed to the rocky walls. Countless pallets of beer barrels were huddled around the various tunnel paths that led in all directions.

"Which way did dey go?" Polly whispered to Hindin.

The malruka said nothing, but pointed to Will.

Polly looked over at the tendikeye. He paced around, looking at the ground. Then he frowned and shook his head. "Too much activity down here. I need everyone to stop movin'. On the count o' three, stop breathin', too. Hold yer breath as long as you can. One. Two. Three." Everyone complied as he closed his eyes. The tiny quills on Will's ears rose and fell like the fur of a cat. He was perfectly still, as if he were a part of the stone he stood on. Several moments passed. Polly and Röger strained to not breathe. Then Will, without opening his eyes, turned halfway around and pointed down a specific tunnel. "They're still alive," he whispered. "Thatta way."

Polly listened the best she could, but heard nothing. "Will, how can you...?"

He put his hand over her mouth and shook his head. "I hark, Polly," he said. "Now, it's yer turn to hark me. Elai NcRay is ramblin' his philocreed nonsense to over fifty terrified people just down that passage as we speak. Since you an' me got the lightest feet fer sneakin, this is how it's gonna go down."

Polly removed his hand and replied, "Whatever you have in mind; it won't work. Dat passage leads into a large open area. Dere will be nothing to hide behind and he will see us coming."

Will grinned as he looked down at her. The look in his eyes made her nervous. "He won't see all of us, Pol."

❁

"Our souls are like heat!" declared the Pyrotheurge. "When it gathers it becomes the fire we all know as life! But no flame is eternal, my dear friends. That has been a hard lesson that I've only recently learned. All of our flames will eventually go out. But there is hope, I say! We need not let our flames burn out slowly into obscurity and old age. If our flames are to one day burn out, then I say let be this day! Let our sacrifice become a glorious inferno to be remembered by all of Doflend! It will be a gift that we share not only with each other; but the entire city! Together, every soul in Embrenil will shine its brightest!"

As Elai NcRay spoke to his captive audience, smoke and flame shot out from his eye sockets and mouth. He was a gaunt, skeletal version of his old self. His hair and lips had been burnt away. And his robe smoldered with wisps of smoke.

He had his captives trapped inside a huge ring of blazing flame. The sixty-seven employees of the NcRay Brewery trembled in the sweltering heat. They looked upon their long time employer in sheer terror. Many of them wept. Others screamed. Some begged and cowered. His fiery prison left no room for hope or bravery.

"Through self-immolation, self sacrifice, I have achieved power far greater than my Master, Lurcree. My blazing soul keeps me alive long enough for this last act of destruction. My time, and yours, will soon be over. And as the remnants of our souls scatter like cinders in the wind, all will be new again!"

Elai NcRay stalked around the burning circle like a hunting wolf. He raised a thin claw-like hand, and slowly started to make a fist. As his fingers closed, so did the burning circle. The people wailed as the flames closed in on them. They huddled together, sharing the same fear and fate.

And that's when *they* stepped into view.

Will had his rifle aimed at NcRay's head. Hindin and Röger both carried a beer barrel under each arm. Polly was nowhere to be seen.

NcRay's head turned when he saw them several yards away. The flames spouting from his head changed from orange to bluish white. "You three!" he muttered. Then his charred teeth formed something like a smile. "I was just about to fire my workers!"

Will made a sound that was half groan, half growl. "Shoulda picked better last words, Elai!" His trigger finger flickered, causing one of the five bullets within to break loose from its brass shell. The hot spike of lead screamed its way through the barrel like the first crack of lightning.

NcRay was ready for it. By concentrating his will, he swerved the bullet off its course and into the wall behind him.

As Will slid back the bolt on his rifle to eject the expended shell, Röger took two quick steps and launched one of his barrels in NcRay's direction.

Elai began to duck, but his worry disappeared as the barrel missed him by several feet. He did not even bother to watch it crash and splash onto the floor behind him.

Will slid the bolt forward and fired another round. Once again, Elai curved the bullet off its path.

Hindin flipped his two beer barrels onto the palms of his hands. With perfect form and all his might he pushed the barrels into the air. They crashed into a section of the Pyrotheurge's fiery circle, devouring the flame in a cloud of beer-flavored steam.

"Everyone! Leave this place!" Hindin called out to the hostages. His emerald eyes shifted to NcRay. "We will see to this coward."

Some of the people knew these three men as the slayers of the Sizzagafiend. Others recognized them as the ones who thwarted the Mystic Mafia or for battling assassin post-morts, fearsome golems, corrupt detectives, and insidious theurges. Either way, the people knew that help had arrived. They flooded out of the broken circle and ran with hopes renewed.

Elai NcRay bellowed angrily *"A burnt child fears the fire!"* A huge ball of flame erupted from his hands and shot its way to the three Excursionists. Roger took his last remaining barrel and tossed it in front of Hindin, screaming "Here it comes! This better work!"

Hindin stepped forward shifting his weight from one foot to the other, twisting his waist in a whipping motion, and shooting his arm out with a devastating palm strike to the airborne barrel. The wooden keg exploded, sending beer in all directions. The sudden splash quenched the fireball before it could reach them.

Will fired another round. Elai barely had time to react, but managed to steer it away.

At that moment the broken pieces of barrel that had landed behind Elai began to stir. The liquid that had been in that barrel was not beer. It was blood. Polly Gone rose up from the puddle, naked and seething with fury. She sneaked behind the distracted Pyrotheurge and summoned the veins from her arms. Without hesitation or mercy she coiled the barbed veins around his neck and arms and constricted with all her power, all her will. Elai opened his mouth to scream, but his throat was tied shut. He tried to move his arms, but the muscles in them were being torn to shreds.

"Will! Now!" she screamed.

Will fired his fourth round. It took the top of NcRay's head off in a bursting flash of sparks and shattered bone. NcRay's body erupted into flames and fell limp to the stone floor. Polly shrieked in agony and quickly took her veins off him, sucking them back into her arms to be healed.

"Yeah! History is ours to write, people!" Roger exclaimed, pumping his fists in the air. "The bad man is dead and Polly is naked! Happy ending!"

Polly covered herself as best she could with her arms and yelled "Turn that helmet around and toss me my clothes!" Hindin gave her clothes back and she quickly threw them on.

The four of them took a moment to watch the burning skeleton at their feet.

"It was a good plan, Will," Hindin admitted.

"A great plan!" Roger added, glancing at Polly.

Polly sneered at the human, drew her knife, and quickly jabbed it into his thigh. "Not another word!" Roger screamed at first but then started to laugh as the wound closed up.

Hindin looked at them both and shook his head in disappointment. "Come. We must go. This is a funeral pyre that no one should attend."

Not wasting any time, The Four made their way down the long, winding tunnel in a matched pace.

"I can hear the people up ahead," Will said. "Sounds like they made it to the hatch."

"This complex is gonna collapse any minute!" Roger shouted. "Maybe we'd be safer if we stayed down here, find a deeper cave or something."

"We can make it if we hurry!" Polly replied.

Just then, there was a loud explosion behind them. The concussive force knocked Polly, Roger, and Will onto their stomachs.

Hindin stumbled, but steadied himself quickly. He turned, clenching his marble teeth. It seemed odd to him that he was not surprised by what he saw. The charred bones of Elai NcRay walked towards them in a menacing gait. Surrounding the bones was an aura of flames that burned with many colors throughout the length of his form.

"*Chakras!*" Hindin thought. "*They are manifesting into a visual state!*"

The broken skull of Elai spoke. "I have transcended the flesh. I live only to destroy now. Consuming only led to my downfall. Your weapons, your clever tricks; they cannot stop me as I am now. I have sworn by my *philocreed* to destroy this city. If I cannot live to see it forever, then it will die with me."

Will rolled onto his back and fired his last round. Two of NcRay's vertebrae broke away, but the skeleton still stood.

"Leave us! The three of you must go now!" Hindin ordered his friends. "Make sure the employees have escaped. Make sure the authorities outside know what has happened."

"Rev...!" Will began to argue.

Hindin picked him up by the scruff of his neck and set him on his feet. "Go!" he ordered. "This is a battle between theurges. Chimancy and Pyrotheurgy. We discussed this on the way here. Only I can stand against him."

Will gritted his teeth in defiance. "You'd better make it quick!"

Hindin watched as his friends continued down the tunnel before returning his gaze to his enemy. "You are the one who betrays those who would protect you. You caused the death of your own brother and his beloved. I will take no pleasure in killing you, nor carry any guilt. Your new found purpose of destruction shall be in vain."

The burning skeleton's face contorted into an expression of disgust. "Even if you are a real Chimancer, you can't hope to harm me. My nerves have burned away. Your fancy pressure point attacks won't work!"

Hindin shook his head. "You still have a mind, Enemy. And even though it is twisted and shallow; it is still vulnerable to my theurgy."

NcRay tilted his broken, burning skull in curiosity. "In all my studies of other theurgies, I have never heard of Chimancers casting maxims.

"Because, we do not!" Hindin declared. "Maxims are words of so called wisdom and power that create mystical effects. They only serve to attach us to our desire to control reality. What I cast are *koans*."

NcRay's spine slowly straightened, "Koans? What is a koan, pray tell?"

Hindin raised his chin and stood with relaxed authority. As he began to speak his emerald eyes faintly glowed. *"If one hand claps in the forest, and no one is around to hear it, what is the sound it makes?"*

For three seconds, Elai NcRay was at a loss for words. For three seconds, the words of the Chimancer's koan cleared his mind and paralyzed his thoughts. In those three seconds, Hindin closed the distance between himself and his enemy and answered the question of the koan. He *clapped* the Pyrotheurge's rib cage with an open palm, shattering the blackened bones. Elai flew back like a burning boulder from a catapult. He ricocheted off a sidewall before hitting the ground and rolling several feet.

The Pyrotheurge sat up, laughing maniacally. "Was that supposed to kill me?" He rose up back to his feet. Several bones were broken or missing. But Elai did not care. He looked at Hindin, ready to melt the malruka into a puddle of molten rock and steel. But his flaming eye sockets caught sight of something that the Chimancer was clutching. It was a round piece of green flame.

"What...What is that?" NcRay asked.

Hindin held out the green flame so it could be better seen. "It is your heart chakra, the part of your soul that regulates your emotions and life force. I stole it from you before you flew back."

NcRay gazed at the captured flame in Hindin's hand. His bones trembled with fear and rage. "Give it back. Give it BACK!!!" He reached out with his hand.

Hindin felt NcRay's will trying to tug the flame from his grasp. He clenched his fingers around it in a vice-like death grip. "Why would you want this heart back, NcRay? It has done nothing but plague you with want and unhappiness. It has caused others to suffer, as well!"

The Pyrotheurge raised his hand and shouted "*It is better to die in action than sitting still!*" A cone of steam erupted from his palm. "Rust and crumble, you bastard!"

Hindin reacted by dropping into a sitting cross-legged position. As the steam engulfed him he retorted "*Stillness IS action.*" As he spoke the koan, the steam dispersed into nothingness. "Your master used that same maxim against me before he died. This time I was ready for it. It is a pity your theurgy is not more original."

Elai's eye sockets seemed to blink in disbelief as he watched the sitting Chimancer roll the captured heart chakra in his hands. In a flash of motion, Hindin shrank the blazing ball into a smaller, brighter bead of light.

"Our chakras are the organs of our souls. Your momentary transcendence of the flesh is meaningless. This is no mere battle of fire and fists. This is a war between spirits, Enemy; and you have wasted yours on petty vengeance. Your heart is guilty of bringing about needless destruction for the sake of vanity. Were you to have achieved immortality, it would have only served to prolong your own misery and suffering."

Elai could still feel his own heart in the Chimancer's hands. It felt heavy with something he did not recognize; Remorse. "Y-Y-You cannot judge me!" he cried out defiantly.

"I make no judgments!" Hindin answered. "No judgment need be made when the Truth is self-evident. Farewell, Elai NcRay! I will leave you with one last Koan: *Where does fire go when it goes out?*" With that, the green flame in Hindin's hand disappeared.

337

The flames engulfing Elai's skeleton roared in a lackluster flash and went out. The charred bones became husks of gray ash, and fell to the ground like feathers before crumbling into dust.

◎

Will, Polly, Röger, and every last hostage escaped through the dock area before it collapsed into a mountainous heap of smoke and rubble. The once majestic NcRay Brewery had fallen to ruin. The flames on the surrounding buildings had spread horrifically. Every structure in a five block area was burning. And even though the police and fire department had done a great job at evacuating the remaining residents, thousands of hearts were heavy from losing their homes.

Will stood diligently, watching the ruins of the brewery smolder and burn. Polly and Röger stood by him, lost for words. They glanced back and forth at the destruction and the stern-faced tendikeye.

"We ain't got all day, Rev!" Will shouted at the blaze. "Yer honor-bound, remember? 'Course, you do! You remember everything!"

Polly's throat got tight. She placed a hand on Will's shoulder. Röger did the same.

"He ain't dead," Will muttered. "He just likes to take his sweet time, is all." His face trembled as he drew air through his nose. Again, he screamed "Rev! We still need to go find Brem an' set things right! I ain't smart enough to figure things out without you! Hurry up an' come out!"

Röger hung his head and hid his eyes. Polly looked at the burning rubble. A tear went down her cheek and the nearby heat dried it almost instantly.

Then.

Every flame and every glowing ember on every building, every trace of heat started by Elai NcRay; utterly vanished. Not even a single brick in all the surrounding area was warm to the touch. The smoky atmosphere cleared and disappeared in a matter of seconds. The danger that had swept so quickly throughout a dozen buildings left sooner than it had come. With the abrupt end of the destructive fires, there came the ear-numbing sound of cheering in the streets. Thousands of voices rose in a cry of joy and relief. People hugged and cried together.

They marveled in amazement of the sudden miracle. Embrenil, the Bone Brick City, was saved.

But Will paid no mind to any of this. He stood and waited for his partner like a loyal hound. Hope had already left Roger and Polly. But they had not the heart to tell Will that Hindin had perished.

Polly sat on the sidewalk and wept openly. She thought that she would never again meet a kinder and gentler soul than Hindin. Röger sat next to her and wrapped an arm around her. She leaned in and cried harder. To breakdown and be comforted in such a way was a new and strange thing to her. All her life, whenever she dared cry that hard it was always in solitude.

Röger comforted the girl while looking at the motionless tendikeye. He did not feel half as bad for the malruka who died a hero than for the loyal friend he left behind. *"Who's that kid gonna take advice from now?"* he thought. *"Me? What do I know? The kid's lost now. We all are. Hindin made things work between us all. Without him, we're all just going to get sick of each other and go our own ways, I know it. These two kids are gonna get themselves killed one day with how wild they are. And me; I'll just keep on roving from place to place, watching the Huncells get older and friends coming and going in one way or another. I really thought that THIS TIME, I could be part of something worth going long term for."*

Will had it in his narrow mind to wait until his legs gave out and he lost consciousness. But he did not have to. A large section of fallen brick wall began to slowly slide out of place. Will leapt to it in two quick long bounds. "Röger!" he called, "Help me!"

The Black Vest and Polly stood in disbelief. They ran to meet the tendikeye. Will was already sitting on top the rubble, trying to push the fallen section with his strong legs. Röger was soon beside him. Together they pushed with all their might. Polly looked around to see what she could do. She saw that the fallen wall rested on a chunk of crushed metal.

"Down here!" she cried. "Move dis... dis whatever it is!"

Röger slid down. "It's a piece of smoke stack funnel, I think."

Polly growled. "I don't care *what* it is! Just move it!"

Röger complied. He yanked hard at the piece of debris and it came out with a scraping squeak. The brick section slid violently down the heap as Roger and Polly moved out of its way.

Hindin Revetz stood in a shallow recess where the section had been. Under his arm was a large barrel of beer.

Will picked up a brick and chucked it at the Malruka's head. "What took ya, ya dirt baby?!"

Hindin calmly swatted the brick out of the air and answered. "I had to rescue at least one barrel of beer, since you fleshlings covet it so passionately." He tossed the barrel to Roger, who caught it graciously. The label on the side read *NcRay Select*.

Röger looked up from the barrel. "It's a miracle!"

Polly ran toward Hindin with her arms outstretched.

He quickly held out his hands in protest. "Wait! Please, do not hug me! I'm sorry. But I am still very hot to the touch!"

She stopped, smiling warmly. "Hindin," she sighed. "I'm glad you're okay."

"NcRay dead fer good?" Will asked.

"He should be," Hindin answered. "I used three koans to defeat him."

Will's eyes widened. "You used THREE on the poor guy? Dang! Glad I wasn't there to hear 'em. You know how them brain-teasers give me a headache!"

Röger put the barrel of beer on his shoulder and stood proudly. "You saved the city, big man. All the fires went out. We're heroes again!"

Hindin frowned. "Yes, it seems we are. But let us not boast of it, please. The police and fire department are more deserving of praise than us."

Will arched an eyebrow and grinned. "I don't know, Rev. It'd be nice to get our names an' faces in the paper again."

Hindin smiled and shook his head. As he began to walk down the heap, the others followed. "I am sure that the people we just saved will spread word of our deed this day. The news will evolve into a local legend. And as that legend is told and retold, we will gain notoriety with the good people of this region..." He glanced back at the mountain of rubble. "...and infamy amongst the evil ones. Come, my friends. The next day is waiting for us."

The following morning, Mayor Krouslin called for a public conference in front of City Hall. A large platform and podium were erected. Upon it stood every available member of the Council, many firefighters, several high ranking police officers including Leal NcRuse and Waltre Taly, and of course, Four Winds-One Storm. To the platform's right were special seats reserved for the blinded victims and their families, everyone the team had interviewed. Even the kin of Davil Pert and Dahms Capgully were in attendance. On the left side of the platform, two huge glass clock faces twenty feet in diameter had been neatly stacked on top of two stone slabs. The black painted numbers 1 through 10 encircled the pearl tinted disks.

A huge crowd had turned out. It was a sea of curious purple faces. Dotted throughout that sea, tall malruka stood out like shining islands. The crowd buzzed with speculation until the Mayor took the podium.

"My people of flesh, bone, metal and stone. I am here today to tell you all that a great conspiracy has been uncovered and trounced. It has recently been revealed that Secondary Councilman Elai NcRay was indeed a ringleader and mastermind behind the sinister activities of the Mystic Mafia, as well as yesterday's fires. Furthermore, two more officers of the Police Department were found to be in league with him. Together, they had devised a plot to curse the new Clock tower and compromise the safety and security of this fair city's people. And when this plot was uncovered, the Councilman attempted to destroy us all. It is a shameful disgrace that such a prominent public figure and four officers of the law would fall to such corruption. But I can promise you that justice has been served, and they are no longer a threat. Tomorrow, a more detailed explanation of what went on will be printed in the Gazette.

But the main purpose of this gathering is not to dispirit you with bad news. I am indeed pleased to say that the blinded victims of this conspiracy need not continue to suffer or despair!" He raised his long arm, gesturing to Hindin. "Mr. Hindin Revetz, would you be so kind?"

The Chimancer stepped forward and bowed respectfully. He stepped smoothly off the platform and went over to the glass clock faces. Squaring his stance, he focused his eyes on the massive disks. He raised his right hand slowly like a heron raising its head from water. Then with the speed of a whip, his palm slapped into and through the giant plates. A thousand fractures went throughout the numbered faces, and they crumbled into minute shards. Many of the nearby onlookers would later swear that the malruka's hand was burning when it came down.

The Victims could not believe their eyes. Chan Burster was the first to rise from his seat. "I can see! I can see!" he rejoiced, waving his hand and hook in the air. The others quickly joined in his elation. The crowd cheered ecstatically for several moments on end. Then the Mayor raised his large, clean hands and masterfully hushed the crowd back down.

"Indeed, it is a fine day for heroes, dear citizens. We will never forget the courage put forth yesterday by our local civic guards and firefighters. But the heroes that stick out here today are not local, nor had they any personal stake in our city's plight. Four foreigners came together to lend us a helping hand. By working together and with the city, they uncovered the snake's nests and struck the vipers down. They were not afraid to cover their hands in villainous blood for the sake of our continued safety. They visited with the blind-struck victims and offered hope when there was none. And more importantly, they put out the theurgy-fed flames that threatened our lives and homes. And it is my great honor to present to you these four young people that will live on evermore in our collective hearts and memory: Four Winds-One Storm!"

The crowd roared so loud that it startled all four of them.

Waltre Taly leaned over and whispered in Polly's ear. "But you did most of the work, right? Those three lugs would be lost without you."

She looked up at him and smiled. She felt something bloom inside her, like a flower of hope. She knew that it might wilt sooner than later. But a part of her argued that it may be sustained forever. She could see the cured victims stepping onto the platform. They were coming to thank her and her teammates. She was probably going to get hugged and thanked over and over again, invited to meals, introduced to single relatives, and offered opportunities to go shopping for clothes.

"No, tank you," she whispered to herself. She leapt off the platform, and disappeared into the cheering crowd. Only a few people were able to briefly notice her. Everyone was too focused on the stage to bare her any mind. Well, almost everyone.

"Hullo, Miss Gone!" a voice called to her. She felt a hand touch her shoulder.

She turned her head. It was Dale Yonoman, the Barber at Yonoman's Barber Shop.

"I thought it was you!" he called out with a bright smile. "Polly Gone, right? Well, I just wanted you to know: You can get your hair done at my shop anytime! Free of charge!"

Polly's throat started to swell. Her eyes and lips trembled. She latched onto the nice man and squeezed him tightly. She couldn't stop the tears from escaping. "Tank you!" she cried. Somehow she knew; that if there was any good in her, it was there because of this man. She would never let herself forget that. She then turned and ran away.

Officer Feyna leapt into Röger's arms, wrapping her legs around his waist. "You're the best thing I've seen all day, baby!" she told him. They kissed long and hard, with her firm round butt supported by his hungry hands, neither of them caring who saw.

Will and Hindin had their hands full in a different way. For over an hour, they stayed with the people they had helped. They even greeted the entire crowd. By the end of the day, their names would be secured in the minds and hearts of the whole city.

Will did his best to inform the swarming crowd that he didn't shake hands with strangers. For him, it was like hugging and kissing them all. But that soon went out the window. He adapted to their custom with the number of offered shakes. Gratitude was gratitude, after all.

Then there was a face in the crowd he recognized. And by the look of that face, he was expected to do a lot more than shake hands.

"Rhowshell!" he exclaimed, stepping to her.

She was even more eye-catching than he remembered. "I thought you left town," she said with a dynamite smile.

Will laughed nervously and scratched the back of his neck. "Uh, well, I was. But it turned out we had more bad guys to catch an' spank."

She looked down. "It must have been quite a spanking with hands like that. What are you doing tonight?" She bit her bottom lip and fidgeted cutely.

Will raised one of his quilled eyebrows. "Ain't decided yet. How 'bout you decide for me?"

She took his hand and they ran off together. Once hidden and enclosed in the comfort of her apartment, they surrendered their affections to each other for the rest of the day. Her bed was constructed much like a large circular cot or hammock. They lay together naked in the center of it as if cuddled in a large cloth bowl. Night fell.

In the arms of the drakeress, the tendikeye put the last week's madness behind him. It was a week of meeting new people in a new place, making new enemies and killing them, and putting aside useless prejudice. The learning experience was an overwhelming distraction that he had secretly welcomed. It distracted him from the same tattered thoughts that he usually dwelled upon.

He held her tenderly, running his large fingers through her hair and nuzzling her forehead with the bridge of his large nose. Her perfume was like strawberries and vanilla. Her violet skin put silk to shame. Her body was strong when it wanted to touch him. And it was soft when it wanted to be touched. He slid one of his thick hands down her waist, over her shapely hip, onto her bare thigh and gave it a playful squeeze. He felt her arms and hands on his back and shoulders, gliding over his tan skin.

He looked down at her face. Even in near darkness she seemed strangely exotic, yet genuinely down to earth. He had always found Drakeri eyes a little unnerving until that moment. Each eye looked like three gold plates fixed to a shining black sphere. Beautiful. Natural.

"Will?" she asked, breaking him out of his trance.

"Huh?" he replied.

She looked like she really wanted to ask him something, but was afraid to.

"Please don't ask me to stay," he thought.

"Will, it is all right if I ask you something?"

"Uh-huh," he answered, lying.

She licked her lips, looked away for a second, then looked back. Finally, she asked. "How come you don't have wings like other tendikeye?"

A flood of relief washed down his spine. "Oh. You mean why I'm a bukk?"

"Yeah. Are you a different breed or something? Or...were they cut off as a punishment?" She looked cutely nervous as she asked.

Will turned his head and laughed at the ceiling. He could not help it.

"Don't laugh!" she groused, pinching his arm. "I'm curious."

He smothered his laughter and grinned. "Okay, okay. It's a fair question. Let's see. Yer in the medical profession. You ever heard of *limbatic vestigia*?"

She shook her head.

"Well, it's when a set of limbs don't grow or form right. I was born with it. My buddy Rev calls it a genetic defect. By the time I was three, my wings just fell off like old arthritic fingers."

Her face grew concerned. "Did you face...mistreatment?"

"Not fer bein' a bukk. A kid gets a lot of bad luck out early in life that way. Bukks get treated like livin' luck charms. The great general Tidsla Childoon was the first bukk to prove it could be overcome. Most of 'em even become commanders. In fact, I—" Will stopped himself just then. He did not want to say anymore. Saying meant remembering. He did not mind sharing his present time with this woman. But his past was another issue.

Rhowshell looked at him thoughtfully and kissed him under his right cyc. "It's okay," she whispered. She stroked his face and quills until he felt at ease.

He smiled and sat up on his elbow. He let out a sigh. "'Kay, now I gotta question fer you: Why ain't *you* got wings?"

She raised a curious scythe-shaped eyebrow.

Will shrugged a shoulder. "I mean, you Drakeri claim you come descended from fairies *and* dragons. Shouldn't you have wings of some kind, like bat or dragonfly kinda wings?"

She tilted her head, looking at him adoringly. "Well, I think that because dragon wings and fairy wings are so different that they just didn't mesh. And we Drakeri aren't the only drakeri in the huncell. Our Miccan and Chume Fey neighbors are drake-fey, too. Although, most of them deny it because we all have different histories."

Will sat up all the way. "Izat a fact? Tell me *yer* history. All I've heard is hearsay up till now. If ya please?"

She sat up straight and crossed her legs. "I'll tell you the story my grandmother told me."

"I like stories," the tendikeye grinned. His eyes dropped down to her spectacular rack. "I like them, too."

She grinned and gave her perky purple boobs a playful shake for his viewing pleasure. "Let's see. A long time ago, before this huncell had countries, there were three tribes of fey: The LeMay, the Tesson, and the Chuma. Then the three dragons came. Now, the fairies reasoned only with their hearts. And the Dragons reasoned only with their minds. Naturally, they became enemies.

A great war was fought. The fairies' numbers were many, but the dragons were too powerful. Each dragon took and enslaved a tribe for itself, ruling over them like cruel tyrants. Retaeh the Pyrodrake took hold of the LeMay fey, Lios the Geodrake took the Tesson, and Kar-Lin of the Woodlands took the Chuma.

It was Queen Shanja of the LeMay who saw a way to overthrow Retaeh. As a false sign of her submission, she offered her body and the bodies of her thousand and ten handmaidens to be used for his pleasure. And the temptation of a fairy queen is a hard thing to resist. She and all of her handmaidens conceived children and bore them in secret. Each half-drake child was raised with one goal in mind: To kill their father. Queen Shanja told her plan to the Chuma and Tesson fairy queens, and they did the same.

When the half-drakes were fully grown, none were near as powerful as their fathers. But together, they fought side-by-side and slew their sires, freeing their fairy brethren from bondage. Then each and every half-drake took an oath: To only breed with other fairies and not each other. It was feared that the power they inherited might lead them into corruption. And so, the power of the dragons was spread and diluted into the veins of every fairy down the countless generations.

The power in the dragon's blood prolongs our lives to this very day. And we Drakeri, descendents of the LeMay and Retaeh the Pyrodrake, can reason with both our hearts *and* our minds.

Many of us can even use pyrotheurgy because of it. But, sadly, because we carry the blood of a dragon, none of us are without sin. Drakeri like the ones that you brought to justice inherited and thrived with the evil of Retaeh."

Will furrowed his brow in thought as he studied the woman. "So that explains it then. You seduced me the same way them poor dragons got seduced by yer fairy ancestors. I was powerless to stop you."

"*I* seduced *you*?" she asked, pretending to be offended. "How dare you! I was a proper young woman before you blew into town with your big rough hands, lean body, and that grammar-raping accent of yours!" She pushed him down, straddled him, and kissed him madly. Her tongue lashed around inside his head like a wet, slippery caged animal. And long into the night, the two temporary lovers lost themselves in a cloud of ecstasy and exhaustion.

Rhowshell the Belle woke up the next morning to the smell of sweet chives in an empty bed. While changing her sheets, she found a small blonde quill by her pillow. She placed it in a box full of junk jewelry she had collected since she was little. And there it stayed.

◈

Later that evening, Will met his teammates at the Green Dirt Battle Arena, formerly known as the Red Dirt. This time, they were spectators.

"Did I miss it?" Will asked as he took a seat they had saved for him.

"You are just in time," answered Hindin, passing him a small bag of concession chips. "Here. I bought these for you. The match begins in ten minutes."

"That's what they said ten minutes ago," Röger groaned. He slumped in his seat with his big arms crossed, bored out of his mind.

"Dis isn't right!" Polly bitched, rocking impatiently in her seat. "Dey're only giving him a C class battle because he was willing to cooperate. All he did was confirm everyting dat we had already found out. We never even needed his help!"

"Ah, don't be so down, Polly-pop!" Röger teased. "The other three thieves are going to prison for a long, long time. But

347

this Drew Blood guy wants to test his mettle for a chance at freedom. And you told us he's not that good of a fighter to begin with, so why worry? He's gonna die out there like he should. Blind Bitch's Bane! I heard that they're gonna pit him up against a pack of wild stray dogs!"

Polly bit her bottom lip and frowned. "Dose dogs may or may not attack like a proper pack. I've heard dat city dogs can be more dangerous dan wild ones because dey aren't as afraid of people. But on the other hand, dey may not attack en mass. He still might have a chance."

Will raised an eyebrow. "She makes a good point. Too bad the new actin'-chief took it easy on him." He reclined and popped some chips in his mouth.

Polly glared at the empty arena, gritting her teeth. She shook her head defiantly and stood up. "I refuse to watch dis!" She turned and walked out of the stands, fists clenched.

"Where's she headed?" Will wondered aloud.

"Probably went to go cry in the restroom," Röger replied with a shrug. "Girls do that sometimes."

A few minutes later the announcer spoke.

"Ladies and gentlemen! We now present our main event! A local boy you all know and hate! A convicted member of the notorious Mystic Mafia! Ladies and gentlemen, I give you Drew Blood!"

A large door opened on one end of the battleground. Drew Blood emerged holding a short double-edged sword. The thousands of spectators that surrounded him booed with their every breath. He felt their hatred, took it in, and made it his own. He had resolve and confidence. He decided that any fear he would feel during the fight would be replaced by the pure rage of survival. He raised his head high to the crowd, so all could see the pride on his freshly scarred face. He would laugh at them all after he won.

"And his opponents!" the announcer bellowed. "Courtesy of the Embrenil Pound! The Green Dirt Dirty Dozen!"

The second door on the other side opened, releasing thirteen large, ill-tempered canines with their fangs exposed (although, no one in the vast crowd really took the time to count them). They barked and growled insanely as they charged Drew. He answered with a screaming charge of his own. The first mutt leapt at him. His blade flashed into its eye socket. The mutt

348

yelped and fell to the ground twitching. Another two mutts went for his legs. He slashed down at them, splitting one's skull and cutting into the other's shoulder by pure luck. The rest of the dogs were trying to surround him. He began to run from them, slashing wildly as they drew close. He ran, dashed, slashed, and dodged, fending against the disorganized pack of strays. After four short minutes, he had laid a mortal wound on every mutt but one.

Drew was already exhausted and sweating. Blood from a half dozen dog bites dripped from his forearms and legs. He breathed heavily as he circled the last dog. But the uninjured mutt showed no signs of aggression. It only kept its distance as Drew caught his breath.

The thief chuckled as he inched closer. "Come'n, girl!" he called. "Let me put you out of your misery so I can leave this city behind!"

The mutt only looked at him, no expression in its dark eyes. Then its tail began to wag.

"That a girl!" Drew encouraged. "I'm your friend, yes! A friend that's gonna chop your bitch head off!"

The mutt's tail kept wagging. Its eyes looked right at him, and suddenly flashed red. Drew stopped in his tracks, his eyes widening with sudden fear.

"*Blood for blood,*" he heard the dog whisper. His body shook and his nose started to bleed. The dog's tail kept wagging. He tried to scream, but nothing came from his mouth but drool and gore. His sword fell to the ground. The dog leapt at him, sinking its teeth in his neck without making any kind of growl. Drew fell over with the dog on top of him. Its tail kept wagging as its jaws crunched around his arteries and wind pipe. The mutt jerked its head to the side, ripping everything loose in a spraying burst of red. Drew Blood went still and died.

The mutt looked up at the astonished crowd and charged the battleground wall. In one great leap it bounded to the top, causing many frightened spectators to scatter. Before anyone could react, the mutt ran away through the stands and out a nearby exit. Gone. Never to be seen again.

A few minutes later, Polly returned and sat down with her teammates. She looked down at the battleground as a group of arena employees were cleaning up the mess.

"You missed a helluva fight," Röger said flatly before sipping his beer.

Hindin looked at her with caring eyes. "It is over, Polly. The thief lost and justice was done upon him. There is no more need for concern."

"Tank you, Hindin," she answered. Her eyes shifted to Will, who was peering at her knowingly.

He raised his hand to his face and brushed at the corner of his mouth, as if to say "You got a little somethin' on yer lip."

She raised her hand and mimicked his movement. Looking down, she saw the faintest bit of blood on her finger. She looked back at Will with shocked eyes.

The tendikeye made a slight grin and winked at her. But there was something cold in his expression, like a kind of warning.

"Excuse me? Four Winds?" came a booming voice.

The four teammates turned their heads to see a polite-faced malruka in a fine tailored gray suit standing on the isle steps. "My employer would like to meet with you," he said with a smile.

"Who?" Will asked suspiciously.

"Secondary Councilman Erloy Aundi. You interviewed his daughter, Yrot, during your recent investigation."

The four exchanged silent glances before rising to follow the massive messenger. He led them outside to a huge covered wagon hitched to a team of four well-bred bileers. A middle aged Drakeri man with a comb-over haircut sat at the reins. Yrot sat beside him in the shotgun seat. They greeted the team with bright smiles as they stepped down to meet them.

"Ah, ha!" the Councilman exclaimed with his arms spread. "Here they are; the four people who saved my daughter's eyes! Blessings to you all!"

Yrot gave them a shy wave. "Hullo. Thanks again, all of you."

Will gave the woman a humble bow before addressing her father. "Councilman, how may we be of service? Please, don't tell us you want us as bodyguards."

The man laughed and shook his head. "No, sir. I am here to reward you for services rendered."

Hindin raised an eyebrow. "But, Councilman, is it not illegal for a public official to reward excursionists? Even if they aid the local police?"

"Yes, Mr. Revetz, it is. But I am not rewarding you as a member of the city council. I am rewarding you as a father. I don't know or care why you four banded together to investigate and settle this matter. I'm sure you all have your own reasons. All I know is this: My daughter and I had been growing apart. It took this to bring us together again. Family is the most important thing. One tends to forget that when tending personal goals."

He turned to look at the bileer-drawn wagon. "As a Secondary Councilman, I am also one of the richest business owners in Embrenil. This wagon and fifty others like it help me with my transport service. They are built strong to last for years of shipments. Everything from grain to meat to textiles, Aundi Liners delivers." He turned back to them. "It should serve you well on your future travels."

"Sir!" Hindin exclaimed with shock and gratitude. "I do not know what to say!"

The Councilman pointed at him. "But you knew what to *do*, son. And that's all that matters."

Will stepped forward. "Them're fine animals, Councilman. And I want you to know they're in good hands."

Yrot stepped to Will, smiling. "I'm sure they are." She then placed a lingering kiss on his cheek. She did the same to Hindin and Röger before stopping at Polly. "You play the piano beautifully, you know."

"Tanks," Polly returned. And the two shook hands.

Former Chief Justice and *Frigorifist* Waltre Taly retired for real this time. He resigned himself to become a full-time family man. Often, during family gatherings, he would entice his many great, great, great grandchildren with stories of his adventures while on the police force. And to them he taught the virtues of his philocreed, *The Path of Cold,* and how it is good at preserving things like food and peace.

Coroner Leal NcRuse, who had never married or had children, took a year off from his duties. Chepsu the post-mort fetus assassin remained in his care.

Richard Armbakk, inspired by the heroes he had met, sold his taxi-wagon. He became an Excursionist and headed North, swearing to spread the glory of his family name.

Officer Feyna returned to the force. But after her scandalous behavior with Röger, she was no longer allowed to watch over prisoners. She eventually became a Detective who had a talent for gathering information.

Chan Burster, upon learning that his favorite beer maker had been behind the cause of his blindness, gave up drinking beer all together and lost 34lbs.

Darb Wesley's broken leg healed sooner than expected. He moved to the 5th Ward because the rent was cheaper. Dympner Bhakta became his landlord.

Yrot Aundi the art lover and Horce Roland the artist met and really hit it off. He had acquired a large fortune auctioning off his artwork. Together, they opened their own art studio and married the following year.

Sinala Ettessi never really got over her scar on her face. But eventually, she saved up enough to have it removed at the 3rd Ward Temple of Health. She then got a job as a chorus girl in the Westpear District. Rather than forever live in fear by always taking a taxi cart, she still prefers to walk everywhere she goes.

Cecil the Fleshbroker, lacking his two front teeth, lost the respect of his peers in the flesh trade business. He tried to have new teeth put in, but made the mistake of goosing his cute female dentist. He ended up losing three more.

And as for the four misfitting heroes who pitched fits and missed fists; they said goodbye to the Bone Brick City of Embrenil. Shortly after receiving their new wagon, they found a small wooden box in the back that held fifty *One Hundred Grotz* gold coins. With only a few, they bought clothing, bullets, books, and other supplies. Röger was unable to retrieve his sword and axe from the ruins of the NcRay mansion. He did not bother to buy replacements.

"That's okay," he said as he climbed to the wagon's front. "I might know a place out of town to get an axe, at least." He sat down, took the reins, and shouted back into the wagon. "Are we ready?"

"Almost!" came a voice from around the side. It was Will. With an effortless leap, he landed in the shotgun seat next to the human. He seemed well rested and in good health. But deep down, something still bothered him.

"Ready," Polly answered. She was sitting in the back, curled up in a blanket.

"Ready!" Hindin shouted back from inside. He sat cross-legged, reading one of his new pyrotheurgy books.

Will looked back at him, sighing with disappointment. "Rev, are you really thinkin' of pursuin' that fire-starter gut snake? I mean, it's bad enough we got one maxim-chucker."

Polly rolled her eyes.

Hindin turned his head to his old friend. "Correct me if I am wrong, though I rarely am. But was it not *you* who used mystical petrifaction bullets to keep himself from burning alive?"

"That's differ'nt!" the tendikeye defended. "I used them fancy-pants mystic rounds fer a purpose other than what they was intended!"

Hindin smiled and shook his finger in the air. "That is still relying on theurgy, Mr. Foundling! Now, if you will excuse me. I need to teach myself pyroglyphics to better comprehend the maxims of this *philocreed*."

"Aw, shut up an' read yer book!" Will took out a cigarette and a fliptop lighter that was brand-spankin' new. "Where we headed next?" he asked as he lit up.

Hindin paused. "Hmm. Coming to this city *was* your idea. You wanted urban experience. Did you get it?"

Will noticed Röger grinning at him. Rhowshell the Belle came to mind. "Yeah, I got it, Rev. Now, it's yer turn to choose. Where to?"

"Why not Wraith County?" Röger suggested. "It's just to the South-West of here."

"Wraith County? What's dat?" Polly asked.

"Its official name is Apple County. That's just what the people call it now. Supposedly, the whole county is haunted with ghosts. Any of you ever had to deal with cursed, disembodied spirits?"

He heard no answer.

"Well, the way I see it; if we're ever going to make our mark, we need to take jobs that others won't. Mercenary work? Bodyguarding? Escorting wagon trains in exchange for rides? That's all kid's stuff. The real adventures are found where no one else will look. What do you say, lady and gentlemen?"

Hindin nodded with approval. "I second your motion, Sir Röger. Paranormal ecology would be a good thing to study firsthand."

Will shrugged. "Might as well. If we manage to rid a whole county of its curse, my ol' mentor oughta catch wind of it."

"South-West is good," Polly agreed. She turned her head to look out the wagon's rear. As the steeds started to pull, she watched the many different bone-laced buildings pass by. She then made a silent promise to herself. If by some chance she were to ever escape her mother for good, she would return to this city for another haircut. Until then, she would let it grow.

And so, the Four Winds traveled as one to their next Excursion.

Epilogue

For the last time tonight, Dale Yonoman's broom passed lazily over the floor. Dusk descended over the city as he finished with his last customer. After a long day of snipping, he swept the last of the trace hairs from his patrons. The bristles of the broom dug into every nook and corner. The shop was poorly lit by two dusty oil lamps. Because of the bad lighting, he obsessed a little about how well he swept his floor. He went over the entire floor once, twice, and now a third and final time.

The entrance door behind him opened, striking the brass bell that hung over it.

"Didn't I lock that?" he pondered beneath his breath. He turned with a tired smile. "Sorry. The shop is closed."

The lady in red stood at the door. She wore a hood that shaded her face. Her eyes shifted from left to right, surveying the shop and everything in it.

The barber squint his eyes. "Miss Gone? Is that you?"

He felt it, but never saw it. Something like a barbed whip cracked against him. A line of fiery pain ran from his chin to his sternum. The momentum of the lash knocked him onto his back. He halfway sat up, casting a fearful gaze at the woman.

After a long, tense moment she drew back her hood. The woman did indeed resemble the mysterious girl who had saved the city. But this woman's hair was longer, fuller, with streaks of red that resembled crimson lightning.

The man looked down to see that his shirt had been split open as well as the skin beneath it. An overwhelming sense of self-preservation shot through him. He reached for his broom. "Whoever you are, this is my shop! And I will not have—"

Her wrist flickered and another painful lash tore the skin off his knuckles. The prone broom became splattered with his blood.

Before he could even scream, she was on him. A dozen barbed veins slithered from her wrists and ankles. They coiled harshly around his arms and legs, pinning them down. He tried to shout again, but her plump, soft lips pressed against his own. The vibration of his screams buzzed through her mouth and skull.

She sat up, straddling him like a smug harlot. Her eyes were lit with a crazed mix of amusement and frustration. She smiled with clenched teeth. "Where is she?" she demanded.

"Who?" he replied.

"Her," she answered, her upper lip flaring. She pointed at the picture of Polly Gone. "She came all dis way to see you, Dale. I told her it was a waste of time. Dat you never even knew about her."

"I don't understand," the man cried.

The lady in red snarled and leaned down. She ran her tongue up the bloody gash on his chest, ending seductively on his chin. She looked in his worried eyes, tasting his blood and the memories within it.

"No," she muttered, disappointed. "She told you nothing." The woman took a deep breath and sighed sadly.

Dale Yonoman glared at her. He looked down to see a septegram tattoo on her arm made of red lines. Then a dusty old memory floated to his mind's surface. *"Her face," the* man thought. "It can't be!" he exclaimed in a whisper. "I remember you!"

"You had better, you dog!" she hissed with a furrowed brow. "Although, I should not blame you for not recognizing me. We weren't exactly facing each other when I took your boyish innocence. Did *she* remind you of me, Dale? Is dat why you cut her hair for free? Did you have a soft spot for de little wretch? Or was it a hard spot, hmm?" The woman laughed sickly in a deep, hoarse cackle.

Dale shook his head in terror. He was too afraid and confused to make sense of the witch's words.

"Which way do you tink she went?" she asked playfully. "I have lost her trail. You will help me find her."

A sudden right cross knocked his head into the floor. The woman got off him, leaving him in a dizzy stupor. She sauntered over to Polly's picture and picked it up. She looked lovingly at the image. "So, you have chosen a name for yourself, my agave?" She stepped over to the counter and picked up the barber's largest pair of scissors. She went back to Dale, who had rolled onto his hands and knees. She gave him a swift kick, sending him back onto his back. "Down, boy!" she ordered.

She set the picture down and snatched his wrist. She jabbed the blades into his palm, holding it over the picture. The man screamed and tried to pull away. But she would not let him until enough blood spilled onto the glass image. "Your blood," she said, letting him go. "Plus *my* blood. Dat will suffice." She jabbed the scissors into her own palm, letting her blood fall and mix with his.

He scooted slowly away as she stared blankly at the blood covered picture.

Her eyes flashed red. "South-West," she whispered. Her head tilted thoughtfully as she regarded the picture. "I'm coming, my darling baby girl." Her cold gorgeous eyes shifted to the barber.

He saw her raise her hand. He heard the vicious crack of her whip once more. Then, there was silence and darkness.

The saga continues in

FOUR WINDS — ONE STORM

THE GEOHEX
OF
WRAITH COUNTY
BOOK II

Glossary

Anima Husk: the soul's skin or outer layer.

Archdrake: one of three legendary dragons that once ruled over Burtilbip.

Billblade: a greatsword tipped with a large hook.

Bionomist: a chimancer who specializes in the science aspect of their theurgy, such as acupuncturists.

Black Vest: a state employed urban monster hunter of Fevär. Given a knightly honorific to mark status.

Blind Bitch's Bane: a Fevärian expression for disapproval of the obstruction of justice.

Blood Theurge: a Crimson Theurge / Hematologist / Hematonomist, a disciple of a philocreed based on ritualistic assassination/murder, emotional manipulation, and the circulatory/cardiovascular system. They refer to their spiritual path as The Red River.

Bukk: a tendikeye without wings.

Bullpie/Merde/Brown Gut Snake: nonsense or lies compared to and named after feces.

Chakra: spiritual organs through which chi flows.

Chi: the blood of the soul.

Chimancer: one who brings their spirit and body closer together through complex combat training and supernatural meditation. A theurge of martial arts and personal well being.

Code of Word and Deed: the code of conduct upheld by Black Vests.

Cryotheurgy: theurgy based on the abstract perception of Cold being a force in reality.

Dan Tien: the stomach chakra.

Drakeri/Drakeress: a member of the drakeri race who originate in the country of Doflend in the Huncell of Burtlbip. Hair and skin pigmentation range in various shades of purple, violet, indigo, and lavender. Recognized by their eyes with three irises, double-pointed ears, hands consisting of one thumb and three fingers, and feet with two large toes. According to legend, they are hybrids of prehistoric dragons and fairies. However, their mundane culture offers little to support this claim. Drakeri reach adulthood at age 18 and typically live 10 to 12 centuries.

Dreamweed: a smokable herb that induces relaxation and serenity.

Eagleton Sphere: also called an eagle egg or handmine. A ball-shaped bomb covered and loaded with spike-like bullets. Can be used as a grenade, landmine, or short term timer bomb. Fevärian in origin.

Excursion: in ancient times this word meant vacation or holiday outing. But as the huncells grew more dangerous such trips became hazardous and unpredictable the word slowly became synonymous with adventure or heroic trial.

Excursionist: one who goes on excursions.

Fevärian: also called humans. Indigenous to the huncell of Fevär.

Fleshbroker: a pimp.

Fleshling: a malrukan term for people made of flesh and bone.

Frigorifist: a disciple of cryotheurgy.

General Tidsla Childoon: tendikeye bukk historical figure. Revolutionary hero.

Geotheurgy/Geonomy: The theurgy of soil, stone and metals.

Golem: a construct, usually bipedal in shape, that is animated and controlled by a piece of a theurge's soul. While some are intelligent, they have no will of there own.

Harker: a tendikeye woodland reconnaissance and bushwhacking specialist.

Hell: a place, usually a pit or low point, outside a community where garbage is burned.

Hemogoblin: a laich that consumes the cardiovascular /circulatory systems of living creatures to maintain their own.

Hemopathy: reading or tasting blood to divine information.

Huncell: a natural enclosure, part rock and part flesh, vast enough to sustain gravity, atmosphere and life. The Cells of Reality. Georganic in nature, part flesh, part rock.

Hunvein: one of many vein channels that house a lava/blood-like substance called skault. The source of light and heat in a huncell.

Hunwalls: the walls of a huncell.

Hurklyone: a large wildcat native to Micca. Known and prized for its extremely tough hide.

Hydrotheurgy: the theurgy of Water.

Jubube: (pronounced jew-booby) a type of large, plump nectarine.

Krilp: a beast-like native of Gurtangorr, resembling hulking cats crowned with massive horns.

Ruan: a tendikeye guitar.

Septagram: a 7-sided star. Although, stars do not exist in this reality.

Shunt: a term for sexual intercourse.

Stonebro: stone brother, a friendly term for malruka.

Tendikeye: the native race of Cloiherune, marked by their large hands and feet, quill-covered heads and wings, and tanned skin.

Theurge/Theurgess: a disciple of one or several forms of theurgy. They are also called mystics by some.

Theurgy: the mystical practice of defining and redefining reality as one sees it. An effort in spiritual, scientific, and artistic influence.

Tuntrum: a tendikeye word literally meaning proper or kosher. The term is used for weapons that can also be used as tools, as well as wild game that was hunted using such weapons.

Laich: a powerful amortal being that feeds on the living to sustain their potency. They come in several varieties, some with unique tastes and abilities.

Magmacock: a huge domestic male chicken enhanced by pyrotheurgy to be wreathed in flames without harming the bird. Used in Doflend penal combats. Usually slain after combat because giant flaming cocks are so hard to handle. The meat is already cooked as it is butchered and is sold to spectators.

Malruka/Malrukan: a people constructed from metal and stone. First created by tyrannical geotheurges as warrior slaves during The Omni-War, now a self-perpetuating race under rule of Slate in the huncell of Tomfeerdon. Exact life span is 200 years. Their most common philocreed is geonomy. Sexless, but most identify as male.

Maxim: a phrase of theurgical wisdom used to generate metaphysical epiphanies that alter energy in people, places, and things.

Medicine: one's personal ability to decide and steer their own fate, particularly when others oppose them.

Monster Abater: one who specializes in the removal of monsters.

Necrotheurge: a disciple of the theurgy of Death and/or Amortality, necrotheurgy. Notable philocreed sects include The Bone Ladder and Zerothism, enlightenment through oblivion.

Necro-Receptive/Necroactive: able to use necrotheurgy.

Nyupe Shan Zahn: a historical drakeri Life Theurge from the Age of Technology.

Omni-War: the first and only war that included the entire Draybair Cluster.

Perceptionists: an illusionist theurge.

Petraround: a geotheurgically-enhanced bullet that turns a living target into stone temporarily. Fashioned from serpent fossils.

Philocreed: a spiritual doctrine that draws meaning from a specific aspect of reality (such as elements or other natural things) and holding that aspect in the highest regard. Most philocreeds have a related theurgy.

Pnuema: soul, spirit, anima.

Post-Mort: a post mortum being with a physical body.

Pyroactive: able to use pyrotheurgy.

Pyroglyphics: the written/visual language of Fire.

Pyrotheurge: a disciple of pyrotheurgy, the philocreed of The Sacred Flame. One in a supernatural relationship with fire and heat.

Retaeh's Breath: a drakeri expression of shock, usually toward something negative.

Sizzagafiend: also known as The Scissor Monster and The Shear Terror. There was once a Lemuertian Legba who enjoyed eating snakes, spiders and scorpions. One day, he had his cook chop up all three into a creepy critter salad. The legba consumed his meal happily, but was soon plagued with a terrible stomach ache. The ache turned to agony as an amalgam of the three consumed critters sheared its way out of the Legba's abdomen. The monster grew to become a menace to all beings throughout known history. Although it has been slain repeatedly, the Sizzagafiend always mysteriously returns.

Slate: the Pharaoh of the Malrukan race. A being composed solely of spiritual energy and living lightning. Their Father-in-Spirit.

Socionomic Revolution: when Doflend ceased to be Feudal Goldocracy once controlled by the now defunct Buresche social class of Drakeri.

Thunderjug: a chamber pot.

Vaughn: cobalt.

Werekrilp: a sentient being infected with a lycanthropic curse of transforming into a murderous krilp.

Witch: a slur or rural term for theurges.

Witchworks: a negating term for theurgy.

Yashinin Machete: a tendikeye tuntrum blade used to clear wild overgrowth and for skirmishing. The blade is crescent shaped, ends in two points, sharp on the outside edge, with a hole-slot on the inside edge to create a handle grip. Yashinin literally means "voting blade" in Old Tendikeye because the tendikeye show and use their weapons as a means of electing leaders.

Yestermorn: yesterday morning.

Yesternight: yesterday night.

Zodiologist: a disciple of zodiology, one who searches for patterns in history and sentient being behavior.

Geography of
The Eight Huncells of
Draybair

Draybair Cluster: the eight known huncells, first mapped out and presented by Prof. Sävva Draybair of Fevär.

Fevär: the Huncell of Humanity. Currently divided into the purely human kingdom of Karsely and the Free Republic of Meodeck.

Burtilbip: the Drake's Cradle. A huncell consisting three separate realms. **Doflend**, a confederated capitalist democracy home to the Drakeri race. The Wilds of Chume, a forest expanse populated by the Chume Fey. And Micca, home of the subterranean Miccans.

Cloiherune: the Huncell of the Tendikeye. A swordocracy composed five sovereign states; Meramac, Tarkio, Bourbeuse, Cuivre, and Wyaconda. Produces more crops than all other huncells combined.

Ses Lemuert: the Everdying. The Cancerous Huncell. Populated by various clans of Lemuertians.

Tomfeerdon: huncell of the Malruka. Originally inhabited by the now extinct Kesslar. Ruled by the entity known as Slate.

Ocsnart: the Dead Huncell. A radioactive tundra littered with ruins. Former home of the now extinct Lonya race and former realm of the Laich Khan Arthar.

Gurtangorr: huncell of the Krilp Tribes and some Fevärian settlements.

Sodara: the Trembling Sea. An oceanic huncell peppered with a few sparse island states. Below its quivering waves, secret sexy things slither and swim.

Cities, Counties, and Towns

Embrenil: the Bone Brick City. One the seven major cities of Doflend, known for its fossil-laced architecture. Literally means "The Enduring Ember".

Vempour: the Stained Glass City. One of the seven major cities of Doflend, known for its architecture composed of natural, colored glass. Named for the Beresche goldmonger Idech Vempour.

Apple County (aka Wraith County): a once prosperous rural county famous for its abundant orchards, now a haunted land plagued by ghosts, crime, and poverty.

Weapons

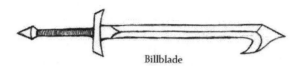

Billblade

Great Axe

Yashinin Machete

Holly Leaf Sword

Nagamaki

Stone Lion Tooth

Web Handle Dagger

About the Author

Aaron William Hollingsworth was born and raised in Jefferson County, Missouri near St. Louis. He lives in Kansas City, Missouri with his wife and two sons. He invites his readers to visit "Aaron Hollingsworth - Science Fantasy Writer" and "Four Winds – One Storm" on Facebook.

Made in the USA
Charleston, SC
31 December 2014